Venus Examined

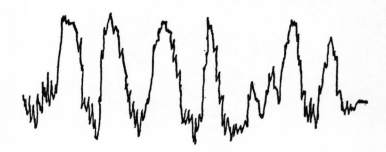

BERNARD GEIS ASSOCIATES

Venus Examined

A Physiological Novel

BY ROBERT KYLE

Distributed by Grove Press, Inc.

to the volunteers

*To all those
enrolled in formal
investigative programs
in Cambridge,
Massachusetts, New York,
St. Louis and
Bloomington, Indiana,
And to those others
who prefer to conduct
their research
in their own way,
on their own time,
in private—*
THIS BOOK IS DEDICATED

Venus Examined

chapter 1

The dynamic early-shift disc jockey was warning his public that all was not well in the Queens Midtown Tunnel, but the news came too late to help Harry Royce. He was already committed. One of a half million people who had spent the summer weekend on Long Island and decided to drive back on Monday morning to avoid the crowds, he crawled toward the tunnel opening in low gear.

His maroon Ferrari, which could do 110 without strain, was not at its best in this kind of traffic, and neither was his girl. She was a television actress with exceptional skin, which seemed less like real skin than a substitute produced in the artificial climate of a cosmetics laboratory. She pressed forward against the belt, taking quick bites at her cigarette. In the hard light after entering the tunnel, her face was no longer especially attractive, all shadow and bone.

She shook the ash from her cigarette. "Well, it's a man's world," she said hoarsely. "Four years of Hotchkiss. Four years of Yale. Three at Harvard Law, two in the Air Corps. None of them coeducational. So it's small wonder—"

"Whose biography is this?" Harry said. "Maybe I know him."

"Not funny," she said flatly. "Do you realize you've been humming for the last twenty miles? I mean like Muzak in the elevator. 'Some Enchanted Evening,' for God's sake. It was enchanted, all right. For you."

He touched her shoulder lightly. "You were with me a couple of times."

"I was not with you a couple of times. You went your merry way."

"Well, the law of averages, after all. Sometimes you win, sometimes you lose. I seem to remember other nights when you went off like a hand grenade."

"Because you didn't hurry me!" she cried. "You get selfish when you drink, Harry. You forget everything you ever knew."

He started to say something, but turned it into a half laugh.

"And what's that little snort supposed to convey?" she demanded. "Sometimes you lose, sometimes you win. But that's the female, isn't it? The male always wins. That dates back to before women's suffrage. We're supposed to be more enlightened today. With some people I wouldn't feel so let down, but I thought I could count on you."

She coughed up some carbon monoxide she had taken in along with the cigarette smoke. Harry reached back and pulled up the top.

"Back to the womb," she remarked bitterly as it settled over them, "and if there's anybody I don't want to go back to the womb with right now—"

"You'll be home in a minute."

"I doubt it," she said. "I think I'll be stuck here all day. I may even die here, unshriven, in a state of unresolved sexual tensions." She pulled despairingly at her cigarette. "Didn't they ever give you any sex education at Hotchkiss? Didn't they tell you what happens to a woman when you do certain things, and what doesn't happen when you don't do certain things?"

"God, no."

"They let you rely on instinct, I suppose." She breathed out smoke. "I have an announcement to make. Instinct isn't enough."

She was beginning to get to him. She had been watching for it, without looking at him directly, and she showed a glint of satisfaction. He suppressed the remark he had been about to make and turned on the blower. The truth was, he had read the recommended books and could find a clitoris in the dark as readily as the next man. He had always assumed that what pleased him pleased his partner. As far as he was able to tell, the response had usually been good.

The line of cars ground forward a short way, and then they sat some more. The girl was absolutely still, her eyes closed, and Harry had a feeling that if he touched her now even the seatbelt wouldn't be able to hold her.

Their next move took them out of the tunnel and up into Manhattan. She lived in a handsome egg crate in Kips Bay.

"God, I hate that tunnel," she said when he stopped to let her out. "Thanks for the weekend, I suppose."

"My pleasure."

"I'll say it was your pleasure," she said, returning to her grievance. She opened the door, but didn't reach back for her suitcase. "Do you feel like coming up for a fast cup of coffee?"

"Sorry. I have a Foundation meeting and I'm late as it is."

"I'm not trying to get you inside me again. It's just—" she made a strangled gesture—"I'm so full of juice I'll have to take a couple of barbs to knock me out, and that's such a lonely thing to do when nobody's with you."

He made a small movement. She said quickly, "I know. I had my chance. I take back some of the things I said. I've got an audition this afternoon, and it's bothering me. I couldn't stand all that euphoria! 'Some Enchanted Evening!' That's what sex is supposed to do for you, but with me, even when I make it—" She put her hand on his knee and looked at him intently. "You're pretty damn competent, as a matter of fact, and that's really what scares me."

"I'll call you tonight."

She hesitated. "Well—better not. I think I'll do some comparison shopping, if you don't mind, before I panic."

She twisted upward, taking his face in both hands, and kissed him hard. Harry's hand, with the watch on his wrist, stayed on the steering wheel. The watch faced him. God, he was late.

"We'll meet," she said, drawing away. "It's a small town."

She pulled out her suitcase and clicked into the lobby without looking around. She was marvelously put together, and in some other century, before women were given their independence, before the discovery of Dexamyl, which was all she had eaten all weekend . . .

Harry breathed out. He was relieved, on the whole. He pushed the stick into low and the full-throated exhaust blew him away from the curb.

Harry had the careless assurance that usually goes with a good golf game, combined with inherited money. He had been shooting in the mid-70's since he was fifteen, but he wasn't consistent enough on the greens to win many tournaments. He was beginning to believe that you couldn't be rich and also a dangerous putter unless you made your money yourself. He was now thirty-one, with a responsible job—a laugh, in some ways—and he was beginning to see that his putting would never improve unless his father went bankrupt, which wasn't likely. The day before, after one of the pleasantest Saturday nights he had spent in some time, he had shot a terrible 84, three-putting most holes. Did it actually matter?

Somebody has to be first in every law school class, and somebody has to be last. Harry was last his year. He had done exactly the right amount of work to stay in, getting three C's and one D each of his three years. This had required a certain coolness, a good judgment of human nature, and a certain amount of luck; but if he ended up knowing less than his classmates about the law of contracts, he knew more about Boston girls, who were no less cooperative than girls elsewhere except that they had more of a tendency to consider themselves courageous.

He grew a cavalryman's mustache in the Air Corps, shaving it off when he became a civilian again and went to work for the family stores. Royce's, founded by his grandfather and greatly expanded by his father, broke even at its old Fifth Avenue location but coined money at its six shopping-center branches. Harry started at the bottom, as vice-president with vague responsibilities in the fields of personnel and publicity. Soon he found himself doing some of the talking for the management side during labor negotiations. He proved to be good at this, for many of the same reasons he was good at golf. He represented the family on one of the mayor's emergency task forces (on traffic and transportation—they had prepared an eloquent report, including some sensible recommendations about the Long Island Expressway, and the report had been accepted with thanks and placed on file). He raised money for Lincoln Center and muscular dystrophy and Planned Parenthood. He was the only Royce on the board of the Royce Foundation.

He occupied a six-room apartment in an East River cooperative, with a fine view of the industrial chaos of Greenpoint and Long Island City. In the lobby, he picked up Saturday's mail. There was a lot of it, and he gave it a fast first sorting in the elevator—bills, checks, junk, solicitations, finally a few letters. He called his answering service and learned that his father had called him three times over the weekend, most recently half an hour before, while Harry was mired down in the Queens Midtown Tunnel.

The older Royce always left home at the same time. Harry called the mobile operator and gave her the number of his father's car phone. While he waited he tore open an envelope postmarked Cambridge and addressed in a familiar handwriting, that of an old friend, the wife of a Harvard Law professor.

His father's voice, breaking in, caused him to stiffen slightly. As far back as Harry could remember, he had been handling his father by detouring around him. Eventually Harry would succeed to the big job, if he wanted it, but meanwhile there was no question about who ran the stores. Steven Royce believed himself to be flexible and open to argument, but on important matters he was as solid and as firmly rooted as a stump, and Harry had never had the delusion that he himself was a bulldozer.

"When you're away for the weekend, Harry, leave your number. How many times have I told you?"

"I was out on the water most of the time when I wasn't playing golf. Dad, today's the day we give away your money. I'm supposed to be downtown in half an hour. I still have to shave. The traffic was murder."

"This is Foundation business," his father said. "Tommy Gevorkian called me last night about a grant that's up for renewal. I know they sent you an agenda, but if you've been out on the golf course all weekend, did you read it?"

"I glanced through it, but there didn't seem to be anything too spectacular."

He put the phone down quietly, found his attaché case, and brought it back.

"—when it comes up for a vote," his father was saying.

"You faded out for a minute," Harry said. "What grant are we talking about?"

"Some people with some kind of connection at Manhattan Medical. They're doing sex research, and why we ever got involved in it in the first place—"

"I remember the one you mean," Harry said. "They're planning a new approach to the treatment of sex-offenders, or something of the sort. They didn't want much money."

"They want a hundred and fifteen now, Tommy tells me. People in my generation used to call that money."

The agenda for the quarterly meeting, due to convene at ten o'clock that morning, was stapled to a folder containing far too much material supporting the recommendations of the executive director, a man named Peter Hixon. One of Hixon's devices for getting what he wanted was to give the board more statistics and sociological prose than any amateur could possibly absorb. Harry clamped the phone in the hollow of his shoulder and thumbed through the pages quickly until he found what he wanted. Dr. Chalmers S. Prescott, professor of obstetrics and gynecology at Manhattan Medical College, was indeed asking for $75,000 to finance continued research on a project known as "Human Sexual Inadequacy, Its Connection with Overt Sex-Offenses and Certain Nervous Disorders"—a hell of a broad mandate. There was a further $40,000 item for laboratory equipment.

"I was wrong," he told his father. "It isn't treatment they're interested in, it's facts. They take individual sex-offenders and try to find out what makes them tick. How they differ from everybody else, if at all. It sounded harmless. They had some money from National Health to start with. We gave them fifteen or twenty—no, fifteen—to evaluate what they'd done so far and make up their minds what to do next."

"By sex-offenders, Harry, don't you mean whores?"

"I guess so. Sex-offenders sounds better. I think they have some arrangement with the courts, as part of the probation process. But we didn't spend that much time on it. National Health, Manhattan Medical—pretty good auspices. I know it sounds pretty far-out, but we've given money to a lot of goofier things."

"According to Tommy, there's more to it than just an interview and a pelvic examination. This doctor wants to find out what happens during intercourse. Sexual intercourse. Period. All the rest of it's window dressing. He's been using male prostitutes as well as female—was the board aware of that? They choose up sides and perform in a laboratory in front of a movie camera with this so-called doctor taking their measurements at various stages."

"Now Dad. Seriously."

"I'm quoting Tommy. Why not? Where do you draw the line? That seems to be the way the world is going, like it or not, and the fact that I don't like it is beside the point. The point is, we run a retail business. We try not to offend people. Of course, I have nothing to say about it, it's up to the board. But there's a hell of a big difference between a planning grant of fifteen and a performance grant of a hundred and fifteen. The stores are bound to be associated with this thing if there's any publicity on it."

"Let me get this straight. They used our fifteen thousand to stage sex episodes in the laboratory?"

"According to Tommy."

Harry whistled softly.

"That was my reaction exactly," his father said. "Hixon's a fancy operator, but how did he sneak it through without any questions being asked?"

"I'd have to look at the minutes. What's Gevorkian going to do?"

"You never know with Tommy. He wanted to startle me and he succeeded. But he may end up by voting for it—freedom of science and what have you. I think the thing for us to do is to move to table. It's a little late to hope to vote it down outright. This is a big departure for us. Do we have all the facts we need to make a decision? Doesn't it raise some fundamental issues which require more consideration? And so on and so forth."

"I'll try," Harry said doubtfully. "But now I'd better be going."

"They won't call the meeting to order before you get there."

Harry wasn't sure of that. He shaved in a hurry and was dabbing at a cut on his chin all the way downtown in a taxi. He had brought the minutes of the last few meetings. Hixon, of course, had been in the business too long to be caught in an open misrepresentation; now that Harry knew what he was looking for he was able to find it, smothered under a blanket of unfamiliar nouns. In the current agenda, the item was considerably more simple. Dr. Prescott requested $75,000 to enlarge his research population. He wanted to go on with what he was doing, in short, but with more people. The additional sum of $40,000 was for equipment to measure and record physiologic variables in the duration and intensity of intravaginal reaction patterns developed in response to changes in sex-tension increment.

Harry read that sentence again—and then read it a third time. Intravaginal reaction patterns? What the hell were *they?*

The Royce Foundation, with assets of $25 million, mostly in Royce Company common stock, had been established five years before under heavy tax pressure. Peter Hixon, its executive director from the start, had made a specialty of mental health grants. This field was crowded, but because mental health was such a difficult thing to define, almost everything anybody tried seemed to work, and even the smallest experimental success could command major publicity. For the first two or three years, the Royce Foundation was rarely offered anything until it had been rejected everywhere else first. This was bad. When reports of a Royce success appeared in the press, other foundation people were able to say truthfully, "Yes, interesting, if a bit inconclusive. We had a chance at it but we turned it down."

J. Howland Wharton, chairman of the board, was a senior partner in a securities law firm with offices in a comfortable Broad Street building, solid, airy, spacious, the kind of building that instills respect for the humanity as well as the power of the law. It had outlived its depreciation and was about to be torn down. The board's quarterly meetings were held in the Wharton, Wharton & Andrews partners' room. Wharton waited ten minutes after the specified time before opening the meeting. Harry slipped in while the secretary, one of the army of anonymous middle-aged ladies in this part of town, was rattling through the minutes of the previous meeting. He gave the chairman an apologetic shake of the head and took an unoccupied chair near the foot of the table.

He exchanged silent greetings with the trustees facing him. Dr. Gevorkian, seated near the head of the table, gestured with an unlighted pipe, his usual prop. He looked younger than Harry's father, though they were contemporaries. He with an English professor at Barnard, a famous lecturer on the lesser Elizabethan dramatists—everybody but Shakespeare. He had written a book about Christopher Marlowe that Harry intended to read sometime. While Harry was growing up, he

had had Gevorkian at Sunday dinner, Gevorkian on Christmas afternoons, Gevorkian at the Yale Bowl. Harry had liked
Mrs. Gevorkian better than her husband. A stern, preoccupied
woman, she was one of the few people during his childhood
who had been willing to listen to what he said. She had been
dead now for several years.

Wharton, with a strong sense of time and the kind of voice
that carries half the length of a railway coach, was an excellent
chairman. As he moved the meeting through communications
and reports and on into old business, Harry was wondering
how he would make out with the motion to table. Unlike his
father, he didn't think that any Royce motion was sure to be
adopted. They were spending Royce money, but they had
legal authority to spend it in any way they pleased, within
the limits of the exemption. There were seven trustees present.
Harry could be sure of only one vote besides his own: Frank
Brennan, a banker, seldom opened his mouth on these occasions
except to vote "aye." (The Royce account was his bank's biggest.) And Gevorkian? Harry's father had wanted a humanist
on the board to liven things up, to keep the executive director
on his toes. Gevorkian always managed to find unconven-
tional reasons for his decisions, but the decisions themselves,
Harry had noticed, were usually conventional.

Peter Hixon, a small man nearing forty, with a neat paunch
like a robin's, had set up an overhead projector to help explain
an elaborate teaching machine, a computer crossed with a
typewriter out of a television receiver, which was designed to
help retarded slum children who resisted any suggestions made
by human beings. The cost was $100,000. It was a character-
istic Royce Foundation idea, occupying the shadowy region
where education, psychiatry, and sociology converge. It was
eye-catching and almost sure to work. It was approved with
a murmur of ayes.

The chairman then called Item Nine, the Human Sexual
Inadequacy Project, and a kind of static electricity ran around
the table. Apparently Gevorkian had alerted the others to
what was coming. While the secretary read the item aloud in
her rapid drone, Gevorkian folded up the outer lenses of his
double glasses and looked at Hixon mildly.

"This is listed as a renewal," he said when the secretary had finished. "Isn't it in effect something new? If it's sex research why don't you call it sex research? Why smuggle it through under the guise of a rehabilitation program or a mental health program?"

Hixon fussed with his papers, getting the bottom edge precisely parallel with the edge of the table. "Surely you would concede that much mental illness is of sexual origin? But I don't wish to quibble. Call it anything you like. One of the big improvements we've made since you joined the board, Professor, is that we're much less impersonal in our grant program than we once were. We try to back the person as much as the proposal. Sometimes we have to gamble, and today I'm recommending to you that we gamble on Dr. Prescott."

"All right, that's a good place to start. Who is he?"

"I consider him one of the genuinely great scientists of our time. He has published only a few papers in medical journals and his work is not yet widely known. He has a large gynecological practice, and he and his associate, a Mrs. Martha Freeman, operate a well-known gynecological clinic."

"Does Manhattan Medical have any real connection with his research?"

"Not at present. His project uses laboratory space in their Research Building, for which he pays nominal rent. This was his own decision, to protect his independence. Financing research of this nature is a difficult problem. Everyone in the medical and scientific community will agree that too little is known about the human sexual process, and research is necessary and valuable. Parting with cash to support it seems to be another matter. He had to come in, so to speak, by the side door. Mrs. Freeman is a psychologist, formerly attached to Probation Court. The Division of General Medical Sciences of the Public Health Service made the initial grant for an exploratory program, under which they compiled case documentation on sex-offenders, referring them, whenever possible, to the Prescott-Freeman clinic for further evaluation. From the clinic, many have joined the laboratory study subject population. When Dr. Prescott first came to us to discuss his needs, he emphasized the mental health aspects, knowing that mental health is one of our preferred areas of concern. That's the way the game is played."

"Sometimes. But continue."

"Medical science can tell you precisely what happens when a calcium deposit closes a ventricle in the heart, and how to go about repairing it. Thousands of articles about the heart appear in the literature every year, about the stomach, the gallbladder. Only two regions of the body remain relatively unexplored— the brain and the genitalia. They are separated in space, but perhaps they are more closely related than we imagine. The sex act is initiated somewhere in the recesses of the neurological system. For much of the way it is controlled by the brain, by fantasy. Is it so farfetched to imagine that the quality of sexual performance will have a reciprocal effect on the level of mental and nervous adjustment? Nobody knows."

Gevorkian snorted. "Nobody knows? Hixon, you're talking about something that's part of the received wisdom of mankind."

"I'm afraid I don't agree with you. Dr. Prescott has already established that much of the received wisdom of mankind is pure myth, with no foundation in fact. I must tell you, in all honesty, that Dr. Prescott is not greatly interested in practical results. He is interested, quite simply, in establishing what happens physiologically during the full reaction cycle, from the onset of excitement to postorgasm disengagement."

He let a bubble of silence float by. From an oil painting on the wall behind him, an early partner, wearing a 1910 cravat and a stiff collar, glared down at the table. This man, Harry was sure, would have recoiled in horror from the suggestion that anybody lay out $115,000 for research into such a private matter as what goes on inside the vagina.

"Are we ready for a vote on the item?" Wharton asked.

Harry started to speak, but Gevorkian forestalled him.

"I'd like to hear whether Hixon shares Dr. Prescott's lack of interest in practical results."

"By no means." Hixon pulled down his vest, which he wore as a background for a Phi Beta Kappa key. "In my five-year term as your executive director, I have never recommended a program with more obvious possibilities of a practical nature. Dr. Prescott is asking us for the tools to open up a new field of investigation. He is attempting something that has never before been done. Kinsey and his group of investigators were aware that their statistics were based on secondhand evidence, and in the Kinsey archives, Dr. Prescott tells me, there is a vast amount of observed material—but not laboratory material, not recorded under laboratory conditions. There's a laboratory in Cambridge, another at the Washington University School of Medicine in St. Louis, conducted by a Dr. William Masters, but there's no serious threat of competition. There's enough here to keep a hundred laboratories busy."

"Specifically."

"Fertility studies—exactly how does conception occur? When two fertile people fail to conceive, what did they do wrong? How effective are mechanical contraceptives?"

He pulled a sheet out of his folder. "I've jotted down a few of the questions we're hoping to answer. What about sex during pregnancy? After the baby is born? Is there any danger that orgasmic contractions will bring on a premature delivery? How do vaginal and clitoral orgasms compare? Is there such a thing as a female multiorgasm? Sex during menstruation. Sex in old age."

He looked up. "What about phallus size, as opposed to the size of the vagina? Do the dimensions of the phallus have any true relation to sexuality? Millions of people are sure the answer is yes. But how do you go about finding the truth? The traditional technique would be the interview. The sex-interviewers had to battle every kind of prejudice and suspicion, but they have done their work and I think most people will now admit its value. But how limited it is. You ask a sample of fifteen hundred American males to rate the size of their penises, and correlate that data with their place on the orgasmic frequency scale. Still you have nothing that goes to the heart of the matter—which is, if you have a small penis and your performance is poor, how much of that is the result of your belief, possibly fallacious, that a small penis equals low sexuality? If you are a woman conditioned by centuries of gossip—"

"I think we take your meaning, Hixon," Gevorkian remarked. "And if I've been substandard all these years, I would hate to be enlightened this late in life." He leaned forward so he could see the secretary at the opposite end of the table. "You needn't put that in the minutes."

"I'm not taking down *any* of this," she said with spirit.

Hixon smiled thinly. "A better example—the heart patient who asks his doctor how much sexual activity is permissible. Needless to say, that is not part of the received wisdom of mankind. Heart specialists differ widely. How can they give their patients sensible advice when they have no exact knowledge of what happens to the heart when a sex act occurs? If sex was never important to the patient, he is told to abstain. If he doesn't consider life worth living without it, the doctor will tell him that a moderate amount of sex may even have a therapeutic effect. But what is a moderate amount of sex? Again, nobody knows. Sex becomes one more thing to be careful about."

Wharton made a small movement, and Harry remembered that he had missed a meeting the previous year because of a heart attack. Hixon's hands were flying among his papers.

"The old man who dies in his young bride's arms while striving for orgasm—it's part of the folklore. How much truth is there in it? The biostatisticians will tell you to construct a sample. Have as many heart patients as possible fill out a detailed questionnaire. Follow them over several decades, hoping they keep in touch with you and tell the truth, and eventually a pattern will begin to emerge." He made a brusque gesture. "All nonsense. The effect of orgasm on the heart is a physiological question, to be answered only in a laboratory equipped with an electrocardiograph and other recording apparatus. Dr. Prescott will have the answer inside of six months."

Gevorkian's lighter flared. "With an assist from the world's oldest profession, I believe?"

Hixon's smile ate more deeply into the flesh around his mouth. "It is quite true that his laboratory subjects at present are professional prostitutes."

"So people have told me. Your doctor has assigned himself the task of discovering how much strain sex puts on the heart, so he can advise heart specialists who can then advise their patients. And how is this scientific breakthrough to take place? As I imagine the scene, a male and a female prostitute, being paid their usual rates, wearing only a blood-pressure sleeve and a few electrodes, will couple on a laboratory table while Prescott and his white-clad helpers hover about with stethoscopes and stop watches. The lights blaze, cameras whir, commands are given and acknowledged, the sensitive little penis of the cardiograph jiggles across the paper—"

"That's a highly colored picture," Hixon said, breaking in angrily. "He isn't recording emotion, he's recording anatomical changes. Undoubtedly the genital and extragenital reactions of a male prostitute during orgasm will be the same as those of any other human male. He possesses the usual masculine organs, routinely distributed. I don't suppose you would maintain that he digests his food differently from other people?"

"If his profession required him to eat highly spiced foods or to swallow without chewing, he might. It's a poor comparison, Hixon. The question is one of attitude. There's more to sex than physiology. You can pay a male prostitute to have sex with a woman, but emotionally the experience must leave him cold. How can that sort of encounter compare with lovemaking between husband and wife? You used the word 'undoubtedly.' I doubt it, for one."

Brennan, the banker, was anxious to be heard. "Do you mean to say this is actually going on right now, Hixon, on a Royce grant?"

"Yes. But of course prostitutes sleep late. Probably the first session today won't take place before noon."

"But where, in God's name?"

"In a laboratory suite in the Manhattan Medical Research Building on West 158th Street."

Harry was having trouble taking this seriously. Was there any grown person who didn't know that the heartbeat quickens during sexual intercourse? That sometimes it beats faster than other times? He had once witnessed a copulation in a Paris brothel between employees of the house. Both the man and the girl had reached orgasm, at least ostensibly, but Harry would have guessed that their pulse had remained fairly normal throughout.

"It's an age of professionalism," Gevorkian said. "In his clinical work Prescott may pose as an expert, but of course he's a sexual amateur compared with his stable of prostitutes. The neighborhood name for the clinic, I'm informed, is the Prescott Center for the Performing Arts. Can you give us more definite information on that, Hixon? Is it true that whenever he runs into a particularly stubborn problem he invites the couple to a session in which a pair of professionals demonstrate how the thing really ought to be done?"

For the first time Harry saw a crack in the executive director's self-possession.

"Not to my knowledge," he snapped. "In any event the clinical program is quite apart from the physiological research, which is what we are asked to support."

Harry raised his hand. This was as good a time as any. "Mr. Chairman, I move to table this application."

Hixon swung around sharply. Wharton was holding his left wrist loosely in his right hand, perhaps taking his pulse.

"You move to table?"

"It's a new field for us," Harry went on. "As Hixon says, we'll be pioneering. He made a couple of points I agree with, but I'm inclined to go along more with Professor Gevorkian. I don't know about everybody else, but this didn't really register on me when I looked through the agenda."

"It certainly didn't register on me," Brennan said.

"And I must have been asleep," Harry continued, "when we voted that first fifteen thousand. I just didn't make the connection—I don't think any of us did. I'm not blaming you, Hixon. It's our own fault for not asking questions. I want to think about this some more. Even if it's okay to do this kind of research, do we want to be the ones to finance it? Maybe I'm being too finicky, but I don't like the idea of hiring prostitutes out of Foundation funds."

Wharton called for a second.

"Second," Brennan said strongly.

"Until the next regular meeting," Harry added.

For a man usually in complete command of himself, Hixon seemed more than surprised. He seemed disconcerted. He pushed his papers out of symmetry with the edge of the table.

"May I have the floor? I won't object to Mr. Royce's motion if he's willing to shorten the time limit, if we could convene a special meeting in, say, a few days' time. If we let it lie over, we'll lose it. Ben Burns of the Knowlton Fund, to mention one, would give his front teeth for a chance to take this over. There are others. It seems to me this is precisely the kind of problem we're set up to handle. We're small enough so we have room to maneuver. As I understand our purpose, it's to keep an eye out for the small, low-cost experimental program which can have an impact out of proportion to its size. I hope no one thinks I have tried to mislead the board—"

"I didn't say that," Harry said.

"I try to provide full information on all grant requests. I thought you agreed with me that what Dr. Prescott is doing ought to be supported. On the point about the use of professional prostitutes, which Professor Gevorkian has objected to, I agree that there is something distasteful about this. And as study subjects in a long-range program they fall short of the ideal. They leave town or they fail to appear for appointments. With some of them there is a certain amount of—well, pelvic abnormality, perhaps it could be called. They have been of enormous assistance in the early stages, but Dr. Prescott has decided to phase them out gradually as soon as it becomes feasible."

"You take a weight off my mind," Gevorkian said. "And who will he get to replace them?"

"He's calling for volunteers from the academic and medical communities. He already has a small nucleus from his clinical program. But we can't expect him to mark time for three months while we debate the matter." He hesitated, bringing his papers back into line. "I'm afraid I indicated to him, on the basis of our previous vote, that the board was in sympathy with his objectives. I feel strongly about this recommendation. So strongly—" his voice had recovered its usual assurance—"that I would have to consider adoption of the motion as a vote of no-confidence, calling for my resignation."

"Don't be a prima donna, Hixon," Gevorkian protested. "We accept ninety-nine percent of your recommendations."

"I know of no other way to make clear how important I think this is. It will be funded by somebody, of course. The world hungers for the truth about sexuality. All the old taboos are falling. Professor Gevorkian used the word 'breakthrough' —sardonically, perhaps. But this *is* a breakthrough, a real one. I want the Royce Foundation to be a part of it."

He laced his fingers, tightened his lips, and waited for the vote.

"On the motion to table," Wharton said. "Those in favor."

Two hands went up, Brennan's and Harry's. Gevorkian's rose more slowly.

"I'm opposed to sexual hypocrisy too, Hixon, but I think we need to know more about this project, a great deal more."

"Opposed?" Wharton said.

There were three "nays." At least two were not votes in favor of putting money into laboratory sex but against going through the laborious business of finding a new executive director. Hundreds of new foundations were created every year, and there were too few good people to go around. Hixon might be a pain in some ways, but there was no denying his efficiency. This was his first crisis in five years.

"Three in favor, three against," Wharton said. "The chair votes nay. Motion's defeated. Further discussion."

Hixon kept his eyes down, careful not to seem pleased.

"I'd like some further discussion of this forty-thousand-dollar apparatus," Gevorkian said. "Will you enlarge on that, please, Hixon? Your style became a little more murky than usual at that point, I thought. I'd like a description of this expensive piece of equipment in ordinary English."

Hixon looked at him coolly, now sure of his control. "In ordinary English, it is an adjustable mechanical device to be used by female subjects in artificial coition."

There was a faint rustle. The secretary gripped her notebook hard. Her eyes were closed, and there was a possibility that she might be praying.

"Do you have a diagram to put on the projector?" Gevorkian asked. "No, that would be pornographic, under the statute. Is this what Dr. Prescott counts on to bring the women flocking into his laboratory?"

Hixon continued to hold himself in check. "He uses a system of tests and interviews to screen out exhibitionists and others who are merely looking for a new sensation."

"But why does he bother? Wouldn't he contend that an exhibitionist would respond to any given stimulus in the same way as a nonexhibitionist?"

"To a degree. Naturally he wants to come as close as possible to the norm."

"Do you honestly think there is such a thing as a sexual norm?"

Hixon looked surprised. "There has to be."

Wharton put in, "I don't want to cut off discussion, but we've had an exhaustive explanation of this item, and we still have a heavy agenda. I now call the question."

"Mr. Chairman, excuse me," Brennan said. "I want to ask Mr. Hixon how many volunteers they expect to get?"

"Hopefully, about one thousand."

The banker's eyes were trying to come out of their sockets. "A thousand people will agree to let him watch while they—"

"He intends to pay fifteen dollars an hour. Many medical students are married. They need the money, and they're already oriented in the direction of medical research. Actors and actresses, perhaps. Some of the more forward-looking staff people at Columbia."

Gevorkian's mouth twisted ironically. "I think I'm a little less concerned about this than I was to begin with. All at once, everywhere I go, people seem to be talking about Dr. Prescott and his strange laboratory. It's the number-one topic on Morningside Heights. But in all the conversations I've had on the subject, I have yet to hear of one single person who is willing to climb up on the table with his wife or his girlfriend, or even with some beautiful stranger, to have his movements observed and recorded for the benefit of the marriage-counseling profession. Would you do it, Hixon? Would anyone here? I'll contribute a dollar to charity for every so-called normal person who asks him for an appointment. He'll have to junk those screening procedures to get any data at all. He can't screen out the abnormal because who else would apply?"

"All in favor of Item Nine," Wharton called, "signify in the usual manner."

"One more question," Brennan said.

Several others were trying to speak. Wharton rapped the table.

"Order, gentlemen, please. All in favor of the item, raise your right hand."

The real vote had been taken on the motion to table. Amid some confusion, four hands went up. Harry voted nay, Gevorkian abstained, and Wharton declared the agenda item carried.

chapter 2

Hixon prepared his agendas carefully, leaving as little as possible to chance. He knew more about his trustees than any of them suspected. He tried to throw each of them a fish, so they could leave a meeting satisfied at having made a small contribution to the forward movement of mankind. Professor Gevorkian, for example, was a longtime socialist. For his benefit Hixon had promoted a grant for a psychiatric study-in-depth of a low-income block in the Hough district of Cleveland, to find out if there was any correlation between economic and mental stress. Gevorkian had snapped it up, as Hixon had expected, and perhaps that explained his abstention on the Prescott grant.

This much preparation, Hixon knew, was probably a little pathological. Friends of his in the business, who believed in doing no more work than they had to, looked on him as something of an old lady. But Hixon believed in doing every job as well as it could be done. The Royce Foundation, coming into the game late and bringing only $25 million in chips, was still getting the leftovers. When Hixon told someone where he worked, he usually got nothing but a polite stare. People had heard of the stores, of course, but not of the Foundation. He was beginning to think about moving on. If you changed jobs too often you got a reputation as a foundation-hopper, but to stay put for longer than five years showed lack of initiative, a tendency to settle.

He shoehorned himself into the crowd at the bar. After every quarterly meeting, he met his wife for lunch at some restaurant which they couldn't really afford. Today she was late. He ordered a Campari and tried to look like someone who came here habitually. But he was too short. He had never learned to blend with his environment, a knack so many other people seem to inherit. The ideal setting to display his gifts—it was an old dream—would be a private, discreetly paneled dining room in which a group of distinguished men from different walks of life could lunch quietly while discussing ways of patching up various leaky social problems. Hixon had a flair for steering such discussions. It was one of the things he did well.

He knew that the performance he had put on that morning had been close to brilliant. His ploy on Harry Royce's motion to table! No professional matador ever worked that close to the bull. Poor old Howie Wharton, who had recently surprised everyone by marrying for the third time—Hixon had discovered that his doctor was one of those who subscribed to the mild-exercise-and-no-strenuous-sex-after-a-heart-attack school. One of the other pro-Hixon votes came from a trustee who was supposed to live in Riverhead, Long Island, but who actually stayed most of the week in a Manhattan apartment where he probably didn't spend all his time reading the *Wall Street Journal*. And as for the lecture on the mythology of penis size, that had been a shot in the dark. Being unable to order the board to report to the Prescott laboratory to be measured, he couldn't be sure whether or not it had struck home.

He felt exhausted, drained. He was being jostled at the bar from either side by bigger men who had the moral advantage of having someone to talk to. He finished his drink. If he could have caught the bartender's eye he would have shifted to gin, though he didn't actually believe in coming to a first-class restaurant and stunning himself with martinis before he could taste the food. The bartender refused to look his way, as bartenders and waiters had a habit of doing with Hixon. He must lack charisma, if that was the word.

He saw Julia.

She was nice-looking, nothing sensational but certainly very nice-looking. She was now more or less a blond. When Hixon gave her permission to color her hair, he had known she wouldn't do anything too outlandish or weird. She was a few years older than Hixon. That gave her an incentive to watch her weight.

"Let's have our drinks at the table," he said. "It's too noisy at the bar."

They hadn't been given a bad location, for once. Julia's eyes kept sliding about to see if she recognized anybody.

There was no point in looking at her husband, she could do that at home. She saw several professional television guests as well as one host. When the drinks were delivered they took the first ceremonial sip together, celebrating the passage of three more months without disaster.

"So how did it go?" she asked.

"I had them eating out of my hand," Hixon told her. "A couple of small fires, but—" He shrugged.

"Darling, I wish I could watch you work. Couldn't you smuggle me in disguised as a charwoman or something? Any trouble with Gevorkian? Did he try any of his usual rabble-rousing?"

"He cleared his throat a few times, but I think he's finally beginning to realize that I've got the votes."

"He's such a bore. Did you say anything to them about money?"

"We talked about nothing else. No, I know what you mean, Julia, but we didn't get around to discussing the starvation wage they pay their executive director. It wouldn't have been a good idea."

"You've been working practically an eighty-hour week!"

"I know, but all the board sees is the finished product. They don't realize the staff work that goes into processing applications, including the ones we turn down. *Especially* the ones we turn down. Perhaps I'd be happier if I didn't have such an abhorrence of shoddy workmanship."

"What you need is more staff. I know Roland comes through with the occasional inspired suggestion, but he's not that good on the pick-and-shovel level, is he?"

"He's really not too bad. I need a sounding board for my ideas, and he's good at that. Actually the typing service has worked out fairly well."

"I don't know why I couldn't brush up on my stenography. I used to be quite good."

"The secret of a happy marriage, darling, is the wife in one place from nine to five, the husband in another. Here's the menu at last."

They were handed two oversize menus. Having dispensed more than $300,000 in two hours that morning, Hixon gave the prices only a passing glance. Julia wanted crab Florentine.

He chose the blanquette of veal, and then they discussed what they would have first. Julia had never tasted snails. Did she dare? She let him persuade her.

"What happened at the Dalton interview?" he asked.

"Oh, Peter, I just don't know! Everybody was so nice to us, they couldn't have been more cordial, but Ellen got the impression they didn't *quite* consider her Dalton material. Of course they're swamped—two thousand applications for I forget how many places. Ellen says she couldn't care less, but she doesn't fool me. One of the things they asked was what she thought of the Beatles! Apparently they use it as a kind of inkblot test."

"What did she say?"

"I thought it was rather cute. She said she loves their music but she can't stand the boys themselves."

Ellen, the Hixons' only child, had suddenly become a large, sloppy, lank-haired adolescent, utterly transformed from the impertinent little sprite Hixon had formerly adored. Her sprite-hood had ended abruptly at almost the same moment that her education started costing $2,000 a year. What a terrible city —fantastic rents, fantastic taxes, foul air, chaotic schools.

Julia's stream-of-consciousness was moving along its usual route. If they gave up their apartment and transferred their base of operations to Connecticut, they would all have adjustments to make, no doubt, but at least Ellen could get a good free public education among people of their own sort. Adjustments? Yes, Hixon would have adjustments, and sooner than make them, he was willing to enter Ellen in P.S. 251 or whatever and let her *get* pregnant, not that he didn't think the pregnancy propaganda was greatly exaggerated.

To Hixon's astonishment, Harry Royce, holding a bloody mary, appeared suddenly at Julia's elbow.

"That was nicely played, Hixon, as usual."

Hixon had just taken a bite of warm buttered roll. By the time he swallowed and touched his lips with a napkin, he had Scotch-taped his official expression back together. Harry Royce was somebody he didn't happen to dig, as a type or as an individual. Either he was a mental flyweight or else he was extraordinarily well adjusted to his position as heir apparent to a merchandising fortune. Hixon's chief gripe about the man as a trustee was that he refused to take serious things with the right amount of seriousness. Right now he ought to be furious about that threat to resign, but here he was smiling, and the smile was clearly authentic. Of course, in fairness, he also seemed a little stoned.

Hixon introduced his wife and came close to blurting out something to explain his presence in a restaurant so obviously beyond his financial reach. He was saved by a sense of his own human uniqueness. He had a *summa* from a good Eastern college. His name was listed in *Who's Who*. He had every right to spend his insufficient income any way he pleased. Perhaps his wife had money. (She definitely didn't.)

As a matter of cold fact, Harry didn't seem surprised to find him here. The rich were insensitive people, almost by definition.

"What's the game plan now, Hixon? Do we get out a press release?"

"We used to, routinely, but nobody ever printed it. Now it depends on whether there's any special angle."

"Why don't we skip it this time? Gevorkian's sure this is going to turn out to be a major fiasco. Let's see how many volunteers they manage to line up. I know they wouldn't get any data if they had to depend on me. I'd be too tongue-tied, to use a figure of speech."

"Dr. Prescott's amazed by the early response. Perhaps that old taboo isn't quite as potent as people think."

"It's not the taboo I'm worried about being potent." He gestured with his glass. "You've got a persuasive husband here, Mrs. Hixon. He had a tough audience and he persuaded everybody but me. God knows everybody wants to find out all they can about sex or they wouldn't be human. Those male prostitutes shook me for a minute. I hope they're out of the way by the time this gets back to the president and chairman of the board of the Royce stores." He added, "Not that I think a machine is too much of an improvement. Keep our fingers crossed. Nice to've met you, Mrs. Hixon."

And having done a maximum amount of damage, he moved away.

"That's about his third bloody mary, in my estimation," Hixon said. "I told you about Dr. Prescott, didn't I?"

"No, I don't think you did, dear."

"He's a Manhattan Med College professor. He's running a small sex investigation. Not in our usual line, of course, but it looks promising. We gave him a small exploratory grant to perfect his lab techniques, and this is a one-year extension." He shook his head. "I never hope to understand people like Harry Royce. I happen to know he has girls galore. Somebody different every weekend. Actresses, models. And yet mention the word 'sex' and I think he's shocked."

He poured more wine. She said hesitantly, "I've always thought you had such a sure instinct about avoiding anything that was likely to—"

"Julia, it's research. I was much impressed by this chap Prescott. If he doesn't end up as one of the most distinguished men in the field—"

"Darling, what was that reference to male prostitutes?"

Hixon decided it was time to remind her who brought the money into the house. "I've had this all morning and I don't want to go through it again right now, do you mind? Controversial? Of course this is controversial. The Foundation has been digging itself into a first-class rut. It's only as high as my armpits now, but in another six months I shudder to think— You'd like me to play everything safe. That's the wife's role in our culture. But don't forget that charitable foundations exist at the whim of the United States Congress. If we go on avoiding risky decisions, taking no chances, putting money into the same bland studies of the same safe subjects—"

"But couldn't you take risks in some other area?"

He began to get angry. "I'll tell you this much. Ben Burns has been trying to hijack Prescott for the Knowlton, and Ben has a well-deserved reputation for picking winners."

"I don't consider Ben Burns much of a recommendation. I don't like the man and I don't like his mannerisms."

The waiter served their snails with a flourish. Julia tasted one and said doubtfully that she thought it was good.

"Peter, darling, I know I'm stupid, but how can a study of male prostitution—"

"It's not a study of male prostitution! I'll explain the whole thing some other time, when we aren't eating a twenty-dollar lunch."

"I must be a congenital worrier," she said miserably. "But if you alienate Mr. Royce just when your contract's coming up for renewal—"

"He has no real power."

She looked really alarmed at that, he was glad to see, and she didn't come back to the subject until the plates had been removed.

"I don't know why everybody nowadays seems so pre-occupied with sex. It's sex, sex, sex. You'd think they never saw a sunset or really looked at a flower."

"Even flowers reproduce."

"I know!" She had decided to try gaiety. "Isn't it scandalous? Darling, reassure me. You won't have anything to do with this project personally, will you?"

"All I do is sign the checks." He put his hand on hers. "Funny face."

She gave him a quick smile. "I'm thinking of Ellen, really. I had such an odd feeling this morning with the Dalton people. They were like gods that have to be propitiated, and the terrible thing was that I didn't know what sort of sacrifices they preferred. They don't have to give us poor humans any reasons at all, just a simple 'yes' or 'no.' I do know that anything startling—"

The main course arrived, and Hixon had a brief respite while the waiters whisked about pouring wine and clattering dishes onto the table. The butter boy brought butter. The water boy poured water. For an instant Hixon had thought Julia was on the verge of making an intimate statement, something she rarely did. He felt a wave of tenderness for her. She was much too anguished about this Dalton thing. He would ask around about their admissions procedure. A word in the right place was often the equivalent of fifty points in Scholastic Aptitude. Thank God the child was a WASP and thus part of a minority in New York. He knew the advantages of having a daughter at a good school. It was almost worth the bloody tuition. But if they turned Ellen down on the specious grounds that her father worked at a foundation that was putting money into *in vivo* sex research,

Julia would have to learn to live with it. He was sorry, but that was the way it was.

They took their time over dessert, a lovely, gooey bombe. They were in a good mood when they left, and this part of the city, which received better maintenance than most, seemed semibenign. That it was a jungle nevertheless, Hixon knew.

After they parted he crossed Park and strolled to the Waldorf. Roland, his helper, was getting into the three-martini habit and he probably wouldn't be back from lunch, but there was no point in taking chances; Hixon needed privacy for the call he was about to make. He found an unoccupied booth in Peacock Alley, gave the operator his code number so she could charge the call to the Foundation, and asked for a number in an academic suburb of San Francisco. Moments later he was talking to an old friend, Dennis Cullihan.

"Lamb!" Dennis exclaimed. "You haven't called me for months. And with direct distance dialing it's such a simple thing."

Hixon refrained from pointing out that it was just as simple to dial New York from San Francisco as it was to dial San Francisco from New York. The phone calls lately, since Hixon began to disappear into the Royce rut, had all gone one way, east to west.

Dennis had been his section man in Psych I at Williams, and Hixon had decided soon after his first section meeting that here was the most brilliant person he was ever likely to know—brilliant and, at the same time, for an ambitious freshman from Toledo, Ohio, somewhat dangerous. Listening to Dennis—and for a year or two Hixon did hardly anything else—he had constantly found himself catching his breath. Dennis didn't care deeply for culture, but he knew how to talk about it—culture in the sense of Stockhausen, Ronald Firbank, John Donne, and silent pictures. Hixon imitated him for a time but soon realized that that was possible only if you also had Dennis' outrageousness and sense of personal style. They were five years apart in age, and Hixon was definitely the protégé.

They vacationed in Mexico the summer after Hixon took his M.A. By that time he understood that a break was necessary, unless he wanted one of those careers that go downhill steadily after triumphs at college. He carefully suppressed all witty remarks, confessed a secret fondness for Eisenhower and the astronaut John Glenn, and finally made Dennis see that he was really only a Midwestern dullard *au fond*.

They separated without a quarrel. Dennis could be a vicious enemy and he already had a not-bad job as an educational consultant. Squares excepted, everybody was enchanted by him and he got every plum he went after. When he moved into foundations, he considered only jobs with a considerable degree of autonomy and rich patronage. He had an unerring instinct for the subjects people were going to be talking about the following year. He financed the first LSD research in 1959. 1959! He rediscovered poverty long before anybody else and he was the first important foundation man to turn against educational television.

But a manner that worked at thirty began to creak a little at forty. He was high in a foundation with a bigger annual budget than the city of Los Angeles, but it was beginning to look as though he would remain basically a speechwriter. If Hixon hoped to cash in on their old connection, he couldn't afford to wait.

"And how is Julia?" Dennis asked, sweet and nasty. "No, on the whole I don't think I want to know about old Julia. Tell me about the brat. As elfin as ever?"

"Elfin? You're kidding. She weighs one-five. She had her Dalton interview this morning. It seems they have a new screening technique, Den, you'll be interested in this. They asked her which Beatle she liked best and why, and it went into her profile. Are they looking for Ringo people or George people? You ought to commission a paper on it."

"Baby, we've already commissioned a book. A probing sociological treatment of admissions criteria and what they reveal about the assumptions of society. To answer your question, they aren't looking for Ringo people or George people, they want equal representation from all four. Where've you been? This is known as heterogeneous grouping. And speaking of heterogeneous groups, do you see much of Benny Burns?"

"Just at parties."

"In confidence, love, my advice would be to duck if he tries to get you for lunch. They're greasing the chute for Ben."

"Gee, that's awful," Hixon said sarcastically. "What happened?"

"He couldn't keep his hands to himself, that's what happened. It would be perfectly understandable and part of the great American tradition if he happened to like girls, but unfortunately that's not what he happens to like. He's been on the hooter to me a couple of times. I can't do a thing for him."

Hixon's grip on the phone tightened. "And that brings me around to why I called. What can you do for me?"

Dennis' responses were usually so rapid that when he hesitated for even an instant it was conspicuous. "Trouble?" he said quietly.

"Den, repress those conspiratorial tendencies. Nobody's called me in to ask me which Beatle I like best, if that's what you mean. I've got a funny board, but they seem contented. Everything's smooth as silk. But have you been in New York lately? I'm attracted by California's salubrious climate and salubrious money. I'm also a bit fed up with the oddballs and the mental retardates we've been giving our money to. They're God's creatures like anybody else, but dull! Dennis, you don't know."

"There's an opening in Publications," Dennis said in a chilly tone, "but outside of the climate and the money, neither of which is all that good, would you want it? The reason I mentioned Burns, I understand they pay thirty, and I do have a glancing contact on that board. I'd be glad to give him a tinkle."

"I hear Ham Wickham wants to retire."

Silence followed, which always sounded more intense at long-distance rates. Dr. Hamilton G. Wickham was president of the Institute for Constitutional Policy Studies, a tiny jewel in the cluster of organizations thrown off by the great foundation where Dennis worked. It had a low budget but huge prestige. Other foundations financed books. This one financed multivolume studies, to be published over a span of decades. The president and his rotating fellows lived on a cliff overlooking the Pacific, in elegant houses designed by a prize-winning Chinese. Guest thinkers were impeccably housed and fed. The Institute's chef, imported from Paris, gave them a big advantage over the competitive tanks around Santa Barbara and farther down the coast.

"I know," Hixon said. "I haven't suddenly gone into regression because of the strain of living in the world's number-one city. I was wondering how you'd phrase it, but that was one of the most eloquent pauses since George M. Cohan went to his reward. Do you have anybody in mind as a replacement?"

"We've sounded out one individual whose name I shouldn't mention so I won't. One of those culture *cum* real estate men, more real estate than culture if you know what I mean, and thank the sweet Jesus he said no. It's not supposed to be general knowledge that Wickham's leaving, and I know you won't tell me how you found out. He's given us a year to come up with somebody. But the requirements are, shall we say, stiff. Guessing the name of the right Beatle isn't enough."

"Don't belabor the obvious. If you go into your board and nominate Peter Hixon, who's doing a bang-up job at the Royce Foundation, they'll think you're psychotic. Nobody's heard of me. Nobody's really heard of the Royce. You need somebody with special panache, plus courage. The president of a university who defies the Un-American Activities Committee. No, that's not enough. Say a university chancellor who defends the right of nonstudents to paint phallic symbols on the chapel walls."

"What have you got up your sleeve, lambie-pie?"

"I can't tell you right now."

"Yes, you can. I make no commitments unless all the cards are on the table."

"It may not come to pass. A lot of gears have to mesh. I assume you'd have no personal objection if I got the job?"

"Lordy, no. We'd have a ball. But I consider myself a virtuoso in the art of the possible, and buddy, unless something's going on in the big city that I don't know about, this ain't possible."

"You used to tell me anything was possible, given the right

mix. I'll need the full year. What I want you to do in the meantime is disparage any and all other candidates. You'll enjoy that, unless you've changed."

"Thank you, dear. Now to be serious. Totally serious, Peter. In one way you're not asking much, and in another way you're asking for the moon. The court jester can't make mistakes. I'd adore you to have the job. I know you could handle it, because what's to handle? I won't ask for any recompense except to be allowed to install one of my friends as a temporary fellow from time to time, and I'm known for my moderation. Now I need to know how your mind is working. In subheadings *a*, *b*, and *c*."

"If I must," Hixon said with resignation. "Den, I'm getting the feeling that all I'm doing at Royce is carrying on a dialogue with myself in an empty ditch. You and I know that the Royce has done some fine things. But nobody else knows it, except for a few shrinks and a few school superintendents—and they only talk to one another, in their own dialect. We've beaten the Fund for the Advancement twice —by a mile!—and did anybody notice? Mental illness is okay, I suppose, but you can't get an argument about it. Nobody's really for it."

"I'm weeping. So to cope with this sad state of affairs—"

"I gave a hundred and fifteen thousand clams to a slightly deranged scientist. And I had to crack the whip to get it through—I've got a couple of real fossils on my board. The doctor's name is Chalmers Prescott, and I do believe you'll be hearing it. He's a sex-research man, and with our financial help he's about to go into orbit. He's been using prostitutes —male and female, white, black, and Oriental, and what handsome creatures some of them are, to be sure—but the Philistines have been howling about that, so he's shifting to ordinary citizens, even as you and I. He puts on the complete act in the laboratory, in its infinite sweetness and variety. He let me look at his films. It's all on a high scientific plane, naturally, and Den, the sight of those boys and girls wired up to the machines aroused me to the point where I was giving the Nazi salute. I didn't dare stand up for fifteen minutes."

"Gulp."

"Exactly. He has a tenuous connection with a med school,

which gives him a thin academic patina, but the way it's set up they can disavow him if necessary, and I'm betting it's going to be necessary. This isn't something you can keep quiet, and, needless to say, I'm not interested in keeping it quiet. I expect to be denounced by both Cardinal Spellman and Norman Vincent Peale, which will give ecumenism a boost. My trustees will come under heavy pressure to withdraw support. I intend to stand on the Bill of Rights, waving the bloody banner of freedom of scientific inquiry. This may take a certain amount of intellectual courage, but I'm just immodest enough to think that I'm up to it."

Dennis giggled, which he only did among friends. "You're a blue-balled wonder."

"Then you're with me?"

Dennis considered. "To this extent. The day after *The New York Times* runs an editorial backing you, I'll submit your name to the board. Can you get me a print of those films?"

"Possibly."

"I'm so glad to be in touch. Baby, do you think this thing is actually going to take place? What kind of people would volunteer?"

"Nobody we know, thank God. But there's one thing I can say about Dr. Prescott. He has a hypnotic eye."

chapter 3

Once upon a time Fletcher Williams had been able to lose himself in Debussy, but that period in his life was over. Trying to explain this to his wife, he had harked back to the Hardy Boys adventures, which he had read voraciously in the fifth grade. She had almost hit him. Tonight he was playing Debussy because Hanna wanted to play Debussy, and a marriage, after all, is a partnership.

Fletcher had the viola. First fiddle was a girl named Mary Jane Mosberg. There wasn't an ounce of fat on Mary Jane's violin. Her fingernails were broken and invariably dirty. With dirty fingernails, Fletcher himself might have made first chair at Boston or Cleveland. Mary Jane playing the violin always made him think of an eagle eating a coyote. After tearing her way through the flesh, she cracked the bones to suck out the marrow. And yet, adept as she was, she had few musical opinions. She played every kind of music with equal fury.

Dr. Max Sultan, a look of intense pleasure on his cherubic face, was mistreating an expensive cello. He was a stomach surgeon. A realist with a knife, he was a sentimentalist with a bow. A man's bowing technique, Fletcher believed, was a key to his personality. Max affected an elaborate wrist motion. He breathed deeply and dreamily with his eyes half-closed, and rolled his shoulders as though doing a slow frug. The music that came out, not surprisingly, was mincing and coarse.

Hanna, Fletcher's wife, played an acceptable second violin. They had an excellent marriage that was the envy of their disorganized friends, but Fletcher no longer enjoyed playing quartets with her. When she was working through the easy parts of a piece, the parts she could do without taxing herself fully, she had the same expression on her face as when she made love.

Debussy, meanwhile, was trying to get under his scalp and the son of a bitch finally succeeded. It was artificial, but what artifice! The pyramids were put together in the same manner, to a simple abstract design, one stone at a time. Fletcher could feel himself receding farther and farther from the four ludicrous little figures toiling up the face of the pyramid toward the one logical stone at the top, which would justify the climb. They hadn't quite made it when the piece ended.

"That wasn't so bad, was it?" his wife said.

Mary Jane sat still, digesting her coyote. Max mopped his face with a handkerchief.

"Hanna, if you want to know what I think, I think we're beginning to go places. We accomplished something that time. How about some Schubert? 'Death and the Maiden,' as a special favor?"

"No," Hanna said regretfully. "I have to live with this man."

"Fletcher," Max said, real entreaty in his voice, "one more?"

"Let's have some coffee."

Her bow and fiddle in the same hand, Hanna put her other hand at the back of her husband's neck and kissed his mouth. The kiss had a signal inside it. She was warm and excited. That happened with Schubert and Debussy, and most of all with Tchaikovsky—but at Tchaikovsky Fletcher drew the line.

"Thanks for the music, darling," she said softly.

"We hit quite a few clinkers," Mary Jane commented. "Max, you're improving. You made those thirty-second notes. But I wish somebody'd put you up on the table sometime and cut out that schmaltz."

"Schmaltz?" Max said equably. "That's soul. No surgeon could find it. Give me a kiss like the one Hanna gave Fletcher."

"They're married," she said, escaping him.

They moved into the dining room, and Hanna lit the candles. She had brought a set of Canton china to the marriage. Their silver, a wedding gift from a rich aunt who in the end had willed her money to Christian Science, was simple and good. There was a platter of petits fours, which Hanna herself had baked that afternoon. Did any other amateur cook in Manhattan bake petits fours?

They had a big Riverside Drive apartment, luckily rent-

controlled. Fletcher held an associateship at a nearby conservatory, and like every musician in the world he gave
lessons. He was choosy about his pupils—it was his life, after
all, and those were his nerves. Hanna had done wonders with
the apartment, considering that they also had a baby, a four-
year-old named Jennie, who was taking lessons in ballet,
creative dramatics, and the recorder.

Max picked up a handsomely bound first edition of the
poems of Gerard Manley Hopkins. "Did you do this?" he
asked his hostess.

"You pay the nicest compliments. No, I haven't done anything since the Montaigne." She went to the end of the table,
where a silver coffeepot sat over a tiny flame. "But I want
to get back to it as soon as Jennie's a little older. I came
across some marvelous Italian endpapers in a little shop in
Brooklyn Heights. Mary Jane, you'll have coffee?"

Mary Jane was looking at the portraits of composers on
the wall. Hanna had happened into an auction and picked up
an autographed letter from Schönberg—it didn't really say
much—and that too had been framed. Mary Jane's hand with
its dirty fingernails rested lightly on Fletcher's shoulder, but
she was thinking about something else, and nothing came
through.

Max poured a whiskey, which he offered to Fletcher.
Fletcher took it, needing some medication after climbing that
pyramid.

"You have a lesson at eight-thirty, don't forget," Hanna
said.

"It's Joe Ben—how could I forget?"

Max and Hanna had met in the Reform Democrats. Hanna
had only stayed through one campaign—you had to be polite
to such dull people, on the political principle that once inside
the voting machine their votes carry the same amount of
weight as anybody else's. Max ate two of the little cakes
before bringing her up to date on the latest vacillations of
their congressman, who didn't feel he could afford to offend
anybody. Max was a signer and a joiner, and quite often his
causes won. The Food and Drug Administration had actually
reformed a few of its procedures. Negroes did elect a sheriff
in Alabama, and the auto companies had promised to install

collapsible steering wheels. The power of Tammany Hall was a thing of the past. So why, Fletcher wanted to know when Max tried to get him to sign a petition or a *Times* ad, did the quality of life in New York get steadily worse and worse?

"Fletcher, Hanna," Max said. "It's time to admit I had an ulterior motive when I suggested quartets tonight. I have something I think is right up your alley."

Hanna smiled at him. "Don't waste any breath on Fletcher. I'm the one member of this family who believes there's any point in going to meetings. Jennie agrees with her father."

"This isn't a committee. It's a way you can make some money—agreeable work in clean, well-lighted surroundings. A research team up at Manhattan Medical." He started on his drink, his mouth moving at one corner. "They're studying fucking."

Hanna's spoon rang against her saucer.

Max laughed. "I knew I could make you jump. They don't call it that, they call it coition. I tried to talk Mary Jane into joining—"

"I wouldn't sleep with you in private, let alone in public," Mary Jane said.

"Max, you're putting us on," Hanna said.

"Fletch, you get around. You've heard about it, haven't you?"

"Nothing but rumors."

"You didn't tell me!" Hanna exclaimed.

"I didn't know you'd be interested."

"Dog."

Max took a long drink. "As a matter of fact," he said seriously, "it's completely legit and I'm very much in favor of it. I don't know the doctor who heads it up, but the woman who works for him, Martha Freeman, is a friend of mine. They're trying to find out what happens, and by that I mean exactly what happens in physiological terms, in terms of the human anatomy, in the course of sex. I don't blame you for dropping a spoon. It takes time to get used to the idea. But my God! We study the structure and pathology of the genital organs, why shouldn't we study the way they function when they're actually being used? Some of my colleagues at St. Clare's are running around as though the world is coming to an end. Attitudes that astound me! In Mozart's day, which wasn't so long ago, the anatomists were still robbing graveyards to get human bodies. The ignorance, the ignorance in the medical profession is appalling. Don't take a problem of sexual malfunction to a general practitioner. You'd do better to consult a witch doctor in the Congo. There's less prudery there."

"Max, I love you," Hanna said.

Max took off his glasses and rubbed the pressure marks on his nose. "And this isn't something we can put off. It's urgent. We've got to find out about it in a hurry, while there's still time. Sex isn't an isolated process. The sexual function can get so screwed up and blocked and distorted—"

Mary Jane put in, "Max thinks we never would have dropped the bomb if Truman's sex life had been really successful."

"Yes, wouldn't it be lovely if everything was that simple?" Max said. "All I meant when I said that was that American social pathology is the sum of the two hundred million pathologies of individual Americans, and unless we get some understanding of the individual it's going to be too bad for mankind. I didn't say sex is the only thing we don't understand. But it's at the top of the list, and how many people are working on it? Damn few."

Hanna's excitement was growing. "But Max—"

Max put his hand over hers. "Don't say anything right away. I met Martha Freeman at somebody's house the other night and we had a long talk about it. The thing has a fascinating history. It started as an inadequacy clinic, dealing with problems of impotence and frigidity—highly relative terms. A man or a woman fails to reach orgasm, or does so less often than normal. But what is normal? When you come right down to it, what's an orgasm? They decided they had to find out before they could give any advice that would mean anything. They started with prostitutes, and they had some really melodramatic adventures while they were rounding them up. Now they want to move out into the general population. I didn't offer to volunteer. I have the usual inhibitions. I grew up under the privacy-while-defecating taboo, for example. When I walked into my first army latrine and saw those naked hoppers lined up cheek by jowl, my bowels turned to stone. I never did succeed in adjusting. I taught myself to wake up at three in the morning when I'd have the latrine to myself. Well, they have a number of volunteers coming in from the clinic, but the question is, how representative are they? They're desperate for a half-dozen happily married couples to use as a control. You two would be ideal."

Fletcher said, "It's nice of you to think of us, Max, but I'm afraid I'm already spread pretty thin. Of course Hanna might be able to spare a half hour, and if you can overcome those inhibitions—"

"To make a serious comment," Max said, "which that remark doesn't deserve, it isn't a case of a spare half hour. They want to record continuity of response over a period of time. Here's a way in which someone with no scientific training can help advance the frontiers of knowledge. Well, that may be enough proselytizing for one night. Will you think about it, Fletcher? Hanna? I've watched enough marriages fall apart to know a good one when I see it. I know you make love often, with joy. If you want to find out more I'll introduce you to Martha Freeman. Okay? Changing the subject, Fletcher, what did you decide about Darmstadt?"

"It's still up in the air, but I don't really think I can take the time."

An orchestra in Darmstadt, West Germany, had recently written, out of the blue, offering to do a difficult piece of music he had written, *Interlude for Oboe and Strings*. Like most of Fletcher's work, this contained passages that made heavy demands on both the performers and the audience. String players he had talked to in New York didn't believe it could be done. The Darmstadt people wanted him for three weeks, but all they could pay was transportation.

"Everything's upset at the Conservatory since Teddy took the Iowa job," Hanna said. "Did Fletcher tell you they've asked him to take over?"

"It's nothing but hints so far," Fletcher said.

"Darling, don't be naïve. They want to be sure what you'll say before they ask you formally."

Perhaps, but Fletcher still hoped he wouldn't be asked.

Becoming director of a conservatory of music had never been one of his career goals, and he knew that Max would blow up, as a matter of principle, being a strong no-compromise man in his off-hours, even though he didn't seem to object to making money during the day. He had to be guaranteed $500 before he would pick up a scalpel. Fletcher had discovered abruptly, after many years of going about in corduroys and sneakers, that he felt healthier in good clothes. He was a changed man after his first Viyella shirt. He walked the streets of the upper West Side with a lighter step in Peale shoes. These artifacts of civilization cost money. Things he couldn't afford now he would be able to afford easily as director. His administrative load had increased sharply after the previous director was made cultural czar of Des Moines, Iowa. Having dodged administrative work for years, he learned that there was nothing so arcane about it, after all. He could do it, and do it well.

Max reacted with unexpected mildness. "Wouldn't that mean giving up composing?"

"Why?" Hanna said. "The job isn't that demanding. He can easily set aside a block of time every day for his own work. The man who's sure to get it if Fletcher turns it down would be a real disaster. A Goldwater type named Swinburne, of all things. Half the staff would run for their lives."

"You're nuts to consider it," Mary Jane said, standing up. "Hanna, thanks for the coffee and cake."

Hanna looked at her watch. "Is it that late?"

"I'll drive you in a few minutes," Max said without moving.

"I'll take my chances on a taxi. I've got an early rehearsal tomorrow."

Knowing Max, Fletcher was aware that he wouldn't get off with a mild look and one inoffensive question. Before the end of the evening he was going to have his nose rubbed in the God-Mammon dichotomy. Hanna, too, realized that the sooner she left the men alone the less Scotch would be consumed and the sooner everybody would get to bed. She looked in on Jennie and left a peanut butter sandwich and a glass of milk for her waking-up snack. She came back to the men in a dressing gown, her hair loose, looking her absolute best.

"Max, can I get you anything?"

"I'm going in a minute, Hanna."

"I think I'll read for a while. I'm really too groggy for Norman O. Brown tonight, but if I don't discover what that man is talking about I'll go mad."

She kissed them both, and thanked Max for the music. The kiss she gave her husband was quick and dry, but it told him to hurry.

When they were alone Fletcher said, without any windup, "I know my composing days are over if I take the Conservatory. Would that be such a loss to the world of music? I haven't written a thing for six months. I'm through with electronics. The last piece I did was so scarey I wiped it off the tape. Some of the effects were incredible."

"I can believe that. But was it music?"

"It was very much music, but it wasn't mine. The console took over. All the things that have been bothering me—Robert Moses, Huntley-Brinkley, the bombings, that sex project you're talking about—it was all there, and the hell with it."

"I wouldn't have liked it."

"Did I say I liked it? But it was beautiful, in a way. What do I do now? I'm beginning to wish I'd never seen a mobile. They're going to destroy modern music unless random composition does it first. That oboe and string piece is a Calder, forms moving freely through three dimensions but controlled by a central pivot. How long since you've seen an aspen in a breeze?"

"Years," Max said, drinking.

"Now that's what I call a mobile. They're wonderfully engineered—each stem comes in at a right angle so the leaves are never entirely still. Everybody in education isn't a bureaucrat, Max. I might like the job."

"Doesn't that worry you?"

"Why should it?"

Max went to the sideboard and poured more Scotch. Hanna would moan in the morning—couldn't they drink the Calvert's?

"Fletcher, one more thing and then I'll let you go to bed. That little hat with the Hawaiian feather band—"

"That's a great hat."

"It's a bureaucrat's hat. For a musician like you, that little cock's feather is sickening."

"I always considered the homburg the bureaucratic hat."

"In your case a homburg would be better. It would be an obvious disguise. The director of a music school doesn't wear a homburg. Your choice is inspired. The feather's a sop to the liberals. You disarm the conservatives because the thing is so damned expensive. You don't want to spend your life chairing meetings and keeping student protest to a minimum and writing money-raising letters. If you aren't careful you'll end up with a string of honorary degrees."

"Max, everybody has to live."

"That's my point. This is a dangerous course for you, Fletcher, just because you might be good at it. I know that good conservatory directors don't grow on trees, aspen or any other kind, but does it matter if they're good or bad? And while you're doing this outstanding job as an administrator, what do you expect would be happening to your emotional life?"

Fletcher moved angrily.

"Who am I, etcetera," Max said gloomily. "I know that most of my emotion is forced and bogus. Sometimes I open up a patient and smell the mess inside and close him right up again. I've had days when I operated for sixteen hours, and it was nothing but cancer, cancer. You have two things I don't have. You have talent and passion. There's a kind of anarchy inside you. I think you'll come out of it, but that's not something that just happens. You have to kick and scream and fight dirty. I'm a little drunk. Stravinsky likes your music. Bernstein likes your music. I know what you think about Bernstein, but he's no fool. Why do you think the Germans want to do that piece? Not because it reminds them of a mobile. There's passion in it. There's passion in all your music. Let it out. Resign from Consumers Union. Have you ever given Hanna an ultimatum in your life?"

"God, no."

"Every man ought to give his wife at least one ultimatum. I like Hanna, but she thinks the world can be fixed with intellect. She's never been in Bellevue's emergency ward on a Saturday night." He drank off the rest of his whiskey. "How much schmaltz did I put in that Debussy?"

"To be honest, Max, too much."

Max sighed and put down the glass. "I had a little girl die on the table this afternoon. No reason at all. She just went."

He picked up his cello. "There's no schmaltz in Mary Jane. But can she take out a simple appendix? I doubt if she even knows where to find it, on the left or the right. They tell me she's a tiger in bed."

"It wouldn't surprise me. It goes with the fingernails."

"Think about Darmstadt, Fletcher. Go. Then decide about the Conservatory job when you get back."

"I might, Max. I'd like to. They won't do the music unless I'm there to prepare it. But you're wrong—there's no feeling in that piece. It's technique."

"Use your ears, for God's sake."

Fletcher and Hanna always made love at the end of a musical evening, but tonight, as much as he looked forward to it, he would have preferred to listen to some tapes. There was no reason he should let his friend's remarks affect him, especially on the subject of hats. Didn't the fact that he could pay thirty dollars for a hat and wear it without guilt prove that he had no real desire to write serious music? Hanna thought the hat was fun and she had never seen anything in his music except what Fletcher had told her was there. Max was a propagandist by nature. He didn't care what arguments he used, so long as they convinced.

Naturally, the things he said had been somewhat flattering. Writing the Darmstadt piece, listening to the music in his head before distorting it in the form of notation, had been a painful experience, and Fletcher would never know how much of the pain had survived unless he went to Germany and took it out of the notation and back into sound.

As for that crack about honorary degrees—each spring the faucets were opened and witty, graceful remarks came trickling out while the stuffed shirts rewarded the other stuffed shirts for the remarks they had delivered on other ceremonial occasions. If Fletcher did take the Conservatory job —the chances were that he wouldn't—he would be careful about accepting speaking invitations. He could hear the rounded sentences becoming rounder and emptier and more complacent over the years. But if you were aware of the danger you could control it. Hanna had been skeptical the first time she heard him speak at a dinner, but he had won her completely. Their lovemaking afterward had been one for the sex doctor's books.

He added more Scotch to his drink. He would go in soon. The trouble was, when Hanna had been reading something serious before putting out the light, their first moves tended to be a trifle forced. Once under way, of course, it was invariably satisfactory. He had never made love to anybody else since they married, the day after he graduated from Oberlin. They never had arguments, let alone what you could call fights. They were truly compatible. If he hadn't been married, if they didn't have a child—large ifs—he wouldn't be giving the directorship any serious consideration. But for a lovely, imaginative daughter like Jennie, for the kind of life Hanna had made for him, he had to give up something, and all his renunciations so far had been easy.

He undressed in the bathroom and went naked into the bedroom. They believed in domestic nudity, so Jennie would get off to an uncomplicated start, but whenever the light was on Fletcher always thought guiltily that he ought to get more exercise. He hadn't gained much weight—a few pounds—but it had distributed itself badly.

Hanna's hair was still down, which settled it. She would have to get up afterward, unfortunate woman, to put in the metal and plastic that would make her look her usual self in the morning.

She took off her glasses. "I didn't think he would ever go."

"He knew you were waiting for me. He likes to set up these little tensions."

She turned out the light and slid down in bed with a slithering motion. Usually the sound of her naked flesh against the sheets started something in Fletcher, but tonight for some reason he was going to be hard to rouse. He wasn't a nightcap man. The two heavy Scotches, plus the talk about Darmstadt, had sapped his strength.

"I'm so stiff," she said. "I ironed too long this afternoon, foolishly."

"Do you want me to rub you?"

"I hate to ask you, darling, it's so late."

Fletcher switched over to his reserve oxygen as she turned on her stomach. "Should I get the alcohol?"

"Just your hand. Darling, you're tired, I know it's an imposition—"

"Don't be silly. Where?"

"Right there. A little lower. Yes. Lovely."

He rested his forehead on one hand, and came close to dozing off. Her skin was as smooth as butter.

"Lower," she said after a time.

This was a formula, and he told himself to wake up. The Scotch, at the same time, told him to go to sleep.

"Lower," she said. "A *bit* lower. Darling, what did I ever do to deserve you?"

"Ironed."

"Honey, this is luxurious. I feel so elegant and whorish. Depraved."

These were obligations he could discharge in his sleep. Tonight he wasn't up to any creative innovations. She told him she felt the beginnings of the sweet rush, which he already knew; the tactile sensations in his fingertips went both ways. But the information he was collecting with his fingers stopped in his brain, too tired to go further.

Her conscience awakened. It was time for activity.

"No, darling, stay where you are," Fletcher told her. "This is nice for me too."

"Are you sure?"

"Yes."

"Darling, your fingering's so skillful. It comes of playing a stringed instrument. There. Not too hard!"

"Sorry."

"Yes, like that. Fabulous."

He dozed as she accelerated. His mind circled and slipped. Why should honorary degrees be looming so large, all of a sudden? The problem, such as it was—it was tiny!—wouldn't become acute for another thirty years. If some unknown college in Wisconsin decided to offer him an honorary Doctor of Laws, in recognition of a distinguished career in music education, he could always turn it down. Of course it was only a symbol—it would please Hanna as much as he was pleasing her now with his hand—she would make the same sounds. . . .

She slipped away from him, in an access of selflessness.

"Darling, you're not with me at all!" she exclaimed. "Roll up your sleeves, old girl. Time I got to work."

She knew where to apply friction, how to change and intensify, and before long he began to catch fire. There was nothing like sex, after all.

His brain was soon invaded and overcome by a cool fog, smelling of cologne. He couldn't be expected to give this up. If Max Sultan had anything like it, he wouldn't be so quick to give disinterested advice. Darmstadt would be a battle-field—all musicians are hostile to new arrangements of sound —and would Hanna, a pacifist, understand? She would hear only the torment in the music. Sexual pleasure, of the smooth, gliding kind, was what she loved. Why would any rational person turn his back on pleasure and go looking for trouble?

Satisfied that they were equally ready, Hanna guided him in, whispering to him in their private language. There was only one change Fletcher would make in their lovemaking if he could start over. It was no longer possible, of course, because it would condemn too much, but he wished that at some early point he had found a tender and diplomatic way to let her know that he would rather not be told how she felt. They had always experimented. Whenever they heard of anything new they tried it, and Hanna felt that to get the full benefits they needed to describe their sensations as they occurred. And so a lovemaking argot had developed, a mixture of Anglo-Saxon and Latin and words that had somehow coined themselves.

With part of his mind he was miles away. The same thing had happened during the final movement of the quartet—the copulating couple, he and Hanna, became smaller and smaller until finally they were tiny protozoa dancing ritually in a drop of water at the far end of a microscope. Muscle group-ings gripped and relaxed, and finally held. In the drop of water a tidal wave curled, collapsed, and receded.

"You came hard," she whispered as he slipped away.

"So did you."

"What a wonderful lover!"

She backed in against him, in the arrangement they knew as the double questionmark. Later he heard her say, "Darling, asleep?"

"Almost."

"We can talk about it tomorrow."

"About what tomorrow?"

"What Max was saying."

She shrugged closer, in contact all the way. One of his hands lay on the smooth prominence of her hip. The intersecting curves.

"How do you think he knew we're good in bed?" she said.

"Sixth sense."

Another long, delicious shrug.

"I was reading Norman O. He writes about sex in such an unsexy way—"

The sentence ran downhill. Why was she still awake?

"Trying to decide if I could do it. Could you, darling? Make love with people watching?" She laughed softly to herself. "Well, listen. I was ticking away at ninety miles an hour. Imagining what it would be like, with the doctors in their white gowns— We'd be in a hard hospital bed, I think, with the head tilted, and we'd be quite naked and the whole approach would be so serious and dedicated—"

He was waking up. "Sort of like the Nativity. Only instead of the Wise Men—"

"Fletcher, no jokes. And bang! I came! Holding *Love's Body* in both hands, with my glasses on. I throbbed for ages. Couldn't you tell when you touched me first?"

"You were slippery but I thought that was me. I didn't know any medicine men were involved."

"Dearest, it was you I did it with. The laboratory just added a small fillip. I was on you, and we were doing it that revolving way. You were licking my nipples. But darling, the really wild thing was something you did when you were getting me ready. There was this low murmur of amazement around the room. Isn't it absurd?"

"Are you trying to get me excited again, by any chance?"

"Certainly not. What I really want is a glass of cold milk. I wouldn't dream of asking you to get it."

"That's lucky, because I wouldn't dream of getting it."

"Darling—" She stopped, but he knew from the surface tension of her hip that she would continue in a minute. "I could, you know. I really think I could. Now don't say the first thing that comes into your head—"

He pulled away slightly.

"You're against it?" she said.

"Damn right I'm against it. I wasn't thinking about it in terms of us."

"Are you cross?"

"No, but I'm surprised."

She broke the pattern by rolling on her back. "I had a silly ambition once. When I was a girl I had a real crush on Madame Curie. I never got anything but A's in math and science. And then you walked into the Commons, you beast, with a hole in the elbow of your sweater. You know I don't regret a second of it, but I've already decided, I'm going to General Studies and get my A.B. I don't want to be nothing but a wife. All I need is ten credits, and I can get those standing on my head."

There was a brief pause.

"Conceivably," he said, "just barely conceivably, I might have done it when I took a thirty-two waist. There wouldn't be any awed murmurs now when I undressed."

"Fletcher, you're beautiful."

"You're a loyal wife, and somewhat dotty. I'm not beautiful."

She laughed. "Now you don't know what to believe, do you? Was I serious or not?"

"You were half serious."

"Was I? Perhaps I was. The hard part would be getting started. Certainly it wouldn't be possible if either the man or the woman had any secret reservations."

"I don't have any secret reservations. I have open reservations."

She sat up and turned on the light. "Who do you think they'll get? People with a completely cynical attitude, I suspect. Who believe in getting in and getting it over with fast, without any tenderness or respect. And then they'll publish the results as the definitive word on married sex. What a distortion! You and I would be so perfect."

Yes, they'd probably get A's, Fletcher thought, perhaps

eventually an honorary degree. He went to the kitchen for the milk. Hanna had her rollers in by the time he returned and had taken on her nightly resemblance to the Statue of Liberty.

"Thank you, sweetheart."

After the light was out they returned to the double question-mark.

"Good night."

"Good night, dear."

They didn't worry the subject any further, but they were too much in tune with each other not to know that they were both still thinking about it.

chapter 4

Jake Burgess wanted two things: to be a playwright and to find a girl who understood what it meant to want to be a playwright. Both seemed impossible.

Everybody knows the Broadway statistics. Five thousand plays are written every year. Five hundred are considered seriously for production. To an author this means being kept dangling from month to month, by producer after producer, until finally, concluding that he has been lied to by everybody, he surrenders and goes to work for a paycheck. And yet a hundred or so plays are optioned or announced, and fifty are actually produced. Twenty reach New York, three make money.

So why would anybody in possession of his senses set out to buck these odds? Girls, Jake had found, weren't even willing to listen to an explanation. It was one of the ways they were built differently.

He grew up in Maine, where his father owned a boatyard. One of the summer people in the cove was a playwright, the author of a long-ago hit, with one set and a large cast. It still returned royalties from high school performances. Jake did some caretaking for this man, and they became friends. When Jake started writing plays as an undergraduate at the University of Maine, he wrote a dozen the first year. One was accepted by the Drama Club, and the summer playwright agreed to come to the opening. Before returning to New York he spent an afternoon trying to steer Jake into some other profession, but he had already drawn the sting of his arguments by the look he had given Jake in the lobby the night before, after the final curtain.

In the Army, Jake worked out a number of plots while he was walking guard. Three of his college plays were being considered by New York producers. Two more were tied up in fellowship contests, from both of which he emerged as the runner-up. He went to work for his father after surviving twelve months in the Mekong delta. He intended to write before work and on weekends; in two years he finished one play. The letters from New York continued to be encouraging, but two production offices followed up their compliments by losing his scripts.

He had a shock of black hair, generally in motion. He was a good dancer and owned a good car. He was completely at ease in his own part of the world. The girls he had dates with assumed that he would inherit the boatyard, the hundred-acre saltwater farm, and the island; that he would give up his pose of being independent and register Republican; that sometime in his late eighties—it was a long-lived family—he would end up in the Burgess burying-ground. Before any of this could happen, he wrote an article about a war between the lobstermen of two offshore islands and mailed it to a New York literary agent whose name, Judah Sutro, he had seen in a writers' magazine. Five days later the piece was sold.

The same mail that brought the check brought a letter about his last play but one. Read through glasses with a special kind of optimistic correction, it was as good as an acceptance. All he had to do, the producer told him, was bring one of the four characters up a little. But what did that mean, precisely—up a little? The producer didn't explain. If producers could express themselves, they wouldn't be producers. Jake took three weeks off, worked twelve hours a day, and submitted a revision. This time the producer thought he had come very, very close. But it still wasn't quite . . . It didn't capture just the right . . . There was a faint blurring of focus, an obscure failure of nerve.

After reading this letter, Jake slammed out of the post office and down to the cove. He had a choice. He could forget the whole thing or go at it full-time. After several hours on the rocks, listening to pointless advice from the sandpipers, he called his current girl and invited her to a double-feature at the drive-in. It was the best sex they had had to date, so good Jake didn't see how it could be improved upon by years of practice. It stopped, finally, as such things do. Feeling more harmonious than he had since that moment, six years before, when the playwright gave him the ambiguous look on his first and only opening night, he settled back and looked up at the big screen.

The movie was a leading candidate for that year's Academy Award. Brendan Gill had liked it. It starred a famous actress, nobly built, in eye-catching clothes. The director had been celebrated for years. The settings reeked of money. But the screenplay was atrocious, the dialogue jejune and unreal. If Jake couldn't do better than that . . .

He left for New York the following week.

His unspoken understanding with his father was that if he wanted money from home he had to come back and earn it. He took a room without bath in a house with an elegant exterior, a few steps west of Central Park. All he really needed was a bed and a low table for his typewriter, and that was what they gave him, at a staggering monthly rental. He walked a lot, partly to see the city, partly to work off the cafeteria food.

His agent made time for him one morning. He was short, erect, simply and soberly dressed, with only one sign that he made his living under duress—a vertical line between his eyebrows, so deep that Jake feared it might go through into the brain. He thought it was fine that Jake was now within reach, and he hoped to have another sale to report very soon.

Jake met a half-dozen producers and found them, on the whole, a slippery lot. He saw the final two acts of every play on Broadway, mixing with the paying customers during the first intermission, wearing his one good suit. If an usher bothered him, Jake gave him fifty cents. For most people this would be a maddening way of seeing plays, but Jake had most of his trouble with third acts.

For twelve months he didn't sell a line. Occasionally, when he was out of money, he looked in the classified section for listings under No Exp Nec, and worked for a few weeks as a counterman or messenger. Finally, his agent, who had given no sign of life for months, asked him to stop in, again not for lunch.

The Judah Sutro office was on Fifth, in a sliver of a building two windows wide, dating back to the 1920's boom. Air-conditioners had been added, but nothing could be done about the old-fashioned elevators without encroaching on the rentable space. Sutro immediately began telling Jake about an interesting deal he was negotiating with MCA and the Russians.

The Russians in Russia? That was the way it sounded, but Jake thought it would be cooler not to ask.

"How are you making it, Burgess? You haven't copped out and gone to work for anybody?"

"No, I'm still free-lancing."

"We have something that could interest you. Only a hundred a week, but don't walk out yet. This is for Bobby Quinby."

He paused, and Jake said politely, "I've seen his by-line."

"You know magazines," Sutro said. "Five years ago I couldn't peddle him for dog-meat. Everybody said he was too flippant. Now they've decided flippancy is what the readers want. He took home eighty G's last year. But they could change again, and we'd like to get him a hardcover success, for some long-term status. He's busy and he needs an assistant, somebody who can write a decent English sentence. He liked that *True* piece of yours about—" he snapped his fingers, the line between his eyebrows deepening—"about—"

"The lobstermen?"

"The lobstermen. You'd interview people for him, be a reporter and general factotum. Nothing menial, no typing. If you're interested, I'll set up a date."

Jake laughed. Sutro, startled, laughed with him and instantly seemed more intelligent and likable.

"All right, it's not great. Bobby was thinking initially of a no-pay apprenticeship. We jollied him out of that. If he can up his production by half a piece a year he'll end up making money."

The phone rang. He picked it up and began talking about large sums and how to lessen the tax bite on one of his clients. Jake, having no particular tax problems of his own, felt like an outsider. The voice at the other end of the connection offered an advance of $125,000, whether for a novel or a shipment of neckties there was no way of knowing. Jake looked around while he waited. Sutro was apparently the kind of person who keeps lists, in the hope of imposing some limits on life's natural disorder. Reading upside down, Jake saw his own name, followed by a question mark. Burgess? It was a question Jake sometimes asked himself.

After rejecting the $125,000 deal with scorn, Sutro returned to Jake.

"What do you want me to tell Bobby?"

"A hundred's pretty low."

"He might go one twenty-five," Sutro admitted, using the figure that had been quoted on the phone, but without the zeroes. "He's on the Coast. Due in Monday." He put his hand on the phone. "Monday afternoon? Drinks at five?"

"Drinks at five would be fine," Jake said, "except that I'm not sure I want the job."

The agent reflected for a moment, and decided to release some more information.

"Random wants a fact-crime book on the order of *The Boston Strangler*. Bobby would be right for it, and the deal is more or less set. But, in confidence, he's got a new girl. He doesn't think he has time to do the legwork."

The phone call he had just heard had reminded Jake of a basic truth about negotiation: in every financial transaction there is a buyer and a seller.

"And the reason he wants somebody who can write a decent sentence is so the man who does the legwork can also do the writing?"

"That would be between Bobby and yourself. If you block out the first draft, he might give you a point."

The usage was unfamiliar to Jake. "A point?"

"One percent royalty. Two would be tops. You're without a name, Jake, and there are things you have to learn. Whatever you do in the future you're going to market through us because we've got you on contract. You're no good to us now. We want you to grow."

"I never said it was my ambition to write magazine articles. I want to write plays."

"Then God damn it," Sutro exclaimed angrily, "what are you doing in this office?"

Jake laughed again, and again he surprised the agent into looking like a human being. "Why would anybody in his right mind want to write magazine articles?"

"Hundreds of *thousands* of people want to write magazine articles."

"In their right mind?"

"Well, you may have a point there. Do I call Bobby?"

In any Quinby-Burgess collaboration, Jake knew, Burgess

would be doing most of the work and Quinby would be pocketing most of the money. But Bobby did several kinds of pieces. One was the quick interview with the hot theatrical personality. The more important they were, the sillier he made them sound. He must know his way around in the world Jake was hoping to enter.

"Tell him I'll talk to him, but he'll have to persuade me."

Sutro gave him a thoughtful look before dialing. He talked to the writer in California and hung up muttering. "He's having trouble getting his teeth in the new piece. New piece is right. He's got that girl of his out there."

The phone was ringing. He reached across to shake hands and let Jake find his way out for himself.

Jake passed through a long room filled with typing tables beneath a large electric clock. Men and women were typing furiously, as though they would be lined up and shot if they didn't finish the day's quota by five in the afternoon. These were the fee-readers, and on his previous visit Jake had turned down an opportunity to join them.

At a desk in a little clearing facing the elevators, a secretary slid her glasses down her nose and looked at him with a nice smile.

"You're a hard man to reach on the phone, Mr. Burgess."

"Sometimes they give me the message and sometimes they don't."

She regarded him pleasantly, in no hurry to get back to work. Her fingers grazed the keys of her typewriter, which gave off a low, encouraging hum. She wore a crisp blouse with three vertical pleats. Not having had a single productive date since arriving in New York, Jake had already noticed that the two outside pleats exactly bisected two very nice breasts. She was no doubt also a good typist. Jake, personally, was a butter-fingered typist, and one of his daydreams was that someday he would meet an attractive girl who would type his scripts for nothing because she loved him.

Possible lines of dialogue skittered through his mind. How did she like working in a literary agency? Did the money-making clients ever come into the office, or did Sutro meet them in restaurants? Had she ever run into an article writer named

Bobby Quinby, and what did she think he'd be like to collabo-
rate with? Was she free for a drink after work?

But it would have to wait. If she accepted the invitation, one
drink would lead to another, until it became apparent that she
expected to be asked for dinner, not to mention a possible cab
fare . . .

He went on to the elevator, and she resumed typing. The
old-fashioned elevator danced to a stop, failing by six inches to
line up with the floor.

"Watch your step," the operator warned.

With less than ten dollars in his pocket, watching his step
was what Jake had to do. Before the summons to the agent's
office, he had been planning to spend the afternoon writing
dialogue on the Staten Island Ferry. Instead, he went to Room
315 in the Public Library and looked up Quinby in the most
recent volume of *Reader's Guide*. The entries filled half a
column.

Thirty minutes later, after watching the numbers on the call-
board blink toward his and jump past, he got his six slips back.
The titles he wanted were either in use or they couldn't be
found. Eventually he received a single bashed-in volume well
on its way back to wood pulp. The Quinby article, as it happened, was an interview with an enormously successful producer who had been holding one of Jake's scripts for eighteen
months. Quinby always went into the ring with a load in each
glove. He hit the man freely, finishing him off with a few hard
kicks where they would do the most damage. Jake enjoyed it.

That night he went to a new play from England—imported,
as a matter of fact, by the same producer Quinby had interviewed. Having missed the first act, Jake found it hard to
follow. The theme seemed to be the difficulty of communicating in the modern world, and certainly the playwright was his
own best example. Jake's attention was divided. He had his eye
on two girls who were also standing. The fantasy dialogue,
with himself handling all three roles, crackled with wit and
authority, a big improvement on the dialogue coming from
the stage. But nothing came of it in the end.

After the play broke, Jake went to Third Avenue. Here, on
a two-block stretch in the low Sixties, young men and women
of a certain type, most of them college graduates and recent

arrivals in New York, milled about every Friday night looking for a Saturday-night date. Jake had written some of his best boy-meets-girl dialogue here, but he always went home deploring his own high demands. Did a girl have to be as stylish as Audrey Hepburn for a one-night episode?

Tonight, once more, he was unable to force himself to speak that first line. He watched several successful encounters. The girls wouldn't be here if they hadn't wanted to be approached, so how much brashness did it take, after all? He drifted off about 1:30, still unattached, beginning to believe that the great population explosion must be a myth. How did all those new family units get together?

Two hours later he was in a bar downtown, drinking dark beer served in a heavy, false-bottomed mug. He had spotted the girl the moment he came in. She was wearing a black turtleneck and butterfly earrings. She didn't seem part of the group at her table. Jake studied them covertly from the line of silent single men at the bar. The table didn't seem to be organized in pairs. The young men were all bearded, and one was reading an Anchor paperback, an affectation in that light.

Another girl came in from the street. To Jake's intense surprise, she turned out to be the secretary from his agent's office, still wearing the blouse with the three pleats. She was smiling straight at him.

Coming closer, she changed into somebody else, and the smile turned into a look of indifference. He bit back the friendly greeting he had been about to give her.

When he checked the big table again, the butterfly girl was gone. A pack of Kools and a *Daily News* remained on the checkered tablecloth at her empty place, which might mean that she had gone to the ladies' room.

Without planning any dialogue, he pushed off from the bar, leaving his half-finished beer and change from a dollar, and bumped into her head-on. She was even prettier at close range, with a full, rather sullen mouth. She was too skinny, with breasts that were more like apples than melons, but Jake's standards of excellence had been going down, down, for one solid year. His opening remark was a parody of opening remarks and wouldn't have remained in a script through the first rehearsal.

"Hi."

"Hi," she said, checking to see if she knew him. "Crowded tonight."

"Jammed."

And that might have been that, except that the pressures of the crowd kept them together.

"I've been watching you for an hour," he said. She looked up at him, unwilling to feed him a line. He went on, "Trying to figure out who's with who at your table. Whenever somebody said something, it went on a slant, never to the right or the left. How do you explain it?"

Her glance came down to his tie.

"Pay no attention to the necktie," Jake said. "I'm as uncommitted as anybody here." He fingered his chin, which of course was clean-shaven. "Sorry about the beard. It got caught in an air-conditioning unit and I had to shave it off."

This was fair dialogue, he thought, but the girl seemed unimpressed. "What do you do, work in an office or something?"

Jake hated to identify himself as a playwright, because the next question always established him as a would-be playwright with only one nonprofessional credit.

"When I'm working, which is as seldom as possible, I demonstrate potato peelers."

Her upper lip stiffened. Jake had had just enough beer to do the one thing that would help. He laughed.

"I believe you," she said scornfully.

"I have property rights to a piece of the bar. Will you join me?"

She shook her head. "Thanks, I'm on my way."

"Now maybe I'll find out how that table of yours pairs off."

He sidestepped and let her by. She reached past one of the bearded men to get her cigarettes. She was wearing black openwork stockings and an insignificant skirt. The stockings went up and up and *up*, and finally disappeared from sight. She said nothing to anybody and left by herself. Jake downed his beer and followed.

"You," she commented when he fell in step beside her.

"Do you feel like a short bracing walk?"

"Not really. Not tonight. If you're looking for the IRT, you're going the wrong way."

Jake knew the next line was the critical one, and he hesitated. Suddenly, without waiting for it, the girl began to talk.

"A potato-peeler demonstrator. Oh, yes. College bastards like you give me a pain. Money's no problem. There's always a check in the mail from old Dad every month, isn't there? You ought to take the thumb out of your ass and grow up."

Jake gulped but recovered quickly. "Be fair. Am I that bad?"

"How should I know?" she said irritably. "Tonight I don't feel like finding out. If I wanted a new guy right now—*which I don't*—"

"Now you've said something interesting."

"Don't tell me that was a God damn accident in there. Somebody told you about Mickey and me. I've got eyes."

"Very nice eyes," Jake said.

She looked around and started to say something, but stopped.

"I don't know many people in New York," he said, "and I sure as hell don't have any informants in that bar. I really did demonstrate a potato peeler for ten days in the 42nd Street Woolworth's. And who is Mickey?"

"We're only supposed to be living together, that's all, which doesn't seem to mean a hell of a lot to some people. I had a tooth pulled this afternoon. Do you know how you feel with a jawful of Novocain?"

"Sure."

"Like a zombie. That schmuck of a dentist had to jab me three times before he could get it to take, and naturally Mickey picked the minute it began to wear off to start in on me. Why don't I take the sheets to the Laundromat, why don't I put out the garbage once in a while, that kind of crap. There are other things in life! Music. Vietnam. There are plenty of points I could bring up in my own defense, I assure you. I just had to sit there and take it, with my tongue feeling like a piece of shoe leather. Considerate? Very. Thank God we didn't get married when he came back from the service. The creep. He only cares about one thing, getting laid. Does it ever occur to him to ask how *I* feel?"

Jake was feeling less and less sexually interested by the minute. She went on complaining about the unchivalrous Mickey, for whom Jake was beginning to feel some sympathy, until she stopped at a building that was probably one of the historic landmarks of the neighborhood. The inner door was permanently sprung. The smells were disagreeable. A single word was printed in red crayon on the urine-colored wall: BLOOD!

"You don't want to come up," she said. "You really don't."

She was right. He really didn't.

She went on, "I'm so worn out, I can't tell you. I'm going to take some of those tablets the dentist gave me and go to sleep by myself for a change."

Jake, too, intended to sleep alone, though in his case it would hardly be a change. She peered up at him.

"But I hit the Bistro four nights out of five, and if you wanted to try again tomorrow? I'm not promising anything. I mean you can't predict about Mickey."

"I think you'll get back together and make each other very happy."

"You're sore."

"Why, no. Why should I be sore?"

She sighed. "Males. You guys are impossible. The big trouble with me is, I put myself in the other person's shoes. Just tell me one thing. What about that potato peeler?"

"It could shred carrots and cut up cucumbers. You could also slice off the end of your little finger with it, I found out. It grew back. Point me right for the subway."

"Wait a minute. I guess I'm probably up to it. You went out of your way to say a couple of nice things, which is more than most people. Just don't take all night."

She touched him, simply and directly and on the whole quite nicely, but Jake shied away.

"What am I all of a sudden, repulsive?" she said gently. "Baby, let Mommy hold it for a minute. Give me a little notice next time and I'll put clean sheets on the bed. I don't want to take you upstairs. The place is a mess, and that fucking Mickey has a key."

She put her forehead against his chest while she opened his zipper.

"Put your hands on my ass," she whispered. "Tell me when you're about to come. I just had this skirt cleaned."

The street door opened suddenly behind them, and Jake was

given a paralyzing blow in the kidneys. Someone seized him around the neck.

The girl sprang back, and for the first time Jake saw the raw socket which no longer held an upper canine. She whirled and ran into the building. Hands were at Jake's pockets.

He told himself not to resist. These were experts. They wouldn't kill him for a suit of clothes and a couple of dollars. The arm tightened about his neck, and the night began to close in. The graffiti on the wall wavered and ran. Jake slammed his elbow backward and managed to twist free. The pain spreading upward from his kidneys kept him from doing anything more. He caught a glimpse of something moving toward him and tried to dodge. The lights blazed around him. He dropped through into nowhere.

He was in bad shape when he climbed back. He knew where he was, and what had happened to him. He was lying on his face in a dirty Village vestibule, wearing only a ripped shirt, a necktie, shorts, and socks. Everything else was gone—watch, money, identification, suit, shoes, the picture of his Maine girl. Insects crawled across his face. As soon as he could move his hand, he tried to brush them off, and they changed to blood.

He had a confused memory of a girl, but she no longer seemed to be around. He waited until he had the strength to lift his head from the cold, dirty marble—it was actually marble. There were doorbells next to the mailboxes. Above them an ancient notice was thumbtacked to the wall: OUT OF ORDER. He crawled through the inner door. The building was inhabited. In a moment someone would hear him and come out, making sympathetic noises. Or the girl would come back. She had begun to be more friendly at the end.

"Help me," he said into the silence.

He had crawled as far as the bottom of the stairs when the cops arrived. In the police view, no one is altogether innocent in this kind of building, and they rolled him over roughly. Discovering that he was white, they left him alone. Perhaps the necktie helped. Though of course, Jake reflected, it was the necktie that had got him into trouble in the first place.

Several people came in and stepped over him to get up the stairs. Fifty minutes slipped by before the ambulance arrived.

Jake, without a watch, had no way of measuring the time, but the cops kept talking about it.

He didn't hear a siren. The stretcher simply appeared.

One of the cops said sarcastically, "All the time in the world, boys. We got nothing else to do."

Jake took the plunge again while he was being manhandled onto the stretcher. The motion of the ambulance jolted him back. They still hadn't turned on their siren, and Jake felt it as a reproach. They must know this was nobody's fault but his own.

chapter 5

Victoria Orr, a pretty, unhappy girl of twenty-three, found herself attending another Happening, her third that month. These dreary events were taking place everywhere in New York that summer, and she found them boring beyond belief. She knew the arguments—they were *meant* to be boring, to point up the monotony of modern urban life. People knocked Matisse and Picasso, and where were their pictures now? In *Life* magazine and hanging over the beds in half the motel rooms in the United States. But just the same!

Victoria's roommate, a tall girl called Anne Geselle, was dating an assistant district attorney, Woods McChesney. Victoria had been impressed with this title until she learned that in certain sections of town you couldn't fly a paper airplane out a window without hitting an assistant district attorney. Her own date tonight was a stranger named Matt something; his last name had been mangled during the introductions. He had served in the Army with Woods and came from Chicago. Victoria had no intention of letting him know that she grew up in the same part of the world herself, Winnetka.

She'd been up late the night before, riding the merry-go-round, as usual, and all day at work she had looked forward to a quiet domestic evening, writing letters and washing her hair. But if you didn't go out in thunderstorms you couldn't expect to be struck by lightning, and she had finally agreed to show the Chicagoan that New York was a hospitable town. Woods had suggested that they make a special effort; their out-of-town visitor had never been to an authentic New York Happening. She and Anne gave the men drinks before they left, they had more drinks in a seedy bar, and here they were now in a dirty loft on the fifth floor of a terrible building in the East Village.

The cast of characters was nearly as large as the audience. Two men in Edwardian costumes were piling up a dry wall of cinderblocks, on the other side of which a girl with one breast exposed was pretending to suckle a baby. The baby was actually a doll, a black doll at that. The symbolism was easy. It was almost the only message people were bothering to impart these days: that human relationships were becoming more and more difficult. The trouble with symbols, in Victoria's humble opinion, was that they didn't actually mean very much. She thought back to the time when she had left the Church, with its symbolism, and was trying to extricate herself from that messy affair with Larry Feinstein at college. She had talked at length with a very smart man who billed himself as a lay analyst. Together they had been able to identify the problem. That didn't mean he could tell her what to do about it. Her father had walked out on the family when Victoria was eight. He had worked in a bank, and for a long time she suspected from something her mother had said, or had failed to say, that he had stolen some money. She learned later that there was nothing to it at all. He had simply decided one day that banking and marriage had too much in common and he got rid of both at the same time. Victoria, of course, had been included in the deal. Her mother had never remarried, although she was reasonably attractive even now, thanks to Clairol and Canadian Air Force exercises. She sold real estate and insurance. Her house was too big for one person, but she kept it looking like something out of *House Beautiful.* She had never concealed the fact that she considered a daughter something of an imposition. Victoria had retaliated by leaving clothes around, forgetting to make her bed, and underachieving at school. Her mother didn't like Jews or Negroes, so of course Victoria had two successive affairs in her freshman year at Northwestern, one with a Jewish boy who attempted suicide when Victoria dropped him, the other with a very black, very fierce, very superstitious exchange student from Nigeria. On a superficial level this was all very obvious.

Most New York Happenings had a musical accompaniment, usually good and loud, but in this one the actors went about their work in absolute silence, to demonstrate that the breakdown of communication was total. Matt stirred uneasily beside her, and she put her hand on his arm. Alienation was the big word now in New York, and if he didn't know what it meant she would be glad to explain it to him. At her low point, before she left college in the middle of freshman exams, she had had the feeling that there had been a thin plastic membrane separating her from the outside world. She had torn it away finally, not without difficulty, because she'd been sheltered by it, and for a couple of years now she had been ready for contact. She was sending out signals, but so far no one had picked them up. Never mind what the doctors said, getting in touch was partly a matter of luck.

Twenty-three was a difficult year for a girl. New York was a maelstrom that sucked in girls from all over the country, from all over the world, and for some reason most of them seemed to be about Victoria's age. The competition was ferocious. When she first arrived she had gone three months without a date. Then she heard about a party, put on her best dress and her best perfume, gritted her teeth, and crashed it. Word of mouth did the rest.

For someone in her situation, she had the best kind of looks. She had met a few models, and they weren't constantly being badgered for dates, by any means. Men were too awed. Girls at the homely end of the spectrum usually managed to end up married, but not by being particular. Victoria was between the extremes. She looked healthy. She had brownish hair, which she wore in a slash across her forehead; she had a long, delicate nose and widely spaced eyes, teeth that weren't perfectly in line but had few fillings. Her figure, quite simply, was first-rate.

On the back screen behind the actors, a flickering home movie showed a junkie, a girl in a slip preparing to inject herself. Victoria glanced at Matt. There was an interesting play of muscle along the hinge of his jaw.

"How long do we have to stay?" he whispered.

She turned to see if the others were ready to leave. A young actor holding a live chicken suddenly picked up a hatchet and began trying to hack off the chicken's head. The chicken screeched and fluttered. Matt growled something and, taking Victoria's wrist, pulled her to her feet.

The actor finally subdued the chicken and waved it triumphantly, its partially severed head dangling. He was blown on something; he had the craziest eyes Victoria had seen in a long time. Blood spurted over the people in the first row. Waving the dying bird, which continued to pump blood, he began pulling out handfuls of feathers and throwing them at the audience. Chairs went over as people ducked and dodged. The Black Sambo doll hurtled down from the stage and was thrown back. The needle went into the vein. A nude man wearing a huge dummy phallus ran in and began lashing people with it, both actors and audience. The Happening was successful—the line between performers and onlookers, so strictly observed in a traditional playhouse, had disappeared.

"This calls for a few drinks, or something," Matt said as the group emerged into the dirty street.

"Do you have anything like that in Chicago?" Anne demanded.

"God, no! That boy could use a lesson in how to butcher a chicken."

"Will you look at that?" Anne said, examining the spots on her dress. "Blood's the hardest thing there is to get out."

They walked uptown on Second Avenue in search of the right kind of bar, without too much crud on the floor. Victoria's heartbeat had begun to fade, but she didn't want to calm down all the way. She was nursing a frail little spark, knowing it would flicker out in the first adverse wind. She had her hand inside Matt's arm. As part of the initial buildup, she had been told that he had played four seasons as corner back for the Bears. He had a pigeon-toed walk. His sports jacket was the wrong color, the wrong material, the wrong fit, but couldn't she be open-minded about clothes for once in her life?

They found a bar with an empty booth. Victoria and Matt ended up across from each other with their knees grazing. There was enough light to make out the black tufts of hair in his nostrils.

"And something else you don't have in Chicago," Anne said when the drinks were ordered. "Woods, tell our friends what you told me. It's not secret, is it?"

"To a certain extent. But whenever I start to tell somebody, it turns out they've heard about it already. Vicky, listen. I'm trying to persuade Anne to— Vicky."

Matt had set up a little knee-to-knee chafing motion. She was trying to imagine the reality beneath the unfortunate jacket. She knew you had to be tough to play professional ball. The flicker of excitement took hold and began to spread. And it was too soon; they still had some drinking to do. Making an effort, she turned toward Woods.

She knew his biography. He had grown up in Brooklyn, where his parents owned a tiny drugstore, and he had worked like a demon to get where he was. He worked his way through NYU, then through the University of Pennsylvania Law School. He was more harassed than usual at the moment because he was trying to give up cigarettes. He was smaller and older than Anne; most of her social life was with older men. He was probably fairly handsome, if you cared for that type—carefully weeded mustache, glasses, small, neat bones. You only noticed his eyes after you got to know him quite well. He had something bottled up inside him, and Victoria didn't want to be around when he pulled the cork.

The drinks arrived. Matt sent the waitress back for another round.

"We're talking about sex," Anne explained. "It's one of Woods's many interests." She patted him fondly. "He's a Renaissance man."

"Hell, I know this guy—I soldiered with him."

"Take a hypothetical case," Woods said, "except that it's not hypothetical. A doctor. Somebody gives him the use of a laboratory, and he decides to discover something. Other people are working on the common cold. What else is there? Headaches? Backaches? Too trite. And then he gets an inspired idea. Copulation!"

"You've got to be kidding," Matt said.

"I'm definitely not kidding. It's going on right now. People come in on a regular schedule. He tells them what position to do it in, and by God, they get undressed and do it."

Matt was no longer moving his knee against Victoria's.

"Is it *legal?*" Victoria asked.

"Well, now," Woods said, enjoying himself. "Legal. If you go strictly by the book, hardly anything's legal, except face-to-face connection between consenting adults of the opposite sex who not only have to be married, they have to be married to each other. And how often does that happen? They're violating seven different sections of the Penal Code. We know what they're doing, and they know we know what they're doing. But what a bitch it's going to be to prove. Naturally they don't sell tickets. They lock the doors. And while we're breaking in, the man gets up off the woman and puts on his pants. 'Sex research, officer? Not at all, just a routine obstetrical examination. You're invading our privacy. Get out.' "

"They must keep some kind of records," Victoria said. "Seize them."

"You need prima facie evidence that a crime's been committed before a judge will give you that kind of subpoena. I've talked to three people who I know for a fact have been going to the laboratory two or three times a week, and they look at me as though I'm some kind of Peeping Tom."

"I'll be glad to volunteer," Matt offered. "What do the babes look like?"

Woods waved in disgust. "What you'd expect. No, actually they don't look any different from ordinary people. But they aren't using many single men except on special projects."

"Tell them about Mooney," Anne said.

"One of the smartest investigators on the D.A.'s Squad, a hard man to fool. He's infiltrated the Minutemen, the Communist Party, you name it and he's been in it. But he said something wrong. We still don't know what. He never got that postcard to appear."

"Don't go so fast, Woods," Victoria said. "Not that I believe a word of this, but do you mean they don't have to be married?"

"Some of them are," Anne put in. "No, go ahead, honey, you explain it to her."

"They keep a dozen knives in the air at the same time," Woods said. "I was going to say balls but Anne doesn't like me to be lewd. I'm not too interested in what he's got the married people doing. This thing is ticklish. I not only have to get some live testimony before a grand jury will indict, I have to convince the office that we won't get our fingers burned. This is New York and by and large it's a permissive town. In the first place, are they bothering anybody? In the second place, do we want to look like the State of Tennessee in the Scopes trial? He's a scientist. I happen to believe, personally, that he's a joke scientist, but there's no doubt that he's got the degrees. I can't touch it before it's been cleared on a policy level."

He exchanged his empty glass for a full one. "I need something that even the *Village Voice* will think is going a bit far. One of his main laboratory tools is motion-picture photography, and the trouble there is, he can't photograph what's happening to the woman, can he, if the man keeps getting in the way?"

"I can see that," Victoria said.

"So he got a foundation to give him forty thousand bucks to develop a machine. I'd like to describe it for you."

He was talking mainly to Victoria. From any other angle he probably looked more or less normal, but now and then she caught a glitter that made her think of the actor waving the chicken. He made a shape with his hands.

"It's a case of form following function—this is purely functional. Less is more, as the architects say. What it is, not to beat around the bush, is a mechanized prick. That may sound like a simple concept, but it's a very sophisticated piece of engineering. He had to go to an aerospace company outside Boston. Would you believe that it's transparent, so he can take pictures through it? That its dimensions are adjustable, so it's sure to fit anybody? That there are dials to control speed and depth of thrust? That when the moment comes you can press a button to make it ejaculate?"

"Imagine!" Anne murmured.

"And I'm damned if I'll let him get away with it," Woods said. "We're going to need some more drinks over here."

Anne and Victoria shared a walk-up apartment on Charles Street, in the old Village. The rent was too high, in view of the garbage and hot-water problems, but they wouldn't have lived anywhere else. Both men were pretty potted by the time they arrived. Matt fell to one knee getting out of the cab.

"Street, hold still," he managed to say.

When Victoria put together the drinks in their tiny kitchen, she made Matt's very pale. Anne had switched on Long Jim, the radio talker, their usual after-midnight companion. She was perched on the sofa arm, fooling with the hair at the back of Woods's neck. He never needed a haircut. It was too bad

Anne was so tall. In a scaled-down version, Victoria had thought more than once, she would have been terrific. Unfortunately, outside of *Alice in Wonderland*, there was no way of working that kind of miracle.

The girls had roomed together for a year, and there were some things they didn't have to put into words. After a bit, Anne glanced at Victoria, asking the obvious question. Victoria answered with an eyebrow. Anne put her head down to kiss Woods on the cheek.

"Baby, do you know what I'd like, after all that sexy conversation?"

Woods looked at Victoria from the depths of the sofa. She didn't need subtitles to know he was wishing he could switch dates at the line of scrimmage and send Matt into the bedroom with Anne. One afternoon, about two weeks before, she had come out of the bathroom with her hair in a bag and only a wrapper on, and the wrapper had been wide open. She didn't know anyone else was in the apartment; she wasn't that free and easy even with Anne. And there Woods was, in the same spot on the same sofa, reading *The Reporter*. She had pulled the wrapper together fast, but she wasn't sure Anne believed it had been an accident.

Anne tightened her grip on the back of his neck, with a lifting motion. "On your feet, soldier."

"Just going to give Vicky a small kiss."

She stood still, but didn't contribute to it. The corner of his glasses cut into her forehead. The last look she had from him before he disappeared into the bedroom was slightly out of kilter; his glasses were askew. But everything else was in place. His shoelaces were tied, the knot of his necktie hadn't been allowed to slip, his hair lay precisely where he wanted it to be. He made her think of those hard-working, ordinary boys who do everything the world expects, up to the point where they take a shotgun and start murdering people.

Matt was listening to Long Jim, who was carrying on as usual. He was strongly anti-Establishment in everything, and one of the things he was down on currently was physical fitness. Matt looked angry again. So much the better. Desire by itself, Victoria had found, was far too simple for this day and age. She said nothing, keeping a watchful eye on the little internal flicker. This was an important moment. If she could manage the transitions without interrupting the curve, she thought she might have a chance tonight with this man.

"Turn it off?" she suggested presently.

He turned it off so emphatically that he almost wrenched off the knob. "Somebody ought to clobber that guy. He's sick."

Victoria flicked on the television but turned off the sound, getting a pleasantly psychedelic effect. She silently willed Matt to move quickly and say nothing. The wrong word at this point would put out the fire. There was still a trace of anger around his mouth. His first kiss forced her lips back hard and stopped her breath.

She was afraid for an instant that he might be too drunk. But no, it seemed to put them in the same time zone. There was something sweet and pathetic about the way he tried to find her zipper, which she had already pulled for him. Their clothes came off naturally. By the time they were embracing on the rug, which she had vacuumed that afternoon with something like this in mind, she was on fire throughout her length.

It might have been nice to know his last name, but possibly not, too. This way they could concentrate on the sensations, with none of the distractions that come from knowing people too well. There was a small, lovely curve below his lowermost rib. She traced it with her fingertip, then with the palm of her hand. She had found it in other men. It came only from competitive exercise, and once you had it you didn't lose it in a hurry. His knees were terribly scarred, as though they had been sliced apart and put back together like a jigsaw puzzle. She kissed them lovingly.

It was a time to be very, very careful. Anybody who thought sex was easy was out of his mind. What was being done to you had an effect on the other person as well. You had to be sure to get each essential response in the proper sequence, and you also had to be sure you weren't giving your partner the wrong signals. He could so easily gallop ahead and leave you floundering.

The whiskey confused Matt and made him easy to manage. His athlete's body became a wonderfully intricate machine, completely under Victoria's control. It was far more satisfactory, she thought, than any laboratory machine could possibly be. Because how could anything of plastic and metal . . .

And then she blundered.

She made a small, involuntary sound. The instant she heard it she knew she had booted the best chance she had had in a long time. She was backed up against him at that moment, on her knees. His fingers were opening her, and the pleasure was too intense to be borne in silence. If she could only have kept her mouth shut for another few minutes! The next instant he was inside her from behind. And she wasn't completely ready. She tried to expel him but he was riding his own curve now, which rose far more steeply than hers. They had been together so far, all the way, but now they began to diverge.

She knew the procedure too well. His thrusts would excite her, but not quite enough. She would still have some distance to go when he arrived. The ensuing commotion would prob-ably be somewhat pleasurable, but they would already be antagonists. She would want to move while he wanted only to hold still. He would be going downhill while she was still laboring up the other side, perhaps within a stone's throw of the summit. Then, if he was a typical male, and she already knew that he was, he would withdraw, full of self-congratula-tion, leaving her in such a turmoil, so charged up, so blocked and jangly. If anybody had a choice, who would choose to be a woman?

His fingers were on her nipples. She tried not to let him know how he was pleasing her, because that would speed him up even more. She fell farther and farther behind, but neverthe-less, for a short time, she found this unknown Matt superb, this ex-football player with the ruined knees. If she couldn't succeed with a man like this, with no past and obviously no future, what was she good for?

"Matt!" she cried. "Can you wait? Please, can you wait?"

The answer to that was no.

Suddenly there was a scuffling sound, a stifled laugh. A door opened. Matt froze in midthrust. Her mind formed a wordless question, but no, he was still operational. She tightened down hard. His breath roared in her ear.

"Excuse us," Woods said. "Looking for ice."

Anne giggled uneasily. "Woods, you fool."

This wasn't permitted! There had to be rules. You couldn't just— Victoria felt a shudder start in her throat. Her body was undergoing strange, unwilling contractions—surely not those lovely contractions of orgasm she had been reading about for years.

"Are we interrupting anything?" Anne said, and giggled again.

After a long, tense pause, Matt completed the interrupted stroke and began moving away. She could feel herself losing him. She knew with despair that in another moment they would be separated and scrambling ungracefully for clothes. She had been in different situations in her time, but never anything like this. She wished above all that she hadn't been caught in this position, on her knees with Matt behind her. It was perfectly kosher, one of the recognized variations in Van de Velde, but somehow it would have been less embarrassing to be lying in the orthodox way.

Matt hesitated, all but gone. But it was beyond his power to leave her. Slowly and tentatively, he came back. The action resumed.

Victoria knew from the prickling about her eyes that she must be blushing. She might just fool everybody by staying in this crouch with her eyes shut until they all gave up and went home. Anne, of course, lived here, but Victoria would face that problem when she came to it. She heard only her own agitation for a moment. Woods and Anne must have gone back to the bedroom, where they had always stayed before. Victoria started as somebody's hair brushed her shoulder.

"Woods, you're crazy," she heard Anne say. "What would the District Attorney say?"

"He'd say move over."

Matt was doing something quite elegant. His hands kneaded her hips and his lean flanks clashed against her at the climax of each powerful forward motion. By reaching between her legs she could have touched him briefly whenever he appeared, but he wasn't going to get that refinement with so many people around. The noises close by began to pick up definition. It was all absolutely awful, but at the same time it was interesting. She was being pushed so violently that the breath was driven from her lungs in gasps.

When she couldn't stand not knowing, she opened her eyes. Woods was looking up at her. He and Anne were reversed. It was the first time Victoria had seen him without his glasses. He looked sly and happy.

She bit down hard and tasted blood. She was going to kill somebody for this.

They were crowding her. Matt no longer seemed bothered by not being alone, and Victoria knew he couldn't last much longer. She tried her old trick of pretending to be wrapped in plastic, but in these close quarters it didn't work. The world was in a conspiracy to blur her identity. She was a receptacle. Of course, even under these circumstances she felt an obligation to pretend. It occurred to her suddenly that if she could use her hipbones as a kind of nutcracker she would get back some self-respect, and perhaps he would regret not bringing her along more gently. He was taking it all, in accordance with the laws handed down long since by some virile male god. She was getting nothing.

Or was she? Hope stirred. This whole thing was so precedent-smashing, what if . . .

Woods hitched closer, trying to bite her breast. Her body was wide open to his hand. He hurt her with what he probably meant as a caress. Then he found the right place, and somehow her body was able to tell him to continue, to continue. Somebody else's hand came through her screen of hair to touch her face. It was Anne, for heaven's sake! Fingers fluttered against Victoria's cheek. For an instant they were all four in a kind of mixed-up tangle. Talk about double-crostics! She loved Matt, she loved Woods and Anne, she wanted to join them. Every other woman on earth was capable of it, why wasn't she? Kissing the palm of Anne's hand, she clutched Woods, a man, after all, to her breast with a moaning cry.

Then everything caved in. She found herself crying real tears.

Matt pulled out rudely, without waiting to count ten. She couldn't blame him for wanting to cut this short. The rules had been suspended for a tiny instant, but they were back in force. This kind of thing was prohibited, and for a good reason: when it was over you had to make your way back to the everyday world. Her last drink came into her throat.

Anne and Woods were disentangling. Victoria stayed in her fetus crouch, her face hidden by her hair. *Go away*, she told them silently. *Everybody*.

Matt, at least, did as she told him, and he was the one she could least afford to lose. When she could bear it no longer she looked up. His shorts in one hand, he was looking down at the three of them in disgust. Younger, he would have been blinding, too much of a good thing, but he was still the most beautiful man Victoria had ever seen, and she knew she wasn't likely to see him again.

"One of these days somebody's going to stamp the shit out of you, boy," he said, and started to dress.

"But why?" Woods said. "Where are you going? Make yourself a drink."

Woods lay sprawled on the rug in the fitful light from the television set. In any bodily comparison with his friend from Chicago he came off badly. He got his only exercise walking up and down in front of a jury and he didn't actually try that many cases. He laughed unsuccessfully. The moment was approaching when he would have to put on his glasses and brush his hair.

Matt dressed quickly, his nostrils flaring. With each piece of clothing, he looked more ordinary. He said something savage under his breath and picked up his jacket by the neck. He didn't bother to say good-bye, except by banging the door hard as he went out.

"There goes a meat-and-potatoes man," Woods said. "Vicky, what's the verdict? You enjoyed yourself, didn't you?"

Her breast tingled where he had bitten her. The toothmarks would probably show. She knew one thing. She wasn't going to lie around naked being cross-examined. She filled her lungs with air and stood up. She wanted to run, but to a certain extent she kept her cool. She stalked into the bedroom, one step at a time. That they both were watching her, she knew; she could feel the warmth on her buttocks.

She closed the door firmly and inspected herself in the mirror. She looked pretty much the same, she was sorry to say. Woods had marked her with a crooked circle of red dents: malocclusion. She found tools and fixed her eyes and mouth. On an impulse, before putting the cap back on the lipstick, she slashed a red X across her image in the mirror, canceling herself out. And just what did that accomplish? When she moved away, nothing was left behind the X, nothing at all.

Woods and Anne were shouting in the other room. Victoria's mind was busy, and she didn't bother to listen. The front door slammed for the second time that night.

Anne came in silently and put on pajamas.

"You're crying, aren't you?" she said without turning around.

"No."

Anne sat down on the edge of the bed and put an arm around her.

"Vicky, is it the end of the world?"

"I don't know yet."

"I put some water on for coffee."

Coffee! Victoria didn't see how they could drink coffee and go on as though nothing had happened. Something had definitely happened. Maybe that multisex hadn't been altogether Anne's idea, but she could have stopped it if she'd wanted to.

Slipping away, Victoria began looking for cigarettes. The men had walked off with them, which was typical to say the least. The kettle whistled her into the kitchen. She measured out the coffee and poured the water. When Anne came in she had washed her face and made a few passes at her hair, but she still looked miserable.

"No cigarettes? The bastards." She let Victoria arrange the sugar and cream. "What a hangover I'm going to have in the morning. I can feel it gathering."

"I'll tell you one thing about Woods," Victoria said. "He wasn't as drunk as he made out."

Anne took a sip of her coffee and made a face. "How I love bitter coffee. Matt wasn't too bad-looking."

Victoria thought of a remark. It had the wrong tone for the way she was feeling, but she said it anyway. "Except with his clothes on."

Anne looked relieved at this small sign of a change in the weather.

"Oh God! I feared for my boy's health for a minute. I thought there were going to be some broken bones."

"I wouldn't have lifted a finger to stop it."

Victoria liked her late-at-night coffee very hot. After the first mouthful had scalded away the taste of stomach-whiskey, she began to feel more like herself.

"I never did anything like that before, that's all."

"Do you think I did?"

Victoria took one more sip of the scalding coffee. "All this is very well, but God damn it—"

Anne gave her an anxious glance, and Victoria went on, "There's no point in shouting and screaming, and I'm too tired. I thought it was understood. If I can't count on having the living room to myself once in a while—"

"It won't happen again. I made that clear to Woods—if you heard the fight we were having you know we didn't part friends. I don't even know how it happened! All that talk about the sex doctor—sex for its own sake, outside the regular compartments. There's nothing freakish about *Woods*, as a rule. He goes through the motions, but I wouldn't say he uses too much imagination. And now all of a sudden it turns out he's the master of ceremonies type. I was amazed!"

"In other words, the next time he calls you're not exactly going to hang up on him."

Anne moved nervously. "Most of the time he's not so bad. I know you were the big attraction tonight and I ought to be dizzy with jealousy, but I'm not. He's so square usually! That patriotism of his and so on. Those unsolicited tributes to J. Edgar Hoover. I love him, I guess, but I hate to love somebody I know won't ever surprise me. But after tonight maybe there's hope?"

"Anne!"

"I don't mean this particular thing's going to be repeated. I'm not my usual clear-thinking self right now, Vick. Can we call time and talk about it in the morning?"

"If I'm still here in the morning."

"Vicky, don't *say* things like that. We get along reasonably well, don't we, over the long pull?"

A minute or so earlier, Victoria had been ready to flip a coin to see which one of them would move out. By the simple act of sharing a pot of coffee they had managed to stabilize the situation. Another roommate would be hard to find, and did Victoria want to live alone? Anne did the marketing and more than her share of the cooking. She was good about writing down phone calls. She knew the people to call when things went wrong.

"I don't know how to put this—" Anne said. "But if you know what I'm talking about, that's something else that won't happen again."

"I hope not."

"I don't want you to think I'm dyky or anything. I honestly don't think I even have any tendencies. You just looked so wild—"

Their eyes met for a fraction of a second and skipped apart. It was true that in all the confusion that caress hadn't been entirely one-sided, and perhaps Victoria's best move would be to forget about it.

"It's late."

"Yes," Anne said gratefully. "We ought to get to bed."

Later, lying awake, Victoria thought back over the weird evening. This was her usual practice, after the man had departed or fallen asleep: she went back to the bottom of the curve and started over, to try to locate the point where it had gone wrong. What baffled her was that it was a different thing each time. She had done plenty of reading. Overanalysis, she knew, was as bad as underanalysis; but, being a child of her environment, how could she be expected to stop overanalyzing? There was a catch to it somewhere.

Now, brooding wakefully, regretting her second cup of coffee, she remembered that rush of pride at the end, when all hell was breaking loose. It hadn't been pleasure as much as pure unadulterated conceit. There had been no doubt that she was the center of attraction. She had felt important and with good reason. The feeling had come too late to do much good. Nevertheless, perhaps it was encouraging, looked at realistically. She couldn't afford not to be realistic.

"Vicky?" Anne said hesitantly from the other bed. "Are you still awake?"

"Yes."

"I've got to decide tonight. Remember the laboratory we were talking about?"

"It seems to me the subject of a laboratory did come up," Victoria said, "for about two hours." She rolled over and came up on one elbow. "How much of that was true?"

"Probably all of it. Woods doesn't exaggerate too much. He wants me to go up and volunteer, and I don't know if I dare."

Victoria waited a moment in the darkness. "Volunteer to—"

"I told him I'd think about it. And that's what I'm doing—I'm thinking about it. They're signing up people like mad, and if I don't do it the first thing in the morning they may be filled up."

"Do you want my advice?"

Anne hesitated. "No. I know what you'd say. You're so self-sufficient. You don't like Woods, do you?"

"I'm not crazy about him."

"Well, I'm not *crazy* about him, but if I ever hope to get married—"

"Hey!"

"I know, I'm the jolly one. But I'm twenty-seven. Do I want to sell African masks in Brentano's the rest of my life? Someday I'm going to put on one of those masks myself and scare a few people! Woods has a lot of good qualities. He's on edge with you, Vicky, for some reason—he always has to be such an authority. It's ingrained in him. He hasn't let himself relax since he was twelve. When he was a Boy Scout, of course, he had to make Eagle. I could have grabbed him by the ear tonight and made him stay in the bedroom, I suppose, but I wanted to see what would happen. What he'd do."

"They ought to take away his merit badges."

Anne gave her funny laugh, and Victoria smiled to herself in the darkness.

"Right now he's stuck, career-wise," Anne said. "Number-two man in the Rackets Bureau, and what does the number-two man do when the number-one man is satisfied to stay where he is until he retires? If Woods could work up something a little out of the ordinary—this is confidential, Vicky—"

"So he's willing to throw you to those sex wolves?"

"That's how I reacted when he brought it up. But it's not as though he wants me to have sex *with* anybody. I wouldn't even consider that. This is automanipulation." She paused. "So-called."

"Masturbation."

"To give it its right name," Anne agreed. "I go in and take mental notes on the machinery, and do it once. That's all there is to it. At least, so I tell myself."

"Well, who can join? What are the qualifications, outside of being a woman?"

"You have to be referred. There's a lady gynecologist in Newark who does abortions, Woods happens to know, and she'll refer me. Except for that, there's only one thing. You have to be able to make yourself come at the drop of a hat. And in my case—"

"It's no problem," Victoria supplied.

Anne sighed. "I just wish I didn't do it so often."

Somewhere deep inside Victoria she could feel the familiar flicker. "Don't talk about it if you don't want to."

"Oh, I don't mind talking about it, I guess. Maybe I was brought up wrong. According to what they teach nowadays, I suppose I was. I never even knew there was such a thing until it happened. I woke up with Mother shouting at me that if I did that again I'd end up in an asylum. So naturally I did it again, and I went on doing it. I've got the willpower of a banana. I hardly did anything else for a few years! I know the books say it's okay, but people who write books don't know everything. Look Vicky," she said reasonably, "every moral code in the last three thousand years has forbidden it. Don't you think that ought to mean something?"

"Do you still do it?"

"Do I still do it! I used to think it might help if somebody tied me to the bed, but even then I'm afraid I'd think of a way."

Victoria swallowed convulsively. This was a bit night-marish, like J. Paul Getty complaining of his tax problem to a man who asked him for a subway token. She had always patronized her friend slightly, on the theory that somebody like Anne could hardly fail to benefit from sharing a Green-wich Village apartment with somebody like Victoria. And now it turned out that Anne possessed a skill that Victoria herself was dying to develop. But what was all this guilt busi-ness? This was the sixth decade of the twentieth century.

"Vicky, I'm so useless to everybody. I'd like to do something constructive. And it could be a kind of shock treatment for me, personally."

"Then what's stopping you?" Victoria said unsympathetically.

"I know I should have got Mother out of my system long ago, but I keep thinking what she'd say if she ever heard about it. She'd take off her hearing aid and turn her face to the wall."

"How can she hear about it, dope? She's in Florida. You wouldn't have to get up and testify in court, would you?"

"No, he just wants me to sign an affidavit, if that's what it's called. If I could help put this Dr. Frankenstein out of business —the thing that gets me about him, he probably doesn't even think he's doing anything wrong."

"Do you come with men, too?" Victoria asked casually after a moment.

"Well, sure, when I put my mind to it. To be entirely selfish for a minute, leaving everything else aside, what effect would it have on *me?* It might give me a whole new perspective. God knows I've tried everything else. The one thing they don't seem to make pills for is to stop people from masturbating."

"Then do it, for goodness sake! Just don't come complaining to me afterward."

Both girls were lying on their backs, watching the reflected headlights skid across the ceiling. Anne said quietly, "I'm scared to go up there alone."

"Well, don't look at me. Woods's career can stop right where it is, for all I care."

"Just to lend me some moral support?"

"No. In fact, *positively* no."

After that there was a long silence until Anne's breath caught suddenly. Victoria heard her roll over.

"Did you?" Victoria asked.

"Yes, damn it! It's an addiction. Good-night."

The moment Victoria closed her eyes, a montage of erotic images blurred against her eyelids. She tried to picture the laboratory, but it would have been easier to imagine an intelligent conversation on Mars. The atmosphere would be anything but furtive, though, and conceivably Anne could come back with a new philosophy. She had to be made to realize that an orgasm was nothing to be ashamed of. Again Victoria remembered that moment when everybody in the foursome had recognized her importance. That might be the sensation Anne needed. The sex doctor wouldn't be put off by her size or her bounciness. He was interested in only one thing, and that, it seemed, Anne could do very well.

It was funny. Well, Victoria might be willing to hold her hand as far as the door. After that she'd be on her own.

Victoria rolled and twisted and after a time she went to the bathroom for an oblivion pill. She remade the bed and put on a fresh nightgown.

Sleep closed in at last, with Victoria resisting all the way. Anne had confided in her, why hadn't Victoria confided in Anne? Probably because of the way she had carried on at the end with Matt, bucking and writhing and moaning as though she was trying to deliver a baby. Sexual fakery was the worst kind.

The pill was doing its work deep inside her, melting the ice. But not enough—never enough. She was a paraplegic, with something out of focus in some tiny cell, too small for any ordinary doctor to locate with the most powerful microscope. Now with Matt, if she'd only been able to press a button to slow him down . . .

chapter 6

The voice on the phone sounded promising, Martha Freeman thought. She checked with Dr. Max Sultan, whose name Mrs. Williams gave as a reference.

"Hanna Williams!" Max exclaimed. "I gave them a sales talk the other night, but I didn't think they were really listening. Fletcher, the husband, had a very negative reaction. I wonder how she worked it."

"Tell me something about them."

"Let's see. Well, they frequently display contusions which are obvious love-bites. This is your subject, not mine. How often does that happen after nine or ten years of marriage?"

Martha laughed. "I don't have any statistics on that, Max."

"The point is, they still enjoy physical contact. They keep touching each other. They give off sexual complacency in one of its most maddening forms."

"Is this really a recommendation?"

"Absolutely. Complacency isn't the right word. I mean that sex doesn't seem to have any terrors for them. It's not complicated and baffling and exasperating, the way it is for most of us. I play quartets with them, and that's a good way to get to know people. Hanna's a warm, intelligent, sexy woman, and I'm very much taken with her, which is probably obvious. Fletcher's a musician. I don't know how he'll strike you. As a bit self-satisfied, perhaps, but I'd like to play you some of his music sometime—it's fantastic."

The Williamses made an equally good impression when they appeared in person. They were curious about the laboratory, but not morbidly curious. They were patient during the history-taking. Somehow they managed to look somewhat alike, as husbands and wives were said to do in the old days after a lifetime of marriage; it was Martha's unscientific impression that this didn't happen much anymore.

The research population had more than quadrupled in the last two months. All at once everybody in town seemed to be talking about what they were doing. Extraordinary rumors were circulating. To Martha, the project had moved naturally and inevitably from stage to stage, and it was hard for her to understand the effect it was having on people who heard about it now for the first time. She kept being invited to parties by people who didn't really know her. She accepted as many of these invitations as she had time for, so that she could deny some of the rumors. She heard the project denounced as a kind of electronic circus presided over by crazed ascetics who were using science as a screen for their own perverted tastes. She met women who boasted about taking part in the research but who had never come near it and who wouldn't have been allowed across the inner threshold if they had. Dr. Prescott, thinking about the attacks they would have to weather when their findings were published, was careful to rule out anyone who gave any signs of exhibitionism. Martha believed he was worrying unnecessarily; it was a hard line to draw. There was nothing wrong with wanting to do something well.

By this time they had talked to more than 250 applicants, of whom they had kept about eighty. But the well-adjusted marital unit, with a marriage based on shared interests and mutual trust and respect, was still in short supply. Knowing how much they needed the Williamses, they overcorrected and conducted the interview with more care than usual.

Questioned about motivation, Mrs. Williams said they had always believed that sex was an important part of life and they wanted to help establish the truth about it. If they were accepted as study subjects, they would consider it an honor. Fletcher admitted, with the right degree of humorous candor, that participation had been his wife's idea, and he wasn't entirely sure that he could come up to expectations. This was true of ninety percent of their couples, both in the clinic and the laboratory. The wife was the one who made the initial move, and the husband frequently came along merely to keep peace in the family.

A complete intake screening took six hours, divided into two three-hour sessions. After working together for a year and a half, Martha and Dr. Prescott had developed the screening interview into a sophisticated clinical instrument. Of course there was a tremendous amount of repetition. The thousandth case of female orgasmic inadequacy was much like the first, and yet any sign of boredom or inattention would impair the therapist-patient relationship. These were touchy people.

Martha and Dr. Prescott, as scientists, were like actors sentenced by a run-of-the-play contract to repeat the same performance over and over, telling the same jokes, preparing the same effects, resolving the same situations in the same stale way. Lines and gestures, even the way they looked at their patients and each other, became habitual. Approaches that failed were quickly discarded. Sometimes a new variation, introduced by accident, would prove effective, and then they would fool around with it, tinkering and adapting, until they were satisfied and it became a part of the performance.

This was inevitable. Martha would hear Dr. Prescott making an offhand comment that had worked on other occasions, with the same slight hesitation while he sought the exact word—a word he had sought and found many times before—and the only thing that worried her was whether it was working now. They played well against each other. She was tall, dark-haired, indolent in appearance. She never seemed excited. She was interested in people, whereas Dr. Prescott, by contrast, was interested in the symptom, the behavior, the stimulus, the response.

"Could I ask one question before we go any further?" Hanna Williams said. "How many people have access to your records? This isn't the only thing we're worried about—is it, darling? But if you could reassure us—"

Dr. Prescott was the one who usually explained their security system. It had been devised by a lawyer who had once worked for the CIA. The names and addresses of the volunteer study subjects were recorded only once, on data cards that were kept in a locked file in a safe in another building. No one had the combination to this safe except Martha and Dr. Prescott. In the unlikely event that they were both killed at the same instant, in an airplane crash, for example, their executors had instructions to burn the cards immediately. All the records in this office were filed under code numbers. If Mr. and Mrs. Williams were accepted for the program they would be known only as Numbers 149 and 150. Two large safes were built into the wall of the consulting room. One of these held schedules and current records, the other the collated data. Again, only the two project heads possessed keys. When it was necessary for other members of the investigative team to record data, it was done on unnumbered forms. The code numbers were added just before the forms were locked in the safe.

Hanna followed the explanation carefully and asked several questions before she looked at her husband to see if he was satisfied.

"That gives me one more number to remember," he said. "And I haven't memorized my zip code yet."

The questioning resumed, and check marks accumulated on Martha's data sheet. Average frequency of coitus per week. Percentage to orgasm. Time involved in foreplay. Manual techniques. Oral. Coital positions. Nudity. Maximum frequency, ever, in a single week. In a single twenty-four hours. Mouth-genital contact to orgasm. Anal intercourse. Anal insertions. Group heterosexual activities. Observation of coitus—of friends, of parents, of professionals.

Martha and Dr. Prescott had been over this ground so often that they could confer without looking directly at each other, like top bridge players. When an interview was clearly non-productive, there were prearranged shortcuts to bring it to a conclusion. They rarely failed to agree. They had differed on only one case recently, about a girl a week ago named Victoria Orr. They had been far apart on that one, for almost the first time since they started working together. About the Williamses, of course, they were in complete accord. Working so much of the time with problems of clinical distress, Martha had her pessimistic moments about American marriage. Here, finally, were two people who made her feel there was something to be said for the institution. Their sexual harmony was obvious, and from that everything else followed. They completed each other's sentences. They were intelligent, uninhibited, born experimenters. Hanna especially seemed to have a talent for describing physical sensations, which was precisely what the project needed at this point to supplement the data they were getting from the machines. She was frequently multiorgasmic. Her husband had never experienced erective difficulties; he had failed to attain orgasmic release only after repeated exposures in a single episode. They were questioned more thoroughly on their sex histories and patterns in separate sessions, Dr. Prescott talking to Hanna and Martha talking to the husband. Everything jibed. The results of the Minnesota Multiphasic Personality Inventory and the Cornell Medical Index were excellent, easily the best so far.

Martha would have to send Max Sultan a bottle of Old Grand-dad. The Williamses were definitely a find.

Martha Freeman's own sex history was not a part of the project records. Though less eventful than many she and Dr. Prescott had taken, it had had its peaks and valleys. She grew up in a beach community near the tip of Long Island, where her father taught history in the local high school. There were seven children. Martha received her proportionate share of her parents' attention, approximately one-seventh, which was probably enough. Her summer life and her winter life were opposite sides of the coin. The summer adolescents attended savagely competitive schools, they had money, most of the parents were divorced. Every boy over the age of fifteen considered that any year-round girl would be glad to make love in return for being noticed.

Martha had the best grades in her high school class, but that was during the winter. In the summer she wore the most advanced bathing suits available, staying in the vanguard of the slow advance to total nudity. She tanned nicely, and played a good game of tennis for a girl. She soon found that the surface arrogance of the summer boys concealed the usual teen-age hang-ups, a phrase not yet in use. After failing to persuade her to have sex, they talked to her. She listened.

On a National Merit scholarship, she went to a Rocky Mountain college with a strong psychology department. She stayed to take a Master's and then came back to the main arena. She worked for two years as a psychologist in the city schools. She tested, tested, tested, and had innumerable ten-minute interviews with children who needed new parents and new apartments and probably special schools. She began to feel like a pebble on an exposed beach and resigned before the incessant wave action had worn her smooth.

She married a personable young man named Joe Freeman, a friend of one of her brothers. He was a union lawyer, interested in city politics. They stayed married five years, a period during which they made their way from Peter Cooper Village to East 65th Street, between Park and Madison. She realized gradually that every move he had ever made, including his marriage to her, had been taken after careful consideration of its effect in some future political campaign. When Martha wanted to take the trouble, she was capable of dressing well. There were times, arriving at a party or entering a restaurant with her husband, when she was conscious of creating a stir. Joe, at those times, gave the game away with a little crinkling around his eyes, which to Martha denoted pride of ownership. She had the kind of good looks that would still be effective in her forties and fifties, when Joe would be shooting for the top jobs, or if he had taken a wrong turn in the political maze, for the big retainers. She was twenty-nine, and he thought it was about time to think about having children. Beginning to be a little wary of the man she had married, she decided to wait. She wanted children, but not so that they could be used in campaign publicity.

He began attending American Legion meetings. Martha had recently found a job she liked with the Probation Department, working with people charged with sex crimes. Joe, of course, was nervous about it. There were all kinds of ugly possibilities, and he didn't want his name to appear in that context. They broke up after a month-long argument over the case of a retarded Puerto Rican accused of incest. The daughter who brought the charge was clearly psychotic, the police handling of the case was bad, and Martha saw to it that the man was acquitted. It didn't make the papers, but by that time her own divorce was under way.

A magistrate she liked and worked well with asked her to talk with someone who had a suggestion about the rehabilitation of convicted prostitutes, Dr. Chalmers Prescott. They met at a Fulton Street fish restaurant. Dr. Prescott gave her an appraising look as she sat down, but it was clear to Martha that he didn't see a dark-haired, somewhat drawn-looking woman who had just been through a bad divorce; he saw a probation worker who might help him win over a magistrate.

He looked about thirty-five; actually, he was ten years older. He seemed to be burning calories even sitting still. She learned later that he played a murderous game of four-wall handball, and when he couldn't get an opponent he matched his right hand against his left. The right hand always won, but the score was generally close. He had an abundance of sand-colored hair, of the shade that can turn gray without being noticed. Glasses. Sharp, observant eyes.

"Do you have mackerel?" he asked the waiter impatiently.

"Very nice mackerel."

Martha smiled at the waiter and hunted through the menu for some obscure and expensive fish. Dr. Prescott finally switched to reading glasses to peruse his own menu. He also gave Martha a second look. He stayed with mackerel in the end.

"I understand you want to talk to me about a plan for a rehabilitation program?" she said.

"No, not at all. I need suitable subjects for a research project I'm attempting to develop. I want you to recommend to Judge O'Toole that women convicted of prostitution have their sentences suspended on the condition that they report to my clinic for a period of observation."

"What do you mean by observation?"

"I want to subject them to physiologic and anatomic study while they're reacting to sexual stimulation. I'll pay fifteen dollars an hour. This may be the only social function these women have ever performed, and some degree of rehabilitation is certainly a possibility, but only as a by-product."

"Dr. Prescott, will you repeat that? You want to subject them to anatomic study—"

"During masturbation and coitus, yes, using standard research-laboratory techniques." He added, unnecessarily, "As far as I know, this has never been done."

Martha's first thought was of her ex-husband. If he considered her allegedly incestuous Puerto Rican dangerous, how would he react to this? The thought predisposed her in its favor.

"It sounds impossible. Tell me more about it."

The waiter came and went. Martha had ordered red snapper in butter sauce, and soon her plate was empty except for a few bones. She couldn't remember eating anything. She had learned that Dr. Prescott still kept an obstetrical practice in the New Jersey suburb where he lived. He no longer took much interest in the routine emergence of infants from their mothers' wombs after the specified period of months, he had seen it happen too often. A young assistant now handled the uncomplicated deliveries, and Prescott hoped that before long the mothers of Leonia would be willing to contribute to the rise in population with no further help from him. He and another doctor named Gunther Levy ran a gynecological clinic in Manhattan. This made quite a bit of money, but Prescott was more and more dissatisfied with it. His partner had psychiatric leanings. Prescott had recently discovered that Dr. Levy was almost fully engaged in counseling his female patients about methods of transferring their orgasms from the clitoral region to the vagina. This famous distinction was first made by Freud in *Three Essays on the Theory of Sexuality*, and in Prescott's opinion the analytical profession had made a very good thing out of it ever since. The idea was that if a woman was still getting only clitoral orgasms, of the kind associated with childhood masturbation, she was not yet fully mature and she needed expensive help.

"But I thought—" Martha said.

"And you may be right," Prescott put in. "Who knows? I have a strong suspicion that there's no physiological difference whatever."

He spoke in a confident, carrying voice. A scrod-eater at the next table, Martha noticed, was blinking rapidly.

Dr. Levy, debating the point, was able to cite hundreds of references in the literature in support of his position. There were also a few authorities who agreed with Prescott, but Prescott didn't care about what even the lady experts said they experienced; he wanted to get a speculum inside a few women while it was happening, and see for himself. His partner had backed away from the idea in agitation. They were doing well. Their patients were satisfied. Try a thing like that, and Prescott would lay the clinic open to malpractice suits. To break the deadlock, Prescott refinanced his Leonia house, negotiated a bank loan, and was now in the process of buying out Levy's fifty percent of the clinic.

For the last half dozen years he had also been doing physiological research in a laboratory building belonging to Manhattan

Medical College, where he had a lecturing appointment. The space was inadequate, but it could be made to do. By scrounging around among his hospital connections, he had collected the necessary laboratory furniture. The husband of one of his Leonia patients, a theatrical producer, gave him the necessary lights from a show that was folding. He only had to buy one thing new, a $3,500 Arriflex—a German sixteen-millimeter motion-picture camera—and he believed he had found someone to operate it. He had put in for a grant from the Public Health Service. They seemed to be taking it in their stride. The National Institute of Mental Health was a possibility. All that remained was for someone to produce the orgasms, and that was where Martha came in.

The man at the next table choked on a bone.

"I think O'Toole might be willing to try it," Martha said. "He's willing to try anything. We get only the dregs of the profession and we get each woman many times. From the court to jail to her usual hallway, back to court, back to jail —you realize that they're not very presentable?"

"We won't be photographing their faces."

"But do you think you can get them to cooperate?"

"Why not?"

He was looking at her blankly. Obviously, no prostitute of the kind processed by Judge O'Toole and the other judges in the Court for Vagrant Women had ever found her way to the Prescott clinic or into his private practice. Martha decided to contribute to his education. Sex as he understood it had no relationship to the services provided by the poor needle-scarred wrecks who streamed through the revolving door at 100 Center Street. Sex paid for by the transaction was something different from sex paid for by a joint checking account, and the sooner this middle-class expert found it out, the better. It would be doing the women no disservice. They needed the money to support their pimps and heroin salesmen. They could get it from Prescott without running any of the usual occupational hazards, disease, nonpayment, physical mistreatment, arrest.

While the restaurant emptied around them, Prescott went on talking about the lines of investigation he was eager to pursue. They parted two hours later at the corner of Fulton and Nassau Streets. After she had crossed Nassau, something impelled her to look back. Prescott, absorbed in the train of thought he himself had started, was still where she had left him, although the light had changed. His hair was disheveled; one of his mannerisms when talking about something that interested him was to run his hand through his hair the wrong way. The flow of pedestrians broke around him. She felt a flicker of exasperation. He could use a Seeing Eye dog.

Judge O'Toole, as Martha had predicted, fell in with the idea. He was careful to explain, when he was suspending the sentences, that the women were under no legal compulsion. Dr. Prescott was not a part of the law-enforcement machinery. Fewer than half of the women ever actually showed up at the laboratory, and not many of them really understood what the judge had said. They looked on this as a novel form of punishment; the city was always trying something new.

The histories they dictated were as fraudulent as their professional names. They often had sex with strangers, with other strangers looking on. Why should they care whether it took place in a hotel room or a laboratory? But they seemed to. They were suspicious and uncooperative. They were willing to be photographed by Prescott in any action or series of actions, but they flatly refused to masturbate for the cameras. They were ready to talk lewdly about stimulative techniques, about methods for heightening or channeling sexual tensions, and they offered to demonstrate them on Dr. Prescott's own person for an additional fee, but they refused him the one thing he really wanted, their orgasms. Martha had warned him that there was one point on which prostitutes of all levels agree: they never have a real orgasm with a John—the paying customer. And if Prescott was not, as he continued to claim, a different kind of cop or welfare worker, what could he be but a John with enough political clout to trick the Probation Department into providing the raw material for his quirky rites? He was an enemy on too many grounds—he was white, male, educated, straight, not interested in a good time, at least not with them. There was a cultural gap that he was never able to bridge. They did what he told them, sometimes sullenly, sometimes, when they had managed to get high on something, with a horrible mimicry of professional gaiety.

Martha was able to supply only one male, a weedy, sad-eyed Negro. Some of the girls agreed to go through the motions with him, for the sake of the camera. They yelped and clutched, breathed hard, and produced some impressive muscular gyrations, grading upward into spasm. Dr. Prescott, watching for the telltale detumescence of the areolae and the loss of nipple erection, knew it was all a fake.

He broke through only once, with a motherly-looking lady in her middle thirties, who had developed a disfiguring rash and felt she should drop out of the rat race temporarily. It finally dawned on her after the third session that Prescott, weird as he was, was also no fool, and he wouldn't go on paying her unless she started telling the truth.

He found that she herself didn't realize she had been having less than a genuine orgasm. She had always been curious about it, ever since she was a child. Certain ones said one thing, certain others said something else. Her own idea was that somewhere inside her, in the spinal region probably, there was a small sac filled with fluid, a sort of reservoir which was depleted gradually over the years by repeated orgasms. When the sac was empty, your sex life was over. Some years before, when she was working the conventions, she had exercised the muscle groups at the entrance to her vagina until she succeeded in plucking a folded ten-dollar bill from the corner of a table, an old skill that was rapidly dying out—young girls didn't want to take the trouble anymore. Simulating contractions had never been one of her problems. Being under the control of her will, they were never too early or too late, but always on schedule.

Prescott showed her some film footage of a real orgasm and explained the difference. She applied herself to the problem, while Prescott stood by making helpful suggestions. To her consternation, after a half hour's diligent effort, she rang the bell.

He had made a convert. She did well on the Thematic Apperception Test; the research atmosphere didn't bother her. She had only one stipulation—before she could continue, her old man had to okay the setup.

Her old man turned out to be a small, tight Negro wearing several rings. He listened attentively to Prescott's explanation, tightened up even further during his tour of the laboratory, and asked for twenty dollars a session instead of fifteen.

"Sorry, it's budgeted at fifteen."

"Take it out of your own pocket," the pimp suggested.

"That isn't possible."

"We get fifty a trick when she don't have that mess on her face. Did she tell you she can pick up a—"

Prescott told him that that accomplishment didn't come within the project's scope. The Negro finally agreed to terms— "But it's charity, man—" and said he had another wife he was willing to send over if she could be used before four in the afternoon, when her regular working day began.

"That can be arranged," Prescott told him. "We need men more than women. Would you be interested?"

For the first time the pimp blew his professional aplomb. He looked around as though counting the exits.

"You want me to jerk off or something?"

"I was thinking of intercourse with one of your women."

The Negro carefully picked a bit of fluff off his lapel. "I don't think I care to get mixed up in it."

The woman promised Prescott she would ask around the bars and perhaps she could come up with something. She phoned the next day with bad news. She and her old man had been busted on a narcotics charge, and if Prescott felt like putting up bail it was $2,500 apiece.

"You just buy a bond. You don't have to get up the full—"

"No."

The woman said she'd known he was a prick when she first saw him, and promised to spread the word in the House of Detention that this Dr. Prescott was poison. That ended the experiment of using the Probation Department as a source of supply.

Martha had just completed a probation report on a woman who was about to be sentenced. She liked to be known as Tracy Gaylord—her real name was more prosaic. She had spent fourteen years and nine months of the previous twenty-two years in prison, almost all of it sitting out thirty- or sixty-day sentences for prostitution or loitering. And was there any point in it, including the role Martha herself was playing? Did these women become prostitutes to earn money for narcotics, or did they take narcotics to be able to stand being prostitutes? If prostitution was a medical and psychiatric problem instead of a crime, as Judge O'Toole kept saying, how could the medical profession deal with it when most doctors were almost as poorly informed about sex as the women themselves? Physicists had been inside the atom ever since Tracy Gaylord went to jail for the first time. Chemists were working in the tiny gap between animate and inanimate matter. But Martha Freeman, with an advanced degree in her specialty, could think of nothing more sensible to do with Tracy Gaylord than to recommend putting her back in jail for another sixty days.

Martha thought about it, and when Dr. Prescott asked her if she wanted to come to work with him, she accepted.

chapter 7

The more Martha learned about her new employer, the more he puzzled her. She never found out much about his early life. He was born in Kansas, where his father was a dentist, still in active practice. She had an impression of a childhood that was mostly work. He worked on his basketball two hours a day, summer and winter, in the school gym. In college, an unknown one in Iowa, he became one of the best shooters in the state. His marks were poor, barely good enough to stay eligible. Then something happened suddenly that turned him completely around. Martha heard about this much later. They were having coffee at five in the morning, after an exhausting night. They had been discussing an applicant for a place in the pregnancy-sexual program. Prescott rarely went in for verbal free association, but this time fatigue kept him from suppressing an anecdote from his own history. In his junior year at college his team had completed a successful season by beating its major rival. Prescott scored thirty-one points, a lot in those days, before the invention of the jump shot. After the game his friends insisted that he have a few beers. Later they shifted to whiskey, and he ended the evening in a parked car with a girl he knew only slightly. In the course of their lovemaking he did something that made her bleed. He had never known exactly what had happened. She bled terribly, and lost consciousness. By the time he was able to rouse a doctor, the front seat of the car was soaked with blood, and he was convinced that the girl was dead. She recovered, but she left college soon afterward and he never knew what happened to her.

In his senior year he took the highly unpopular step of dropping basketball to concentrate on his lab courses. The pro-Prescott party on campus dwindled to one, a girl he later married. He squeaked into medical school and did well there.

The first Kinsey Report, establishing the respectability of the zoological approach to sexual behavior, came out the year he was admitted as a diplomate of the American Board of Obstetrics and Gynecology. He read it through in a single weekend, all 700 pages, saying to himself on every page, "But how do they *know?*" The report on the human female followed a few years later. Reading more carefully, Prescott saw that this time not all their information was hearsay, but in the censor-ridden 1950's they couldn't admit it.

Of course, observation by itself wasn't enough. You had to record the exact ups and downs of thousands of sexual cycles under careful laboratory controls before the work could be called scientific. Kinsey, Prescott heard on the ob-gyn grapevine, was anxious to break out of the limitations of his questionnaire. He hoped to organize a physiological laboratory at Indiana University, and he was looking for a man to run it.

Prescott knew he was still too young for the top job. Nevertheless, he wrote, expressing an interest, and he was asked out for an interview. Dr. Kinsey himself was off interviewing homosexual seamen in Galveston. Prescott was seen by an assistant, who took him around the Institute quarters in Jordan Hall and showed him the blueprints of the projected laboratory.

Well, it was hardly a laboratory. Fearing that a too-austere atmosphere would skew the patterns, they had attempted to duplicate the usual bedroom in a college dorm. There were carpets on the floor, pictures on the walls. The cameras were to be camouflaged in the ceiling. The electrocardiograph, the electroencephalograph, the myograph for recording muscle contractions would be out of sight, either under the bed or built into the wall. After the electrodes were in place and the cameras focused, the laboratory workers would withdraw and leave the lovers alone.

In Prescott's view, this approach missed the mark. They would get little except visual material, and they already had millions of feet of pornographic film in the Institute vaults, collected from all over the world—much of it of undoubted scientific value. But he kept this opinion to himself. He was given to understand that he could expect a staff position, if and when the laboratory was activated. The director, for obvious reasons, had to be a physiologist with an established reputation in some other field, just as Dr. Kinsey himself spent twenty-odd years becoming the world's leading authority on the gall wasp. The Institute was willing to go high for the right man, but everyone they approached begged off. They disliked the Indiana winters, they had commitments elsewhere, they didn't think the idea could be made to work. Those were their stated reasons. The truth was, obviously, that they were scared. Dr. Kinsey died of a heart attack, taking histories to the last, with the laboratory still only a blueprint.

Prescott, meanwhile, was building his own reputation and waiting for enough time to pass so that he could enter the field without being accused of doing so for prurient reasons. His own laboratory was beginning to take shape in his mind. There would be no nonsense about a hidden camera. It would be a laboratory, plain and simple.

He joined the Manhattan Medical faculty and was given space in its Research Building. His subject was chemically induced miscarriages in rats. Papers under his name began to appear in the literature.

His obstetrical practice was a success from the start, although he was a long way from the twinkly-eyed baby doctor depicted in Norman Rockwell's *Saturday Evening Post* covers. He was short in his answers, his mothers feared to disobey him, he refused to let husbands into the delivery room. But he seemed to have a kind of built-in X-ray that told him exactly what was going on inside a woman in labor. He frequently called his patients by the wrong name, but that was the only sort of mistake he made.

He was earning $70,000 a year. His own wife had two children during this period, a boy and a girl. He kept their pictures on his desk in the clinic, but Martha never heard him say anything about them. She met Mrs. Prescott only once. Prescott had forgotten that he was supposed to go to the theater, and his wife came to the clinic to fetch him. She chatted pleasantly with Martha while Prescott changed his clothes. She was a well-girdled, still handsome woman, with a little more manner than Martha liked. Inside her, Martha could see the pretty young girl Prescott had married. Her chrysanthemums, Martha was told, had a certain local fame. Her daughter was doing well at Leonia High School and had been accepted by Sarah Lawrence. She hated to pull Dr. Prescott away, but he worked too hard and sometimes she felt it was her duty as a wife to insist.

A little suburban, perhaps? It was none of Martha's business, of course.

Prescott's application to the Public Health Service sailed through, being studied, approved, verified, audited, processed, and mailed—all in the short space of four months. The sum itself was ridiculous, too small to buy many laboratory episodes, but it gave the undertaking a kind of plausibility that would get it a hearing later at the foundations.

Taking inventory after the Magistrates Court debacle, Prescott found himself with very little usable material and a payroll of three, Martha Freeman, a photographer named Nick DiVito, and Lydia Baum, a small, earnest brunette with an M.A. in statistics from City College. Lydia had agreed to come for six months. The six months were now up. She was staying on, but only on a week-to-week basis, until Prescott could find somebody to replace her. She approved of what he was doing, and the job was certainly a challenging one, but she wanted to go on to get a doctorate. Martha handled the interviews and the case records, at the laboratory and at the clinic, but stayed out of the observation suite when it was in use. In Nick DiVito, Prescott had found the perfect technician. He was twenty, a good-looking boy, with the shaggy hair of his generation. He had already made two underground films and he was fascinated with the problems of shooting sex in color. Capturing some of the responses Prescott was interested in recording would take all his inventiveness and ingenuity. There were sports photographers, fashion photographers, portrait photographers. He was the first to enter this new field, which according to all the signs was going to be very big.

He brought in two acquaintances who had performed in one of his films. The girl was a waitress and a semi-hustler. Dr. Prescott had to turn her down because she had gonorrhea. Her boyfriend was disgusted with DiVito.

"You didn't say anything about a physical. Now it's going to be all over town."

It was Lydia Baum, surprisingly, who found their first hundred-dollar call girl. Her name was Lisette Whalen. She was a beautiful girl, elegantly dressed, very jumpy. She and Lydia had been to high school together and they met by chance on Fifth Avenue. Lydia asked her what she was doing, and Lisette, seeing a chance to shock a girl she remembered as being a ninety-six-average student and pretty insufferable, told her she was a whore. Lydia, in turn, had a surprise for *her*.

Lisette was highly verbal, with an IQ of 147. Her sociosexual history, if she was telling the truth about it, was a grisly one. She was known professionally as a girl who would take on anybody, and in her five years in the racket she had serviced some authentic freaks. The initial interview had to be spread over a week, broken into forty-five minute takes; at the end of the forty-five minutes she was fidgeting around the room, anxious to be gone. She agreed to help, a little condescendingly, but refused to take any money for it. She was making thirty or forty thousand a year and naturally she paid no taxes.

"Give the fifteen bucks to Lydia," she said impulsively, with a glint of malice. "For making valedictorian."

Midway in her first recording session, Dr. Prescott came out of the laboratory into the consulting room, where Martha was working on a cross index.

"She wants you to come in."

Martha put down her cards carefully. "Why?"

"I don't know." He gestured toward her file. "The answer's probably somewhere in her history. But she doesn't want Lydia in the room."

Martha hesitated for a long moment. When they went in Nick was changing a lens, and the two girls were talking quietly.

"Hi, baby," Lisette said to Martha.

After Lydia left, Lisette lay back with a sigh, putting an arm over her eyes to shield them from the lights. "Okay, how do you want it, Doctor?"

Prescott showed Martha how to operate the machines, and she monitored all Lisette's sessions from then on. An obvious narcissist, Lisette at times seemed to be seeking approval, particularly Martha's. She made many procedural suggestions, some of which they adopted. Prescott began giving her the books of his famous predecessors. She skimmed through them, annotating the margins with symbols to indicate where she agreed with something and where she thought they were taking too much for granted. She shared Prescott's interest in sexual technique and once she sat talking for an hour and a half, with Martha taking notes, before she came to her feet abruptly and said she had to go. That was the high point of her participation. There were other times when she began making sarcastic remarks the minute she arrived and did her best to upset everybody. She had one joyless coition with their single male prostitute, who claimed he didn't care how he got his kicks, with a man, a woman, or a zebra. She reviled him with anti-Negro epithets all the time, using the insults subjectively to elevate her tension levels. Asked to evaluate the experience afterward on a psychological scale, both partners gave it the lowest possible rating, zero.

Lydia Baum resigned soon after Lisette's first session, and Martha replaced her in the laboratory. She realized now that this had been inevitable from the beginning. The prostitutes they were working with were edgy with Prescott. Their nerve endings were very close to the surface. To restrict herself to the taking of histories implied her disapproval, or at least mistrust. She was in no position to pass judgment on Lisette or the others. Too many judgments had been made over the centuries on the strength of too few facts. She didn't approve of prostitution, but as for the prostitutes themselves, approval or disapproval was simply not at issue. From the great pioneers—Freud, Exner, Hamilton, Davis, Dickenson, Kirkpatrick, Locke, Pomeroy, Calderone, all the others—she had learned that there was no such thing as normal or abnormal sexual behavior, there was simply behavior, which could be described in physiological terms, tabulated statistically, and made graphic in the form of tables or charts. Some people held their fork in their left hand, some in their right; she held hers in her left, but the world was big enough for everybody.

Nick DiVito picked up two girls in a 42nd Street pokerino parlor and interested them in the easy money Prescott was offering. They claimed to be eighteen. They seemed younger. Prescott took their histories, but didn't accept them as laboratory subjects. They were furious and promised to come back with friends and take the place apart. It was a silly threat —some highly classified bacteriological warfare research for the Navy was being conducted elsewhere in the building, and a city cop was constantly on duty in the downstairs lobby.

Prescott, meanwhile, found a promising-looking bar, on Lexington Avenue in the high Fifties. It was called the Chiswick. Darkness came early here, and well-dressed, unescorted women, with "I Am a Whore—Approach Me!" written all over them in invisible letters, began dropping in afternoons around 4:30. By their looks, they were thirty-five-to-fifty-dollar girls, and he knew from the histories that in this bracket they couldn't afford to specialize. They had to accommodate themselves to all perversions, they had to beat and be beaten. He had made out badly with the women from Magistrates Court because of his ambiguous role. They hadn't been able to place him in the adversary culture. The courts were their enemy, and he had some kind of connection with the courts; therefore he was their enemy. But with these bar girls, who had to have a few drinks with the man before they took him off, he would have a chance to explain.

He came to work the next day with four long, deep scratches on his left cheek. A girl who had been referred by Lisette was waiting to be interviewed.

"Fight with your wife?" she said, interested.

"Not exactly."

He told Martha about it later. He still wasn't sure what he had done wrong. He had had two drinks while he was sizing up the situation. Daiquiris, and he seldom drank. Around him, at the bar, men from nearby office buildings were drinking bourbon like cough medicine. Girls came and went, giving Prescott raking looks as they passed. He waited, and chose carefully—a girl who sat by herself at the far end of the bar, smoking cigarettes in a long holder. She seemed attractive, though in that light it was hard to tell. No one approached her. There must be something discouraging about her at close range, Prescott thought, and he decided she would be the least likely to turn him down.

He stationed himself behind her, and when she fitted a new cigarette into her holder he lit it for her. She looked up through her thicket of eyelashes and said she had noticed him and said to herself, "There's a swinger." Her voice was thin and small, a child's voice, which might be what put people off. Prescott didn't care, their films were silent.

The dialogue had followed a predictable path. Was she

meeting anybody? She did have sort of a half-date, she told him, but she was beginning to think nothing would come of it. Was he married? Yes, was she? Certainly not, she was having too much fun. He offered to buy her another drink and she accepted, though, she told him, she shouldn't be drinking at all because of her kidneys. The doctors wanted to cut her open and take a look, but she had told them, "Not this little girl!" And then she said he might find it interesting to come up to her apartment. "Honey, the way you've been studying me for the last half hour, I'm getting so excited. I'm all wet down there, I honestly am. My name's Margot Hornblower, does that give you any dirty ideas?"

He was afraid he had to ask for a raincheck on that. He had to meet some people.

"Oh, hey, just when we were starting to dig each other. Call from my place. Be late for once."

Prescott was sorry, it was a business appointment. But he had a suggestion to make, if he could talk to her for a moment. Could they get a booth?

She looked at him over her uncapped lipstick. "You want to set something up for the future, is that it?"

"Substantially."

"It won't kill me to listen, so long as you realize there are some things I don't do unless you make it very attractive financially."

She steered him to the inner lounge. A pallid man with varnished hair was playing show tunes on a white piano. She pulled Prescott into the booth after her so they were on the same side and lit still another cigarette.

"You don't smoke. I knew the minute I looked at you that you had a healthy pair of lungs. I wish I could give them up, but I can't seem to. My philosophy is, enjoy life even if it kills you. Whatever your preference, I do it. But the way I like it most is with the mouth, don't you think that's nice?"

Prescott decided to clarify his position, and a confused few minutes followed. Her first idea was that he was some sort of psychiatrist who wanted to charge her fifteen dollars an hour to let her talk about her various kinks. He insisted that the money would be going the other way; he would be paying her. He couldn't make out her expression. Where they were, in the back of the cave, there was hardly any light at all. He tried to tell her about the laboratory, but she didn't let him finish. Now she was sure he was a surgeon.

"We spotted you for a psycho the minute you walked in. Everybody wanted somebody else to find out, and of course it had to be me. You want to get me up on that table and open me up, don't you? I know how you mothers hate us. We're shit, aren't we? But you're not going to cut *me*."

Reaching across, she cupped her hand over his chin and held it. Her pointed fingernails dug slightly into his cheek.

"You picked the wrong playmate, sweetheart, because I don't go in for that kind of game."

And suddenly something made Prescott realize that he was not being held by a woman, but by a man dressed as a woman. He wrenched away, and the fingernails raked across his cheek. Everybody had stopped talking in that part of the room, and the tinkle of Jerome Kern came through clearly. A lithe youth, wearing a Thai peasant shirt, narrow yellow slacks, and sandals, blocked Prescott's way.

"Oh, let him go," the transvestite said. "Can't you see he's got problems?"

Martha was laughing helplessly, and Prescott finally produced a grudging smile.

"Well, perhaps it's funny. I'm afraid I let him see how much I disliked having my chin held by a homosexual. It was a reflex, and I'll have to work on it if we ever hope to get any honest homosexual data. I'm not so worried about what the women thought they saw in my face—I assume some of them must have been women. I try not to go to Leonia cocktail parties, but I'm sure I look the same way there."

The girl who had heard about them from Lisette Whalen turned out to be excellent. At about this time Prescott was told about a gynecologist with a call-girl practice. That lead produced two more girls. They were in demand at the moment, at the top of their disorderly profession, and they seemed to consider Prescott's interest in their masturbation habits a kind of confirmation of their status. They treated Martha like a maid. They were bad about keeping appointments. One was injecting amphetamines, and Prescott dropped her.

Thus the project limped along. They were accumulating data, but any kind of publication seemed years away. Prescott by now had reason to believe that some of the statements in the manuals and the textbooks were demonstrably wrong. But the sample was still terribly small and their findings tentative and obviously subject to further verification. They went to the Royce Foundation for a grant of $25,000. Peter Hixon, the executive director, was enthusiastic, but he advised them to cut their request to fifteen and come back for more when they had a larger body of observed material. They continued to run at a deficit, paying the subjects out of profits from Dr. Prescott's clinic. The laboratory equipment was idle much of the time. The whores, with their irregular lives and uncertain motivation, couldn't be depended on. But Prescott had known it wouldn't be easy. All they could do was keep plugging away and hope for a breakthrough. The first Royce money was soon gone.

When the breakthrough came, they didn't recognize it at first. It happened not in the laboratory, but in the clinic. Dr. Levy, departing, had taken two of the nurses, as well as the receptionist and the business manager, but almost all the regular patients had stayed on. Included in this group was a couple named Hallinan, who had come in with a routine story. They had been married two years. During the early months their sexual adjustment had seemed to proceed satisfactorily, with a coital frequency of ten to twelve times a week. Hallinan worked as a printer. He came home for lunch, and for some time they made love regularly each noon. Mrs. Hallinan had known she couldn't expect to reach orgasm right away, but when it still hadn't happened at the end of the first year she began to intimate that it might be her husband's fault. Hallinan no longer ate lunch at home. By the time they reached the clinic they were having intercourse once a week, on Saturday nights, and sometimes not even then.

Hallinan was a short man, with ink-stained hands and a heavily wrinkled forehead. He had been educated in parochial schools and he seemed reasonably well informed, but Prescott quickly established that one of his blank spots was the construction of the female body. On that subject he was as ignorant as a Stone Age savage. Mrs. Hallinan herself wasn't much better. Prescott gave them a quick review of the anatomy of the reproductive system and sent them home.

They were back a week later to report no progress. Martha took Mr. Hallinan into another room while Prescott interviewed his wife. Mrs. Hallinan admitted that sex had always been a painful experience for her. Her husband came at her like a flamethrower, his penis huge and menacing. Their noontime engagements had been particularly swift and savage—he liked to eat a leisurely lunch. It was all very puzzling to her, because before their marriage he had been sweet and considerate.

Martha, meanwhile, was giving Hallinan a short quiz. He maintained that he had studied the diagrams but she saw at once that he still had no idea of the functions of the female viscera, or even where the various organs were located. She got out the Dickenson drawings again, and they went over them together. He kept nodding, but his panic was unmistakable. He wasn't taking anything in.

Prescott opened the door. "Mrs. Freeman?"

"Yes. Excuse me, Mr. Hallinan. Now keep in mind that this is a *cross section*, seen from the side."

She joined Prescott in the hall. He said abruptly, "Lisette Whalen killed herself."

"Oh God."

"She jumped off the roof of a motor lodge at four this morning. She had my name and phone number in her purse. Not the clinic number, my home number. She's never called me there." He made a helpless gesture and said a surprising thing. "She was such a lovely girl."

Lisette had kept a 2:00 A.M. appointment in the laboratory that morning, and Martha remembered now that she had been quieter than usual. After producing her usual multiorgasm manually she had remarked casually to Prescott, "Was that worth keeping the laboratory open for? It's all such shit."

Now Prescott made a visible effort. "What about Hallinan?"

"He still isn't getting it. He's bright enough about most things, and I think he's really trying. But this particular set of facts is something he just doesn't want in his mind."

"Bring him into the examining room."

Mrs. Hallinan, undressed, was lying patiently on the examining table, her feet in the stirrups. Hallinan's step faltered when he saw his wife. They had reported being always partially clothed during coitus, and this may have been the first time he had ever seen her totally nude. Mrs. Hallinan gripped the edges of the table, looking into space, while Prescott repeated his anatomy lesson in a matter-of-fact voice. Hallinan was now in such a state of agitation that Martha was sure he was hearing nothing. Prescott shifted gradually into a discussion of the common stimulative techniques.

"Do you know what is meant by oral-genital contact?" he asked abruptly.

Hallinan clearly didn't. Prescott explained, making no effort to lessen the impact. The blood left Hallinan's face.

He managed to say, "I see."

"I don't think you do," Prescott said brusquely. "Try it. Mrs. Hallinan, be sure to tell him if he does anything right for a change. If you have any questions, call me."

Hallinan swallowed. "*Here?*"

"Yes. Otherwise, I'm afraid I'll have to recommend that you try to get an annulment."

He nodded to Martha, and they left the room.

"That's hardly standard clinical practice," she said. "You don't expect anything to happen, do you?"

"We'll see."

They talked about Lisette Whalen while they waited. The suicide rate among prostitutes, always high, was higher in the period just before Christmas. Did her decision to jump have any connection with what had happened in the laboratory that morning? Prescott definitely didn't think so. She had participated in perhaps fifteen episodes, including the one with the Negro male, always refusing a fee. At the start she had probably been attempting to demonstrate something to Lydia Baum, but she had kept on accepting appointments after Lydia left. Why? She hadn't given a reason. At twenty-three, she had had ten years of unsatisfactory and degrading sex. Her stepfather, a younger man than her mother, had come into the bathroom once when she was seated on the toilet. Nothing further had happened, but her heterosexual history had started that evening with a casual date. Her mother never paid much attention to her. They had moved a lot and she had no friends.

None of this explained why she was willing to have sex with the entire football team in high school, or why, a few years later, she permitted herself to be photographed having intercourse with animals, for the backs of playing cards. She had had relationships of a sort with pimps and with lesbians and had broken them all off. She carried Dr. Prescott's home phone number in her purse. Behind the coldness and the mockery, she had been asking for something, but it wasn't anything either Prescott or Martha had been trained to provide.

He looked at his watch. "Let's see how the Hallinans are getting along."

Martha shook her head. "You've examined them both. You see how they're getting along. I'll take your word for it."

"No," he said seriously. "We've established our authoritative role as a bisexual team. What they need is support and reassurance. Don't start being prudish at this point, for God's sake."

It wasn't exactly prudery that was causing Martha to hesitate. Sex performed by prostitutes in the laboratory was one thing. But Hallinan, poor man—if someone came in while he was carrying out Prescott's instructions, he would go up the wall.

Prescott was holding the door for her. Well . . .

On the examining table, the battle of the sexes was proceeding merrily. It continued even after Hallinan and his wife realized that they were not alone. Mrs. Hallinan showed an unmistakable sex flush and had gone into carpopedal spasm. Only a few seconds earlier, the vibrations coming from Martha would have stopped Hallinan cold, but he had crossed the divide. The repressions of his boyhood forgotten, he smiled up at Prescott.

"It seems to be pretty much okay, Doctor."

"How did it feel coming in, Mrs. Hallinan?" Prescott said. "Any better?"

"No comparison!" she gasped. "In fact, I think I'm going to— Oh. Oh. Oh!"

chapter 8

That afternoon Prescott attended a conference at the Waldorf-Astoria on postmenopausal hormone-replacement therapy. The reading of papers went on into the evening.

At dinner he found himself seated next to a fat-mouthed obstetrician from South Carolina, whose tag gave his name as Samuel ("Sam") Dawkins. Someone had told him about Prescott's research. He had a voice like a bullhorn and a loud, nickering laugh. If Prescott was having trouble getting volunteers, he offered to ship in a few truckloads of handkerchief-heads from his home county.

"Give them a dollar and a snort of corn and they'll accommodate you in front of the cannon in the courthouse square, I swear to Jesus. But they don't go in for any far-out stuff. If you want it dog-fashion that's twenty-five cents extra."

Prescott gave him a hard look, which conveyed his message. The Southerner's grin faded.

"I humbly beg your pardon," he said sarcastically, and turned to pass the time with the doctor on his other side.

The doctors surrounding Prescott had come to New York from all over the country. Their traveling expenses were deductible, and it was one way of getting out of range of the ringing phone. They were almost all slightly overweight and slightly complacent, and to a certain extent, Prescott thought, their complacency was justified. They were doing good work. They would live to an untroubled old age. Prescott himself could have had that kind of life. At one time, when hormones were first being synthesized, he had considered doing progesterone research, and if he had taken that path he might have been reading one of the papers at the conference. Instead, he had chosen to wonder one day about the effect of steroid withdrawal on female sexual performance—and before he knew what had happened he was clawing his way through a tangle of berry bushes at the edge of a quicksand.

When the meeting broke up, Prescott hesitated on the sidewalk. A light rain was falling. He began walking, thinking about Mrs. Hallinan. After her orgasm, the first in her life but a fine one, self-consciousness had returned with a rush. She had covered her face with her hands, and, when her husband swung down from the examining table, she dressed hurriedly. Not so Hallinan. He was delighted with himself, delighted with Prescott. After putting his clothes in order, he had lighted a cigar with immense satisfaction. Mrs. Hallinan had been smiling shyly when they left.

The terrible failure with Lisette Whalen was balanced by the Hallinan success. Then perhaps that was where Prescott should make his contribution, in the clinic, not the laboratory?

He was crossing Lexington. Chance had brought him to the neighborhood of the bar where his face had been scratched by the male whore. He gave it a wide berth. He didn't want to run into Margot Hornblower or any of his friends tonight.

But if, out of conviction or simple stubbornness, he stayed with the laboratory, there was one basic piece of equipment he had to have. He needed a machine to simulate actual coition. Self-manipulation had obvious limits. The big problem, of course, would be angle of thrust. Hundreds of measurements would have to be taken. The question of materials . . . the Kinsey Institute had a huge dildo collection, artificial penises of every imaginable kind of fiber, but none of them would be suitable for laboratory use. The glans of a laboratory penis had to have the optical properties of glass. The machine could remain in a state of vasodistention when not in use, but its circumference would have to be adjustable, within a limited range. Ideally, it should be self-lubricating.

But these were technical problems, which the technicians could solve. And who would use such a machine when it was finished? With Lisette dead, his female study subjects had been reduced to three. One of these kept talking about how she was about to leave any day for Las Vegas.

He was on Third Avenue. Ahead of him a big man in a wide-brimmed hat came out of a black car that was equipped with a buggy-whip aerial.

"You set here a spell," he said, in an exaggerated Texas drawl, "and I'll see if I can shoot me a little quail."

"Don't you mean tail?" a man in the car said.

Unlike his friend on the sidewalk, he wore ordinary New York clothes. As Prescott passed, he saw the bulge of a gun under his arm.

His companion cocked the huge white hat, spat into the gutter, and walked away on the outsides of his feet. The man in the car laughed.

"Rod, you got a great future on *Gunsmoke.*"

"Shore appreciate them words."

He entered a bar in midblock. Prescott continued along Third Avenue, then turned and came back.

The bar had an Irish name and a chipped shamrock on the window. Prescott went in. The physical appearance of the interior hadn't changed since the bad old days, before the yellow-brick condominiums, but most of the customers were new. The detective pushed back his big hat and took a stand near the beer pulls, hooking one thumb into his belt, which was sapphire-studded with an ornate buckle bearing a bas-relief of a steer's skull. He called for rye and ginger. Prescott, when the bartender got around to him, asked for a beer.

A drink and a half later, a girl settled herself comfortably against the bar beside the Texan. Prescott was glad to see that she definitely wasn't a male in drag. Her skin was a delicate olive color, her eyes were slightly slanted. Above, on the television screen, several exquisitely dressed people were discussing, with every appearance of seriousness, whether it was wise to give children pets for Christmas presents.

"—all alone in the big city," Prescott heard the Texan say. "Haven't had a woman in four days. So don't give me any of those sexy looks. I'm in a delicate condition."

His laugh boomed out. She smiled pleasantly, showing white, even teeth. Five more minutes passed before she made her proposal. The Texan pretended to consider.

"Do you French? I'm funny that way."

"I've been known to," she said dryly. "It'll cost another ten bucks."

"No, ma'am. Forty's as high as I'd care to go. Down home I get it for nothing, and those little old gals come flocking back for more."

Without waiting for the bargain to be struck, Prescott went outside, where he shut himself in a phone booth.

Presently the man and the girl appeared. He had his arm around her, one big hand low on her hip. When they turned the corner, the waiting detective followed on foot. Returning for his sedan a few moments later, he drove around the block and double-parked. By that time Prescott was posted in a doorway farther along the block. He had never done anything remotely like this before, but for some reason he didn't feel furtive.

He waited nearly an hour before the man in the big hat brought the girl down, put her in the sedan, and they drove off together. Prescott returned to the phone booth, where he called Martha to tell her he thought he might be on to something.

At ten the next morning, Prescott and Martha were in Women's Court for the girl's arraignment. Judge O'Toole allowed them inside the baffle, an arrangement of wallboard panels across the middle of the courtroom. From the spectators' side, nothing could be seen but the tip of an American flag and the motto "In God We Trust," with the final *t* in *Trust* missing.

A toilet had backed up in a nearby lavatory, and the floor was awash. There was considerable traffic in and out through the baffle, from the clerk's office and the officers' room. One by one the offending women were called in from the cage. Prescott recognized one from his first batch, a corpulent Negro lady wearing dark glasses with elaborate costume-jewelry rims. She pleaded guilty saucily. On her way back to the cage she made a small detour to pass Prescott. Lifting a curled little finger, she remarked, "And fuck yew tew, Professor."

The girl Prescott had seen being arrested was named Lillian Shaw. She was twenty-two, with no prior record. She stood in front of the bench with her eyes lowered while the complaint was read.

At 11:10 the previous evening, the accused had accosted Officer Roderick Shanley and offered to commit a lewd and indecent act for the sum of forty dollars. She then took him to an East 58th Street apartment, where she proceeded immediately to disrobe. At this point Officer Shanley identified himself as a police officer and placed her under arrest.

Now no longer a Texan seeking a forty-dollar fellatio, back in his true identity as a Vice Squad detective, Roderick Shanley raised his right hand and swore to the facts contained in the complaint. A court officer advised Lillian Shaw of her right to counsel and to an adjournment to procure counsel and asked if she pleaded guilty or not guilty. Hearing a plea of not guilty, Judge O'Toole remanded her to the House of Detention pending trial.

A week later Prescott and Martha were back in court to observe another series of arraignments. Several women, previously found guilty, were sentenced. Lillian Shaw was brought in from the cage and charged with violating the vagrancy statute, Section 887 (4) (a) of the New York Code of Criminal Procedure. One of the peculiarities of this court was that the District Attorney's office would have nothing to do with it. The Police Prosecutor, a florid, heavy-jowled man with a fine head of white hair, conducted the case for the People. There was the usual indiscriminate milling around while the complainant, Officer Shanley, stepped up nimbly. This was his home turf. He laced his fingers across his stomach, ready to carry out his accustomed part in the rigamarole.

The Prosecutor glanced at a copy of the complaint and asked Shanley whether, at approximately 11:15 P.M. on such-and-such a date, at a certain East 58th Street address, he had arrested the defendant, Lillian Shaw.

"I did."

"Tell the Court the circumstances that prompted you to make this arrest."

Shanley looked at the ceiling and recited rapidly: "Entered McNeill's tavern and took a place at the bar. Seeing I was by myself, defendant engaged me in conversation. Said, 'Are you lonely, Jack?' Crowding me and attempting to slide her hand into the fly of my trousers. Said, 'I'm part Chinese. My mother was half and half.' Then stated, 'I like to go down. My mother taught me to French. People tell me I'm the best blowjob artist in town.'"

"Did she mention a price?"

"She did. Forty dollars regular, ten more around the horn."

"Proceed."

"Defendant conducted me to her apartment. Proceeded to disrobe, removing all clothing except for a garter belt. I thereupon identified myself as a police officer, informed her of her constitutional rights, and placed her under arrest."

The Prosecutor nodded to the judge. He had taken two minutes of the Court's time.

The defense, as usual in this court, was in the hands of the Legal Aid Society, as personified by Aline Cohn, a peppery young woman with untidy brown hair that she probably cut herself. With a faint grin, she called Officer Lee Metcalfe.

Calling anyone but the defendant or a character witness was an unusual tactic in prostitution cases, and two plain-clothesmen going through the baffle bumped each other. Officer Metcalfe, who had been working with Shanley the night Lillian Shaw was arrested, came forward to take the oath. He looked apprehensive, as though someone he had thought he could trust had suddenly turned on him.

All Miss Cohn wanted the witness to do was confirm his partner's story. Together they took Shanley into the bar, to look for violators of Section 887 (4) (a), out of it again in the company of the defendant, around the corner, and into the defendant's apartment building.

"Now," Miss Cohn said briskly. "How long did you wait until Officer Shanley and the defendant reappeared?"

The witness had been answering warily. Miss Cohn repeated this question, and asked the Court to direct him to answer. He finally ventured that he didn't recall.

"I'm not asking you to be precise," she said. "I'm trying to get an impression, a very rough impression if you will, of the length of time Officer Shanley was in the defendant's apartment. Was it on the order of five minutes? Half an hour? Was it longer than half an hour?"

All the arresting officers who were waiting in the probation room had crowded into the doorway to see what was happening. Judge O'Toole, for once, looked almost benign. Again Miss Cohn repeated her question.

"I didn't take any notice," Officer Metcalfe told her unhappily. "It was my night to drive. I just wasn't too conscious of the time."

"You have had twelve years' experience as a police officer, is that correct?"

"That is correct."

"How many years have you served on the so-called Vice Squad?"

"Going on five."

"I believe I've seen you in this court frequently in the role of arresting officer. How many prostitutes have you been instrumental in bringing to justice, thousands?"

"Not thousands. Maybe hundreds, a lot of them repeaters."

"Then let's say, shall we, that I've called you to the stand as an expert witness. Officer Shanley has testified that the defendant disrobed upon entering her apartment, whereupon he identified himself and made the pinch, not neglecting, of course, to inform her of the rights which even professional prostitutes enjoy under the Constitution. How long, based on your considered opinion, after twelve years in the Police Department and five on the Vice Squad, should it take a prostitute to remove her clothes?"

The witness squirmed. "Depending on the circumstances."

Miss Cohn pounced. "The circumstances in this case, if the previous witness is to be believed, are as follows. The defendant solicited the witness to commit a single lewd and indecent act. It was then approximately eleven o'clock, which would indicate that her working day was far from over. Presumably, if she could dispose of Officer Shanley in a hurry — He was pretending to be a lonely Texan that night, was he not?"

"I can't testify to that of my own knowledge. I mean, I was outside in the car."

"Wasn't he wearing a large white hat? Speaking with a Texas drawl?"

"He may have been, I wouldn't want to swear to it."

"I know you wouldn't want to, Officer. But to return to my previous question, and I must now respectfully request an answer, would a prostitute under these circumstances take her time getting undressed? Or would she simply slip off her clothes and assume the indicated position?"

"I suppose that's what she'd do, as a regular thing. Remember I wasn't there."

"Would five minutes cover everything?"

"Maybe she made him a drink."

"Officer Shanley didn't testify that she made him a drink. In your experience—"

"Like I say! She could get some music on the radio, give him a little striptease. It happens!"

"A striptease. I don't have your experience in these matters, Officer. Is that what is meant by the verb *to French?*"

There was laughter from the public side of the screen. Miss Cohn commented that she herself, with no financial incentive for hurrying, rarely took as long as five minutes to disrobe. She released him at last. The Prosecutor passed up a chance to cross-examine, and she called Dr. Chalmers Prescott.

Prescott identified himself. A reporter, summoned by some kind of jungle telegraph, slipped in and took a seat at one of the tables. Miss Cohn led Prescott into an account of the meeting between the defendant and the arresting officer. Lillian Shaw drummed the fingers of one hand soundlessly on the table. Shanley himself had pushed into the group of onlookers and listened while Prescott testified to the Texas hat and the steer's-head belt buckle.

"Now are you in a position to state, Dr. Prescott, at what time the officer and the defendant entered the defendant's building?"

"I am. At 11:07."

"And when did they emerge?"

"At 11:58."

"An elapsed time of—"

"Fifty-one minutes."

Everybody had known what was coming. Miss Cohn let it sink in for a moment, then gave the Prosecutor her witness.

The Prosecutor advanced. A policeman himself, he could be expected to come roaring to the defense of a fellow officer. But Prescott's stare seemed to unnerve him. Prescott knew, from the Kinsey material and the law of averages, that the Prosecutor himself was not without guilt. Of course, there were questions that could have been asked. For Prescott to interest himself to the extent of waiting fifty-one minutes on a rainy night in December, he must have overheard the dialogue in the bar, and so he could corroborate Shanley's statement that she had offered to perform the

French variation for forty dollars. But this was risky ground. In sumptuary-law enforcement, everything depends on who makes the initial move. Was it the disguised cop or the person he suspected of being a criminal? Shanley's actual first words had been, "Haven't had a woman in four days," and Judge O'Toole, who had a reputation among the police as an anti-police zealot, would be sure to interpret this as proof of entrapment. The Prosecutor decided against taking a chance. He turned away with a disgusted movement and told the judge that the People would have no objection if the defense should now move to dismiss on the grounds of insufficient evidence.

The corridor outside was very crowded. The reporter overtook Prescott as he was leaving. Prescott answered his questions politely. It seemed to him, he said, that the way the police secured evidence in prostitution cases was worse than the offense itself, and if Officers Shanley and Metcalfe and their colleagues were transferred to traffic duty they might be more useful to the city.

chapter 9

The Women's House of Detention might not be the most comfortable place in the world, but it wasn't as horrible as the papers made out, either. Still, Lillian Shaw was glad when the week was over. She had been given plenty of free advice from the other inmates. On a conscious level, none of them considered that they had done anything wrong. They had made a mistake and they hoped to be more careful the next time. Lillian, with a clean sheet, was sure to walk, especially if she was lucky enough to get O'Toole, who for some reason didn't despise whores. She would be found guilty, of course, because not even O'Toole could take a whore's word against a cop's, but he would suspend sentence.

Prescott, when he showed up with the Legal Aid lawyer, was a puzzle. After the interview, her cellmates crowded around to find out what his angle was, but she couldn't tell them. He seemed sincere enough, but why should he bother? The defense was sure to work if Prescott would agree to switch the dialogue around and forget he had heard Lillian mention the forty dollars. He refused to do that. The cops would just ask for a postponement and bring in somebody else to testify to the actual words. The bartender, for example. He probably hadn't heard anything, but if he didn't do what they said the Liquor Authority would jerk the license. What it came down to was a question of whether Prescott could succeed in scaring them enough. On the streets, the Police Department had the power, and if it fell through who would take the pounding? Not Prescott. Not Aline Cohn.

One of the girls had heard about Prescott—he was a surgeon who entertained himself by sterilizing prostitutes, a humane Jack the Ripper. Lillian checked this with Miss Cohn. Finding that he was actually a professor who ran a marriage-advice clinic, she decided to gamble on his looks. He had impressed her, and she was fairly sure he would impress the cops.

Prescott had a woman with him during the trial, and Lillian couldn't place her, either. Courthouse characters kept trooping in and out, passing through the well of the court under the judge's nose, and they didn't bother to lower their voices. Nobody was writing anything down. The clerk was reading a racing form. O'Toole, on the bench, might be a fair-minded man, as the girls said, but he also looked a little crocked. At least they had fixed the toilet during the intervening week, so water was no longer running across the floor.

After it was over and they returned her belongings, she came out of the courtroom and looked for Prescott. She didn't see him at first. Was that all there was to it?

Then she saw him talking to Shanley. The detective was red in the face, and of course he would have felt naked without his .38.

"I'm a married man," he was saying threateningly. "What's my wife going to think if that gets in the papers? You didn't happen to think of that, did you?"

"Nothing was farther from my mind," Prescott said, staring at him.

"Just because somebody happens to be a cop—"

"Well, here we are, deep in the heart of Texas," Lillian put in. As Shanley swung around she added coldly, "You owe me forty bucks, buster."

"I owe you a couple of broken legs."

Lillian had intended to do no more than divert Shanley from Prescott, but when he took her arm and started to squeeze she kicked him beneath one knee. He let go, his face crimson. Metcalfe, Shanley's partner, came quickly through the crowd and put both arms around the detective.

"Cool it, baby. This is neither the time or the place."

He wrestled his partner into the crowd.

"Well, it worked," Lillian remarked to Prescott. "And I better not cruise any more cops for a while, don't you think?"

"Let's have breakfast. I hear the coffee in the House of Detention isn't too good."

"The coffee in the House of Detention stinks." She gave him a sideward glance. "And what happens after breakfast?"

"I want to talk to you about a job."

"Great. Can't you see by looking at me that I'm not the job type?"

"Do you enjoy sex?"

"I can take it or leave it. Why?"

"That's the job."

She didn't comment on that, because she was sure to say the wrong thing. He didn't mean that he wanted to pay her rent, she hoped, because the answer would have to be no. She didn't go in for getting involved. But it had to be something else. The one thing she was sure of by now was it wouldn't be ordinary.

They went out through different sections of the revolving door.

"I knew there had to be an angle," she said. "You don't disillusion me one bit. Well, I've still got a perfect record as far as convictions go, so what am I being snotty about? You've invested a certain amount of time in this. I feel too grubby to go to a restaurant. What's wrong with my place?"

"Fine."

He was parked illegally but safely, thanks to his MD plates. He had a big black Olds, a real doctor's car. He fastened his seatbelt, a trait she didn't like in a man.

"Miss Cohn says you run a marriage clinic. Where would I fit in? As a consultant?"

"I also have a research study going, and I need volunteers."

"I begin to get it. You want the gory figures. How many rim jobs a night, and am I subconsciously a lez?"

"Are you?"

"As a matter of fact, I'm not. Though a couple of times this past week I was sorely tempted."

"Do you reach orgasm?"

"Doctor, you're kidding."

"No, I find that when I ask a prostitute that question, the answer isn't always yes."

"It's yes with me."

He was driving fast, making up time. "But the point is," he said without looking at her, "can I believe you?"

Gong. Now she understood why he had been willing to take on the New York City Police Department on her behalf. It hadn't been social conscience after all. That she might not have been able to handle.

"You want to watch," she said.

"Yes. In the laboratory, where we have the setup to do it properly."

"If that's all," she said, "I'll be glad to help."

That pulled his eyes around. Probably most of the girls he asked giggled and had to be persuaded. But what Prescott didn't know, and what she didn't intend to tell him, was that Officer Roderick Shanley was only the fifth man she had ever solicited for money. This last week in the House had been an education. Did she want to be a prostitute? Not if there was some more edifying way to make money, and it was beginning to seem there was.

She shrugged. "But first I'd better hear about it."

He stopped fighting the traffic and went with it while he began telling her the kind of things he and his assistant, the woman Lillian had seen with him in court, were trying to discover.

She had two rooms on the fourth floor of a remodeled building. She used the front room as a studio, where she made peculiar objects of brushed aluminum and brass.

"Find a place to sit down," she said. "I'll put on the water for coffee, and then I want to zip in and out of the shower."

After showering she brushed her hair and gave a moment's thought to her appearance. She decided to leave it alone, without lipstick or anything on the eyes. She went out barefoot, in a gray wrapper.

"I had some Danish, but that was last week. They're hard as a rock. And I'm sorry to say the cream's sour."

"Just black, thanks."

He was examining a four-foot-high aluminum construction. It wasn't finished yet, but why should she tell him that?

"Do you sell these?" he asked.

"They're for sale. Nobody's bought any yet. I had one show, or a sixth of a show—there were six of us. Nobody reviewed it."

"How much is this one?"

"Quit it. You've done your good turn for the week. Do you like it?" she couldn't help adding.

"I don't know," Prescott said slowly. "What's it supposed to be?"

"Does it have to be anything?" she said irritably. "It's just what it looks like, a shape."

"Was that the wrong thing to say?"

"Maybe not—everybody says it." She moved a welding unit from the end of a long pine table and arranged two place mats facing each other. "I forgot to thank you. It was pretty heroic, when you come to think about it. You're going to be well-known around town, in certain circles."

"I hope so. I need some good publicity. There's a rumor going around that I'm a psychopathic surgeon, looking for victims."

"I heard that one," she said, pouring the coffee. "What kind of guys would you give me?"

"That's one of our problems. We only have one male, and he's pretty terrible."

"What about you?"

"That might be nice, but it wouldn't be a good idea. Somebody has to operate the equipment."

"But why go to this much trouble? I mean, I'm glad you happened to come along just when you did, but that was a hundred-to-one shot. Why not go into the open market and hire a couple of dozen pros?"

"That's a marvelous suggestion. What do you think I've been trying to do the last ten months? I'm used to dealing with middle-class pregnancies. The prostitute community is as closed to me now as when I started. For some reason everybody seems to think I'm a threat. Bit by bit I've collected quite a body of material, but from the scientific point of view a lot of it's worthless."

"How much money have you got to play around with?"

"Not nearly enough. We can't get an important grant until we can demonstrate that the thing is feasible, and I'm beginning to have some doubts about that myself. I've been hoping to complete a color film on the physiology of the clitoral function. We've had one woman who was able to give us a satisfactory series, exactly one. She had a high orgasmic capacity, she wasn't inhibited by the laboratory atmosphere, and she was willing to carry out instructions most of the time. And she resigned from the program a week ago by jumping off a roof."

"That must be Lisette—everybody was talking about her. Sort of ticky, wasn't she? Somebody said she didn't jump because she was depressed, she wanted to see if she could fly."

He reacted as though he'd been flicked. So the man had feelings?

"All right, it's a tragedy," she said. "But if I had a dollar for every girl in the life who's ended up on a slab— Tell me about the movie you want to make—I might have some ideas. But go easy with the words. The only science I took in school was geology."

She poured more coffee and listened attentively. At last she interrupted.

"That's all I can take in one dose. When do you want me to start?"

"Right away. This morning."

"There's one thing we didn't cover. Price."

He explained their fee schedule. She shook her head.

"That's not realistic. And maybe that's half your trouble. With somebody in the racket it's too close to home. How much cooperation can a John expect for fifteen bucks? Pay me one-fifty a week, and I'm yours. It has to be something definitely different from turning tricks. I know a couple of girls who might be interested, but I'll need some kind of title. I want to say I'm the coordinator or something. Think up some high-sounding name. We need some special talent that not everybody has. Do you see what I mean? You won't lose by it. I'll guarantee you a minimum of ten orgasms a week. I've got them to burn."

She stood up and pulled the knot of her robe so it hung open. "And if you'd like an audition—"

"I don't think so, thanks. One-fifty a week, then. How much do you want for the sculpture?"

She brought her robe together and said nervously, "Do you want to buy it because you like it, or are you just trying to—"

"I've already hired you. My wife's birthday is next week, and I'm trying to decide how that would look in her garden."

Lillian was confused for a moment. "Aluminum's expensive. Would two hundred be too much?" She made a quick correction. "One seventy-five."

He took out his checkbook. "Is Lillian Shaw your real name?"

It wasn't, but it was the name she'd been using, so she went on using it. She soon discovered that the woman she had seen with Prescott at the counsel's table, Martha Freeman, was at least fifteen degrees warmer than their common employer. Then she was introduced to Nick DiVito, the photographer, and the mercury fell again. He was Lillian's age. Wearing a T-shirt and chinos, dark and compact, with the build of a very good shortstop, he was one of the chilliest fish she had encountered in a long, long time. How many people who had looked at her that day had really seen her? Aline Cohn, perhaps. Certainly not Shanley or the Police Prosecutor or any of that crowd. She wasn't sure about Judge O'Toole. To Prescott she was a case history, to DiVito an object. He didn't care, so long as he could get an image on film. He might have been photographing clams.

She found the laboratory a queer, cluttered place. If they could get some money, Prescott told her, he intended to knock out a wall and put in a couple of dressing cubicles. As it was, the subjects undressed in the room and hung their clothes on a hook. But the atmosphere, even with the equipment not in use, had its own excitement. Lillian felt that she was going to do well here. She had always wanted to succeed at something; that was the way she'd been brought up. Prescott needed her more than he realized. She had a feeling she could put this thing over.

They took her history. She didn't tell them too many outright lies, but she switched things around and exaggerated the extent of her experience, as most people do when applying for jobs. Prescott examined her. She passed. Why not?

The story of her rescue from the jaws of the Vice Squad didn't make any of the papers or the news programs, as it turned out, but nevertheless it was around town before nightfall. It was the big topic in the Women's House. When Lillian went into McNeill's that night, she was greeted cordially. The advertising-agency types came over. For twenty-four hours, at least, she was a celebrity. The girl who had bet her ten dollars she didn't have the nerve to hustle Roderick Shanley apologized for that mistake and wanted to hear about Prescott. What did he do in his laboratory, really?

Lillian was able to see how Prescott himself, going up to a hooker and asking her to come up to his place for a scientific orgasm, wouldn't get to first base. But Lillian's week in jail had taken her out of the amateur ranks, and the women were willing to give her a hearing. Gradually, she built up a list. Men were harder to get hold of than women. The police felt that they could be rougher on male whores than they dared to be with women, and there was a good deal of pounding done in isolated hallways around Times Square. Lillian kept circulating and tracking down leads, and finally Nick DiVito had a day when he changed magazines twenty-two times and shot almost 9,000 feet of film.

The program had a few spontaneous walk-ins, its first. Prescott was working on the design of a gadget which Lillian, in the privacy of her own mind, was referring to as the fucking machine. They spent endless hours on vaginal-barrel angulation (she soon picked up the project's terminology). Her pelvis was mapped and photographed in every coital position, and the measurements were transferred to a series of working drawings. It was Lillian who suggested X-rays. They called in one of the new males and daubed him with a radiopaque substance with adhesive qualities, and then took a series of lateral shots while he was inside her, possibly the first pornographic X-rays ever made.

A man named Hixon from a foundation came to look them over. Lillian had just completed a manipulative session and was wearing only a wrapper. Hixon gave her an interested glance, but Nick got the real glance a moment later. What thoughts ran through his head while Prescott explained the concept of the machine, Lillian couldn't say; but she was sure they weren't heterosexual thoughts.

They were asking for $115,000, $40,000 of which would go for the machine. Hixon, bringing his mind back, said he was sure he could swing it.

The grant went through. Prescott was already in touch with a research and development firm on Route 128 outside Boston, which had designed a prototype heart valve for Manhattan Medical. The specifications now were fantastically detailed, but still the engineers had trouble. Prescott spent a good deal of time in Boston. They were trying to use systems analysis, which as Lillian understood it meant breaking down the design problem into hundreds of tiny bits that could be fed to a computer for yes or no answers. This worked well enough with anything with rigid dimensions, like supersonic aircraft or missiles, but in the end they had to subcontract the penis. The new engineers made a light skeleton of an aluminum alloy and covered it with a flexible plastic closely allied to the simulated skin used in the Barbie doll.

The bugs were worked out of the design over a four-month period, and finally the working model was ready. A tool-and-die man came down from Boston to make the installation. His name was Lester, and he worked with the dead stump of a cigar in his mouth.

The crate had been fastened with machine screws instead of nails, and all the working parts were numbered. Lester drilled the necessary holes in an examination table that had been stripped of its usual furniture, and installed the mounting. He put the machine together from the blueprints. This was a big moment, and all the project personnel had collected to see if it would actually work. There was no sound but the clink of metal and a low, preoccupied humming from Lester. Finally he installed a twenty-ampere fuse and turned a switch. The stainless-steel arm stroked forward and back along its carefully plotted arc.

Lillian said softly, "I don't believe it."

Lester cut the main switch, unscrewed the fuse, and began tying in the rheostats. All at once his humming stopped. His jaw dropped and he almost lost control of his cigar. He smiled uneasily.

"You know what I thought it looked like for a minute?" His eye met Lillian's. "Me and my dirty mind."

He went on with the rheostats, but didn't resume humming. He dropped a wrench and a moment later had to chase a nut across the floor. It was only when he was testing the ejection mechanism that he burst out, "But what's the God damn *point?*"

"Didn't they tell you what it was?" Prescott asked.

"No, they didn't tell me what it was! I'm supposed to know

how to read a blueprint. No wonder there was always a crowd around in that end of the shop. All the brass from the front office, the Harvard and MIT guys."

The electrical connections were all in. He began working from a checklist, in a hurry to finish.

"I guess it's none of my business, but they're going to be asking me. You mean you're going to use it, I mean like on a real woman?"

He looked at Lillian for an answer. She said tartly, "No, we've ordered a plastic snatch. You didn't get that contract."

"Jesus!"

"Let's squash that rumor before it gets started," Prescott said. He turned on the power, and the device made a slow, delicate forward movement, on a ten-centimeter thrust, then withdrew into mounting position. "We aren't going to use it on just one woman, but on a succession of women, to establish the basic human sexual reaction patterns. We're attempting to reproduce as far as possible the conditions obtaining during actual coition, except that the operation of the device is wholly controlled by subjective demand. The right-hand rheostat governs the rapidity of movement—these calibrations on the dial indicate the number of stroke-cycles per minute. The left-hand dial controls depth of penetration. If the thrust encounters any appreciable frontal resistance, the shutoff switch will trip automatically. At present the arm can be set for only two positions, the supine and knee-chest, but that ought to be adequate."

Dr. Prescott turned back to the machine. He brought each dial through the complete range of choice. At the higher speeds there was a distracting little clack whenever the arm reversed direction, like a windshield wiper.

"You'll notice this machined bracket at the base of the shaft. That's for a Minox camera and a high-intensity light source. For the present, we'll have to be satisfied with still photography."

Lester watched with a drugged look. "You mean you're going to take pictures inside, while she—"

Prescott looked at him curiously. "That's the entire idea."

"But Doctor, how's a woman going to manage to—well, go all the way? I mean, come? Feel it—it's cold plastic."

"That's going to be no problem at all," Lillian told him flatly. "Do you have any brochures or anything I could take back? They're going to ask me and I'll get it all wrong."

"I can let you have a reprint of an article from a medical journal," Prescott said. "I'm afraid you'll find it hard going."

"So long as I have something I can show."

Lillian was the first to try it. She knew that if anything came of all this, Prescott and Freeman would get the credit and she would be only a statistic. Nonetheless, she herself would know she'd been the first woman in history to have had intercourse with a machine.

It was much better than she'd expected. The volunteers were going to be crazy about it.

They definitely had to get rid of that clackety noise. Over the next few months she recommended other design changes, based on her own experience and on interviews with other girls during the postclimax phase—some of them really took their hair down—and eventually the machine was dismantled, repacked in its original crate, and shipped back to Boston, where the thrust was made smoother, with a slight pause at the moment of maximum withdrawal. With the help of transistors and a tiny printed circuit, the pause was made to vary slightly from stroke to stroke, disappearing entirely at a certain speed. The windshield-wiper noise was eliminated by using ball bearings.

These were minor problems. The major problem was the penis.

Lillian was surprised to learn how much vaginal dimensions vary from one woman to the next. The original working model had come with a number of different parts, in various sizes. But to ensure a comfortable fit, the match had to be made at the end of the arousal phase, and for a multitude of reasons this was unsatisfactory. It broke the momentum, and a number of cycles were spoiled as a result. Later, if anything went wrong, the subject tended to blame the equipment—it was either too long or too short, or the angle wasn't right. How much better if the machine could be equipped with a single all-purpose organ, the size of which could be adjusted by the subject herself.

This was an extra, running the cost well over the $40,000 appropriated by the Royce Foundation. The engineers, in consultation with Prescott and Lillian, finally came up with a solution. The overall length was left at nine inches. The differences in the longitudinal axis, that is, the distance from vaginal entrance to cul-de-sac, were taken care of by varying the thrust. The diameter, or degree of lateral tumescence, was controlled by means of a series of aluminum disks, each made up of well over a hundred overlapping parts, made larger and smaller on the same mechanical principle that governs the lens aperture of a camera. DuPont provided a plastic skin with the same tactile properties of the old one, but distensible. The enlarging mechanism was powered by a tiny motor with its own circuit. A third control dial was added, near the subject's right hand.

And this proved to be the machine's most popular feature. The size adjustment could be made at any time after entry, and most subjects, to Prescott's surprise but not to Lillian's, availed themselves of this option. As the act proceeded, they not only stepped up the speed and the depth of penetration, but the size as well. With a human partner, of course, this was beyond their power.

For the first time, the project had more applications than the facilities could handle.

Four months went by. Lillian's salary was raised to $250 a week. The film on the behavior of the clitoris under different forms of stress had been finished and was now being edited. One evening, after working late, Lillian was approached by two men outside the Research Building. They were immediately identifiable as cops.

"Miss Shaw?"

She admitted that that was her name.

"If you have a minute, the assistant D.A. would like to talk to you."

"Some other time."

She turned toward Broadway. One of the cops walked with her while the other crossed the sidewalk to their Chevy.

Her pulse had escalated to 175 beats a minute, a rate she usually reached only on the approach to orgasm. "I don't want to be antisocial. If he still wants to talk to me tomorrow I'll come down on the subway and bring my lawyer."

"He'd like to talk to you tonight, and he said if you gave us any trouble to mention Flint, Michigan. There's a circular out on you."

She gave a half-sigh and turned toward the police car. There was no conversation going downtown. They pulled up in front of the huge Criminal Courts Building. On her last two visits to this place, she had arrived in a prison van and she had hoped she wouldn't be seeing it again. The assistant D.A. who had sent for her occupied a small bleak office containing a battered desk and several battered chairs. There were several framed diplomas on the walls, and the walls needed painting. His name was Woods McChesney, and unlike his furniture he himself was in pretty good shape, a neat little suit, neat tie, neat mustache.

She asked for a cigarette.

"Are you sure you want one?" he said. "I'm trying to give them up."

"That's your problem, isn't it?"

He went out for a minute and came back with a single cigarette and a match. She breathed smoke at him and watched his nostrils open.

"What do you want us to call you?" he said. "Lillian Shaw or what?"

"I don't care."

"We've had a tap on your phone," he explained. "You shouldn't have given your sister your number. Will you make a statement for us about what you and the other girls are doing in the laboratory?"

"Not unless I have to. Does my father know you found me?"

McChesney nodded toward the phone. "Not yet. He can hear about it in one minute."

"Blackmail."

"Then, too, you're an escapee from a mental institution. That was a legal commitment."

"Balls. My father signed me in because I was embarrassing him. I did it on purpose because he's such a prick."

"Lillian," McChesney said wearily, "I've been sitting in this office for seven years and I've heard most of the stories. I'm sure you're as sane as Dr. Prescott, which may not be saying very much. I'm trying to build a case for the grand jury and I need everything I can get. You wouldn't be using a fake name if you weren't worried about that Sanity Commission. You'll want to know how we'll handle you if you exercise your constitutional right to remain silent. We'll arrest you for procurement. 'Procuring another to commit lewdness, fornication, unlawful sex intercourse or any other indecent act.' You've been procuring in half the bars on the East Side, in front of witnesses. You've already got one arrest—"

"I wasn't convicted."

"Honey," he said reasonably, "everybody knows that nobody gets arrested for prostitution unless she's a prostitute. So if Michigan wants you, they can have you."

Lillian was trying to keep a cool exterior, but beneath it she was rattled. Some of the things she'd done back home had been pretty outrageous, and her father's reactions had made them worse. She had had the bad luck to be caught boosting a handbag. But that was all behind her, and she didn't want to go back.

"That's the either," she said. "What's the or?"

"You make a statement and then you go on doing what you're doing, except that you call me every few days. The main thing I need now is up-to-the-minute information."

"Are you sure you could believe me?"

"You wouldn't lie to me."

She wouldn't? She started lying five minutes later. She tried to get twenty-four hours to think it over, so she could ask Aline Cohn for advice, but that wasn't the deal he was offering her. She was better about making decisions than she used to be, so possibly she was finally beginning to grow up. A few years before she would have begged him to give her a break, which would have pleased him immensely. Needless to say, he wasn't in the business of giving people breaks. For the first time in her life, she had been doing something useful. They were a team, she and Dr. Prescott and Martha Freeman —even Nick DiVito. Together they had produced something that any straight person would have said was impossible. She knew Prescott approved of her. Things might have been different if she'd grown up in that kind of atmosphere. His daughter, whose picture stood on his desk, didn't know how lucky she was. (Her own father neither approved or disapproved of sex. He didn't know it existed.)

To torture McChesney, she made him get more cigarettes and smoked steadily while she told him wild tales of what went on in the laboratory. His eyes sharpened when she started on the machine, so naturally she enlarged on that. She told him it was able to contract during ejaculation, and he seemed to believe it. The one lie she regretted later was that she and Prescott, working together, had demonstrated various sexual maneuvers for patients in the clinic. She probably shouldn't have included that.

After it was typed up she signed it and made them give her a lift home. Lillian still had a lot to do. She packed three bags. One habit she'd picked up from the girls in the business —she always kept cash on hand. If she'd had a couple of hundred the night she was arrested by Roderick Shanley— but then of course she wouldn't have met Prescott, would she?

She started to dial the TWA number before remembering that McChesney had told her he had a tap on her line. That was her old trick—doing something in such a way that she was sure to be caught. She went ahead with the call, but asked the girl who answered about planes to California. She carried her bags downstairs and over to Second Avenue, where eventually she was picked up by a passing cab.

At Kennedy, she bought a ticket for San Juan. She still had her passport and she could arrange the visas there. Rome might be a good place to start. She wouldn't have to stay away forever, just until Prescott's project surfaced.

She looked up Prescott's number. Deciding against that before she dialed, she called Nick DiVito. He answered finally —it was five in the morning.

"Nick, this is Lillian. Are you awake enough to take a message?"

"Is anything wrong?"

"I guess so! Tell Dr. Prescott something out of the past has caught up to me and I have to leave town. Good luck and all that crap."

"Okay."

He waited to see if there was more to the message. She

waited to see if he would warm up and say something human.

"My rent's paid through the month," she said. "Prescott owes me a couple of hundred. Tell him to give it to the super to put my stuff in storage."

"Yeah, okay."

When he remained silent after that, she hung up. What an ice cube!

She had a half hour's wait, which gave her time to wonder if she was behaving like the cliché whore with a heart of gold. No, she decided. She was just being practical, and, on top of that, was she really a whore? She hadn't been convicted.

chapter 10

Martha Freeman, caught up in the excitement of running two innovative programs, the clinic and the laboratory, was working harder than she had ever worked in her life. She was enjoying herself intensely, although she wasn't following her own clinical advice about the resolution of sexual tension— she didn't have time.

They prepared a carefully worded paper about their bisexual counseling technique, including a veiled reference to their success with the Hallinans, the couple whose marriage had been patched up by a joint orgasm in the examination room with the bisexual counselors urging them on from the sidelines. This was published by a gynecological journal and provoked no comment at all. Nobody called. Nobody wrote indignant letters. None of the gynecologists Prescott encountered in his hospital practice mentioned having seen it.

Nevertheless, the news got around among laymen on the grapevine provided by the New York Telephone Company. Soon the clinic was doing standing-room-only business. Every new success enlarged their surreptitious fame. When they began getting their first patients from outside the metropolitan area, they instituted a seven-day crash program. People who had a two-week vacation would spend the first week at the Prescott-Freeman clinic and the second on a new and more satisfactory honeymoon.

The money from the Royce Foundation, which at the beginning had seemed inexhaustible, was gone in six months, and again the research was being financed out of the earnings of the clinic. Hixon wasn't sanguine about getting a renewal —that was his word, sanguine—unless they could arrange some public notice. Thanks mainly to Lillian Shaw, they had material enough for a half-dozen papers. It was a question of finding time to write them. Martha and Prescott were still doing all the interviewing, although Martha now dictated the cases to a tape recorder. Two new doctors had been hired

134

to help in the clinic, and DiVito had the assistance of a professional film editor.

A medical textbook firm asked them to contribute a chapter on the motility of the cervix for use in a book about the pelvic viscera. Prescott forced the facts into the tape recorder in two desperate all-night sessions. Martha shortened some of his sentences and added punctuation. Two papers on uterine reactions followed. They not only made no waves, they made no ripples. It was like dropping stones in a dry well. Finally, Prescott received an invitation to a two-day symposium on the external genitalia, to be held in Chicago under the auspices of the Midwest Academy of Sciences. Thirty-five people, including the leading personalities in the field, had been asked for papers. Prescott's topic was "Secondary Stimulation by Movements of Clitoral Hood during Intravaginal Penile Thrusting." He obtained permission to present visual material to support his findings.

Martha went to Chicago with him. He held the can of film on his lap on the plane, taking no chances with the airline's notorious inability to keep track of its customers' luggage. Prescott had brought a stack of medical journals containing articles by other participants in the symposium. Any doctor who hopes to keep abreast of his specialty has to develop an ability to read only the important words in each sentence. Concentrating hard, Prescott was able to move through the journals nearly as fast as he could turn the pages. He read one piece more carefully, a report by a St. Louis man who was reputed to be tilling the same field.

Martha had a novel, but, unlike Prescott, she read more and more slowly and finally stopped altogether. Quiet moments like this were rare in her life now, and she knew she should use them to try to define her feelings about her job and about Prescott himself. She kept wishing she could get him to submit to one of their intake interviews. There were innumerable questions she wanted to ask. What did he think about life outside the laboratory? If she asked him, he would think she had gone out of her mind.

He paced himself well, finishing the last journal just as the no-smoking light went on—unnecessarily, in his case, as he didn't smoke. He snapped the lap belt and remarked, "I don't know if I told you, Martha. The press is going to be here, from *Time* on down. A man from Johns Hopkins is going to be reading a paper on the sex-change operation."

He gave her a wry look. If newspapermen were going to be present at the screening of the clitoris film, they were in for a major surprise. Hixon, the Royce man, had been trying to promote a press conference, but Prescott had refused to agree to that. The story had to work its way out through professional channels. And was that why he had wanted Martha along? So she could be with him when they emerged into the glare of publicity? Was it possible that he was worrying about how he would stand up under a drumfire of questions? He was tapping his knee, but it was probably only his usual impatience with having to sit still doing nothing.

Martha knew these genital-area people. They were the most cautious members of a profession not known for its recklessness. Their subject was cemented in a matrix of mysticism and superstition. Before sexual responses could be examined and understood, that matrix had to be smashed—the whole mass of sentiment, male superiority, fear and frustration, religious precept, morality, and that most absurd of the absurdities, romantic love—which must exist because every jukebox in the country said so, but which had never been photographed in any way at all, let alone through a transparent artificial penis.

Prescott could handle his fellow doctors. The facts were on his side, the facts and the whole history of medical inquiry. Newspapermen were another matter. They cared less about facts than appearances, about how the facts could be made to look. The questions themselves would be easy. They would all be variations of the standard one they had been asked ten thousand times: "Do you seriously maintain, Dr. Prescott, Mrs. Freeman, that a professional prostitute and a virgin bride will react to sexual stimulation in the same way?"

But, to deal with it properly, Prescott had to be allowed to set the tone. A slight shift in emphasis changed a simple statement of observed fact into a vicious attack on everything the American press holds sacred. Prescott had very little experience with that side of America.

The Prescott-Freeman contribution—they had signed the paper jointly—had been scheduled next-to-last on the evening program. That gave them the whole day to prepare their ground. They decided to separate and to keep moving. Martha was wearing a new dress and she knew she looked fine. There was a scattering of other women present, but the competition wasn't terribly severe. She had been at one other conference with Prescott (the subject then had been the vagina) and she knew a few people. She was the center of a lively group in the bar during what was listed as the get-acquainted hour and she was glad to see a certain jockeying over who was to have her for lunch. Halfway through the afternoon program, the young doctor seated next to her suggested that they cut out and have a drink. They were joined soon afterward by several others. The conversation kept coming back to the title of their paper: "Secondary Stimulation etc.," the only paper on the program that dealt with the genitalia in action, and by the third martini Martha was afraid that everyone at the table had stopped thinking generically and had begun to personify. It was a loaded subject.

She had dinner two tables away from Prescott. He seemed completely absorbed in conversation with a California neurologist, an extremist in sex education. When they began reading the papers, Prescott hitched his chair around to listen, and Martha could tell he was really listening. He wasn't human! There were four men at the press table, coping with occupational boredom in the usual ways. But they would come to life when they saw that first shot of Lillian.

As was frequently the case at these things, the papers went on much too long. But there was no question that some of the people here were brilliant. They wouldn't ask that foolish question about prostitutes. The last paper before Prescott's went on interminably. The subject was an old standby—hormones. People began leaving before it was over. Finally, the chairman called Prescott's name and asked that the room be darkened. Prescott made his way to the projector. He was wearing a tropical-weight suit, the jacket wrinkled across the back.

"I can hardly wait," Martha's dinner partner said.

Without actually saying anything, she told him to shut up. The projector began to whir. The film was in color, with an all-female cast. Lillian's midsection played the lead. They had decided against using titles. The screen flickered for an instant, then suddenly showed an overhead shot of a naked woman, lying prone. Neither head nor feet were showing, and their absence gave the woman the look of a mutilated Venus. This was Lillian Shaw, who had communicated with the project only once since her abrupt disappearance—with a card postmarked Naples, showing a mural from the Pompeii brothel, and a jocular message: "Thinking of you, gang.—L."

Strictly speaking, her external proportions were of no scientific interest. Nonetheless, they seemed to interest this scientific audience. Her hand was at her mons. For a long moment, while Prescott explained in a matter-of-fact tone what they were about to see, the shot was frozen. Then the camera zoomed in slowly, and the hand began to move.

There was a stir in the room.

From this point on, it was all closeups. Some were wonderfully ingenious, especially those shot from beneath. Nick enjoyed tricky effects, but at the same time there was never the slightest doubt about what he was photographing. Lillian's clitoral region was the focus of attention throughout. At the end of fifteen intensive minutes, there was no longer much mystery about that elusive organ—in Lillian's case, measuring only four millimeters in the transverse axis at the best of times and retreating from view entirely as her tensions rose and blood poured into the area. Many of the most telling shots had been obtained during machine episodes, but the machine itself was never shown. By now everyone connected with the program accepted it as an invaluable research tool, but for the time being they knew it would distract attention from what they were trying to show. At each stage in the developing cycle, shots of other clitorides, responding similarly, were cut in, to indicate that the phenomena were not unique to the single reacting individual glimpsed briefly in the opening. Quick shots of nipple erection, vaginal lubrication, labia engorgement were used to establish the time sequence. Tumescence of the clitoral shaft and glans was made more obvious by the use of six-power magnification and time-lapse photography. As the clitoral body retracted and disappeared behind the labial hood, the cuts came faster. The climax was a long closeup of Lillian in orgasm. And then the clitoris reappeared, seemingly no worse for the experience.

When the lights came on, a sense of unease was immediately apparent. Only a few faces turned toward Prescott. He looked exhausted. The chairman called for questions or comment, and after a moment's silence announced the final paper. A dapper, somewhat diabolic-looking Johns Hopkins surgeon rose and began to read.

Prescott slipped the film back in the can, the can back in its cardboard mailer. When the speaker announced the number of male-into-female operations he and his colleagues had performed, the men at the press table began to scribble furiously. Martha noticed that her knees were trembling. Prescott, gripping the cardboard mailer tightly, joined her when the session broke up. The newspapermen had converged on the Johns Hopkins man and were peppering him with questions. Two people spoke to Prescott as they made their way toward the door. "Interesting paper," one said, and hurried off. The other said, "Will we see you in New Orleans in June?"

"It seems we stunned them," Martha said.

A stout, mannish lady overtook them, wanting to pump Prescott's hand. "Emma Fitzgerald, Kansas City. Doctor. that was the most courageous presentation I've heard in thirty years of going to medical conferences. I like a fighter. There's only one thing to do with these dinosaurs, and that's take them by the scruff of the neck and rub their noses in the twentieth century. Male chauvinists, every last one of them. The female orgasm still has a long way to go."

With a final squeeze, she released his hand and barreled away. Martha laughed nervously. If their only support was going to come from the mavericks . . .

A tall, gawky doctor loomed up in front of them. She had met him in New York. He was a professional one-man minority, an early proponent of Medicare.

"We'd better have a talk about strategy, Prescott. The big thing is not to wait around for the axe to drop. Get some grass-roots support and they won't be able to touch you. Breakfast tomorrow?"

"I'll be glad to have breakfast with you," Prescott said, "but whose axe are you talking about?"

"Not here. More AMA stooges to the square foot—"

He nodded and moved away. Prescott shrugged slightly, watching him go. He suggested coffee, but Martha looked around at the milling delegates and decided she wasn't up to any more arguments tonight. The clitoral glans of a prostitute may show a tumescent reaction in response to rising tension levels, but how can you be sure the same thing happens to an inexperienced bride?

"I think I'll go up. I've had enough of the medical profession for one day."

They joined a man and woman at the elevators. At the sight of Prescott the man's mouth opened in the rictus of senility. His badge identified him as Dr. Samuel J. Dawkins, Charleston, South Carolina. The woman with him was obviously his wife. Steel-rimmed glasses kept her face together.

"God damn it, Prescott," Dawkins said, "if I'd known you were going to inflict that filthy—"

The woman murmured, "Now Sam."

"Why do you consider it filthy?" Prescott asked quietly.

"You don't even realize what you did, do you? What about the fellows who brought their wives? This was supposed to be an open meeting. And without a word of warning the lights go off—"

"Sam!" his wife protested. "Why give him the satisfaction?"

"This is a great scientific investigator, honey. He runs a laboratory in New York where five-buck streetwalkers, male *and* female, commit fornication frontwards, backwards, and sideways, while he takes their temperature with a rectal thermometer. It's the truth! After all the pelvic examinations I've done in my life, I think I know a whore's ass when I see one."

"Sam, I've had enough of that language!"

Prescott had tightened his grip on the film mailer. "I believe you're a gynecologist, Doctor. I was hoping you might learn something about the clitoris you didn't already know."

The angry man's face and speech thickened. "What do you mean—from the way a white floozy has connection with a black Harlem buck? I learned something, all right! Not about the clitoris. About the state of medicine in New York City!"

"Several of the subjects were Negroes," Prescott said, "but did you actually think there were any men in that film?"

"I was sitting there looking at it, wasn't I?"

"How did you think we took the pictures of vaginal

lubrication, with a colposcope? Think about it for a minute."
He was looking at Dawkins intently, seeming less angry with
the man than curious about the way his mind worked. "We
didn't use a black Negro penis, Dawkins, we used a machine."

The elevator door opened, and Mrs. Dawkins stepped in.
Her husband looked at Prescott in consternation. He extended
a finger.

"You're no doctor! I happen to be proud of my profession.
You ought to check into a sanitarium and find out what's
wrong, because you're sure as hell a long way from normal."

"That's a sufficiency, Sam," his wife said firmly.

He let her pull him into the car. "I want to tell you some
of the boys are thinking of hauling you up in front of the
Ethics Committee. God damn sex pervert—"

His lips went on working convulsively until the door closed.

"Will you come in for a moment?" Martha said. "If I don't
talk about it I'll never go to sleep."

Inside her room, having picked up the phone, she kicked
off her shoes and continued: "That terrible man. How did
he ever pass his medical exams? The minute he got the idea
that he was watching sex between a black male and a white
female his brain stopped working. Such as it is. I still don't
see how it happened. It must have been one of the knee-chest
shots."

"He's a bigoted moron. We can't worry about reactions
on that level."

"No, of course not. I'm going to order a drink. Do you
want anything?"

"No, I still have some reading to do. That sex-change paper
was full of ambiguities—I think he put them in deliberately.
I want to talk to him tomorrow."

Martha ordered a drink from Room Service and put the
phone back. "Do you mean you actually listened to that paper?
I didn't hear a word of it."

"You didn't miss much."

She sat down across the room. He took off his glasses to
rub the bridge of his nose. He was very tired.

"You were expecting something dramatic to happen," he
said. "But they won't move until they have a consensus. An

obstetrician depends on hospitals because nobody has babies at home anymore. And did you ever hear of an open-minded hospital? But wait a bit. I hope Dawkins does take us to the Ethics Committee. All we'll have to do is run off the film again and ask him to point out the Negro."

Martha pushed back her hair. "But they're all such sheep! You'd never think Queen Victoria's been dead sixty years. And what about the reporters? I thought they'd be writing frantically, rushing out to the phones. I thought we'd have to spend half our time from now on defending ourselves, and how I've been dreading it. But now it seems they're just going to ignore us."

"I don't understand the reporters. Poor Hixon. He was counting on that film. Well, we'll survive."

"We have slightly over thirty-five hundred dollars in the bank."

"The clinic's still making money."

"There's one thing I do think we ought to try. The people I've been talking to all day aren't in a class with Dawkins, that goes without saying, but it seemed to me they were all stopped by the same thing—the prostitutes. I know," she said as he started to speak. "It's not a valid objection scientifically, but I think there may be something to it, all the same. They ought to know better, but when prostitution is mentioned they still think in terms of the old red-light district and the army brothel, with some woebegone working-class girl entertaining a stream of customers all night long. There's certainly nothing clinically pathological about Lillian. Millions of happily married women have sex more often than she does. And I also think there was some exaggeration in the history she gave us. That's not the point. When people asked me where we get our female subjects, of course I had to say among the professionals, and there it stopped. They all wanted to know if I'd used the machine myself. Perhaps I should. The people at this conference must want to know the truth about sex or they wouldn't be here. Well, they'll just have to get used to the idea that there's only one way to discover that truth, and that's our way. First they have to shed a few taboos. That may not be too hard if we can get them over the prostitution hurdle."

She wanted a drink badly. What was the matter with Room Service? "I keep remembering the Hallinans," she said. "They owe us something."

Prescott's eyelids seemed very heavy. "I doubt very much if they'd do it."

"I talked to Mrs. Hallinan again yesterday. Her husband's out on strike so he's home most of the day, and apparently they make love just about all the time. She said she wished she could help other people make the breakthrough, and I almost suggested that she come in and let us explain the lab program. I wanted to check with you first."

There was a knock on the door—her Scotch at last. Prescott was fast asleep in his chair by the time the transaction was completed. She spoke his name gently, but he was gone. She wasn't really surprised. He had slept perhaps four hours in the last forty-eight.

She watched him while she finished her drink. His lips were parted and he was snoring softly. She had once thought there was a kind of vulnerability about him, but she had been romanticizing, of course. He wasn't vulnerable, even when asleep. Any kind of personal interaction between them might prejudice his laboratory results, and that was the main thing he cared about. If they responded to each other in any way, what was to prevent them from responding to the volunteers? They had to remain as indifferent, as omniscient as their machines.

And yet, if he had opened his eyes and asked her to come to bed with him, she would have nodded and begun to undress. Had she fallen in love with him? She wasn't sure. Her head was spinning, and not from the drink. She shook his shoulder, forcing him to wake up enough so that she could get him to bed. She took off his jacket, his necktie, and his shoes. She felt in his trouser pocket for his room key. He moved abruptly in his sleep and touched her breast. She froze for an instant, feeling the course of her blood quicken, and then she removed the key, covered him with a blanket, and went down the corridor to sleep in his room.

chapter 11

The first question Jake Burgess was asked was how he had heard about the project.

"From an intern at St. Agatha's." He crossed his legs, uncrossed them again, and leaned forward. "Last Friday night I met a girl in a Village bar and walked her home. We were saying good night in the vestibule when a couple of colored kids jumped me. I'm sorry to say I lost. They didn't leave me much, and I needed an ambulance. The hospital kept me overnight and almost gave me another concussion when they presented the bill. If I'm giving you too much detail, it's because I'm nervous. Isn't everybody when they come in here?"

The woman named Mrs. Freeman laughed. "Without exception."

She had a pleasant voice. The way she sounded when he talked to her on the phone was really what had got him this far. He had wanted to make sure, first of all, that he would have a chance to back out if the atmosphere proved too alarming. She assured him that they would pay him for his answers to a questionnaire even if he decided to contribute nothing else. They agreed on a time, and he arrived at the Research Building ten minutes early.

He walked up and down the sidewalk the full ten minutes before he was able to force himself to enter. A city policeman was yawning in a cubicle beside the elevator. Were they afraid of crashers? Jake skulked into an elevator. He had been given a floor and a room number. The number, 1806, was the only thing on the frosted glass. He hoped the door would prove to be locked, so he could knock lightly, wait five seconds, and light out for home. Unfortunately, when he turned the knob it opened.

A bell sounded. Jake entered a small waiting room containing a leather sofa and two chairs. A few battered copies of *Reader's Digest* and *Hygeia* lay on a table, and there were several spurious-looking diplomas on the walls. These were the very props Jake would have chosen to confuse first-timers like himself into thinking they had stumbled into the office of some friendly G.P. who delivered babies and set an occasional broken bone and prescribed either aspirin or penicillin for every ailment. There was one anachronism—an oddly shaped chunk of highly polished brass. A woman's figure? A bird?

Martha Freeman appeared. She was as pleasant-looking as she had sounded on the phone. She took him into a consulting room. The main feature here was a pair of locked safes. She explained that these contained the project's records, which were filed under code numbers to protect their study subjects' anonymity. But anonymity wasn't the thing that was worrying Jake.

Presently Dr. Prescott came in and took a seat across the table. A part of his mind was obviously elsewhere, but there was nothing vague or uncertain about his manner. It had the same fizz and intensity as dry ice.

Jake had never had much to do with doctors and he had been a patient in a hospital only twice in his life. Skiing a difficult iced-up trail when he was fourteen, he had seen a girl come bombing out of a side chute, headed straight at him. Drifting up out of the anesthetic sometime later, he had heard a doctor referring to him as a Compound Femur. He had been placed in a semiprivate room with a Kidney. In St. Agatha's the previous Friday night, he had given up his name the minute he was carried across the threshold and had turned into a Concussion. Here, he had answered less than half a dozen questions before he realized that to Dr. Prescott he was not Jake Burgess or even a number. He was a Possible Orgasm.

"My wallet was gone," Jake continued, "and I couldn't have paid that bill even if I'd had it. I'm too young for Medicare. I decided the only way to get out was to sell them some blood. I'd had so many X-rays I probably owed them a couple of quarts, but they settled for a pint. Afterward, the intern took me down to the cafeteria for coffee and told me about you people. There's a limit to how much blood a person can give— Well, I suppose there's a limit here, too."

"Is he anybody we know?"

"I don't know, Mrs. Freeman. His name's Maguire. He said he and his wife have talked about coming up, but when he goes off shift he's always too tired. He thinks they might when he goes into residency."

"How long since you've had sex, Jake?"

He groaned. "A year. That's how long I've been in New York. I've had trouble meeting girls. And the first time I got as far as necking in a hallway I lost my only suit and my only good pair of shoes."

"How often do you masturbate?"

He gulped, mentally. But he probably should have known they would ask that kind of question, and there was nothing to do but give it an honest answer.

"Two or three times a week, and I don't get much enjoyment out of it. I don't mean I think it's wrong, it's just—well, nothing. Like scratching a mosquito bite. Still, as long as you're paying me good money for it, why not do it here? If I can. I'm not sure I can. I hope so, because I owe a week's rent. I may be starting a new job, but I won't get paid till the end of next week."

"Don't you know anybody who can lend you some money?"

"Not in New York. I have an agent, but I don't want to borrow money from him. It would give him an edge. I don't want to ask my father—he'd tell me to come home and go to work. But if I can manage to produce a couple of specimens for you I'll get by okay."

Mrs. Freeman took out a printed form. "All right, Jake, here we go."

She recorded his name and address on a separate card, and the questioning began.

Her voice was still friendly, but the content of the questions made them seem abrupt at first, almost hostile. As soon as Jake adjusted to the terms she was using, he became interested and answered without evasion. Homosexual contacts? Nothing overt. But having done considerable hitchhiking as a boy, he had often been courted and he had learned how to deal with it without demanding to be let out of the car. His cultural patron, the one-play playwright, may have had homosexual intentions, Jake wasn't sure; there had been no declaration. The man was dead now. Had Jake received homosexual invitations in New York? Only from strangers. He had never seriously considered a homosexual outlet to his social difficulties. To be truthful, there had been one or two fantasies during masturbation, so vivid that he had nearly written his hometown girl to ask her to visit him. She still wrote regularly —disturbing letters with tiny wriggling spermatozoa in the margins. She had even drawn the same picture on the backs of the envelopes until he told her for God's sake to stop it; they weren't the only ones who knew what the symbol meant. He was carrying her most recent letter in his pocket now. It was all but radioactive.

"You don't want her to join you?" Mrs. Freeman asked.

"I do and I don't, Mrs. Freeman. I have to be careful what I say in my letters. If she came down, and the lovemaking was one-tenth as good as it was the last couple of times before I left, she'd be wearing a wedding ring inside of six months. If she was willing to live in New York, I'd be a Wall Street trainee."

The questioning continued, and Jake began to see a simple system of checks and balances operating here. Dr. Prescott alone would have made him uneasy. The man was obviously dedicated—but to what was the question. Mrs. Freeman took off the pressure. By the time they reached the end of what was known as his sociosexual history, the topic had no more emotional charge than if these were cancer researchers asking about his cigarette habits. Did he shape the wet end of a cigarette with his tongue? Did he vary his smoking according to his emotional demands? Was it a social thing, or did he get just as much physiological relief smoking alone, and was he sure there was no residue of guilt after it was over?

They moved to another room, where Prescott gave him a physical. Jake was still at his college weight, in spite of all the bread and spaghetti he had eaten in the last year.

"Do you ever play handball?" Prescott asked while he was dressing.

Not since college, Jake told him. Prescott said he was always looking for a game, if Jake was interested. Jake was surprised by the offer, until he understood that now Prescott was regarding him not only as a Possible Orgasm, but as a Possible Handball Victim. Jake declined politely. It would mean getting up at 6:30 in the morning, a near impossibility, and he had a feeling that if he and this middle-aged man were locked up in a four-wall handball court, only one of them would walk out alive, and it wouldn't be Jake.

Mrs. Freeman showed him the laboratory. It was austere and purposeful, and did he think the atmosphere would have a negative effect? He replied doubtfully that he hoped not, but he didn't really see how any normal person could be expected to come through under these circumstances.

"We have nothing scheduled for this morning," she said, "so why don't you just browse around? The room is yours. We have a fairly extensive erotic library. Look it over and see what happens."

"There's no time like the present."

"It's not as grim as all that," she said with a laugh. "Sex is a funny thing, Jake. It can surprise you. If you hadn't been mugged the other night, that girl could have taken you through orgasm, don't you think? And yet it wasn't a nice spot at all, and the girl doesn't sound particularly nice either."

"She wasn't bad except for the missing tooth."

Mrs. Freeman laughed again and left him alone.

He investigated the library. They had all the pornographic classics, as well as several folders of photographs and a small cabinet filled with objets d'art. Jake had never needed that kind of crutch; after glancing through the photographs, a little appalled at some of the combinations, he wandered around looking at the equipment. The coition machine was the only interesting one. There were penises aplenty among the art objects, but nothing resembling this one. It was clearly a product of twentieth-century technology, in a class with color television and electric razors. He touched one of the dials, wondering if he dared. No, it would probably burst into flames. It wasn't lifelike, exactly, it was an exaggerated statement of what life might be like in some utopian society. He decided to press a red button—an alarm of some kind?— and see what happened. To his amazement, the machine ejaculated! Like everything else, the ejaculation was heroic, continuing as long as he held his finger on the button. That alone must have cost a fortune. This was obviously no mass-production item. Few frustrated women could afford to order one for the home. It had to be used right here, and Jake tried to picture the scene.

It would have to be something on the order of a space launching, except that in this case the astronaut would be a female and she wouldn't be wearing a space suit—or anything else, for that matter. Almost hidden in a tangle of wires, her naked form would be depersonalized by electrodes stuck into every bodily cavity. Would her head have to be shaved? White-clad technicians would circulate around her, murmuring to one another in their incomprehensible scientific slang. The room would become tense as the countdown approached zero. The machinery would whir softly. The lewd plastic would caress her internally while she gazed up at pornographic movies projected on the ceiling. Lights would flash, the gauges would register varying degrees of panic. Sweat would be apparent on the astronaut's naked brow. Four . . . three . . . two . . . one. Would she make it this time? Would we beat the Russians to the supreme blast-off, the perfect orgasm?

When Jake let himself out of the laboratory fifteen minutes later, Martha Freeman looked up from a desk-model tabulator.

"So you didn't find our research quarters inhibiting after all."

"How can you tell?"

"I don't know. Perhaps you look a little sheepish."

He sat down and stretched his legs. They both laughed. She pushed some money toward him. He fanned the bills and gave her a questioning look.

"What's the idea? There's a hundred bucks here."

"Fifteen of that is your fee. The rest is an advance. Nevertheless, I don't want you to feel any compulsion about coming back. I'm glad you heard about us, Jake, but this really isn't like contributing to a blood bank. You give them a pint of blood and they give you a check. No emotional overtones. We're trying to isolate the physical side of sex so it can be studied. But sex is a subtle and mysterious process. If you're here just for money, there's going to be a little extra pressure. We'd wonder about it. If you do decide to come back, you can work it off. Or pay us when you can. There's no rush."

"I've already decided to come back. I won't say I look forward to it, but it may not be as painful as I expected."

"I'm glad. Now I'd like to talk about how we want to use you. All right? With men there isn't the huge deficit of knowledge that there is with women. Much of the male genital system is right out in the open where even the most hidebound physician can't help seeing it. And of course the vast majority of doctors are men themselves. So there are fewer unknowns. We have fourteen programs under way. In six we're using single women. In three, single men. In five, family units. Now we want to develop what is known as a comparison control. We need a way to check the data we're getting from our married couples. We want to add a fifteenth program, using unmarried men and women who meet for the first time in the laboratory."

Jake was silent.

"You see," she went on, "married responses tend to become formalized over the years. The husband and wife condition each other. They learn shortcuts. Every index of female orgasm rises in proportion to the length of marriage, forty percent within a month, seventy percent within a year, and so on. There's nothing surprising about this. But we're not so much concerned with the frequency of orgasm as with the orgasm itself. Is it different in an unrehearsed contact between strangers? If so, in what way?"

He shook his head. "I doubt if I'm your man."

"First let me finish, Jake. We're beginning to get a very definite pattern. All the hundreds of sexual cycles we've observed here have had certain things in common. Certain physiological changes occur—not ninety-nine percent of the time, but all the time. And yet this tiny doubt remains. Before we publish our findings, we have to be sure. Have we established a human sexual pattern, or are these merely the conditioned responses of several hundred married couples, white, English-speaking, ten pounds or so overweight, who read the same newspapers and magazines and live the same patterned existence in one corner of a particular American city? Nine-tenths of our female subjects need to wear glasses. Does that make a difference in how they respond to tactile stimuli? I don't see why it should, but we want to rule out the possibility."

"I see what you're driving at, but you don't want me. You want some hotshot Casanova. I'm a guy who hasn't slept with a girl for a year."

"If Casanova came back to life I don't think we'd want him, Jake. He was too atypical. We're having trouble finding the right people for this. We won't learn anything from sex between two people who consider each other repulsive. That's not how sexual selection works. They have to be fairly personable." She interrupted herself with a laugh. "Not repulsive, anyway."

"Thanks for the compliment, if that's what it is."

"We're scientists. We report the facts as we see them. Will you think about it?"

"I'd better say no right away." He hesitated, trying to sort out his reactions, not that he wouldn't like sex with a girl for a change. "So far the hardest part was opening the door and walking in. You didn't turn out to be nearly as spooky as I expected."

"Compliments are flying in all directions around here."

"When I was a freshman at college I put in six hours a day at the fatigue lab for a while. I reported in track pants and running shoes and climbed up on the treadmill. Those people were a lot stranger than you. Fanatics. Fatigue was the one thing in the world they were interested in. There was a presidential election that year, and one of the graduate students asked me which was the Democrat and which was the Republican. I guess it was partly a pose. I'm beginning to think there's a faint chance I won't disappoint you. I'll shut my eyes and pretend I'm back on that treadmill. But Mrs. Freeman, I just don't see how I could do it with a girl."

Jake had made love to a number of different girls in his time—perhaps seven all told. He had chosen them himself. If the choice of partner was put in the hands of somebody else, that would make him an automaton, like the machine in the laboratory. Somebody set the controls, turned a switch, and you went into action. And sex was one of the few things in life that wasn't like that.

He dreamed about it. The girl in the dream wore horn-rimmed glasses and looked a little like Mrs. Freeman. He woke up feeling confused. The thing that was beginning to appeal to him was that there would be no complications. It would be confined to the laboratory. There would be no arguments, no reproachful phone calls. It wouldn't be taken for granted that certain nights were reserved for certain types of dates. No references to how wonderful it would be to have a baby.

Mrs. Freeman had hinted that she had a particular girl in mind, someone attractive. And, even if this unknown creature turned out to be less than gorgeous, did it matter? To join the program in the first place, she would have to be independent, with an independent interest in sex, free from all those pruderies you keep running into in real life. Such a girl was bound to possess a certain allure, even though Jake might not have given her a second look, fully-dressed and walking down Madison Avenue.

When he called Mrs. Freeman he told her about his dream, without mentioning her resemblance to the girl, and proposed that he try a session or two alone while he debated her other suggestion. She agreed willingly.

At the end of a week, having earned forty-five dollars and found the laboratory less forbidding each time, he told her he thought he was ready to move on to the next step. She seemed pleased, and made an appointment for him for Sunday morning.

"Sunday morning!"

"At nine. How about that fatigue laboratory? Weren't they open on Sunday?"

"Sunday was their big day."

"Sunday's also our big day. Most of our people do other things during the week."

Sunday at nine was easily the least sexy hour she could have named, and he wondered afterward if she had chosen it deliberately, to kill any foolish hopes that this might prove to be something that would make a difference. It was a way to kill an hour and earn fifteen dollars, at the same time contributing to the advance of knowledge. He stopped worrying about how he would do. Why should it be any different from his solo performances?

Sunday arrived, and he found himself on the wrong subway. It reversed itself above 145th Street, and he had to go back to 96th to change to the Broadway train. He knew the

subway system better than that. What was wrong with him?
He reached the laboratory ten minutes late.

"Hmm," Mrs. Freeman said, looking at her watch.

"Just trying to worry you," Jake said. "Is everybody else
here?"

"She's waiting. So are the technicians."

He hesitated. "I'm not feeling so hot all of a sudden. If
nothing happens, she'll realize, won't she, that it has nothing
to do with her?"

"I don't think you'll have any trouble."

"I'm a realist. I expect to have trouble. Nine o'clock Sunday
morning!"

"Nine-fifteen, Jake. Get undressed."

After undressing he put on a striped cotton wrapper and
clogs. He hadn't had time for breakfast, but his stomach lining
felt as though he had drunk cup after cup of bitter coffee.
Before going into the observation room, he rested his forehead for an instant against the cool metal of the locker door.

Dr. Prescott and his cameraman were talking in low tones
about a lighting problem. The overhead lights were on full,
a bank of 150-watt bulbs, and the blaze kept Jake from seeing
the girl. Even after locating her he felt it would be wrong
to stare. Dr. Prescott shook hands. Cutting the lights, he and
DiVito left the room.

The girl came around the center table.

Jake was staggered. She, too, was wearing a skimpy striped
robe, a standard laboratory item, but on her it looked like
something by Dior. Her hair was long and blond, lighter in
streaks. She had an elegant tan. She was easily the most
spectacular object Jake had seen since arriving in New York.
Compared to her, Rockefeller Center was nowhere.

The way he was looking at her made her smile. "This is
your first time with someone?"

She spoke with a faint accent. Scandinavian?

"Very much so. I didn't know I was going to draw anybody like— Are you Swedish?"

"Yes. I wish I could lose the accent, but this is not so
easy. You aren't supposed to ask such questions, by the way."

"Do we introduce ourselves, or what?"

"Assuredly not! Your number is One Thirty-seven. As for

me, I am an old soldier." She sketched a salute. "Eighty-nine."

She put out her hand. Jake was still so rattled that he fumbled and grasped only a few fingers. The only line he could think of was the old one, which he had the wit not to offer, "What's a nice girl like you doing in a place like—"

"Mrs. Freeman told you what they wish us to do?" she said. "A breaking of the ice. There will be particular things at another time, if today is satisfactory. They will not be with us at the start, perhaps during. The lights will be off and I am happy about that. It is the lights I cannot adjust myself with. To?"

"To."

Her teeth were marvelous. He felt a pounding behind his eyes. He had been afraid she would be too homely. This was the opposite problem.

She unknotted her belt without self-consciousness. "Now, my dear One Thirty-seven, shall we begin?"

"Shouldn't we have a drink or something first?"

She smiled. "That's quite another program, the effect of alcohol on desire. It will be all right, really, after the first moment. A little courage."

Courage was only one of the things he didn't have. Vertigo overtook him, and he sat down abruptly.

"My dear," the girl said gently. "Did you eat breakfast?"

He shook his head, and thought he heard the hardware rattle.

"These nine o'clock in the morning things are definitely not a good idea. Look—let me talk to Mrs. Freeman. We'll have coffee, perhaps a drink of whiskey after all. If we upset their schedule, so much the worse. It can't be the first time such a thing has happened."

The dots separated and allowed him to see her. Something had changed about the expression of her eyes. She was looking at him for the first time, seeing him as a person who probably, outside the laboratory, even had a name.

"Though the trouble with coffee, you know," she said, "it will mean we must sit still without talking. For what can we say, do you see? It would be much better if—"

He made a slight motion to indicate that he was ready. She bent down with one hand touching his face and gave

him the sweetest kiss he had ever received from another
human.

All in all, it was a huge success.

Jake enjoyed himself and pleased both the girl and the
research team. When it was over he couldn't remember exactly
what it was he had been so afraid of. It had been roses all
the way. She knew more than he did, though he guessed she
was about his own age. He had been playing over his head
here, as sometimes happens against stiff competition at tennis.

Mrs. Freeman asked him to comment. He was glad to, over
a cup of coffee and a cigarette in the consulting room. She
made notes while he talked. At one point she looked up
questioningly, and he assured her he wasn't exaggerating a bit.

But he shouldn't have answered so fully. By the time he
was dressed, the girl was gone. That jolted him out of his
postcoital daze, reminding him that what had happened in
the observation room had been only an interruption. The
hour was over, their separate lives had resumed.

He was given another appointment for Wednesday at 9 P.M.,
eighty-three hours away.

On Monday, Jake had his interview with Bobby Quinby,
the magazine writer. They met at a midtown restaurant
known as the Absinthe House. Quinby was easy to pick out
of the murk because he was wearing a beard. So far it hadn't
made him look especially distinguished. His eyes and hands
were constantly in motion. Most of the conversation between
Quinby and his inferiors went one way, outward from Quinby.
He addressed Jake as "baby," and told him about some of
the well-known people he had been thrown in with lately.
He put Jake on the payroll in the middle of the fourth
highball.

Jake's Tuesday assignment was to badger the ex-girlfriend
of a teen-age singer, who wouldn't talk to Quinby himself
because he was known to be violently opposed to teen-age
music. Jake had been told to say he was from *Billboard*, and
the girl talked to him without embarrassment all afternoon.
Dr. Prescott would have been interested in the story.

On Wednesday he typed his notes. When he went to

Quinby's house to turn them in, he had his first glimpse of Mrs. Quinby, a sleek blond in tight pants. Jake didn't seem to interest her. The teen-age singer was opening that night at the Copa, and Quinby wanted Jake to cover it for him. Unfortunately, Jake said, he already had a date. This was the laboratory night, of course. Quinby told him to take his girl and put her on the expense account. Unfortunately, Jake told him, they had other plans.

This time he was early, hoping to intercept the girl as she arrived. A half-dozen other girls passed him and entered the building, but not the one he was looking for. He waited as long as he dared before taking the elevator. He was getting a recurrence of his Sunday symptoms, dizziness and nausea.

The instant Mrs. Freeman greeted him he knew something had gone wrong.

"We've had to switch things around, Jake. The girl we paired you with Sunday is no longer available."

He sat down, lining up the creases of the slacks he had bought that afternoon.

"I really am sorry," Mrs. Freeman went on. "We only got the tail end of that cycle, but for a first meeting it was extraordinary, we thought. I was hoping we could continue from there, to see if it became more or less intense with familiarity. It's too bad."

He said with difficulty, "Did she give any reason?"

"No, simply that she didn't want to continue. We're using her in another program, and she's staying in that. We'll discuss it the next time she comes in. If she found something objectionable about the setup, we certainly want to know what it was so we can change it."

"She didn't seem to object at the time."

Mrs. Freeman made a troubled gesture. "Nobody's crazy about this phase, Jake. It's something we have to get through. We knew it wouldn't be easy, and perhaps it's harder for a woman than for a man. Would you consider starting over with somebody else?"

Jake hesitated. "Why not?" he said at last.

It was perfectly clear what had happened. It had been a joyful experience for both of them; he hadn't needed to look at any dials to know how she was feeling. She wasn't the kind of person to give way to remorse when it was over.

They had remained together for long minutes after the cycle ended, and as he slipped away she had kissed him with tenderness and love. But afterward! When she was by herself she would take a realistic look at this encounter and decide there was too much risk that he would break the rules. Their brief exchange of dialogue had shown her what he was—essentially a jerk. With their clothes on, the mismatch would be evident. He wasn't in her league at all, and she had realized that in time to get the hell out before anyone was hurt.

Mrs. Freeman was studying him. "Jake, it was impersonal sex. If you start taking it personally—"

"Maybe there's no such thing as impersonal sex."

"That's a silly thing to say!" she said sharply. "I think we'd better drop the subject now. Think it over and call me. How's the job working out?"

"It's something like here—all the people I've met the last couple of days have had sex on their minds. Mrs. Freeman, if you've got somebody lined up for tonight, why not go through with it? Wouldn't that be even more scientific? I was all keyed up for one person, and you send in a substitute. What effect will that have on how long it takes me to come?"

He met her eye and laughed bitterly. "It's funny. I was going to double-cross everybody and ask her to have a drink with me afterward. I realize you aren't running a single-mingle operation. Everybody has to be very tough or you won't come up with the right patterns. I fell for that girl, and I'm disappointed in myself. It won't happen a second time, I can guarantee."

"The complications!" she exclaimed. "All right, let's try it."

"Can I ask you one thing? Did Number Eighty-nine have any episodes with other people or was I the first?"

"I can't answer that."

"I know, and what difference does it make?" He stood up. "Don't worry about me, Mrs. Freeman. I'm one of the most rational men about sex since George Bernard Shaw."

He undressed in a hurry, still very angry. The observation room was empty. It didn't matter a damn bit to Jake what kind of girl they had provided for him. She could be a real grub—even grubs have a sex life, and in the interests of scientific completeness it probably ought to be recorded.

He heard the sound of another pair of clogs. A girl entered.

There were dents on the bridge of her nose. With nine-tenths of the volunteers wearing glasses, the odds had been good that he would draw one of them. She looked all right—plain was probably the word. With luck she would find a mate. Most people do.

"Hello."

She had a shy voice, a rather nice one. So what was a shy girl like her doing in a place like . . .

"Did they tell you what they want us to do?" he said, echoing that earlier exchange.

"Just in general." She shivered lightly. "But I don't know! Have you ever done it before?"

"Yes, but don't hold it against me."

She moved out from under his hand when he reached for her.

"I'm trying to make up my mind. Is it possible—I mean, is it a physical possibility—to take you inside me without knowing who you are? Without even shaking hands? Couldn't we have a couple of minutes of general conversation?"

Jake shook his head. "You're thinking about the way it works in real life. This has to be separate, with its own rules." She let him touch her shoulder. "After it's over, you may not even be sure it really happened."

"I wouldn't like that. Have you ever read Martin Buber?"

She stood still, trembling, and let him run his hand inside her robe. Her breast shivered away from him, but came back.

"One of the weirdest things about this," he said more gently, "is that you're about to be made love to by somebody who's never read a line of Martin Buber."

"That's all right. I just had to say something. It wouldn't be possible to do it without saying anything, would it?"

After a moment she said, "Yes. Yes, that's nice. I think I can after all."

chapter 12

Victoria Orr rode uptown with Anne Geselle, her room-mate. Their initial interviews for places in the Prescott-Freeman project had been scheduled at two-hour intervals.

Anne was so nervous she had eaten off her lipstick. Out-side the Research Building she was attacked by hysterical hiccups.

"Vicky, I don't think I'm going to be able to go through with this."

"I'm not impressed," Victoria said. "You're going to march in, look them straight in the eye, and say, 'I'm just the girl you're looking for.'"

"I don't know if I am or not. I might turn around and go home." She hiccuped.

Victoria patted her between the shoulder blades. "Try hold-ing your breath and then swallow."

"Damn that Woods! He dosn't own me. What am I going to say if I don't like the looks of the place?"

"Tell them you don't think Mother would approve."

Anne hiccuped and said unhappily, "I'll say she wouldn't approve! What did you have to bring *her* up for? Vicky baby, I know it's all arranged, but couldn't you go first?"

"Definitely not. I didn't talk you into this, you talked me. Now go ahead. Do something about your lipstick."

Anne gave her a stricken look and hiccuped again. Victoria wasn't feeling too self-possessed herself, but she knew she had no future in the laboratory because she was the girl who didn't have orgasms. She didn't even know what the word meant, really, though of course she had read countless descrip-tions, some of them probably not too scientific. Dr. Prescott required three things of his females: they had to be normal physically, which Victoria was; they had to be verbal, and there was no problem there, because she always knew precisely where she was on the curve; and they had to be fully orgasmic, standing, sitting, or lying, using the right hand or the left.

That utterly ruled Victoria out. She planned to sail through the interview, modifying the truth wherever necessary, and then, during the demonstration, pretend it was the aseptic environment that was slowing her down. Let them take the blame for her unexpected frigidity. Of course you couldn't be one hundred percent sure. Somewhere in the back of her mind, in those dim depths she never entered except at the dead hour of the night when sleep was impossible, she kept remembering what Woods had said about the machine. . . .

She said good-bye to Anne, patted her on the back, and went to the pizza parlor where she and Anne had arranged to meet after Anne's interview. She ordered a Coke and a wedge of pizza. It was a Saturday, the place was crowded with Puerto Ricans. She had come fairly close with a Puerto Rican once, a nice boy but unfortunately a great believer in the *machismo* mystique. She exchanged silent fantasies with the youths around her, and time passed quickly.

Anne, a big girl, usually walked with a slouch, to camouflage her height. When Victoria saw her coming, her shoulders were back, her stomach was in, and she looked great. Victoria hurried outside to meet her, feeling a slight twinge that was probably envy. There had never been any doubt about Anne's success. She was practically a walking orgasm.

"They turned me down!" Anne cried when she was still several steps away.

"Baby! How could that happen?"

Becoming aware that most of the Puerto Ricans in the neighborhood were looking her way, Anne went back into her slump. Victoria took her arm. They found an empty bench on the mall. It was a narcotics location; addicts dozed peacefully all around them.

"Now tell me exactly what they said and what you said," Victoria ordered.

"Woods is going to turn purple." Anne drew a deep breath that was nearly a shudder. "But they're nice, Vicky! I thought they'd be something out of science fiction, but they're not. You know how conflicted I am about calling a spade a spade. You should have heard me after about five minutes! I was tossing around masturbatory techniques—with me it's easier to do it than pronounce it. I thought I was going over in a big way."

"Couldn't you do it with people watching?"

"I never got that far. The kiss of death—we got onto the guilt thing. I had to admit I wish I didn't do it so much—for heaven's sake, I wish I didn't do it at all. And that's the specialty of the house, just what I feel so guilty about. They don't want somebody who produces a nice multiple orgasm and then bursts into tears."

"I don't see how they could pass you up, Anne. I really don't. Why did you tell them the truth?"

"I couldn't stop myself. And if you want to know something, I'm just as glad, because now I won't have to fink on them for Woods."

"You don't think they suspected anything?"

"They're not the dumbest people in the world, that I do know. Don't think you have to go up there for my sake. If you want to call it off—"

"As long as I'm here," Victoria said thoughtfully. "Now start over at the beginning. Tell me everything they asked you."

Victoria leaned toward Dr. Prescott. "It sounded like exactly the thing I need!" Her manner was just right, she thought, a blend of eagerness and apprehension. "I want to enjoy a few years of freedom before I get married. I only stayed in college a year. There was a boy I had to get away from. I got involved for the wrong reasons, or trapped would be a better word, and he thought I was his forever. I talked my mother into letting me come to New York."

Dr. Prescott was doing the questioning. Mrs. Freeman was taking notes. With Anne it had been the other way around.

"How many sexual partners have you had here?"

"Too many! I suddenly realized a while ago that I was getting to be quite promiscuous. The word sort of scares me. I don't go in for feeling guilty—I don't think I've ever really felt guilty about anything—but I know what men think about promiscuous girls. They don't even like to make love to them, really, not to mention marrying them. So publicly I've got to slow down."

"You realize," Mrs. Freeman put in, "that we don't use many unmarried subjects in coital programs?"

"Well," Victoria said doubtfully, not wanting to sound too

well informed, "I don't mean I thought I was going to jump up on the table the minute I walked in the door. But isn't that what you do?"

She motioned toward the closed inner door, beyond which, at that very moment, who knew what scenes of wild sexuality were taking place?

Dr. Prescott explained, "We're conducting one comparison study, contrasting the reaction patterns of random couples with those of husband-and-wife units. There are no openings in this program at present. Most of our female data is developed by means of auto-manipulation or coition with artificial equipment."

Victoria's heart, that Distant Early Warning system, gave a sharp double thump. She said carelessly, "I'm pretty orthodox. Sex to me means sex with a man. But if you want me to try something else and it's important—"

She let it hang.

"On the question of frequency of outlet," Dr. Prescott said. "How many episodes of all kinds do you average a week?"

"Maybe five? Three or four of those are dates. I do it by myself once in a while when I'm falling asleep."

"With what percentage of orgasmic return?"

Victoria knew her Kinsey, having boned up on it during the past week. She wanted them to think she was above the median, but not in the genius category; that would be too hard to sustain. "Sixty percent? And afterward, if I didn't come and he's feeling kind-hearted, sometimes he'll stay with me until I do. Maybe seventy percent in all."

"And during masturbation?"

"Oh, unless I'm really exhausted," she said, and it was lucky they didn't have her hooked into a lie-detector or she would have blacked out this whole section of upper Manhattan, "a hundred percent, I guess."

He asked if she had multiple orgasms, and here her hesitation was genuine. "I'm not sure if I do or not, Doctor. Some are longer and harder than others. They seem to switch on and off, but during the best ones I go sort of haywire, I don't know what's happening. So I don't know what to answer."

She liked to read case histories, testing her own guess against the diagnosis at the end of the chapter. Going into training for this interview, she had concocted an interesting story, based on a patchwork of actual cases. Anne, by contrast, had stuck to the truth, and look what had happened to her.

She was making more of a dent on Dr. Prescott than on Mrs. Freeman, Victoria noticed. She could recognize a look in a male eye when she saw one, or was she imagining things? After all, thousands of women had gone through this mill, and she wasn't so special, really, unless she appealed to his gambling instinct. Later, she went into another room, undressed, and stretched out on the examining table. She watched him carefully while he examined her. No, it was definitely only a professional interest.

Prescott and Mrs. Freeman conferred. They kept her waiting, but when they returned she saw that she was in.

Mrs. Freeman showed her around the laboratory. They arrived finally in front of the coition machine, which had been radiating impulses at Victoria since she came into the room. It was something to see!

"This must be the—"

Mrs. Freeman told her how it worked. Victoria listened with the right air of interest, like a tourist at the Metropolitan Art Museum being told the price paid for *Aristotle Contemplating the Bust of Homer*.

Before she left they gave her a card for an orientation session two days later. She remained calm in the elevator, but when she emerged into the lobby she couldn't restrain a little hoot of delight. The policeman at the end of the elevators looked startled, dear man.

Two weeks later Martha Freeman called Dr. Prescott in New Orleans.

He was attending one more in the interminable round of conferences that had to be covered to build a record for the next foundation grant. He had delivered a paper on seminal-fluid influence on vaginal acidity. Several intelligent questions had been asked, and the questioners hadn't looked around to see if any FBI agents were lurking in the back of the room. So possibly they were making progress.

"What happened after I left?"

"The main thing was Victoria Orr. You remember the pretty girl we had the argument about?"

"Of course."

"She had her first episode with the machine today. And I'm the one who thought she was lying! I take it all back. You know she only had one subjective success during orientation, and I'm afraid I was a bit of an unbeliever there too. Then the three manipulative failures, which is one more than I think we ought to allow."

"We have to play hunches sometimes, Martha, until we can work out some guidelines that mean something."

"I would have bet we were wasting our time. I didn't intend to instrument her at all at first, but something about this girl piqued my curiosity, and I decided to get an electrocardiogram and a platform recording. I thought the reason for her other failures might be that she was trying to forget she was in a laboratory, and perhaps the electrodes might help. Is there anybody in New Orleans who doesn't believe in *status orgasmus?*"

Prescott said quickly, "You have an EKG?"

"A beautiful one. It took me by surprise. She said, 'There!' quietly. The initial spastic contraction went three seconds. Heart rate up from one-twenty to one-seventy. The entire experience ran fifty-one seconds."

"Fifty-one!"

"With thirty-eight regular platform contractions. The line showed two slight variations, and she felt one definite subsidence, then a return to full contraction. But these dips are so brief that I don't read them as interruptions or a return to arousal levels, but as less severe contractions in a continuous orgasm. The contractile interval stayed at eight-tenths of a second throughout."

"Martha, I have to be sure. Everything's perfectly in synch?"

"Yes, this is one time everything worked. She had considerable muscle tension but good control. Somewhere around the twentieth contraction she checked the electrode to be sure it was still in place."

"What was her own evaluation?"

"A bit strange. Merely good to very good. I think she may have lost consciousness briefly, although she doesn't remember it. She seemed surprised by the fuss we made. She thought it might be a little more intense than her usual coital orgasm but I don't think she wanted to admit it. She's coming in tomorrow after work, and we'll see what we get then."

"Martha, get Xerox copies of that EKG and the platform tracing and mail them to me airmail special. There's a man I want to show them to, Herb Baker from Stanford. A group of his graduate students have been running a small manipulation project, counting their own contractions. One girl reported seventeen, and he thought she was crazy."

Victoria Orr worked for a mammoth insurance company, which occupied its own forty-eight-story building on Sixth Avenue in midtown. Victoria's subdepartment processed loss claims amounting to less than seventy-five dollars. In dollar terms, it cost the company less money to pay these claims than not to pay them. Usually all Victoria had to do was put a card in her machine and strike several keys. One key indicated the amount of money requested, another the nature of the loss. The machine decided whether the person claiming the loss was actually a policyholder of the company and up-to-date on his premium payments. If those two questions had "yes" answers, everything else was automatic. It made out the check and mailed it to the correct address with a canned letter in a self-sealing envelope.

But it was impossible to do away with the human factor entirely. Now and then a claim which somehow seemed fraudulent would reach Victoria. She would strike a different set of keys, activating prewritten paragraphs, and the machine would disgorge a letter asking the claimant for substantiating evidence. When a reply arrived Victoria would pick it up delicately and decide whether or not it still smelled of fraud. After several more winnowings, somebody else in the building might type a letter by hand and an actual tongue might lick the flap of an actual envelope. But of course that was hideously expensive.

The machine was supposed to be switched off when not in use, but Victoria liked to let it run unless her supervisor was hovering around. If you rested your fingertips lightly on the keys, you could feel them tremble. Two red lights like mean little eyes burned on the console, to show that it was eating electricity. All the machines in her aisle looked alike, but when you operated one for thirty-seven and a half hours a week you learned its personality. There was one key on Victoria's console, exactly like the others in appearance, which vibrated a trifle irregularly. Whenever she touched it, and she couldn't keep from touching it, she was able to believe that there was something deep inside that was only temporarily under control. Sometimes the mechanical viscera would give a startling whir and lurch. Victoria had to watch the next few transactions carefully because the little flurry meant that the machine was trying to make a mistake. It did make mistakes, bad ones, but it was probably more reliable than the ordinary person. There was even a list of mistakes it wouldn't permit Victoria to make—she couldn't write a check for more than seventy-five dollars, for example. It was programmed to be suspicious of every fortieth claim, on the theory that spot-checking would keep the public honest.

This company, unlike some of its competitors, allowed incoming phone calls, while making their reception so disagreeable that it didn't happen too often. In the middle of the afternoon after Victoria's first laboratory success—her first success anywhere!—her supervisor buzzed for her. Leaving the power on, she went to take it.

It was Assistant District Attorney Woods McChesney.

"Are you avoiding me, Vicky, by any chance?"

"Why would I do that?"

"That's what I ask myself. You could return a call once in a while. Would it kill you?"

"I don't have much privacy here, Woods. Call me at home."

"I've tried that. Have a drink with me after work?"

"Sorry, I'm busy."

"Tomorrow?"

"Busy. Bye-bye, I have to go now. My machine's calling for me."

"Vicky, what is this?"

"I don't believe in dating my roommate's boyfriends."

She hung up, smiled condescendingly at the supervisor, who wasn't the type of woman to get many personal calls of her own, and returned to her machine.

At 5:10, with a carload of programmers and data-processers, Victoria was discharged into the low-ceilinged lobby. Woods pushed off from a bronze bas-relief and seized her arm.

"This place has so many exits my eyeballs are spinning. Nice to see you, Vicky. What a happy coincidence. How are you? Have a drink."

She didn't try to pull away until they were outside and then she was unsuccessful. "Woods, I'm supposed to be somewhere."

"We have a deal. If you want to back out, say so."

He walked her across Sixth Avenue and into the RCA Building, where she dug in her heels. "I honestly don't have time for a drink. We didn't make any deals that I can remember. I know what you're talking about, but all I agreed to do was go up with Anne and hold her hand if she got nervous. Let me go, please. I keep thinking I'm going to hear from them, but it was one of those don't-call-us-we'll-call-you arrangements."

"You haven't been back since the first time?"

"Woods, if they don't want me in the program they don't have to give a reason. Maybe they don't trust me. I'm not very good at lying."

"I wouldn't say that. No, I'd say you were quite good. As it happens, I was on the other side of 158th Street at ten o'clock yesterday morning. That was a Sunday, to refresh your memory."

She looked at him with loathing. "You bastard, why weren't you in church?"

"If you're going to take that line, I want you to understand the situation. Let's negotiate over a martini."

"There's nothing to negotiate. I can't see that they're doing anything so awful."

For an instant his eyes resembled the red lights on her console. He represented the law, after all, and the law is always conventional. She decided to call time and do some thinking.

"Ten minutes."

He took her into a cavernous bar at the end of an arcade, with a floor space of half an acre, picked an empty corner, and ordered martinis.

"All right, what have they got you doing?"

"It's still at the talk stage, Woods. I haven't seen any of the kind of thing you told us about. Maybe somebody gave you some bad information."

"There's no secret about it. It's been in the medical journals."

"Then it must be in some different part of the building. They've just been giving me tests and questionnaires. I've told them the full story of my sex life, back to whether or not my parents had intercourse when I was an embryo, practically. They show me pictures of things to see if they excite me."

"Brainwashed!" he said, throwing out his hands in disgust.

"I don't know what you're talking about. If it's been in medical journals, why do you need me?"

"I've got to have something personal. That damn language makes it sound too scientific. He's in New Orleans right now, I see from the *Times*. They carried a paragraph about him this morning—one paragraph in a two-column story. Something about changes in vaginal acidity, and nobody on the copy desk bothered to ask how he knew what was going on in that vagina."

"I'll have to remember to read that."

"It might as well be written in Eskimo. Thirty years ago some paper would have printed the full story by now, but it couldn't have happened thirty years ago, could it, so there you are."

"Woods, I don't want to rush you, but you did say something about explaining the situation."

"The situation is," he said stiffly, "that the nominating convention of the Democratic Party in New York County takes place exactly five weeks from now. That gives me a deadline. I've got the D.A. to agree that this is my baby. Do it right, and the people of New York will become aware of the name Woods McChesney."

Well, at least he was candid. Victoria looked openly at her watch. She, too, had a deadline. The waitress was on her way with the drinks, finally.

"What happens at the nominating convention?"

"That depends partly on you. There are a certain number of jobs, and a certain number of people who want them. A couple of congressmen are retiring. The D.A. would like to be governor."

Victoria took the martini out of the waitress's hands before she could set it down. "And you'd like to be D.A."

"I'll take it if it's offered to me. I'm loyal and patient and hard-working, but I'm unknown. I mean the pols know me but the voters don't. I want to break the Prescott case in three weeks at the outside. A girl I was counting on just blew the country, God damn her. She would have been terrific. That leaves you, Vicky."

"What do you want me to say, that they raped me with a machine when I wasn't looking, or something?"

"Or something. But why talk about it if all they do is show you dirty pictures?"

"There's more to it than that," she admitted. "It's like calisthenics. We flip for partners and lie down on exercise mats. They put a four-four record on the hi-fi and Dr. Prescott calls the beat. Sometimes the girls are on the bottom, sometimes on top. One—thrust—*and*—recover. One—thrust—*and*—recover. The object is to all come together at the end of thirty-two bars."

"Hilarious," he said. "If you don't want to talk to me voluntarily, sweetheart, I can always hit you with a subpoena. I can't force you to waive immunity, but you know how these things go. Your name gets in the papers, and people draw conclusions. You might have a hard time living it down."

Victoria was hurrying, but you can't hurry a martini. Sometimes she was pretty astute about people, especially those she didn't care for, like Woods.

"You really think they're immoral, don't you? Not that you're exactly an altar boy yourself."

He licked his lips quickly. "If you're talking about when Matt Hinkle was in town, you know how that happened. We all four had too many drinks, and it happened. We didn't ask photographers in. We didn't claim to be advancing the cause of science."

"I know why you liked it so much, because it was wrong."

"Spare me the psychiatry, will you, Vicky?"

"Psychiatry applies to overage assistant D.A.'s too, you know. If watching sex gets to be respectable, it's going to take away all your enjoyment, and then what will you do?"

"All right, I'm a sexual psychopath, and now let's talk about Dr. Chalmers S. Prescott."

"Woods, cross my heart. Ever since I started going up to 158th Street I haven't had sex with another living creature."

"Maybe I believe you. How do you stand with machines?"

She was putting on lipstick and she finished with a steady hand. "What kind of machine? You mean electric vibrators? I haven't used one of those since I was eighteen."

"Vicky, I'm warning you. I'm going to smash that outfit, and if anybody happens to be around when it happens, they're going to be included."

He was holding a paper napkin in one fist. He broke off, realizing it was only a napkin, and reached for his drink. Victoria studied him as she put her things in her bag. Was there really anything he could do? No, he was like a nonpoisonous snake writhing in fury because it wasn't able to get up any venom.

"We'll have to collect a few couples and go out again sometime soon," she said. "One—thrust—*and*—recover. Thanks for the drink."

She checked her watch again on the way out. God, she was late. But there had been a certain amount of emotion flying back and forth, and she had to see if it had affected her appearance. She detoured to the ladies' room. She was wearing a dress that was a touch too low-cut for the office. She took a rope of pearls out of her bag and put them on, and that definitely ended her business day.

She hesitated. It was silly, because it was only a machine. Yet, why not? She dabbed perfume behind her ears and between her breasts. She ran a comb through the ends of her hair and left, really hurrying now.

A taxi would have been pleasant, but the subway would get her there faster. The rush was still on, and she received two or three cursory feels from a strongly built Negro who left the train at 125th Street. The double standard again—if she had felt him back, he would have jumped out of his black skin.

She wasn't as late as she'd feared. The up elevator in the Research Building was empty, so she could look in her mirror one last time. She checked her stockings and wriggled her dress down over her hips, and as she went down the hall toward the unlabeled room she was almost running.

chapter 13

Fletcher and Hanna Williams turned toward Broadway after leaving the Research Building. Her fingers rested lightly on his arm. Usually, keeping in step was no problem, and it was pleasant when their hips grazed. Tonight the rhythm was off. Hanna gave up and let him walk by himself.

"Fletcher, you know it's an artificial environment. They can't expect everybody to—"

"Damn right it's artificial. They don't want people at all. Did you get a look at that machine? The plastic lingam in a state of permanent erection! That's the sort of performer they want. Tireless. No psychological troubles."

"Everybody knows that in our culture it's more of a problem for the man. It's intimidating at first, that laboratory. And you're not unique, you know, darling. You're not the first man it's happened to. Nonsuccess in Room 1806 has nothing to do with sexuality, with manliness! This is all out of character, Fletcher. It's the kind of thing we laugh about."

"When it happens to somebody else. No, I'm afraid I disappointed everybody. I failed to measure up."

"Failure, success! Stop acting as though this was some kind of test you didn't pass."

"But that's exactly what it was. I know, it all depends on how you look at it. In human terms maybe it's better *not* to get a hard-on in front of a couple of people in white coats."

"I thought they were very nice and reassuring. You didn't make it any easier for them with that lecture about machinery."

They walked on in silence.

"At least," she said with a sideward glance, "it was the first time in our sex life, married or premarried, that that particular problem ever came up."

"Don't you mean failed to come up?"

She laughed and put her hand back inside his elbow. "You had a slight case of erective inadequacy, which is curable, and I love you, darling."

"*You* didn't seem to have any trouble."

She gave another half-laugh and squeezed his arm. "Were you jealous?"

They dived into the subway station, and he decided to leave it at that. He paid their fares, and they moved onto the platform to wait for the downtown local.

"But you must know how different it is for me," she said. "Granted, I made it. But if I'd been a total flop by laboratory standards, I wouldn't think it proved I was unfeminine. So don't be a dope."

A drunk wavered toward them and stopped against the next post to gaze at Hanna. She pressed her husband's arm.

"To be continued."

"No, let's drop it right here," Fletcher said. "Sex as a topic of conversation is beginning to bore me."

The train came crashing down the track before she could ask him to elucidate. *Sex boring!* After they started downtown she put her lips against his ear and whispered, "Like hell we're going to drop it. We're going to get to the bottom of this."

When they came out into the fresh night air at 110th Street, she said, "I wonder what we're going to do when we get home."

"Go to bed."

"That's precisely what we're going to do. We're going to get naked and go to bed and have a highly erotic and mutually satisfactory fuck."

"Maybe," he said briefly.

Fletcher stayed in the hall with his hat on while Hanna paid their baby-sitter, a Barnard girl. Public opinion then obliged him to walk the girl four blocks to Reid Hall because of all the sex-obsessed Latins in the neighborhood. She was hugging a book by Dr. Albert Ellis, which Hanna had loaned her.

He stopped at a bar for a drink on the way back. Tonight, of course, because of her promise, he knew she would be awake no matter how late he came home. Sighing, he drank up and left.

She was in bed, wearing only the tops of her pajamas. Fletcher sat down on the foot of the bed without taking anything off himself.

"Brute," she said. "Take your clothes off. I want to see you."

"Darling, maybe we've thought about sex enough for one night. Couldn't we just go to sleep?"

"What a tone. I'm not suggesting lovemaking as therapy but lovemaking for its own sake. You know we have to tackle this head-on, before it can build up into anything."

"You mean like going out on the ski slope the minute you get out of the cast?"

"Don't be frivolous about it. Maybe I shouldn't have continued by myself. It probably wasn't too diplomatic of me. But just for once I didn't feel like playing the role of the humble, obedient wife. I'm sorry."

"And you had the family honor to uphold, after all."

"I won't allow you to be so sarcastic!" She caught herself and started over. "Fletcher, I know how you feel. But it's not on a par with the bombing of Hanoi, is it? Or Laurence Olivier as Oedipus Rex? It's just not in the same category. You know you're dramatizing. You're potent as hell! What about the night of our anniversary? You were up and down all night long—I was sore for days."

"There were just the two of us present. That might explain it."

"All right, on 158th Street you're impotent, so the hell with 158th Street. They can struggle along without us. I did think we could thrash it out and try again, perhaps, but if that's the way you feel—"

"That's the way I feel, but I don't want to stand in your way. If you think it's so delightful, why not go by yourself? That's what the good doctor was suggesting, or did you miss it? They need females to mate with the machine, so they can find out if the cervix dips into the seminal pool, or does it come to attention and whistle 'Dixie'?"

That made her laugh. "Fletcher, as a student of female anatomy!— I'm sorry, honey. I'm probably handling this all wrong. How can I help if you won't talk to me?"

"Then let's talk. What were you thinking about when you came?"

"Your prick," she said promptly.

"Hanna, Hanna. Nothing was farther from your mind. You were thinking about the machine across the room. What can a man do against that kind of competition?"

She made a small, distressed sound. He left the bed and kicked around the room, his hands deep in his pockets.

"It's not just that. It's the whole God damn business! I don't want to take the Conservatory, and it's closing in on me. If they get me, the only question about what I'll be like forty years from now is how much hair I'll have left. Speeches, speeches. And after the applause dies down I'll come home and we'll enjoy geriatric sex."

"Aren't you jumping the gun a little, darling?"

"I don't want to have sex when I'm seventy! I want to have prostate trouble and rub up against young girls on the subway, the way seventy-year-old men are supposed to."

"Fletcher, what are you talking about?" she said, laughing.

"God knows. It's a funny thing to get mad at, a piece of laboratory equipment. But the whole thing repels me! It sums everything up! The minute I saw the look on your face when you went into orgasm—"

"Darling?" she said faintly.

"It's not you, it's the world! I'm as much to blame as anybody and I don't know what to do about it. Take some kind of pill so I can pretend everything's different?"

She slid to the edge of the bed. "I love you. I love you! Come to bed."

The air was beginning to choke him. He pulled his tie apart.

"Go to sleep without me. You're right. It's not Oedipus Rex. I'll get over it."

She made a movement after him, but she had some sense left and let him go.

He went into his daughter's room. It was filled with the smells and possessions of childhood. He looked down at her smooth brown cheek and trailing arm. When his lungs began to clear, he went into the living room to put a tape on the stereo. He'd behaved like a clown. All that easy oratory about the race between people and machines, with the people three laps behind. And here he himself had a machine, which he couldn't have done without. It was a sweet one. He did most of his own mixing. With a little effort he could reproduce true concert-hall sound in this eighteen- by sixteen-foot room. An ordinary American in the twenty-percent tax bracket, just getting by financially, he had a library of important music within his reach, performed by superb musicians.

Of course, Fletcher hadn't actually listened to much of it lately. How long since he had picked up an instrument and played something for pleasure? There were too many noises in the air. He was fed up with this neat existence, with his neat wife who could be tinkered with in such a way that she produced a neat little gasping orgasm.

Well, that was unfair. He could have vetoed the laboratory visit. Only a small show of reluctance on his part would have made it impossible. But he could see she was dying to go, and if that was the kind of woman he had married . . . He had smelled disaster ahead and he had hurried them toward it. Knowing was better than not knowing. Only a very loud bang would blow the pollution out of his ears. Then he could listen to music again.

He was playing a John Cage composition for mutilated pianos and all at once he began to listen, realizing something about the piece. It was the perfect background music for laboratory sex between women and machines.

chapter 14

To keep the checks coming, Bobby Quinby, the bearded article-writer, ran a sort of assembly line, with a dozen pieces in varying stages of completion at one time, starting with the initial query and ending, a month or so later, after much thrashing around and some internal bleeding, with the absolutely-final final revisions. His office had once been the loft of a nineteenth-century coach house, which he and his wife had had remodeled at enormous expense. His desk had been a roulette table from a pre-Castro Havana casino. He worked in the well where the wheel had been. His current secretary—he changed secretaries even oftener than he changed wives—sat at an IBM Selectric halfway down the table. When he hired Jake Burgess, he made room for Jake's L.C. Smith portable at the opposite end.

If Bobby's end of the table was busy, he expected Jake's end to be busy. Bobby groaned as he typed, fluttering his wrists as though the words were drops of water he was trying to shake from his fingertips. The phone was in use most of the time. Somebody always seemed to be clattering up or down the circular iron staircase.

Jake spent part of each day moving about the city. He was still trying to find an interesting murder for the crime book Bobby wanted them to write. Jake was going through the active homicide files and talking to accused murderers in the Tombs. Bobby wanted somebody with the panache (one of the words he overworked) of the Boston Strangler or Perry Smith and Dick Hickock, the Kansas killers; unfortunately, all the candidates Jake had talked to so far were definitely bush.

Jake blew his first paycheck at Wallach's. The morning the suit was ready, he changed at the store and wore it to work. His shirt, a beautiful pale yellow, had been worn in a *New Yorker* advertisement by a model pretending to be partially blind. Betty Quinby opened the door for him, her hair in pins. There was only one bathroom in the house, and naturally Jake ran into her fairly often, with her makeup half on or missing altogether. She had been friendly but brisk. But with that part of his instinctive life being taken care of in the laboratory, he could afford to be as brisk as anybody.

Noticing the new clothes, she made an appreciative face. "You'll improve the tone around here."

Jake found his employer in good spirits. Two article ideas had been approved; there had been a check in the mail; he had fired his secretary, which always made him feel powerful. Later, after a three-martini lunch, he asked Jake to go to a party with them that afternoon. Jake, who hadn't attended a cocktail party since arriving in New York, the capital of cocktail parties, said he believed he was free.

They rode uptown in a cab, with Betty's warm thighs between them. Fully dressed, with her makeup on, perfumed, she was the kind of woman Jake had always associated with success.

He had been given a drink before leaving, a slug of I. W. Harper over an ice cube, the only drink ever served in the Quinbys' house. The party was boiling when they arrived and it stopped boiling at the exact moment the Quinbys left. Jake found out later that this was one of Bobby's knacks. Jake left among the last, taking along a dark-haired girl who worked for a paperback publisher. She fed him spaghetti in her one-room efficiency in a big new building above 57th Street, and they talked till the clocks chimed midnight. He kissed her lightly and said good night. She seemed puzzled. Was this all he was going to attempt? The truth was, it was Friday night and he had a date at the laboratory.

He soon found himself going to two or three parties a week. These were not simple gatherings of friends. They promoted something or announced something or introduced somebody or celebrated some milestone. Bobby, being part of the world of publicity, was welcome everywhere; his presence made the liquor bill deductible. As soon as people realized that Jake worked at the foot of Bobby's roulette table, he began to be asked under his own name. He learned how to move, how to identify the unattached girls, how to avoid being cornered, how much to drink, how long to stay.

It didn't take Dr. Prescott long to verify the suspicion he had started with: that to the cold eye of the laboratory apparatus there was no physiological difference between the reaction patterns of responding units, whether they were married or unmarried. Jake and Number 187, who had no life together elsewhere, met in the laboratory fourteen times in all over a two-month period. At their final session, after being told by Martha that the control program was being discontinued, she wore her glasses in from the dressing room for the first time. Jake grinned.

"I wanted to see what you look like," she said defensively. "Martha, would you mind if I talk to him a minute alone first?"

Nick DiVito, on a pipe scaffold, was loading the overhead Arriflex with Ektachrome, which meant that tonight they would be working under the lights. Martha had just inserted a spool of ruled paper in the myograph. She and Nick both stopped working and looked at the girl.

"That wouldn't be a good idea at all," Martha told her.

"Maybe not. But so far we've done what we've been told, haven't we? Scientifically it's been a success, I gather. Thirteen meetings, twenty-six orgasms. Just the same, I feel like a zombie." She glanced at Jake. "I don't know about anybody else."

"You know why we have that rule," Martha said.

"I suppose I do. But I want you to make an exception this once because we've been such very good children. I won't eat him."

Martha shook her head. Jake had considered these two women equally cerebral, but now he thought he heard a note of controlled hysteria in the request, something approaching panic in the refusal. What the hell!

"Let's have a drink afterward," he suggested.

The girl continued to look at Martha. "No, there's something I want to say to him now."

After a moment Martha nodded curtly to DiVito. "I still don't like it," she said, and they left the room.

The myograph, which had been left on, hummed faintly. The girl took off her glasses.

"Now I've alarmed you, haven't I? I didn't mean to."

She came up to him, very short in her heelless clogs. She hugged him quickly, her face tilted upward, and he kissed her.

"I haven't forgotten the first thing you said to me," she said. "That after it was over we might not believe anything had actually happened. And that's the way it's been, very existential and pointless, except for the data they've collected, and they knew all along that we weren't going to surprise them."

"Don't forget those twenty-six orgasms. You seemed to enjoy your thirteen."

"I did. That doesn't mean I believe they happened. Darling, do you remember—not the last time, but the time before?"

He nodded, but he couldn't actually think of anything to make that episode especially memorable. Was it the time he . . .

"I made up my mind then," she said. "Now don't look so terrified. I don't want you to do anything drastic like telling me your name. I'm in my second year at Einstein. I intend to be a surgeon and I think I'll be a good one. I'm not going to fall in love with you. You're in no danger. But what I'd like to do, if you're willing, is to make love with nobody else in the room. Couldn't we go to a hotel and register as Mr. and Mrs. John Smith? If your name's really John Smith, we can call ourselves something else. This would be our own private experiment, not Dr. Prescott's or Martha Freeman's. Certainly not Nick's. If it works, perhaps we could continue, with no claims on each other."

"All right," he said, without hesitation.

"Are you sure you want to?"

"Absolutely."

She let out her breath. "I thought I'd have to argue. Will you meet me in the sculpture garden of the Museum of Modern Art tomorrow at four?"

"Sure."

She kissed him again. "I know Martha's in agony. I'll call her."

She went to the door, a competent, passionless, studious girl who hoped to be a surgeon. Coming back, she fainted, falling forward into Jake's arms. Martha looked at him angrily when she came in. Together they got her up on the table.

"You've been working her too hard," Jake said.

The girl came to with a start. For an instant she looked scared and defenseless. She gripped Jake's sleeve and put her face against his arm.

Martha was dubious, but the girl insisted on going through with the delayed program. As it turned out, it was Jake who fell behind. Of course he knew he had to meet her. Their shared sex cycles gave her that much claim on him. If he failed to show up, it would be an admission that he was afraid of being trapped in a continuing relationship. And yet wasn't that exactly what she was trying to do? A Mr. and Mrs. Smith arrangement might work under medical auspices, but it had no chance of survival in the real world. And she wasn't his style! He wouldn't even have noticed her at a party. It was too bad, in a way, but the warm sexuality of the laboratory sessions didn't show up on the surface. People in Jake's position lost standing by dating people like Number 187—an elitist thought, but a true one.

She strove heroically, but, at last, a long time after the 400-foot Ektachrome magazine was exhausted, Jake withdrew from the battlefield. As he collapsed out of her, she took his face in both hands and kissed him gently. Swinging off the table and picking up her robe, she left the room.

Jake took his time about recovering. "You must keep a wheelchair for these cases."

"Jake, this doesn't exactly set a precedent. It happens often."

"Not to me. Better luck with the next couple," he told the cameraman, passing him on the way to the dressing room.

"Where's that cool of yours, man?"

Now, for the first time, Jake was glad he'd be seeing the girl the next day. She could easily misunderstand this nonperformance. He knew it was an emotional thing usually, but there were good physiological reasons: he'd been up till three the night before at a publisher's party and had been forced to fall back on a forty-percent blend when the bourbon ran out. And that faint of hers hadn't helped. It had put the wrong kind of emphasis on this farewell session.

By the next morning he was able to put the event in its proper perspective. Really, the most considerate thing would be to forget the date at the museum. He couldn't explain himself in the middle of a Saturday crowd, and they would undoubtedly end up in that hotel room, pretending to be a married couple. There he would have to explain why an affair as she had outlined it couldn't conceivably work; this had to be the last time. It would be painful for both of them.

But by noon he was back to thinking that he couldn't duck

it just because it would be painful. But what would he say to her? Their lovemaking, until last night had broken the rhythm, had been getting better and better, and he may have led her to believe . . . He decided to draft some dialogue, giving himself most of the major speeches. He had to take command from the opening line, unless he wanted to sound like one of the villains in *Batman*.

It was a hot day, his room was an oven. He was wearing only a pair of ripped underpants. The door was ajar, so any Canadian air that happened to pass through New York would cool off the room on the way to the sea. He finished writing the crucial speech just as a token rap came at the door. Betty Quinby, his employer's wife, walked in. Jake started violently and shifted the yellow pad to cover the rip in his shorts.

"What's wrong with the bastard who's supposed to answer your phone?" she demanded.

"Drunk, probably. Even I have the day off."

She looked around. There wasn't a great deal to see.

"Baby, this is terrible."

"Yeah, no Allen Ginsberg posters on the wall. Betty, you just caught me. I have to be somewhere at four on the dot."

"I want thirty seconds."

She was wearing her usual shades, a striped sleeveless jersey and slacks so narrow that any garment underneath, if she had been wearing any, would have revealed itself by its seams and hemlines. She sat down on the foot of the bed, blocking him from the washbasin, and poked in her bag for cigarettes. When she offered him the pack he took one. Given the uncertainties of the Saturday afternoon subway, he had to be dressed and ready to go by the time they finished their cigarettes.

"Jake, can't we get on easier terms? All this sidling around the house as though if we touched each other the city would catch on fire—"

That was a good description of Jake's behavior, but he hadn't known it was mutual.

"I'm open to suggestions," he said. "If you'll let me by I can be getting dressed."

"I know I seem tense. It's not a matter of life or death, just a party, but for various reasons I'd like to be there. Bobby's sick to his stomach. Will you take me?"

"Tonight? Betty, I can't. I have a date."

She wrote in the air with the burning tip of her cigarette. "Seriously?"

"Seriously," he said, after a half-second's hesitation that told her he was curious and wanted to hear more.

"Hubie Sachs is giving it. You never know in advance, but it looks like the big party of the year. Everybody's trying to wangle invitations. Every hairdresser in town has been booked for days."

"Who's Hubie Sachs?"

"My dear young man. He's in the rag business. He designs great clothes. Some London people are coming over for it, and it's going to be Mod—everybody in minis and long hair."

Sweeping up a brush from the rickety bureau, she darted at him and began forcing his hair over his eyes. The first ash had fallen from his cigarette. There was a fascinating play of movement inside the striped jersey, only a few inches from his face. As she leaned sideward to sight along the part, the tip of one breast grazed his temple.

A little irresponsible sex with Betty Quinby would do his picture of himself no harm. She was part of his fantasy world. Her surface was all enamel and glitter. She had a splintery way of talking, with quick, explosive gestures. Everything about her, including the fact that she was Bobby Quinby's wife, made it almost impossible for him to hold still.

She had the kind of vertical haunches that look well in slacks. The slacks were made of some grooved material, and all the grooves ran in the same direction, upward. She carried her own electrical field, and if Jake should lay his hand on her buttock, as he was tempted to do, he knew he would be rewarded with a shower of sparks.

She gave him a glancing kiss that left little lipstick. "Call her. Tell her your aged grandmother just turned up in town."

"Maybe she *is* my aged grandmother."

There was a good reason why he couldn't call off this date by phone. He didn't know her name or her phone number. He moved Betty out of his way, pivoting her by the hips.

"I might be free by seven-thirty."

"No, this includes dinner. I'm hoping to get a job with Hubie. He likes to have one girl in his group, and the one he has now just came up pregnant. Jake, as a special favor?"

She stretched out on the bed with her ankles crossed, twirling her dark glasses by one earpiece. To commit him to this party, she seemed to be willing to make love to him here and now, in his fifty-dollar-a-month squalor, in spite of the lack of air-conditioning and the used sheets. Either the party was very important, or the sex was very unimportant. He was twenty-five. She was in her early thirties. Something about her expression indicated that she thought it would be a bigger deal for him than it would be for her.

He started the water running.

"This may not make any difference," she said, "but you might be interested in the fact that Bobby took an emetic."

"Took a what?"

"An emetic. Don't expect to understand it all at once—it's a little Machiavellian. Why do you think he asked Judah to get him a male researcher, a year or two out of college, bright, ballsy—"

Jake picked his cigarette off the shelf. "What about the book idea?"

"Oh, that's legitimate, and I hope you find him a nice gruesome multiple murder so he can sell the paperback rights to NAL. Then he could make a cash settlement and be on his way to Juarez the next morning."

Interested? This was close to the bone; Jake had to be interested. He had wondered why Bobby hadn't hired one of the ex-newspapermen who were floating around New York. He sat down beside her; she moved her legs to make room. The logical place to put his hand was around her ankle, and he decided it was time to start being logical.

"Try to be a little less cryptic."

"You probably don't know that before I married Bobby I was considered one of the coming people. Why would you? Three years is an age in the clothes business. The hemline was an inch below the knee. Not down as far as your hand is—" Jake moved on to the pleasant stubble on her calf—"Yes, about there. Bobby's different when he's not married to you. You wonder what personality he's hiding behind that beard. His big trouble is, he has to have a certain amount of intrigue mixed in with his oxygen. There's a fourth Mrs. Q. on the horizon. That's all right with me. I'm, shall we say, disenchanted, and I do wish I could stop using Bobby's words."

"I'm still not with you."

"Well, it's a hot day. I'm willing to be divorced, Jake, but I want a little financial compensation. Don't you think I deserve it? Bobby doesn't either. But *I* think I deserve it. Unfortunately he's already paying two former wives and one more would pauperize him."

"So he wants you to make the first move?"

"Exactly. Judah's been after him to stop doing celebrity pieces and write a book, and he agreed if Judah could find him the right kind of assistant. Judah was number two on the Regents his year, and he hasn't got any dumber since. He didn't have to ask Bobby what kind of assistant."

"He told me Bobby wanted somebody who could write a decent English sentence."

"That too. But they mainly picked you for your looks. And I must say—"

"But my God! Think of the odds against anything happening."

"Propinquity, dear. You'd get used to seeing me before I put on my bra. There would be times when Bobby would be away on a story and we'd have the place to ourselves. I might ask you to hang around and have a drink, and that might be the night when you didn't have a date with your grandmother." She made a sound reminiscent of a rocket being launched. "And, to increase the stress, he's been denying me my conjugal rights."

"Come on!"

"A case of self-induced impotence, for which he's been taking treatment. I'd be greatly surprised if he's impotent outside the home."

Jake laughed. "Tennessee Williams is supposed to be looking for plots. Maybe he could use this one."

She fluttered her fingers. "If you're going to play with me, move a little closer so I can reciprocate."

"Is it really true he hasn't been sleeping with you?"

"Even Bobby can't control his reflexes when I go all out. He wins about half the time. I win about half the time. Further questions?"

"Yes. Do you have anything on under those slacks?"

"No. The zipper's on the right."

"Your right or my right?"

While he was fooling with it she drew his face down to hers. She had green eyes, which were carefully made up. He liked what he saw in them. He could be safe from any emotional storms with this girl. Sex was the first step, and then they would define their terms. She wanted something. Bobby wanted something. There were possibilities here.

He stopped her hand, turning it over so he could see her watch. The numbers were so small it took him a moment to read them.

"Did you bring your car?"

"Yes, and I hope your neighbors aren't stealing the wheels. You smell marvelous." She licked his shoulder. "So salty."

If he could use her car instead of the subway he wouldn't miss by much. He hoped Number 187 would let him deliver at least part of his main speech.

"Now I'll get some benefit out of the pills I've been taking," Betty said.

Suddenly her casual prediction came true, and it did seem to Jake that the city was on fire. It happened very fast. From his laboratory experience he knew the names of some of the things that were happening to him: vasocongestion, myotonia, pre-ejaculatory emission. She was naked now. She had been better-looking with her clothes on, and Jake had a strong suspicion that the reverse would be true of the laboratory girl. Bone clashed against bone as they came together. Intromission was difficult; he was feeling the pressure of time and he couldn't wait. She seemed all points and angles. But she knew what she was doing, and drew his seed with efficiency and dispatch. She didn't go the whole route herself, but she didn't insist on further games as he slipped away.

For an instant he saw a funny look in her eyes. There was an outside chance, perhaps, that she would say the wrong thing. But she stayed in character.

He was standing beside the bed. Turning and coming up on her elbows, she put her face against his thigh.

"I like to make love in hot weather. I'm as slippery as a trout. Did that win you over, darling? Are you going to take me?"

"What time's dinner?"

"Seven. But I want to buy you some clothes first."

"You'll have to let me out of your sight for about twenty minutes. I can't phone this girl because she's already left. And I've got to think up some better excuse than a grandmother."

"She seems to have some kind of claim on you."

"Yeah. I have a date with her."

She sat up and stretched. Jake liked watching the way she moved. It was abrupt and a little overdone, but it was overdone with style. She began getting into her few clothes.

"Is this Hubie a queer?" Jake asked.

"Of course. But don't think I'm trying to ingratiate myself by introducing a new boy. I want you for myself. I'm crazy about you."

"I'm crazy about you, too. What else?"

She laughed. "I knew you'd say the cool thing. I'm older than you are, and we've all read Colette. Maybe Bobby didn't take an emetic. I can't prove it. But there's money at stake, a lot of money. I'd be willing to sign for ten thousand a year. In twenty-five years that's a quarter of a million dollars. That's why we have to be careful. He's such a natural-born conniver. I was in on quite a bit of it while he was married to Number Two."

"How does he get any work done?"

"We all wonder. But I'll be God damned if I let him program me! He won't do anything crude like hiring detectives. I just don't want his lawyer to tell my lawyer that he has a deposition from somebody who walked in when Bobby was supposed to be out of town and surprised the current Mrs. Quinby *in flagrante* on the Noguchi couch."

It was twelve minutes of four by the time he strapped on his watch. Betty was dressed, reading the scene he had written on the yellow pad.

"This is hairy dialogue," she commented, "but I don't get some of the nuances. What's the He character being so hang-dogish about?"

"I'll tell you the plot sometime. Put on your lipstick in the car."

The Quinbys, unsurprisingly, owned a showy car with a powerful motor. Jake was a competent city driver, but there was little he could do on the downtown side of Columbus Circle, where the city always seemed to be in a state of excavation. When he bogged down totally after crossing Sixth Avenue, he left the car to Betty and ran the last half-block, arriving exactly at the dot of four.

He went directly to the garden, where he found the usual dense Saturday crowd. He had to look at faces carefully, never having seen the girl except naked or in a striped robe, and always in the extraordinary light of the laboratory. He concentrated on girls who were by themselves, trying to imagine how they would look undressed. He received similar looks in return.

He moved counterclockwise through the galleries. He remembered times when she had been late for appointments on 158th Street, coming in from the dressing room apologizing and out of breath. He waited till a quarter of five before concluding that she had decided not to come. She was a brainy girl, and he could see now why she had wanted to talk to him before their laboratory struggle instead of after. By failing so spectacularly after she proposed a human connection, his body had given her his answer. His reaction then, as now, had been the exact opposite of cool. His lagging member had done the talking for him. He was ashamed of himself and he didn't really know why. He had played fair by laboratory rules.

He went outside and waited for Betty to come around again. He kept watching the girls entering the museum, especially those who were wearing glasses. But she wouldn't be as late as this. He was angry, a little hurt, and confused, but relieved that it was over.

There was no one in New York Hubie Sachs didn't know. He made clothes for Fords and Whitneys, he had dressed two David Merrick shows and a psychedelic opera, he had been the subject of Talk pieces in the *New Yorker* and an article in *Fortune*. He was the darling of *Vogue* and the *Bazaar*. He could easily have given a huge party attended exclusively by names, but the celebrities would have been snappish and edgy with one another. To provide the proper ambience (another Bobby Quinby word), two-thirds of his guests were always more or less unknown.

He had fourteen to dinner. He lived in a remodeled brown-stone on the edge of Harlem; it was agreed that if anybody could make a district fashionable it was Hubie, but even he had been unable to arrest the process of urban decay. At the same moment, in other houses and apartments about the city, other groups of fourteen were sitting down to dinner. All the invitations had been issued by Hubie himself, and in some instances the hostesses and the guests hadn't previously met. Hubie supplied each dinner with wine and oysters. Otherwise, the individual hostesses were allowed to serve what they chose.

Bobby Quinby had written the *Redbook* piece about Hubie's spring line and so had been invited to the most prestigious table, Hubie's own. Hubie was disturbed to hear about Bobby's sickness, for last-minute substitutions can wreck a party, but when Betty brought Jake in Hubie gave him a flickering glance and kissed her warmly.

Jake was seated between a Kennedy in-law and a nobody. Hubie served no cocktails, only the lightest aperitif; but Betty, knowing about this failing, had strengthened them before leaving with a bracing jolt of I. W. Harper. Putting the Museum of Modern Art debacle behind him, Jake did well. The lady on his right collected a kind of art that was very big at the moment. She and her husband had kept some of the boys from starving—literally—during the locust years. She hoped Jake would visit her collection—the breakfast-food boxes, comic-strip blowups, fun toilet bowls, the statues standing around the living room like perpetual guests.

Somehow Hubie had managed to persuade everybody that by attending his dinner they had become a part of something much, much bigger. Would it be presumptuous to call it history? Afterward they climbed into a Volkswagen bus flying a Hubie-designed flag and started for Central Park. Hubie had hurried them through coffee—he could be a bully—and they were the first to arrive. The scene was a dry fountain at a conjunction of walks. With the help of Jake and the others, he unloaded picnic hampers and champagne. More Volks-wagens appeared, flying the same flag. The new guests were in the same proportion of known to unknown, one to two. Jake saw, or believed he saw, Jane Fonda, George Plimpton, Joe Namath, Murray Schisgal, Elaine May, Sidney Poitier,

Marisol, Harry Royce, Ethel Kennedy, Arthur Schlesinger, Jr., Truman Capote, and Lauren Bacall. By this time even the nobodies had taken on a borrowed glitter.

Two amplified rock-'n'-roll groups faced outward on opposite sides of the fountain, their instruments tied into a common generator. While one group performed, the other drank Hubie's champagne. There was a full moon; Hubie, perhaps, had arranged it. Indoors, this kind of syncopated noise was an enemy of conversation. Here, the older guests, who still believed a dialogue was possible, collected on the opposite side of the fountain from the music.

A disdainful *Life* man, who had covered wars, stood with his camera on one hip. Policemen ringed the party, and beyond was a second ring of onlookers. Grubby young girls occasionally darted past the police for an autograph. Jake, asked for his, signed "George Hamilton." The way Betty had combed his hair, the high shoes, low-slung pants, fruity jacket, all made him feel like an impostor. He belonged out there, not in here. His plays would never be produced. It was too late to marry a Kennedy. Turning homosexual might help, if the tone of this gathering meant anything, but, in the phrase used about professional athletes, he didn't have the desire.

Hubie Sachs dresses were everywhere. The main characteristics of the Mod style were the unconfined buttock and the bared thigh. The girls danced violently. But their eyes were down, their smiles were sleepy. After a sixth glass of champagne, Jake understood the expression—Nick DiVito, the Prescott cameraman, had caught it many times. He glanced around, pleased with the discovery. There again. He himself was dancing opposite a pudgy actress who received $250,000 a picture, but from the look on her face she was bogged down in the arousal phase and wouldn't make it all the way tonight.

Corks blew. The fountain began to spin. Jake should never have tried to keep that appointment at the Museum of Modern Art. He couldn't imagine the laboratory girl at this kind of party, either as one of the guests or as one of the voyeurs. She had probably never danced to this strong a beat. She wouldn't know the moves. The midthigh skirt would look odd on her. The expression on her face just before orgasm—that alone would have fitted in here.

A battery of floodlights had been set up on the fountain rim. All at once, in the blur and dazzle, Jake thought he saw the Swedish girl who had been his first laboratory partner. Her eyes were partly closed. A long necklace was swinging. Delight blazed from her face.

The music banged to a stop. The $250,000 actress lost her balance and toppled against him.

"Why, you're only a child," she said, surprised.

"I'll get you some champagne."

He was hallucinating, Jake knew. The first few days after the initial Sunday morning, he had seen her face wherever he looked. Again and again, they seemed to pass in a crowd. When he was going up an escalator, he saw her on the opposite escalator, going down. Now, moving with the dancers, he peered at faces. He saw somebody who looked like Mrs. Lindsay, somebody else who looked like Mrs. Javits. He saw a television panelist, and Arthur Miller in a Beatle wig. Could it be Arthur Miller? Invited to a party like this, would he dress up and come?

And there she was again.

She was wearing a red dress with a scooped-out back and deep slashes beneath the arms. Using his fingers, he threw his hair back the way he usually wore it and pushed off from the fountain rim. He was in the direct path of the amplifiers, and the beat was insistent and terrible. She turned suddenly and faced him.

"I knew I'd see you again," Jake said softly.

Her hand rose to her mouth. "My God!"

As she whirled away from him, the group succeeded in stamping the number to death, and the crowd closed in. Jake elbowed his way onto the grass and ran to the other side of the fountain, angled back, and worked through the crowd. There were dozens of red dresses, dozens of swinging necklaces. Betty Quinby, appearing out of nowhere, grasped his arm.

"Jake, aren't you glad you came?"

chapter 15

Someday, Fletcher Williams hoped, some enlightened foundation concerned about the mental health of American composers would appropriate a small annual sum so that no serious musician, after reaching a certain stage in his career, would have to give lessons. The problem with an advanced pupil was how to force him past technical competence into the real music, where competence is either taken for granted or beside the point. You had to get down in the mud and wrestle. Joe Ben Fox, an improbable name for an improbable violist, always made Fletcher earn his money. He came from somewhere in the desert country. In a period of long haircuts for men, his was short and bristling. He was strong and quick.

But Fletcher, too, could be dangerous with a viola in his hand. They were playing Mozart. The student, a decade younger than his teacher, was willing to admit that Mozart had had a certain talent, and if he hadn't been so smug about the effects he'd been able to get with it . . . Playing alongside him, using his bow like a whip, Fletcher was making him do things he hated. Joe Ben resisted, naturally.

"No," Fletcher said mildly, breaking off. "Again, from the B flat."

Joe Ben gave him a look with murder in it. That was all right with Fletcher. They owed everybody, as usual, and Fletcher needed Joe Ben's money, but, if Joe Ben was the one who quit, Fletcher's conscience would be clear.

He met the boy's chaotic anger with a disciplined anger of his own. He had more than enough to be angry about, God knew. All at once Joe Ben began playing the instrument the way it was meant to be played. As soon as Fletcher was sure he had him, he let go and began improvising twelve-tone jazz in his head against the melodic line. He hadn't done that in months. Was it possible that the crisis was over?

"That was better," he said, lowering his bow.

Joe Ben looked exhausted. The end of the half hour was

still some minutes away, but they had both reached their limit. Fletcher mapped out an impossible practice assignment and dismissed him.

There was a certain amount of peace in the apartment for the moment. Jennie was at nursery school, where she was being trained for kindergarten. Hanna was on 158th Street, where else? Fletcher was attempting to cultivate an attitude of ironical detachment toward the laboratory, but he wasn't succeeding. He and Hanna had discussed the matter thoroughly, over and over; they were one married couple that had no difficulty communicating. During one of these discussions, he was sorry to say, he had picked up a rib roast of beef and hurled it against the dining room wall. Secretly, he was proud of the outburst, but would Mozart have done it? But then Mozart had never had the same provocation.

Fletcher was being hounded to say something definite about the Conservatory job. The Germans who had invited him to spend three weeks in Darmstadt preparing his oboe and string piece were pressing him for an answer. But he couldn't decide anything in the middle of this running battle with Hanna. Like everybody, she wanted life to have some meaning, and did he have a right to stand in her way, simply because he didn't want to be cuckolded by a machine? Except possibly in the emerging nations, no one used the word "cuckold" anymore. Male jealousy was a thing of the past, a relic of the days before oral contraceptives, when women were property. And to be jealous of something constructed of plastic and stainless steel! It wasn't rational, and he hadn't been able to explain it rationally. What did he object to exactly, she wanted to know. Just the whole God damn thing, that was all.

He was sleeping ten hours a night and yet he had never felt so tired. Whenever he woke up or turned over, he found Hanna awake beside him. In what he now considered the good old days, they had swung into and out of sleep on the same cycle. No longer. Once she sighed and put her hand on his hip. He stiffened; she took her hand away.

The next morning, she made her announcement. She was sorry they disagreed about this, she knew it was bad for them, but she was a sovereign person, endowed with certain inalienable rights, and she had decided not to let her husband's antiquated prejudices . . . This was at breakfast. She was pale, with violet bruises under her eyes. Her voice was even, but Jennie, their four-year-old, knew something important was going on and sliced her pancake into complicated geometric shapes.

"I wish we could do it together," Hanna said, "but I don't see why this has to make such a difference. No two people can be expected to agree about everything. I like Mary McCarthy, you can't stand her—"

"It's hardly in the same category."

"Jennie, eat your breakfast."

"I *am* eating my breakfast."

"You're not eating it, you're cutting it up."

"Mind your own business, Mommy!"

Hanna slapped her hand, and there were tears. Later Hanna came into the bedroom where Fletcher was trying to mate the male and the female tabs of his trick collar.

"If you could give me one sensible reason—"

"I don't want you to! Why isn't that enough? Any ordinary wife would pay some attention to—"

"But it's my decision. I agree with what they're trying to do and I want to help. They're doctors, Fletcher. Scientists."

"That cameraman isn't a scientist."

Their voices were climbing, and because Jennie was still in the house Hanna swallowed her reply and went out of the room. When she came back after taking Jennie to meet the nursery school taxi, her face was determined.

"I'd like to give in, Fletcher. I can't. I think you're being very perverse. Why do we need each other's approval for everything we do? I don't, as a matter of fact, think it was very bright of you to boycott the last presidential election. But I didn't criticize you. Have I put any pressure on you to go to Darmstadt?"

"It doesn't make any difference to you whether I go or not."

"That's not true! I want you to do what you think is best. Darling, I love you. I want to stay married to you. But what do I have in my life? Outside of you and Jennie and Women Strike for Peace—"

"I won't suggest any new hobbies because I don't want to sound sarcastic. But does it have to be public orgasm?"

"That's a loaded description, and you know it. I've made up my mind—I'm going, regardless. I don't see why it has to affect the way we feel about each other. There are places in your mind I know I can't get into. We don't hear the same thing when we listen to music. Fletcher, let's call it something else. Pretend I've signed up at Berlitz for German lessons."

He turned away. "Hanna, please don't do it."

He said it quietly, with an implied "if." If she went ahead with this, in spite of his disapproval, he would have to do something about it. Never mind what, but something.

She phoned Mrs. Freeman and made an appointment.

In most respects their lives continued as before. She now had more spending money. She bought some new clothes and odds and ends she had been wanting to get for the apartment; she bought a tricycle for Jennie. Once, when she came in looking worn out, he said, "Are you sure those German declensions aren't too strenuous for you?"

"I'm warning you, Fletcher."

The phone rang. It was Mary Jane Mosberg, the violinist.

"We want to use a rehearsal room and borrow one of your pianos. They say I need your signature."

"That's the rule. How are you, Mary Jane?"

She had little patience with this kind of routine inquiry. "I'm okay," she said briefly. "How soon do you plan to get to the office?"

"I just finished a lesson. Give me time to convalesce. Around eleven."

"Beautiful," she said. "And if I wait till eleven, how will I get to Juilliard at 10:45? Fletcher, stay where you are, I'll pick it up."

He found a viola tape and dropped it into the machine. It was still playing when Mary Jane arrived, looking like a stripped-down stock car, all power plant and controls.

"You God damn bureaucrats. What are you afraid of with all these signatures?"

Fletcher signed the permission slip and the two carbons. "If anything happened and we hadn't authorized the use of the room, the insurance company wouldn't pay the claim."

"Like if *what* happened? If somebody got a finger caught in the piano?"

"That's a good example. If it happened to a professional pianist, the award could run as high as—"

"Fletcher, you're full of crap," she said flatly.

He laughed. "It's simpler to sign a permission slip once in a while than to keep telling everybody they're out of their minds. Do you have time for coffee?"

"If it's made." Her head cocked. "Who's that on the viola?"

"Don't you recognize the tone?"

"That's not you, unless you had an injection."

He went into the kitchen for the coffee. "Remember the string piece I showed you?" he called back. "You said it couldn't be played."

"You faker," she said when he returned. "Those are two tracks."

"Not only that, I picked up the tempo. But there's a man in Germany who can play it the way it's written."

"Start it over. Let's see the score."

He watched her as she listened, her head cocked to keep the smoke of her cigarette out of her eyes. He felt better than he had in days. Those dirty fingernails were irresistible. She was wearing sandals, and a few toenails showed remnants of paint. After a time, she put the cigarette on the edge of the coffee table and let it burn itself out.

"All right," she said finally. "If I ran around the Reservoir every morning for six months to get in shape. But what's the point of writing a part only one man in Germany can play?"

"Does there have to be a point?"

"It's showing off. I'm Fletcher Williams. Look, everybody —see how brilliant I am."

She leaned forward to get her coffee, and he kissed her. Her lips were chapped.

"What was that supposed to prove?" she said when he pulled back.

Conversation was never Mary Jane's big thing. Suddenly dead serious, he kissed her again, much harder this time.

"Okay, okay," she said. "Let me take off a few things. And if Hanna walks in it's your funeral."

The one thing Mary Jane wasn't was coy. She made love with no cadenzas or semiquavers, saying nothing. Earlier that morning, Fletcher had been trying to get Joe Ben past the barriers set up by technical virtuosity and on into the real thing, and he and Mary Jane were there together for a moment. She was feminine in the important ways. But when it was over it was over, with none of those tender autopsies he had become used to. Had it been special in any way? You wouldn't find out from Mary Jane.

She got up and dressed. "Let's do that again sometime," she said unsmilingly. From her, it was a tribute.

After she left, Fletcher reheated the coffee. For a change no one seemed to be prodding him from behind to get him to produce. To feel really healthy was rare in New York, but he could feel the vitamins coursing through his veins. On an impulse, he did seven push-ups on the living room rug. Hardly up to Marine Corps standards, but not bad for a sedentary musical bureaucrat.

Before he could leave for the office he had to wade through a report about staff workload. It wound up, as such reports do, with a recommendation that he hire more people. Now he had to hunt for omissions and loopholes. He might be able to slip an additional job into the budget, but not five. What kind of music should accompany this chore? Bartók, he decided, and put on a tape of *Bluebeard's Castle*.

When he was finished he tossed the report into the pigskin attaché case Hanna had given him on his last birthday. The *Consumers Union Buying Guide*, open to an inside page, lay face down on the end table, and he picked it up to see what she was considering buying with her illicit earnings. An electric dishwasher.

Suddenly, Fletcher felt a wave of physical longing for his wife. How many times had she washed the dishes since their marriage? Nine years times 365 days times three meals a day. Call it 9,000 times, unless he had brought down too few zeroes. And she hadn't complained about it more than once every two weeks, 225 times, an insignificant percentage.

He decided to surprise her by making the beds. First he worked on Jennie's, which had been struck by a tornado in the night, and then went into the main bedroom, the center ring of what had once seemed an excellent marriage. He straightened the bureau, with its array of organic cosmetics from Walnut Acres. She was impossible. She saw nothing offensive about an orgasm produced by a machine, but he loved her, he supposed.

He smelled her pajama tops and smelled the girl he had had sex with, usually in cars, for two years before they were married; he smelled the trips they had taken, the birthdays over the years, the pleasant times before this trouble started. He wanted her back, on her own terms if that was the way it had to be. So long as she did what he wanted twenty-three hours a day, he could let her do what she wanted during the twenty-fourth.

He picked up a card from the floor. "Mrs. Williams has an appointment at 10:30 A.M. on . . ." It jarred him out of his reverie. He couldn't make love to a woman who might compare him to an electrically driven gismo, designed to produce the dream orgasm, the one that never ends. At this exact moment, while he was mooning around thinking about those early fumblings in the back seat of his old Hudson, she was playing with the dials, making those little adjustments that can turn a so-so experience into a superb one, her forehead filmed with perspiration, her legs lashing . . .

The card was signed Martha Freeman. He had liked Mrs. Freeman and he had wondered how she had brought herself to play a leading part in anything so creepy. Did she know Hanna was performing for them without her husband's consent?

It occurred to him that he had better start being careful, and he inspected the living room thoroughly and removed all indications of Mary Jane's visit. There was nothing he could do about the burn on the coffee table except take the blame for it himself.

What if he went to Mrs. Freeman and explained the situation? They had had the use of his wife for a few weeks, and now could he have her back? He wasn't the space-age man he had tried to seem when they interviewed him. He was only a step out of the cave. Hanna claimed she wanted to stay married, but a divorce was inevitable if they kept sending her those little reminder cards. Would they cut her down gradually, please, and not tell her why? She was just as irrational as he was, though on what they would undoubtedly consider the rational side of the argument.

He thought of little except this rash scheme for the next few days. But gradually the emphasis changed. Why would Mrs. Freeman cooperate in depriving the project of one of its star turns? He wouldn't get anywhere appealing for sympathy. He would have to raise hell. They were running a sensitive operation and they couldn't afford trouble. What Fletcher decided to do was to wait for Hanna's next appointment, go up and force his way in, seize his wife by the hand, and drag her out—whether they liked it or not.

He watched the mail. A card came, reminding her of an appointment at nine o'clock Friday evening. He invented some business to keep him at the Conservatory, left early, and started drinking. The liquor seemed to go down the wrong way. His courage, small to begin with, dwindled with each drink. At 8:45, when he should have been leaving, he was struck by an inspiration. Instead of going directly to Martha Freeman, why not approach her at secondhand through his good friend Max Sultan, Dr. Max Sultan, who had been the first to tell them about the project on that Debussy evening so long ago? Max could put the case to Mrs. Freeman. Did she want to get a reputation for breaking up marriages? Did she want a Molotov cocktail thrown in the midst of her machinery by an angry husband? No? Then send Hanna Williams back to her family, because they missed her.

Enormously relieved, Fletcher plunged into the subway. He left the train a few stops later. Ahead of him on the platform and going up the stairs was a woman who looked familiar. Coming out on the street, she turned west. Fletcher turned west. It couldn't possibly be Hanna, but of course it was. She was supposed to be reporting for duty at the sex lab two and a half minutes from now. Instead, she entered Max Sultan's apartment building, and Fletcher sat down on a stoop across the street and put his head in his hands.

chapter 16

Jake and Betty Quinby came back to his room after the Hubie Sachs party. Half an hour later she left him sprawled, exhausted, on the torn-up bed and went home by herself. He awakened on Sunday morning with a champagne headache and the feeling that too much had happened. He stared up at the cracks on the ceiling; they were as unreadable as tea leaves. Somehow he had to get into his clothes and up to 158th Street. His one laboratory session with Number 89, the Swedish girl, had taken place on Sunday morning. Mrs. Freeman had told him they intended to go on using her, and Sunday might be the only day she had free. It was a tiny chance, little better than no chance at all. But he had to stop drifting. He had drifted into the laboratory, into the Quinby job, into Betty Quinby's vagina. Everybody seemed to be part of a conspiracy to convince him that sex was no more important than a sneeze. He was outnumbered and he would probably lose, but he had to put up a battle.

His head felt as fragile as a Christmas tree ornament. He bought a *Times* and junked part of it so that he would have less to carry. He glanced at the front-page disasters on the subway. Humanity, as usual, seemed to be having its troubles. His own, compared to wars and earthquakes and riots, were trivial, of interest to nobody but himself.

It was a bright morning, and he found a place across from the Research Building where he could sit in the sun and recover. Not many people used the research facilities on Sundays, one or two desperate operators like Dr. Prescott and the maintenance people who came in to look after the animals. Deep in the *Times*, among the marriages and engagements, the committees of jaunty women attempting to stave off middle age by organizing balls, Jake saw a picture of Hubie Sachs, his face creased in one of his brilliant smiles. Some of his celebrated friends were pictured dancing. The *Times* was a sober, careful newspaper, perhaps the most careful in the world, but it had missed the last-minute substitution of Jake Burgess, the nobody, for Bobby Quinby, the writer. One of Jake's partners, if partner wasn't too extreme a word, had been an Italian princess, a fact he found hard to believe.

Screened by the *Times* and the parked cars, he kept watch until two, deciding at the turn of each hour to wait for only one more hour before giving up. His hopes rose only once, when a girl appeared who was the right size, the right age, and who seemed to have the right color hair. He had been reading the drama ads, and the street was out of focus. He folded the paper and set out after her. Hearing footsteps behind her, she walked more quickly. When he caught up to her and she turned to look at him, she changed into somebody else.

"I'm sorry," he said, "I thought you were—"

In an exuberant moment, Hubie Sachs had asked Jake to drop in for tea on Monday.

His clothes were manufactured somewhere else, but they were thought up on the top two floors of his rearranged brownstone. Jake was admitted by an elderly Negro woman who had difficulty getting around. Hubie had tired of his Regency wallpaper and was having it replaced by a paper of his own design, pirated from Saul Steinberg cartoons. Jake squeezed past the paperhangers and entered the big third-floor workroom.

Two bored girls, one Negro, one white, were being fussed over by several decorative young men. Bolts of cloth were piled on chest-high shelves running around two walls. A black and white sketch of a pants suit had been projected on one bare plaster wall, and the young men were attempting to get the same feeling with real materials on real girls. This must be the job Betty Quinby was hoping to get.

The young men gave Jake a hard stare, and one of them directed him to an office where Hubie himself was discovered at a large desk, wearing owlish hornrims.

"Jake Burgess!" Jake was surprised and pleased that the fey little designer had remembered his name. "You came! Wasn't it a *party?*"

"Marvelous."

"It was altogether marvelous," Hubie agreed. "The phone's been ringing incessantly. Jake love, I've got this paperwork, and then we're going to have such a tea. I hope you don't have any waistline problems because we go in for high teas around here. I stopped at the Eclair and went quietly mad. Can you amuse yourself for half an hour? Watch the girls. Or watch the boys, whichever."

"Hubie, I can't stay. I have a question to ask. A girl I met at the party broke the catch of her watch and gave it to me to hold. I haven't any idea who she was."

While not the most ingenious story ever devised, this was good enough to fool most people. It didn't fool Hubie. He shrugged slightly. It was a disappointment, but the kind of disappointment he had learned to live with.

"What did she look like?"

Jake tried to describe her, bearing in mind that Hubie might make clothes for beautiful women, but that didn't mean he admired them.

"I didn't ask any Swedes," Hubie said doubtfully. "One trouble with that party, the only trouble—we were wide open. I remember the dress. It was one of Rudi's. Somebody said she came with the Thants."

He called one of his boys, who went to the phone and returned presently with a slip of paper he handed to Hubie. Hubie handed it on to Jake, and came with him as far as the workroom door.

"How's Bobby?"

"Much better. He's sorry he missed the party, but he made the *Times*, which is the next best thing."

"I love Bobby, one of our real wits. That bird he's married to is loaded with talent. I'm thinking of letting her join the gang. I wouldn't know personally, but I've heard her referred to as a sexpot. What next, I wonder? Bye-bye, Jake."

Outside, Jake looked at the slip of paper, which had a chaste legend at the top, "From the desk of Hubie Sachs." A name and address were written beneath with a broad-nib pen. The girl's name, according to this, was Marcia Clarke. The hell it was! It was either a mistake, or simple bitchiness on the part of Hubie's boy.

Nevertheless, that evening Jake was pressing a buzzer for

an apartment occupied by a girl named Marcia Clarke and two others. The peephole clattered. He passed inspection.

"Is Marcia in?" he asked the girl in the doorway.

"I'm Marcia. I'm in."

He showed her the slip of paper. The Hubie Sachs identification proved to be credentials enough.

"You were at Hubie's party—I knew I'd seen you. Come in and explain."

Two other girls of the same generation were sitting at a card table. One had just washed her hair; her hand flew to her curlers. Jake told the wristwatch story. Unlike Hubie, they believed it and asked him to sit in. They were playing three-handed bridge.

This was a deadend, it seemed. He couldn't go back to Hubie and complain that he'd been steered to the wrong blonde. Jake accepted the invitation to stay, giving the slightest of shrugs, modeled on Hubie's when he perceived that Jake had no ambitions to succeed in the gay world. They cut for partners. Marcia won.

Jake decided to move and, after some searching, found an air-conditioned apartment on the acceptable side of the park at only a little more money than he could afford to pay. Betty Quinby was annoyed with him when he told her about the move. Everybody knew the building; it had been thrown up in a hurry to catch innocents who were willing to pay a rack-rent for the privilege of living in noise and discomfort at a good address. But he had already signed the lease. He bought a double bed that turned into a sofa when lifted and kicked. Betty made a telephone canvas of her friends, looking for hand-me-downs. She had accepted Hubie's offer of a job and she expected to be able to cadge enough fabric for drapes and a couch cover.

One night, during his second week in the new apartment, Jake woke up from his escalator dream, the one in which he saw the Swedish girl on the down escalator while he was going up. The next day he called Mrs. Freeman and made an appointment to see her.

She seemed glad he'd come back. He asked how the project was going.

"We're at a turning point, Jake. We want to get into some long-range studies, but there's some doubt about whether our Royce grant is going to be renewed. We'll know in a week."

He had an uneasy feeling that she knew exactly what he was thinking, but how was that possible, unless she could read minds? "I wanted to ask if you had any openings. What would you think about teaming me with the same girl I worked with before? I know you're finished with that series, but haven't we been together long enough to qualify as an established unit?"

Mrs. Freeman tapped the desk with her pencil. "Does she know about this?"

"No. I don't know how to get hold of her except through you. You probably realize why she wanted to talk to me alone that last time. To see if I was a human being, or just an erection. We made a date for the next day, and she didn't keep it. Three guesses why. If you could tell her I want to try again—"

A phone was ringing in another office. DiVito put his head in the door.

"Long distance, Mrs. Freeman."

She regarded Jake steadily for another moment. "I'll be back."

The instant she was out of the room he whipped around the desk. He had to be quick, because he had a feeling her next word was going to be good-bye. He had a subjective reason for wanting to go back on the payroll, and the big word around here was objectivity.

He flipped the pages of her appointment book, looking for Number 89. If he could find a date listed for her he could be in the lobby downstairs and meet her as she left. He went ahead two months without seeing her number. There were 88's and 90's, but no 89.

The door of one safe was open. Did he dare? If Mrs. Freeman caught him fooling around in her safe, his head would be chopped off on the spot.

He heard voices, a faint clatter. He closed the door to the observation suite and ran to the open safe. Inside, he saw a triple tier of shallow files. The drawers were labeled with code numbers that meant nothing to him. At one time he had known the number of the comparison-control program, but he couldn't remember it now. Back at the desk, he grabbed the appointment book and turned to the Sunday morning when he and the Swedish girl had met for the first and only time. And there they were—Number 89, the girl, Number 137, Jake—in the fourteenth episode in Program 42-A.

He pulled out the file drawer marked 42-A and found the data card. A double line down the middle separated male and female reactions. They had both been breathing hard that morning, but Jake knew that already. Most of the entries were check marks or numbers. Space was left at the bottom for the subjects' own appraisal. In a graded range from one to ten, ten was circled on both the male and the female sides of the divider.

Commenting on the female's reactions, someone had written: "Top evaluation unsupported by phys. data (7 contrs.—subj. consistently attains 10 or better in auto). Vocalization poor this instance, usually excellent. Extragenital response undifferentiated. Onset of O. sudden warmth, feeling of openness, frightened at first, then accepted sensation. 'Pelvic throbbing, heartbeat merged.' Pronounced sensation of 'unfolding.' Unprecedented, never an O. this degree of intensity. *Duration:* 'Seemed forever' (24 sec.). Felt tears (not visible to obs.). Intense awareness male subj.—cont."

There was more on the back: "*Tactile sensation:* muscular flow male s.'s arms and shoulders. Sense of 'possession.' (?) 'Ideal.' 'Incredible.' Completeness for first time. (NB: Initial episode this subj. combination. Mutual 10-scale evaluation calling for further analysis. Initial m. nervousness, extreme. *Watch for:* increased vocalization with greater familiarity. In what way 'ideal?' Other first episodes 42-A rarely satisfactory. Mutuality imp. See No. 89 hist. for low emotional content with previous partners. *Cultural disparity:* m. sociocultural background U.S. semirural, f. Scand. urban, early sex awareness, exp. in academic context. Male shyness provoking teacher-student role-playing? An interesting session!—M.F.)."

He had heard the door open, but he didn't stop reading until he was finished. Martha Freeman was looking at him, her face streaked with anger.

"What are you—"

"I'm reading your private records!" He shook the card. "Do you have the faintest idea what you've—"

"You took that out of the safe?"

"Yes, I took it out of your God damn safe! You've got a very good filing system. It was easy to find."

"That's not meant to be read by anyone but project personnel."

"I know. Where's my semirural code of ethics? I left it in Maine, Mrs. Freeman! What do you think I am, a windup toy?"

She pulled the card out of his hand. "All right, Jake. Please go now and don't come back."

"I'm not going before I get a name and an address. Read what you wrote on that card. Do you think you can organize a thing like that and then pretend it never happened?"

"Jake, it happened in the laboratory between two numbers!"

"Did we act like numbers? I want to know why she didn't come back!"

He was shouting. Nick DiVito opened the door and looked in.

"It's all right, Nick," she said.

"You know it's not all right," Jake said. "It's a hundred percent lousy, and I want to know what you're going to do about it."

"Nothing. This was stupid of you, Jake. Don't you think it's hard enough on everybody without—"

He dropped into a chair. "I have to find her and talk to her, Mrs. Freeman. I knew when it happened that it wasn't just a very good orgasm. It was the sort of thing that may never happen again. But I thought it must have been nothing much for her, or why shouldn't she want to go on? I didn't come here to break into your safe. I wanted to sneak a look at your appointments to see if she's still on the list. I saw her Saturday night."

"Oh God."

"She said the same thing. Then she turned and ran."

Mrs. Freeman didn't speak for a moment. "Was there any truth in the other story you gave me? About your other partner?"

"I don't know. Some. I've been feeling so— I had sex with the girl for seven or eight weeks, nothing like the time with the first girl, but good, mutual sex. You can look it up. And when she asked me what I thought about her as a person I bombed. She knew what my prick was saying.'"

"Thank God we're finished with 42-A."

"You talked me into it."

"I talked everybody into it," she said in a low voice.

"Then don't you think you ought to take some of the responsibility? I can't spend the rest of my life thinking of her as Number 89. I won't keep after her if she doesn't want to see me. Please. Just tell me her name and where she lives."

"I can't, Jake. It happened in the laboratory! It had nothing to do with people who have names and addresses. That was understood by everybody. By you, by the girl."

"If I write her a letter, will you send it to her?"

"No. You have to put it out of your mind, Jake. I'm sorry."

She really did seem to be sorry. He got up to go.

chapter 17

Martha Freeman could feel the unshed tears, almost as if they were trying to burn their way out through her stomach lining. After Jake Burgess left, several minutes passed before she was breathing normally. She forced herself to read everything she had written on the card. She winced at her final comment. An interesting session, indeed!

They had had nothing but trouble with 42-A. Of course, they had had to do it, to plug up an important hole in the research design. To all their 42-A subjects, nonmarital intercourse was a commonplace of life outside the laboratory. None of these people attached much psychological importance to casual sex. So what had suddenly made it seem so important here? It was not only mysterious, but damned annoying and upsetting. The laboratory seemed to add an extra dimension. During laboratory hours, they were all a little larger than life. If Jake had met his girl on the last night of a cruise and they had parted the next morning, he wouldn't have considered himself a tragic figure, for the common-sense reason that enjoying a ten-intensity orgasm was better than having to spend the night alone.

She had noticed a change in Jake, almost from one session to the next. He was a city man now, more sure of himself, and Martha liked him less. How much did the laboratory have to do with the change? Very little, she told herself firmly, and returned the card to its file. There was no question that they had done the right thing in dropping prostitutes from the program, but with them, at least, Martha had always known where she stood. With the volunteers there were constant twists and surprises. The only really consistent, really satisfactory performer, she was sorry to say, was the machine.

She dug out Number 89's file and read her complete laboratory record. The meeting with Jake had been her only bisexual cycle, and she had dropped out of the pH program some weeks later. This was all history now, and there wasn't a thing Martha could do to alter it. To intervene would only make it messier.

DiVito called her to the phone. It was Prescott again.

"I won't be able to get back after all, Martha. Mrs. Prescott needs support in these early stages, and I think I'd better spend the night."

"I'm so terribly sorry!"

"Well, the people here are friends of mine. She'll get very good care."

His voice sounded normal—crisp, a little detached. There was an instant's heavy silence. The previous night Martha had left the laboratory at two, but Prescott had stayed on. And the night before that, she didn't think he had slept at all.

"This happened once before, a very deep depression, and she fought her way out. Well, I ought to be back by noon tomorrow. There's something I want you to cover for me. A few of the Royce trustees want an informal year-end report so they can think about it before they vote on our application."

"I wouldn't be any good at that!"

"I think you'd very good at it, much better than I'd be. I was going to propose that we go together, and that you do most of the talking. I don't seem to have the patience for that kind of thing anymore. Professor Gevorkian will be there, and I know how it would end up, with both us shouting at each other." There was another brief silence. "It's at Harry Royce's apartment. Will you call him, Martha? Give him a chance to postpone it if he wants to. I could make it tomorrow night, but to be honest—" He waited again. "I'd like to get out of it. I'd irritate everybody. I've had that argument too many times with too many other people, and I get worse and worse at it. It seems to me you keep getting better."

"I'll be busy all afternoon. I won't have time to prepare anything. If it's going to have an effect on the grant—"

"It will have a very important effect. I gather that they felt Hixon put something over on them the last time, with his threat to resign. Of course there's more money involved now. I think perhaps if we'd asked for a smaller sum we would have had a better chance of getting it. Martha, informality is the thing. Don't take any prepared material. They'll ask questions. Just try to answer them without getting too technical. I doubt if anything will come up that you haven't heard a hundred times before—the machine, the prostitutes, 42-A, the small sample, exhibitionism—the usual list. Will you do it?"

"All right," she said doubtfully, "but I don't look forward to it."

"I know you'll handle it well. One other matter."

This pause was longer than the others. Martha could feel his exhaustion.

"Victoria Orr. I'm afraid we have to drop her."

"But she's been doing so well," Martha said, surprised.

"Nevertheless." Again he waited. "I think there's one improvement we ought to make in the screening process. Lawyers have a certain number of peremptory challenges when they're empaneling a jury. I think you would have challenged Victoria at the first interview."

"That's true. But look at the way she turned out. I was obviously wrong."

"No—you saw something I missed. She was in the machine last night. I've been struck by the small part fantasy plays in our machine episodes—it seems to be pure physical sensation and nothing else. But last night I suddenly realized that Victoria was fantasizing. Midway through her arousal phase I became aware that she was looking at me."

"Are you sure?"

"Completely. The machine was between us, so from her perspective there may have been a blurring of identities. Just before orgasm, without moving her head, she opened her eyes all the way. She was instrumented for brain pattern, and that made the slight movement more noticeable. I stepped aside, and her eyes followed me. She was well into orgasm by then."

"But that's incredible! She's been with us long enough to know—"

This was another jolt, coming close on the heels of the one she'd been given by Jake Burgess. In their advance briefings, they had never had to warn their subjects against fantasies involving the laboratory workers. It would call into question the whole basis of the undertaking. All playfulness and coquetry were ruled out by the situation itself.

"Even at peak intensity there was little muscle tension," Prescott went on. "It was deliberate, I'm afraid, a deliberate attempt to break restraint. And I remember an earlier time when she touched Nick. He didn't report it, but when I asked him about it last night he said he'd had the impression she was looking at him then, too."

"I suppose there wouldn't be any point in shifting her into another program?"

"No. It seems to me this is a case for a peremptory challenge. We can't afford to take that kind of chance. In all the laboratory cycles you've observed, how often has a subject looked at you during orgasm?"

"Never."

"No. There seems to be a sudden self-consciousness. I don't know what she was trying to tell me—perhaps merely that she herself wasn't a machine. Or perhaps she was trying to get me to declare that I wasn't another piece of laboratory apparatus. There was a kind of wildness about it. No, that's too extreme. But don't you agree that we'll have to let her go?"

"I'm afraid I do. And there's no point in confronting her with it—she'd simply deny it happened. I'll tell her we have all the EEG's we need for the present. No, better still, I'll send her a note that we've had a mechanical breakdown. She won't be able to question that."

Peter Hixon, executive director of the Royce Foundation in New York, put in a call to his friend Dennis Cullihan, executive director of a much richer foundation on the opposite edge of the continent.

"Me again," he said when he heard the familiar voice.

"Lamb," Dennis answered without enthusiasm.

"How well I know that tone. You're depressed?"

"Not depressed. Popeyed with fury! When I took this job I was led to believe there were going to be certain perquisites. I made a nomination for an Institute guestship. Completely on the up and up, Peter, a gifted lad. And what was I told today? That his academic record is a trifle spotty. It's a coward's trick, striking at the patron through the protégé."

"How maddening," Hixon said, grinning. "When a close friend of yours named Peter Hixon takes over the Institute, I'll guarantee you one guest slot for anybody you care to name."

" 'When'?" Dennis said sourly. "Isn't the word you're grop-
ing for 'if'?"

"The 'if' is implicit. I haven't had a really informative com-
muniqué from you in months."

"Oh, at my end we're in fine shape. Ham Wickham has
always been senile, from the age of twenty-one on, but people
are beginning to notice it at last. Last week at lunch, under the
eyes of Nate Pusey of Harvard, Max Lerner, and Adlai Steven-
son, Jr., he dropped a dollop of béarnaise on his tie, and we sat
there and watched it slide down into his ancient crotch. He's
losing his grip—these guest nominations are a case in point. We
talked about the subject of a replacement again at the last
board, but the only names mentioned collapsed of their own
weight. Ham's agreed to stay at the helm on a week-to-week
basis. So we still have a vacuum, which the chaps tell me
nature abhors. And what's been going on at your end? I'll just
remind you that twelve solid months have passed since you
brought up the subject."

"The fuse is still burning, Den. I hope you can give me a
six-month's extension. Unfortunately, as of now, the name
Chalmers S. Prescott is still almost as unknown as the name
Peter Hixon."

"I have to tell you the simplest things," Dennis said petu-
lantly. "When a story doesn't make the press under its own
steam, leak it, for God's sake."

"Odd that you should suggest that. What do you think I've
been doing, gazing helplessly at the calendar? There are newspapermen in town who know more about the Prescott-Freeman operation than I do myself. But they can't print it."

"I don't see that. It's one of the hottest stories since Sodom
and Gomorrah. Sweet Jesus, those films you sent me—"

"It could be I agree with you. I've been trying to talk
Prescott into calling a press conference, but that's not the way
he does things. There has to be something to peg it on. 'A well-
known Leonia, New Jersey, gynecologist, with backing from
Manhattan Medical College and a well-known foundation, has
been photographing and measuring couples in the act of coition
in a 158th Street laboratory, this correspondent learns on unim-
peachable authority.' That's the way I'd like to see it. But it
can't be done."

"Tell me why not."

"Because everybody's against censorship and in favor of sex education and science and untrammeled inquiry. They can report it in a big way as soon as it's out in the open, but they can't crusade it up out of thin air. The only competition the papers are getting these days is from television, and this doesn't quite meet the specs for an NBC News Special, do you think? There's that reticence about saying the word orgasm over the air. The kiddies might be listening."

"You want a peg."

Dennis considered, while Hixon, five years his junior, waited courteously. Den had a first-rate public relations mind, but he wasn't likely to think of something on the spur of the moment that Hixon, who had been thinking of little else for a year, had overlooked.

"How about getting him arrested?"

"That's a possibility. I'm in touch with a man in the D.A.'s office, but they have the same problem. They need a complaint before they can move. I thought I was getting some action in the Ethics Committee of the AMA, but that evaporated. Oh, it's bound to happen. But I'm feeling the pressure of the clock, like you, so I'm changing the strategy."

"I hope it works, dear lad. Because how long I can keep things from falling apart out here I just don't know."

Hixon gave the phone a quarter-smile. So far, of course, all his old friend had done was sit on his tight ass and complain.

"Shall I tell you the idea, Den, or would you like to be agreeably surprised later?"

"I'd like to be agreeably surprised now."

"You may not see the beauty of it at first, but let it soak in. I'm trying to get him to publish a book, under the imprint of a highly respectable publisher, at a price high enough to discourage anybody from buying it."

"How long does it have to soak? Till I'm marinated? If that's what you consider a brilliant idea—"

"I reason this way. Mention the Kinsey Report to a Bantu and he'll know what you're talking about. I've done a bit of research on the origins of that reputation. For years everybody knew what the Kinsey mob was up to, but it stayed in the profession. Then the book was published by a medical textbook firm, without any fanfare, and it entered history. I have a publisher who's desperate to do it, and he'll part with a sizable chunk of cash. The economics are fantastic. He won't need to lay out a penny for advertising, because he can't seem to be exploiting the sensational material. He can charge twelve bucks a copy, and stick the bookseller with the textbook discount of twenty percent instead of the usual forty-four."

"I've read some of this cat's stuff," Dennis said, still doubtful. "It's like trying to peek into a bathroom through a frosted window."

"Baby, the more opaque it is, the better. The reader's going to think he's right in the laboratory. All the prurience will be in his own mind, so the book will be safe from the vigilantes."

"I know I'm being dense, but how will this change things?"

"Book publication makes it an event. Then the papers can cover it and Prescott'll be asked to appear on Johnny Carson. He'll refuse, of course. But one crack in the dike and we'll be up to our chins in the Atlantic Ocean. The quantitative change becomes the qualitative change."

"That's Marxism, kid. Watch it."

"Silly," Hixon said indulgently. "Everything's already written, if you can call it writing. They'll just have to add an index and a glossary. They can have books in the stores in five months' time."

"What has he found out, Peter—anything?"

"Put it this way. His findings aren't as sensational as his methods. He ran some marvelous tests of contraceptive devices, diaphragms and so on. Then the Pill came along, and now nobody cares which diaphragm and which brand of jelly gives protection. To be fair, though, he's probably said the definitive word on the female orgasm. As you undoubtedly know, nine-tenths of all book buyers are women."

"So when does this hue and cry begin, lamb? You think six months?"

"Seven, to be safe. The trouble is, Prescott doesn't want to do it."

"Why not?"

"He doesn't think he has enough supporting data. But without money to buy film and pay his cast of characters, how's he going to get the supporting data? Dig? His application is in at the Royce for a renewal. My board might spring for a modest five figures, like another seventy-five thou. I did the Royces a favor in their proxy fight. I voted the Foundation shares for the management, which was perfectly legal and all, but still it was nice of me, don't you think? A few members of the board want to drop Prescott before the big bang, but seventy-five I think I could squeeze. So I've told him to stop thinking small, it's time to swing. I talked him into putting in for four hundred thousand. Don't worry, they'll turn it down."

"And then he'll have to take the book offer?"

"Then he'll have to take the book offer. Either that or go out of business, and my boy is definitely not a quitter. Some of the trustees are staging a little auto-da-fé tonight, with Prescott on the griddle. I've decided not to be there. Let him handle his own defense. I know the man—he'll scare them out of their socks. Somebody's going to point out that shepherds have been known to have carnal knowledge of their sheep, and does he have any plans for testing the intensity of that kind of orgasm? It's a nice scientific question. And not only that. *Does the sheep respond?*"

Dennis was interested. "Does it?"

"How would I know? I haven't had connection with a sheep in years. The point I'm making—Prescott won't think there's anything wrong with bringing a sheep and a shepherd into the laboratory to find out. But will the Royce board agree with him? I think not."

"One comment, Peter. Isn't all this a little baroque? And aren't you being a touch too solemn about it? You could be losing some of your early devil-may-care sparkle. Which is good!" he added. "It takes care of my last reservation. Whoever heard of an Institute director who wasn't a bit of a windbag? I'll be glad to go out on a limb for you when the time comes, doll, but do let it be soon."

Hixon hung up smiling. Old Den was beginning to show his years.

Everybody Professor Tom Gevorkian talked to about Dr. Prescott's sex laboratory was either militantly for it or militantly against it, and the arguments on both sides were as hard to take hold of as drops of free mercury. Gradually he came to believe that the laboratory was merely an aspect of a much larger problem, and few of the people who were discussing it so warmly really knew what subject they were talking about.

With the help of a poker-faced young woman at the Academy of Medicine library, he compiled a bibliography of Prescott's writings. He ignored the early papers dealing with miscarriages in rats, but he read everything else, not without occasionally breaking out in a cold sweat. Even the briefest paper had the full scholarly apparatus, dozens of footnotes and a lengthy bibliography. Gevorkian, a footnote-and-bibliography man in his own field, began hunting down references and was soon thigh-deep in a study of sexual physiology. At first, he had to struggle along with the help of a medical dictionary, but before long he had enough of the language so he could have ordered a meal in it.

He was told that Hixon, at the Foundation, planned to lay a new application from Prescott before the next board meeting, and this time Gevorkian didn't want to walk in cold, to face Hixon's bar graphs and other audiovisual material. He began organizing his notes. Two weeks before the board meeting, Harry Royce invited him to his apartment to meet Dr. Prescott and Mrs. Freeman and hear what they had to say. Gevorkian, of course, would be asking most of the questions, and the thought crossed his mind of picking up a convenient virus that day and letting the others decide the matter without him. Did it make that much difference where Prescott got his money? Lecturing on Christopher Marlowe, Gevorkian looked out over the bent heads of the Barnard undergraduates who were writing industriously below him, not a one of them, probably, with a College Board score of less than 700 in anything. He had been giving a variation of this same lecture for fifteen years, and what did Christopher Marlowe really have to say to these high-scoring girls? They looked up from their notebooks to see why his voice had stopped, and for an instant he thought one of them was about to say, "Never mind about Dr. *Faustus*, Professor. What about Dr. Prescott? What about the multiorgasm?"

That night he was sorting his notes and the Thermofax copies of Prescott's more outrageous papers when his daughter Paula came into his study.

"We're off to the New Yorker. It's *A Night at the Opera* and *Monkey Business*. Don't you wish you were coming?"

She was a sophomore at Radcliffe. There was another daughter, married to a physicist who worked for NASA and wasn't allowed to say what he was doing, which made him seem somewhat laconic. Paula was still interested in poetry, a fan of Christopher Marlowe as well as the Marx Brothers. She was dressed for a date, but looked as sloppy as when she stayed home. She was a gregarious and a quick-witted girl. She wore her hair parted in the middle and brought down across her face, leaving only a triangle of forehead showing. Gevorkian was proud of himself for never telling her he considered this the least attractive way a girl could wear her hair.

He called a greeting to the boy in the hall. The boy answered respectfully, "Sir."

"Are you still getting up on sex?" Paula said, seeing the Thermofax sheets.

"It's an inexhaustible subject."

"I just read that the Italians call it the affair of thirty seconds."

"Referring specifically to orgasm," Gevorkian said. "I'm in a position to state that it's been known to last as long as a minute."

She burst out laughing. "Dad, you're a wonderful argument for the interdisciplinary approach."

"I'm about to contend that sex is actually not an affair of thirty seconds, but of a lifetime. Though I'm not sure I really believe it myself."

"That's why you're wearing a tie. This is the night you have to—"

Gevorkian nodded. "And they're not like me. They're sure of their position. I have a feeling they're going to wipe up the floor with me."

Paula turned to the boy. "Get a beer, Sid. Be with you in a minute."

"It breaks in twenty minutes if you don't want to get in in the middle."

He faded away. Paula sat down in the swivel chair used by Gevorkian's doctoral candidates and stretched her legs, trying to keep a straight face. She was wearing skinny Levis, and was barefoot. Naturally her feet weren't exactly clean. She swiveled the chair through a short arc, which she had been doing since the age of two.

"I apologize for grinning, Dad. I know there's a lot of money involved, and that makes it serious. But don't you wish the Marx Brothers were here right now? Groucho could be Dr. Quackenbush, the famous sexologist. Harpo could work that machine I've been hearing about. And how about Margaret Dumont? A society lady who needed a blood test and got in the wrong laboratory. All those solemn fornicating couples—"

"I have no evidence that they're all solemn."

"Dad, of course they're solemn. They're the Cotton Mathers of this generation."

Gevorkian laughed. "Somehow I don't think Cotton Mather would—"

"But if he did, he'd do it with *fervor*, is all I mean. Why not stop worrying and let them have the money? It's better than all those grants you've been making for teaching machines and so on. At least this shakes people up."

"It's shaken me. Paula, what about your sex education, was it adequate? A serious answer."

She examined her toes. She didn't seem embarrassed, but since going to Radcliffe she hadn't believed in showing her feelings.

"I know girls whose parents told them about the thirty-seven different positions at the age of ten, and they're the coldest fish in college. I don't mean they don't sleep with people—they do. One of them got pregnant, and I know her mother was astonished. I don't think it matters much what parents say, it's what they're like. I remember when you and Mother were leaving the *Joy of Copulation* around where we were sure to stumble over it—so very subtle. I forget what the real title was. That's what Mary and I called it. Well, I guess that was as good a way as any. The trouble with that kind of book—and the same thing goes for that piece I read by Dr. Prescott—it makes sex sound so easy. Two people are involved, they always skip that. One person has problems enough. Put two people together, and it all gets hellishly complicated. And to get back to Cotton Mather. Don't get the wrong idea, because I could be speaking theoretically. Making love is fun! If they measure what happens when people make love without having fun, does it really mean anything?"

"That's one of the things I've been wondering about."

She hesitated. "Are you interested in whether Sid and I—"

"No! What do you take me for?"

"Don't sound so alarmed." She stood up. "If you aren't sure that what they're doing is a good thing, why not just abstain again?"

"I'm the intellectual on the board, in quotes. I'm not supposed to abstain."

She wished him good luck, kissed him on the forehead, and went off to the world of Groucho, Harpo, Chico, and Zeppo in their early middle age, a world with its own extraordinary rules.

chapter 18

Harry Royce's father was getting harder to argue with each year. Change was one of the laws of survival in the department store business, and he kept himself fairly flexible in business matters. But there was one major change that he hadn't taken in at all. In the years when his attitudes were forming, Internal Revenue people had come into his office with a slight cringe, asking to be bullied. There was a new generation now. These boys had tasted power. The bigger the taxpayer, the more deference they expected him to show. In tax theory, the Royce Foundation and the Royce stores were different entities, in spite of the fact that the Foundation portfolio was loaded with Royce common, a gift from the senior Royce, and a majority of the board had some kind of Royce connection. Royce Stores had just fought off an attack by one of the big discounters, and the shares held by the Foundation had provided the margin of victory. In Harry's opinion, now was the time for his father to lie low. Not being a trustee of the Foundation himself, his father had nothing to say about how the board spent its money. He had heard about Dr. Prescott's sex machine, however, and he had determined that no one who was capable of inventing such a thing should be given another penny of Royce money. As the man with the law degree in the family, Harry advised him to stay out of it, unless he wanted some serious tax trouble. His father couldn't see it. Didn't he have a right to express an opinion?

With some difficulty, Harry dissuaded his father from attending the premeeting discussion that had been suggested by Hixon. Prescott had put in for $400,000, and Hixon was recommending the full amount. This was the first sign that Hixon might be losing his touch. Several of the board members had pet projects of their own that would have to be eliminated or pared down if the Prescott grant went through.

Harry, awaiting the last of his guests, opened the door to a tall dark-haired woman in a black dress.

"Mr. Royce?"

She was a surprise. "You must be Mrs. Freeman. I was expecting someone a little more—" He broke off and laughed. "I don't know what I was expecting."

She must have been used to this reaction; it seemed to amuse her. He introduced her to the others—Wharton, Professor Gevorkian, Frank Brennan. He really couldn't see this woman presiding over the mechanical revels in the Prescott laboratory. Gevorkian was drinking gloomily, convinced that the evening would be a disaster, but he cheered up immediately, as he always did in the presence of a good-looking woman. Wharton, the board chairman, had been complaining about being kept in town to meet Dr. Prescott, only to have a number-two spokesman foisted on them at the last minute. His look of surprise was a duplicate of Harry's. Brennan, a Chemical New York vice-president, not only believed in being cautious—all bankers believe that—he believed in looking cautious. He gave Martha's hand a quick shake and sent an appalled look at Harry. Surely it couldn't be true? Were they going to be discussing the female orgasm with this woman?

"Are you related to someone named Joe Freeman?" Harry asked, making her a Scotch and water.

"He's my ex-husband. Do you know him?"

"Ex-husband would explain it. He was a year ahead of me at law school. He called the other day to find out if we're going to give you people some more money. He didn't seem to think it was a good idea."

"Well, that's Joe. He hopes to be President someday. There've been worse Presidents, Warren G. Harding, for one."

Harry handed her the drink. "Wouldn't a divorce rule him out?"

"He's looking ahead twenty years. Divorced voters may be in the majority in a few key states. He's been trying to get me to go back to my maiden name, but in my work it's an advantage to be a Mrs. The question is, would it hurt him with the voters if his opponent made an issue of the fact that his ex-wife was mixed up in sex research? I don't see why it should, but Joe feels that it's hard enough to win an election even with everything going for you. What did he say about us?"

Harry was more and more taken with her. If this was what sex research did for a woman, he was in favor of it.

"Just that you've been leading a charmed life and it can't last. Nothing definite."

"Joe always did go in for ominous hints. Technically, I'm sure we could be put in jail for twenty years for what we've been doing, but it's too ridiculous to worry about. Of course, if the police do decide to stage a raid, I'm sure Joe will be right in the front car with a fire axe."

They sat down, and Harry gave her time to sample her drink. Then he said, "I think we're complete, so let's get started. Nate Shapiro's going to drop in later but we won't wait for him. This is purely for informational purposes, Mrs. Freeman. No vote is going to be taken. I know we all have questions, but do you want to say anything to begin with?"

"I suppose I should," she said. "I wish Dr. Prescott could be here, because you understand that I'm only a psychologist, not a doctor. There may be questions I can't answer, but I can see to it that you get the answers before your board meeting. You've given us two grants so far, one of fifteen thousand and one of one hundred fifteen thousand dollars, and I think the main question you ought to be asking is whether we've given you your money's worth. Along with our formal application we submitted copies of all of our publications during the year, as well as the manuscripts of papers that have been accepted but haven't yet appeared. We don't really expect you to read them. They're written for a special audience. Many of our observations may seem minor to you, even petty, but they're points the medical profession has been arguing about for years. To me, as less of a specialist than most, our most important finding is that people exist, quite ordinary people, who are willing to participate in a study of sexual physiology under laboratory conditions. We've used a total of two hundred and eighteen women and one hundred and sixty-five men. At the beginning, we didn't really believe it could be done. It indicates to us that many other accepted truths about human sexuality may be equally fallacious."

Gevorkian started to speak. "No, go ahead, Mrs. Freeman, excuse me."

"That's really all I have to say. We've built up a laboratory population of responsive men and women. We've worked out the necessary techniques. We ran out of money a few months ago, and we've been financing the research program with income from the clinic, but even so we've had to cut back substantially. Some of our best material hasn't been recorded because of the cost of processing color film—seven and a half cents a foot! We'd like to take advantage of the present favorable climate to double our research population. We've given examples in our application of the most pressing problems. We want to hire a second photographer, but otherwise continue with our present staff and facilities. We're in a position where there's literally nothing about the human sex act that we won't be able to discover."

"Except its meaning," Gevorkian put in.

She smiled at him. "I'm willing to leave that to you, Professor. I'm not trying to deny that sex has its psychological aspects. How could I? They're self-evident. Sex accompanied by love and affection and admiration is infinitely more satisfying than sex between a prostitute and her client, but who doesn't know that? Many of our married couples, perhaps a majority, are in love with each other. They tell us so and they have lived together happily for years. There's a very subtle difference about the way they perform sex that persuades me— well, that these are the behavior patterns of a loving couple. But the difference can't be measured by instruments. The same bodily reactions take place in response to stimulation, no matter what kind—masturbation by hand or machine, breast manipulation, intercourse with a lover or a stranger. They may feel quite different, subjectively, but physiologically there's no difference at all."

"I don't believe that for a minute."

"And yet it's true. I can show you the records."

Gevorkian leaned forward. "But you don't have any record of the first time your happily married couple made love. Did any man and woman who had sex the instant they met, like dogs, ever end up happily married? No, it's impossible. You have the records of innumerable copulating couples, some married, some strangers to each other—copulating in the laboratory! I put it to you, Mrs. Freeman. Perhaps the responses are similar because the stimulation took place in the laboratory. Perhaps the laboratory setting even provided part of the stimulation?"

"Well—perhaps. Let's say that we have certain investigative

impressions, based on what we ourselves have seen and recorded. Is that any better?"

"It's much better, and I wish you would drop a footnote to that effect every time you use phrases like 'human sexual response,' 'the sexual reaction cycle in the human female.' To me that implies something that happens to everybody, whereas, in point of fact, it happened to a few hundred specific males and females you inveigled into your laboratory with an offer to let them take part in the twentieth-century sexual revolution. People like to be revolutionaries, and this is the easiest revolution of all." He waved his hand. "Inveigled—I must stop using these charged expressions. But do you deny that you're generalizing from the reactions of a very limited and a very specialized laboratory population?"

"Of course not. We repeat it every chance we get. Give us money to expand, and our population will be less limited. Still, data on several hundred responding individuals has more scientific validity than data on one. Would you agree to that?"

"I deny it strenuously, on the strength of my own experience." He drank. "My wife died six years ago, in the twenty-seventh year of our marriage. Physiologically—not psychologically, now, but physiologically—sex in the twenty-seventh year was totally different from the romantic blunderings of the first week or so. You're flying in the face of common sense, Mrs. Freeman. When you measure reactions in the laboratory, you shouldn't be surprised to get laboratory reactions."

Mrs. Freeman had obviously heard this argument before. "I think we're talking about two different things, aren't we?"

Gevorkian drank again, swallowing angrily as though Harry was forcing him to drink brandy against his will. "I abstained on our last vote. I didn't think you could succeed in attracting any significant number of volunteers. And where they come from, how they manage to perform those feats under conditions that would reduce an ordinary person to jelly—it's a mystery to me, and I don't really think I care to have it explained. One thing about your project, no one can hear about it and stay indifferent. You've made us think about our sexual attitudes, and that may be an excellent thing. There's a theory that everybody thinks about sex much of the time, but I don't think it's true. I've been thinking about it steadily for a few weeks, and it's been hard work. I've been reading and questioning people and making notes, and I may as well tell you that I've almost made up my mind to vote against you."

"I'm sorry to hear that."

"But I'm still not sure! You might convince me yet. I have a dozen matters to bring up. I'd just like to throw them at you and see how they sound."

"Go ahead," Martha said. "If Mr. Royce will give me some more Scotch."

Harry, pouring, had his back to the room when Gevorkian said, "For example, I don't find a kiss mentioned in your material."

"A kiss?" Mrs. Freeman said, surprised.

"Every other stage in the sexual progression is described in exhaustive detail. Nothing is beneath notice. But where is the kiss? To me, and I think to most people—I admit I have no data—the sexual kiss is the most important part of the affair. Because it's so intensely personal, so hard to fake."

She took the glass Harry handed her without looking at him. She seemed to be taking Gevorkian more seriously.

"We had to start somewhere."

"But the kiss is more than a beginning. In the most-favored coital position, it continues throughout, changing in ways that should interest sexual scientists."

She drank thoughtfully. "Is this a serious difficulty, Professor?"

"I think so. I might even stop right there. When a male chimp nips and nuzzles and licks a female, it may not matter which particular chimp he's nipping and nuzzling and licking. They aren't monogamous, are they—chimpanzees? It's not my field. But we all know that a human male kisses a human female differently if he loves her. And prostitutes have a rule against kissing their customers at all. So when I read a description of the sex act that contains no reference to a kiss, it seems to me that you're telling me about the kind of sex you were observing in your early days, with our first fifteen thousand dollars, when your subjects were prostitutes."

"We haven't included any prostitute material in our published data."

"Was it so different from what you've been getting lately?"

"By and large, no. On the recording drums, to a pH meter, to a polygraph, the prostitutes and the PTA presidents are twins. And that is why, when a given stimulus is applied and we're able to record a definite physical reaction again and again and again, there's a temptation to regard it as the invariable response of the human female."

"In those circumstances, Mrs. Freeman! In those abnormal circumstances. I understand that some of your laboratory subjects sought you out first in your role as clinicians, because they were having some sexual trouble. Then you exclude the unproficient ones who can't produce orgasms at will, knocking out, at Kinsey's guess, over half the female population. You also try to exclude exhibitionists. And then the final elimination—anyone who is repelled by laboratory sex. The point I'm trying to make for the second time is that your little group is far from the random sample of the Gallup poll."

"We'd love to use the Gallup sample. Unfortunately, it isn't available to us."

"So you're left with a small, statistically insignificant group. Do these people truly represent humanity, or merely others like themselves? You report three kinds of female orgasms—induced by a machine, or manually by the subject herself, or by a male partner in coitus. And the intensity of these orgasms, the physical intensity as recorded on laboratory instruments, follows a sharply declining curve. On top is the machine. At the bottom is intercourse, the main sexual event since the beginning of time. Mrs. Freeman, this is an amazing contention!"

"I see nothing amazing about it," she said. "The machine never loses its erection. It's totally under the respondent's control, as no human partner can possibly be."

"Exactly! But have you considered the possibility that your methods of selection assure you a supply of a certain kind of female, who—in the cold, efficient, objective laboratory atmosphere—is certain to find her most intense satisfaction in the mechanical thrusting of a plastic apparatus?"

"Satisfaction? You won't find the word in any of our papers. The subject's own psychological evaluation seldom correlates with physical intensity."

"I never looked at a medical journal until three weeks ago, but I've known that for years. Sex can be a form of exercise or a form of therapy. You can use it to stop a silly woman from talking. You can have sex because you're afraid of *not* having it, or because the situation calls for a friendly gesture. You can arrive at orgasm in hatred, in contempt for the woman you're with and deep mistrust of yourself. There's considerable masturbation among lunatics. There are uphill orgasms and downhill orgasms. You can have a machine orgasm with a human partner, if you consider either your partner or yourself a machine."

"But in the end, you know, Professor, a contraction is a contraction."

"Are you sure? Perhaps an observed contraction is different from an unobserved contraction. I took one science course long ago, as part of the B.A. requirement, and the single thing I remember was a warning: when you observe something, watch out, you may be changing it by the act of observation. I think man may be the only animal capable of self-awareness. This isn't sex you're describing. It's observed sex."

"I know, I know. And if we ever forget it, I hope you'll keep reminding us. I don't mean that sarcastically."

Harry answered the buzzer and admitted Nate Shapiro, another trustee. He apologized for being late and asked Mrs. Freeman to continue.

"We're jumping around," she said. "We've just taken care of the machine orgasm."

"As I say," Shapiro said, "I'm sorry I'm late. And what is a machine orgasm?"

"I'll tell you afterward, Nate," Gevorkian said. "I want Mrs. Freeman to clarify something for me." He turned back to her. "You say certain things invariably happen, muscle tension as an example. And yet a close reading of your material reveals that this isn't invariable at all. Sometimes it works one way, sometimes another. It varies in different individuals, and in the same individuals at different times. Is it unconscious and automatic, a result of stimulation, or is it done deliberately, to heighten enjoyment? When one subject blushes and another doesn't, and when the blushing subject sometimes fails to blush, is it correct to state, as you do repeatedly, that the sex blush is part of the human reaction pattern?"

Wharton rumbled, "Tommy, you must have more important points to make than that."

Gevorkian pulled at his brandy. "Then skip that one, Mrs. Freeman. I've been trying to determine why it is that people who approve of sex and disapprove of censorship, who have nothing against nudism, who take the Bill of Rights seriously —why so many of these people find the idea of a sex laboratory so distasteful. I think it's because human beings are used in a role we usually associate with animals. White mice, hamsters, rhesus monkeys—those poor laboratory beasts are constantly being mistreated and driven mad and put to death, in the interest of finding out about disease or anxiety states or the learning process. Substituting people for animals suggests the Nazi doctors and their experiments in the concentration camps."

"Now really, Professor. Our subjects are all volunteers. They are under no compulsion. We don't mistreat them or drive them mad."

"I don't want to exaggerate this. But doesn't it debase a human being to consider him as nothing but a biological package of organs and systems, without thought, without emotion, without a sense of personal dignity—without all the things that make him human?"

"We're all of us animals biologically."

"But there's one basic difference. Our behavior is influenced by choice and judgment. We have sexual options. A male salmon will fertilize the eggs of a female salmon, and what we know as love won't enter into it at all. But we've outgrown that stage."

Shapiro caught Harry's eye and shrugged helplessly. Brennan was on the extreme front edge of his chair, his elbows on his knees, occasionally opening his mouth as though he wanted to get in on the exchange. Gevorkian was beginning to show his brandy. Both he and Mrs. Freeman appeared to be listening to each other, which was rare in this kind of argument. Mrs. Freeman was maintaining that in a report of physiological findings to a medical audience there was no reason to keep repeating that there was more to sex than physiology. But physiology happened to be their subject. Of course, a marriage was made up of many more things than sex play. In her own, she and her husband had been compatible sexually, but incompatible in every other way. In many marriages it was the other way around, and those were the ones she and Dr. Prescott dealt with in their clinic. Some couples, in fact, had joined the laboratory program to increase their fund of knowledge, and their marriages were now more stable as a result.

"Perhaps every married couple should spend some time in the laboratory?" Gevorkian suggested.

"We don't go that far. I think the vast majority of people will continue to want to make love in privacy."

Frank Brennan was stuttering. He had downed three brandies in succession, and the rising fumes were bringing a question with them.

"Morality. Do you think s-s-science shouldn't be judged by ordinary moral standards?"

Gevorkian put in, "And I'm sure you've been asked that before."

"Regularly," Mrs. Freeman said. "I don't see anything moral about ignorance, or about judgments based on ignorance. This is an organized scientific effort to discover the truth about an important human function. Neither more nor less. What on earth is immoral about it?"

"But this is sex, Mrs. Freeman," Gevorkian said. "Excuse me, Frank. Did you want to say—"

Brennan shook his head, and Gevorkian continued, "If you were trying to discover the truth about the digestive process, you could forget morality. Moralists have never said much about the stomach except to include gluttony as one of the seven sins. But sex has always been bound up with moral questions. It's been controlled by religion and social philosophy. Now you scientists have taken it over. You say that your only interest is the facts, the kind of facts an electrode can discover. But you can't claim that the facts you've been publishing in the medical journals have no moral implications. You've induced hundreds of people to take part in laboratory sex, on your terms. That in itself is a fact, and it teaches a moral lesson —that sex can be separated from questions of morality altogether."

"It can be. We don't say it should be. The question simply doesn't arise. In every period of history I'm sure there were people who considered sex as sex, neither good nor bad, moral or immoral."

"But they didn't have the prestige of science behind them. That's the difference. In spite of all your disclaimers, you encourage a mechanical attitude toward sex. You isolate the orgasm from the rest of sex, sex from the rest of life. Your measurements are physical measurements. Good sex, to you, means intense and frequent sex. I think you're tragically wrong. Sex is more than a physical twitch. It's a symbol of our membership in the human race."

"A wonderful thing, and it somehow succeeds in making millions of people unhappy."

"Is that what's doing it? Mrs. Freeman, people become more sophisticated about lovemaking and better at it year by year. Meanwhile, the divorce rate rises. I think it's possible to have several intense orgasms a day and still be unhappy."

"What are you proposing, Professor? That the laboratory be padlocked?"

Gevorkian went for more brandy. "Sit still, Harry, I'll get it. Mrs. Freeman, it's that question that kept my mind from working for many months. Isn't sexual physiology a legitimate research subject? Do we want to let the ancient hesitations stand in the way of learning the true facts about a crucial human concern? No, we'd better crowd in all we can before those five-four Supreme Court decisions start going the other way. I think now I fooled myself with that argument. The question to ask is: what do you people want to find out, and how do you propose to do it? If after a certain length of time it can be shown that your results are meaningless—"

"Meaningless!"

"Nine-tenths of your discoveries, in my opinion, are completely without meaning, and the other tenth are wrong or misleading. I've been spending far too much time at the Academy of Medicine and I find to my surprise that a great deal of information on the subject was knocking about before you appeared on the scene. Kinsey's female report had a dense hundred-page section dealing with nothing but physiology— and he couldn't figure out how to handle the kiss, either. If any female is in doubt as to whether she's getting a complete experience, she can buy the Pocket Book edition and look it up. Most of the reactions you and Dr. Prescott report are common knowledge. Almost anyone can fornicate. It's nothing to boast about, even when it's done well."

She gave a quick laugh. "Professor Gevorkian, if you ever decide to leave Barnard, we can use you in the clinic. What you say may be true in a primitive society, though even savages aren't without inhibitions. An aborigine's sex life is riddled with meaningless taboos. But for a twentieth-century woman, after twenty centuries of antiphysical propaganda, I don't think things are that simple."

Gevorkian revolved the brandy in his glass and took a long sip before continuing. Everyone was drinking too much. They were talking, in effect, about scientific masturbation, but Mrs. Freeman's good looks and matter-of-fact manner had somehow defused the subject. Wharton's color had deepened. Brennan was still near the edge of his chair, but no longer trying to get in on the discussion.

Harry was deep in thought. Four hundred thousand was far too much, but perhaps the Royce should give them something. This was obviously not a sleazy operation. His father would raise hell, but the time was rapidly approaching when Harry had to begin making his own decisions. He ought to decide the issue on its merits, however, and not by its bearing on his complex relationship with his father. He had lost the thread of Gevorkian's argument, but Mrs. Freeman, outnumbered by the men around her, seemed to be holding up very well.

"You keep talking about the similarities between male and female reactions," Gevorkian said, waving his glass. "If the woman's nipples engorge, so do the man's. The clitoris is an analogue of the penis, and so on. But my God, Mrs. Freeman, sex is a viable thing only because of the *differences* between men and women. I don't mean simply that one is concave and the other convex. I've been trying to avoid the word love. I know how much it annoys you people. But when you love a woman, she's not only different from you, with a vagina as opposed to a penis, but different from all other women! Don't you see what I mean? You tell us you don't mention love because it isn't your specialty. Actually, you're propagandizing against it."

"But you're mistaken."

"Oh, you make disclaimers. You assure us that you and your colleagues are aware that there's more to love than sex, more to sex than the orgasm. But from what you've published so far no one could know it! When you talk about psychology, which is seldom, it turns out that you really mean those psychological factors which make orgasm impossible. Orgasm is the touchstone. Well, I shouldn't single you out. Your laboratory isn't the only place in the modern world where numbers have replaced names, where a machine is substituted for the living person, where action is separated from feeling and no act has any consequences. But somehow your modernity is a little more vivid! To me your copulation machine stands as a symbol of the other evil things that are being done to us in the name of science. It's too perfect! How skillfully it gives a woman her orgasmic relief, carrying her out of the frustrations and compromises of ordinary life into a condition of perpetual spasm—"

Wharton moved abruptly, spilling some of his drink. "Tommy, what are you saying, that women shouldn't have orgasms?"

"Of course I'm not saying that! Women are entitled to them, just as men are. But I don't think it's the sacred duty of every married couple to produce a mutual orgasm every time they make love. That seems to be the message we're getting from the sex people. When was the female orgasm discovered, Mrs. Freeman?"

"Discovered!"

"Did the Greeks have it?"

"I don't know! I have no reason to suppose it hasn't always existed. Certainly it exists now. We've recorded enough of them to be sure of that."

"Mrs. Freeman, isn't there a possibility that this laboratory orgasm, produced at will by the turning of switches and the manipulation of dials, is something new, something quite different from the female orgasm that has always existed? You put your subjects into a situation where a certain response is expected. They provide that response. If they fail, you don't invite them back. I think that's the biggest flaw in your findings—that your subjects are all experts. They have to be experts to stay in your programs. Your work may be of some value to gynecologists—if I pronounce the word correctly —and to professionals with a background in the subject. But you know it won't stop there. You can't expect an ordinary reader to keep reminding himself that your facts may be distorted by the way they were recorded. The cult of the orgasm was scarey enough before. I hate to think what it will be when your revelations are absorbed into the popular culture. I've been looking at marriage manuals—they're nothing more than treatises on how to achieve the female orgasm. In next year's editions, the orgasm will be scrapped and replaced by the multiple orgasm. You contend, I believe, that a woman ought to be able to go on having orgasms until she crumples from fatigue."

"Professor, be reasonable. All we've done with the multiple orgasm is bring it out in the open where it can be looked at realistically."

"I don't think multiple orgasms ought to be brought out in the open! That's the wrong place for them!" He hurled more brandy down his throat. "I think it's better for lovers to work out their sexual techniques in privacy, even if they achieve only fifty percent of their possibilities. They can still believe that the experience has been unique and special. That's the way love has always been, if we can believe the poets."

"And what if they achieve only ten percent? Or five? When do you think they should ask for help?"

"If they're content with what they have, never. Not everybody can run a three-fifty mile. It's you people and your writings that have made them dissatisfied. I think there were multiple orgasms before sexology became a profession, but only as a part of a larger erotic experience. The orgasms you describe probably also took place—but during masturbation. The moment another person was included, predictability vanished. True lovemaking was an exchange of sensations between human beings. There was playfulness in it. And then the new experts persuaded women that if they missed orgasm their sex was incomplete. It was antisex, not sex at all. Somebody thought up the terrible word 'frigidity.' Nobody worried about frigidity until the disease was named. Now, if a woman doesn't start pulsing on schedule, it shows lack of skill or emotional disturbance. Some people blame Dr. Kinsey, but he was only a tabulator. An orgasm is easy to count. Women look at his medians, and exactly half of them discover they're achieving subnormally."

"Kinsey never claimed—"

"No, he made as many disclaimers as you do. Nevertheless, he went on counting orgasms till the day he died."

"Have you ever known an orgasmic woman who wanted to go back to a preorgasmic condition?"

She signaled Harry with her empty glass, giving him an extraordinary look, both gay and extremely personal. Somehow it made them co-conspirators. It took him a moment to move to take her glass.

"That's a sly remark," Gevorkian was saying. "As a matter of fact I haven't discussed the matter with a great many women. There's a huge difference between no orgasms and an orgasm every time. I accuse you of tearing the orgasm out of its natural context so you can examine and define it. In the process you've given it the sort of radiance the old painters put around the heads of saints. In your world the orgasm becomes not merely the measure of sex, but its meaning. Those heroines of yours, with the indefatigable machine—"

"The machine isn't all that sinister! It's only a laboratory device, to make certain kinds of observations possible."

"No, no," Gevorkian insisted. "It's the leading man in your drama. It's a metaphor for the male you hope to have us become—"

The argument continued until Wharton had to leave to catch a train. The meeting ended soon afterward. At the regular board meeting two weeks later, Hixon moved a grant of $400,000 for the Prescott-Freeman project. The vote was five to one against, with Nate Shapiro casting the single favorable ballot. Harry moved the sum of $75,000. Harry himself, Frank Brennan, and Shapiro voted in favor. There were three negative votes. Wharton, in the chair, broke the tie by unexpectedly voting nay. The sum of $35,000 was then moved, and it was carried with five in favor and only Gevorkian opposed.

chapter 19

The society in Victoria's office was divided into three sexual groups: the overprivileged, the underprivileged, and the in-betweeners, who had sex sometimes, but not on any regular basis. After several months at the laboratory, Victoria began to find her old friends' conversation somewhat repetitious. They only had one subject. Victoria had to keep quiet, unfortunately; she could have told them things that would have chilled their blood.

She was still having dates, but was no longer desperate about it. The men were pretty useless, as always. If she pretended to react, and she didn't bother every time, they took it as a tribute to their sexual prowess, the jerks. During coffee break one day, the girl at the next machine told her about a matchmaking computer. All you had to do was fill out a questionnaire, send in ten dollars, and wait for the phone to ring. It wasn't exactly science, perhaps, but it was better than pure chance. Of course you had to be completely honest. If you liked soul-rock, the machine went out of its way not to pair you with somebody who liked opera. The idea appealed to Victoria, for some crazy reason.

One of the things the computer wanted to know was whether she considered her sexual attitudes old-fashioned, moderate, or contemporary. She finally checked contemporary; being an active worker in the Prescott-Freeman laboratory was probably as contemporary as anybody could get.

A week or so later, the computer supplied her first date. Like Victoria, he was a lapsed Catholic, he hadn't finished college, he liked Hollywood movies better than foreign movies and dancing better than talking. Unluckily, he was one of the most unprepossessing-looking young men she had seen in a long time. He couldn't believe his luck in being assigned a girl as pretty as Victoria, out of the 4,000,000 women in greater New York. He took her to a dance hall that hoped to convince customers on 7-Up they had actually eaten hallucinating mush-

234

rooms. The music was amplified to the pain threshold, and perhaps a little beyond. Underclad girls danced all by themselves in cages. Victoria's date was agile enough, and the psychedelic lighting helped with his complexion problem. She began to catch some of the synthetic excitement. Apparently he did, too. He came at her the instant they were shut up in the front seat of his car. She began to fool with an idea; he was so damn homely that he would have to do exactly what she suggested, for as long as she chose. But how much did he know? This part of town was heavily policed, but she decided to try a few simple moves. She soon found herself in a familiar location, halfway along the curve. In the early stages, any man, even this one, was an improvement on the machine, which lacked lips and fingers and moved in a single plane. Later on, of course, he couldn't compare, but he was so eager to show off his knowledge of bodily mechanics that she thought he might shape up into a pretty good approximation.

Then she pushed him away. She had always insisted on a certain minimum, and he was a long way below it. And she already had one mechanical connection, she didn't need another. He had enough experience with rebuffs to know that the computer had goofed. He looked so let-down that she relented and slid over to take his arm when he started the motor. Another good thing about the machine, she never had to worry about hurting its feelings.

Arriving on her block, she saw a light on in her apartment, which meant that Anne must be home. On an impulse, when her escort moved to take her in his arms to say good night, she asked him up for coffee. Anne had made fudge, which she was nibbling in solitude, watching a dim television movie. Coffee was a matter of minutes. Victoria kept yawning and excused herself after a short stretch of lukewarm conversation. She was asleep before he left.

Next morning Anne brought her breakfast in bed and said nervously, "Vicky, you're going to murder me—"

"Don't be ridiculous. He came out of the computer, and they don't know as much as they think they do. How did it go?"

"Well, I don't suppose he makes love too often."

Victoria congratulated herself. By being generous she had escaped the frustrating climb up the exposed North Face of the big curve, which would have ended with Victoria dangling helplessly from pitons left in the rock from earlier attempts. Even with help from the machine cabinet she wouldn't have fallen asleep for hours. As it was, she hadn't taken a thing, a couple of aspirin and a tranquilizer—oh, and half a tablet a boy from Columbia Dental School had given her—and she had slept like a kitten.

She was a little surprised—even, in the back of her mind, a little concerned—that her facility in the laboratory hadn't raised her achievement level anywhere else. It still stood at zero. She couldn't explain it. She did want to get there with a man sometime, to feel his presence beside her during the slow separation. She wanted to talk to him about it frankly, over a companionable cigarette. A sex life confined to the brightly lighted arena on 158th Street wasn't a rose garden, by any means. The first time or two she had bubbled all the way home. So she wasn't a cold fish, after all! She was a warm-blooded mammal, a member of one of the few species in which a female can share in the celebration. She searched her face in the mirror and decided that she looked healthier. She cut down on the booze and the pills and felt better in every way. And yet . . .

For one thing, it was a long subway ride. Because Dr. Prescott did much of his work at odd hours, Victoria had had some long waits on the subway platform, the bleakest scene in New York. The afterglow eulogized in the marriage manuals didn't last long in the IRT. She was a natural target for the exhibitionists who prowl the subways after dark, sorry creatures who really didn't have too much to exhibit. Sometime, when she caught Dr. Prescott in the right mood, she wanted to ask him to schedule her last some night, turn out those damn lights, and let her sleep on the table. She was still their top scorer in contractions, as far as she knew, so didn't they owe her something?

She had a disturbing moment one night with Nick DiVito, the cameraman. He was working a shutter release attached by cable to the Minox camera mounted on the movable arm. He was concentrating hard, snapping the shutter on each stroke at the exact moment of maximum thrust. By some chance the bottom of Victoria's heel, not a terribly erogenous spot, she would have thought, happened to graze his thigh. And it had been like plugging into a new source of power! Life poured from Nick into Victoria, and that time she really racked up the contractions. The stylus went on zigging and zagging for ages, and the tracing it left on the drum looked like a cross-section of the jawbone of a shark. Nick gave her a hard, unblinking look, a warning not to do it again. But he hadn't pulled his leg away while it was going on, she noticed!

She knew it would be a bad idea to try any such tricks with Prescott. He was all brain, and his aim was to be as objective as the polygraph or the cameras. But ever since he had picked her for the project, she had known that this wasn't the whole story. The fires might be banked, but they were still burning. Something kept picking at the edges of her mind. Any man who was capable of designing that machine, who spent every waking minute thinking about the female orgasm, who knew more about a woman's genital arrangements than any woman alive, ought to be able to set off some real fireworks, to put it bluntly. But she told herself, again and again, to stop thinking about it, to leave Prescott strictly alone.

Unfortunately, some things weren't entirely under Victoria's control. Her attention span had never been too good, starting in kindergarten. And so, a session or two later, she made her mistake.

The ejection mechanism had been giving trouble, and Prescott was making a small adjustment with a jeweler's screwdriver. She forced him to meet her eyes. His irises were dark, almost black, and in the unnatural light they seemed to have no depth and to reflect the glitter of the room. Looking into his head, she thought she could see a small, hairless animal, just born, terrified by the newness of everything. It was a long half-minute.

When it was over, she turned to Mrs. Freeman and remarked in her ordinary voice, "Hell, I moved."

"It's not too bad," Mrs. Freeman said, studying the graph. "Only two or three spikes."

"I thought I ruined it," Victoria murmured, and turned the dial to disengage.

A lot of that had been her imagination, she decided. Of course she was out of line. She was supposed to keep her eyes lowered, like a geisha girl, and swallow any moans and groans. Nobody was doing this for fun. It was science.

There was an unexpected letter from Mrs. Freeman in the mail a few days later. Victoria tore it open in the vestibule. A rheostat was broken. Until they could have it repaired they wouldn't be needing her!

Her first reaction was a surprising one: sheer relief. The machine was so tireless, so potent, so—well, implacable, that anything short of perfection on her part was unthinkable. Face it, Victoria wasn't that good.

And then suddenly she seemed to be caught up in a long breaker, the light failed, she felt cold sweat on her forehead. Something about that curt, three-sentence letter told her they were lying. Prescott had told Martha what had happened. This wasn't a layoff. It was graduation.

She had a hard time that day at work. There weren't many satisfactions for her at the office. It wasn't the kind of job you could do well. You were doing well if you didn't make any horrible mistakes. At the laboratory, when she did something out of the ordinary, they congratulated her. Today her machine was crankier than usual. She forgot to turn the power off during lunch. She kept writing checks for inappropriate amounts. She could have claimed to have the curse so they would send her home, but that would have involved admitting something to herself.

She was functioning almost normally by midafternoon. Rheostats, after all, were delicate things. Victoria's own touch was light and sure, but she knew some women—her roommate was one—who were helpless when confronted by anything mechanical. Anne kept overwinding her watch. She was a real menace in a car. Once she had signaled for a turn so emphatically that she snapped the handle off at the roots. Carried away during orgasm, somebody had obviously given the dial too hard a twist.

Nobody called that night, which was always the way when she needed some human contact. Anne was taking a course at the New School, "Myth and Reality in Hollywood Films of the Thirties," and she wouldn't be home till late. With nothing else to do, Victoria drank martinis. How long would it take them to change a rheostat? She would give them one week.

If they hadn't called her by then, she would have to call them.

By the time Anne came home, Victoria was flying through heavy fog. The television set was on, with the faces jiggling at the end of imaginary rubber bands.

"Martinis?" Anne said. "At eleven o'clock at night?"

"Join me."

"Honeybunch, you're miles ahead of me. You'd better slow down if you're going to make the office tomorrow."

"Fuck the office."

Anne's features jumped around on her face and rearranged themselves in their usual pattern. "What happened? Did you get fired?"

Yes, in a way she'd been fired, but not from her daytime job. She held out her glass.

"I think I'd like a little more."

Anne moved the pitcher out of reach. "Baby, get to bed."

Victoria decided that she loved Anne and would do what she said. But her rheostats weren't functioning. Anne helped her undress. That way they could touch each other without considering it a crime.

"Anne, I'm so scared."

That came out clearly, in a small voice. Anne sat on the bed beside her.

"About what?"

"Something bad is happening to me. I don't like anybody. I haven't had any fun for—"

Anne smoothed her hair back from her temple. "You're gorgeous. You've got millions of dates."

Shedding tears was no problem; Victoria had already cried once or twice that evening. "I think I'm going out of my mind."

"Tell me."

"I never let them down once. I had *status orgasmus* three times, which you probably never even heard of."

"So that's what's bugging you—the laboratory. Did they make you do something you didn't want to do?"

Victoria shook her head, tears flowing down her cheeks. "Anne, would you—"

"What, baby?"

Reaching up, Victoria pulled Anne's head down and

breathed in her ear. She didn't actually say anything. Anne took off her clothes, good old reliable Anne, slipped into bed beside her, and held her until she was able to fall asleep.

She woke up alone the next morning. A message was taped to the mirror: "You'll live through it!"

She managed to dial the office number on the sixth try and told them they'd better not expect her. She slept most of the day. She was in the middle of her first martini when Anne came home from work. With a finger of gin and an antidepressant or two fizzing inside her, Victoria felt almost normal, though there was a core of numbness somewhere that kept moving around. Anne dragged her off to a double bill of Antonioni movies. As far as Victoria could make out—the gin was making her astigmatic—the man was trying to demonstrate that life was pretty empty. Big discovery. Anne's elbow was against hers, and there was a constant flow of electrons between them. Once Victoria turned to look at her, and Anne smiled and patted her knee. Victoria was lucky to have her.

She went to work the next day and managed to cope. She would have to call Mrs. Freeman sometime, but she had decided to wait the full week even if it killed her, which it might very well do. She looked all right, she thought, but she had the impression that her body temperature had dropped. Her blood was running sluggishly. Neither she nor Anne ever referred to her weepy evening. She had made a sort of pass at Anne, she guessed, but that wasn't so awful. Nothing had actually happened.

She stuck it out for six days. She kept touching the phone and finally she picked it up. The number dialed itself.

"Oh, Victoria," Mrs. Freeman said pleasantly. "I was about to call you." (Liar!) "The machine's working again, but I'm afraid we have all the brain patterns we can use." (Thanks mainly to a subject named Victoria Orr, she neglected to add.) "We've had some bad news about our foundation grant. It's been cut way down. We have to take a good look at what we have and set up a system of priorities." (A brush-off, Victoria thought grimly.) "If you could call again in two or three weeks—"

After hanging up, Victoria picked up an ashtray and hurled

it across the room. Mrs. Freeman wasn't much of a liar, and while she was talking Victoria had realized what must have happened. Prescott had been too interested in the sharks' teeth the stylus was putting on the graph paper to notice the look she had given him. But Mrs. Freeman had seen it and she probably made up her mind that minute that she had to get rid of Victoria. Because of course they were sleeping together. Only a regular sex outlet could account for Martha's unhurried air and easy smile. But she would have to be careful. Victoria was one of their best people, whose platform recordings had appeared in the *Annals* of the New York Academy of Sciences. Martha would have to think up some pretext, like a broken rheostat. Now Victoria had to find out if that rheostat had really been broken, if they'd really stopped taking EEG's, and then take the evidence to Prescott and demand reinstatement. And what if Prescott should be so incensed by Martha's childish jealousy that he fired her? There could be an opening in the laboratory!

The next day was Friday. Victoria hurried home from work and fixed herself a therapeutic gin-and-tonic. She was still in the tub when she heard voices, including a man's. She put on her makeup carefully, on the sound principle that you never knew; Anne could have got lucky. But it was only Mr. Assistant District Attorney, Woods McChesney.

"Vicky," Woods said with a movement of his glass. "What have you got on underneath that, anything?"

"Armor. Anne, can I talk to you a minute?"

Anne followed her into the bedroom. Victoria turned on her when the door was closed and said in a fierce whisper, "What did you tell him?"

"How could I tell him anything? You haven't confided in me. He did ask me if you're still mixed up with those people, and I may have hesitated."

"Traitor."

"Now Vicky—would it do any harm to listen to what he has to say?"

"Get me another gin-and-T. More gin, less tonic."

She put on a new black dress and chose her earrings with care. She had herself nicely tuned up for this evening, and Woods McChesney was a distraction. When she was ready she stood in front of the mirror. If you looked hard enough and long enough, you could see she was in trouble, but there were ways she could hide it. She felt tight and dangerous.

She went out smiling faintly, up to any game anybody cared to name.

"You've lost weight," Woods observed. "Too much exercise?"

"Oh Woods," she said lightly. "You're such a lovable clown."

"Where are you off to, the lab? I know Friday's their big night."

Anne handed Victoria her drink and said nervously, "Woods, postpone it, will you?"

"I don't mind Woods," Victoria said. "The last time I saw him he warned me not to go near the laboratory. It was a risky place, he told me. But nothing happened, did it?"

"Vicky, are you still with them? Just tell me that."

"As of this moment," she said, "no."

"Are you ready to tell me how it happened?"

"How what happened?"

He was sitting well down in the sofa, his legs stretched out, sighting over his glass. "If there's any hard feeling, I might be able to help. You don't want to let people kick you, Vicky. It's bad for your mental health."

She cut her eyes at her roommate. So she had mentioned those tears, had she?

She took a diet pill before she left, and the clocks speeded up. The IRT set a new track record getting her uptown. The elevator in the Research Building rose with a whoosh. She heard the bell clang a warning as she opened the unlocked door. She took a step or two into the familiar waiting room and all at once found it hard to breathe. She had come to the wrong place with the wrong personality. She couldn't remember anything, including her own name. Of course, the laboratory people knew her by a number, but she couldn't even remember that. It was somewhere in the low nineties, she knew, for she had been coming here, in all senses of the word, a long time.

Martha Freeman exclaimed, "Victoria!"

Victoria turned cold. "I know you're busy, Mrs. Freeman—"

"We are, as a matter of fact, but come on in."

Something seemed to be wrong with the unflappable Mrs. Freeman. She asked Victoria to sit down while she checked in the laboratory to see if she could be spared. Victoria only needed a minute, to look at the schedule that was always tacked behind the desk. If she could find the number of the brain-wave program it would prove— Was it 37-C? No, that was her apartment.

She pressed her fingers against her forehead, her eyes closed. She knew that program number as well as she knew her own name—which as a matter of incredible fact she had forgotten again.

"Victoria? Do you feel all right?"

She opened her eyes. "I don't know what it was . . . dizzy all of a sudden."

Martha offered her a cigarette. Lighting it and disposing of the match took a few seconds. Composure was important; they had a horror of anything emotional or excessive. But her mind was like a split screen, with two movies playing at once, one a love story and the other a Western with plenty of gunfire. Was that a whir she heard? Was the machine in use?

"I know what an imposition this is, on a Friday night, but I'll try not to take too long. Was anything the matter besides the rheostat?"

Not being a smoker, Martha was calming herself by punishing a ball-point pen. "We gave it a general overhaul. It needed new bearings."

"Mrs. Freeman, the reason I wanted to talk to you in person— I'm dating a man who wants me to move in with him. I definitely don't love him. But I seem to be adjusted to a certain amount of sex. When I was coming here, that was all taken care of, and I could be more objective. I don't like to be a pest, but if you could give me some idea about what are the prospects of coming back—"

"I'm afraid I'm not in a position to say anything definite."

Victoria was smoking jerkily. Afraid her nervousness would give her away, she put the cigarette down and dropped her hands out of sight.

"I've got a pretty good job and I wouldn't want you to

think you had to pay me. The thing is, if I go to live with this man, I'm afraid you'll have to take me off your list. He goes on the theory that what's his is his."

Mrs. Freeman was doodling on a blank pad. "It's not entirely a matter of money. We're winding up most of our long-range evaluations. From now on our programs have to be more specific, using specialized research populations. Menopausal women and so on."

"I admit I'm not ready for the menopause," Victoria said, attempting a laugh.

The door opened, and a girl looked in, small, olive-skinned, with a cap of dark hair. Her glance slid across Victoria.

"Going now, Mrs. Freeman. Do you want me next week?"

"Same time. Many thanks."

"Always a pleasure."

She shut the door. Mrs. Freeman was drawing a large circle around a black point on her pad.

"You've been an excellent subject, Victoria, and you know if there's any way we can work you into the new programs, we'll do it."

Like hell! Victoria hadn't been sure before, but there was no doubt about it now. They actually intended to throw her back into her old life, to flounder until she sank. She had one more weapon—Woods McChesney—and for a brief instant she thought of threatening Martha. No, not yet. First she had to nail down those lies.

She was pleased with the quiet way she stood up, apologized for using up so much time, and listened to one more hypocritical assurance that she would be kept in mind.

Crossing the waiting room, she thought of Nick DiVito. That cat was sure to know whether they had dropped the brain-pattern program. But could she get him to tell her? She remembered the wintry look he had given her the night her heel touched his thigh. He was the essence of something, all right, a member in good standing of the walking dead, and she'd better keep clear of him. But there had to be a way!

The dark girl who had put her head into the consulting room was waiting at the elevators. She stabbed the down button.

"What do they do," the girl said angrily, "turn off the power at nine o'clock in this God damn building?"

A car slid into place and they both got in. As a matter of actual fact, electronic elevators worked better at night than in the daytime. Could the girl have been waiting for her? It was an intriguing possibility. Victoria was careful not to stare, but her approach had to be right the first time, and she gave the girl a quick appraisal. The face was tanned, a bit leathery. The tight cap of hair came forward on both sides, to end in two points. Her eyelids were like withered parchment, and for some reason the eyelids, more than the eyes behind them, made Victoria uneasy. The girl was clearly one of those size-eights with too much energy for a small frame—Victoria could almost see the impatience jetting out of her ears. She stood with a hip thrust forward, watching the lights over the door.

As soon as Victoria finished her inspection, the girl gave her an equally fast look in return. "I saw you with Mrs. Freeman. Was that your interview?"

"Anything but. They're thinking of giving me a gold watch."

"No kidding. What do you think of her?"

"Martha? She's all right."

"I can't make her out. I mean, what does she do after working hours? Which way do you go? I've got a car."

Victoria felt a stir of apprehension. So that was the way the wind was blowing, was it, out of lesbian country? And yet how could she ignore the opportunity? Here was a pipeline into the observation suite.

"My best bet is the IRT."

"Oh, let me drop you. If it's out of my way, so it's out of my way. Unless it's Staten Island or someplace?"

"No, the Village. If you're sure you don't mind—"

"Do you know you're the first living person I ever met from upstairs? It's been in one door and out the other. That's my only complaint."

"It has to be that way, I guess. What have they got you doing?"

"Oh, you know, the mechanical man. If you read about it, would you believe it?"

Victoria started to answer. Better not; she might touch the wrong nerve.

The car was a battered Renault. They ducked into it, the

motor started, and Victoria's new friend said, "Buy you a drink?"

"A drink would be very nice," Victoria answered primly.

"Hey, do you know you're charming? What do we do, go by names or numbers?"

Victoria found that she had forgotten her number again. "I'm Victoria Orr."

"Janie Schlesinger. Hi!"

She worked her way onto the West Side Highway and let it take them downriver. Victoria kept trying to get the conversation back to the laboratory, which was the main thing they had in common, but Janie wanted to move on to new ground. They left the drive at 57th Street and headed across town, drawing up presently on Sutton Place in front of an apartment house with a doorman who greeted Janie by name and took charge of the Renault. Janie's apartment, reached via an elevator with both automatic controls and an elderly operator, was magnificent.

Victoria couldn't sit down before she had seen it all. An expensive-looking jungle grew on the terrace. The living room was like a set in a movie.

"Fantastic?" Janie said, coming up with a bubble glass in each hand. "It's not mine, actually. My friend's in Thailand, and I've been going crazy up here all by myself. I hope you like brandy. This is a thousand years old."

They were edgy with each other at first. Victoria was waiting for an opening. Janie had something to do with the theater —she was vague about what. Her conversation was about people unknown to Victoria. As soon as Victoria got the information she wanted, she was going to get the hell out, not without a certain amount of difficulty, probably. Having started the evening on 158th Street, naïveté and moral outrage would be equally out of place.

Janie relaxed under the caress of the brandy. The couch was wonderfully soft and yielding, and Victoria, who had eaten nothing since lunch and had been up and down, up and down, all day, was gripped by a strange torpor. She tried again, but Janie was definite: she didn't want to talk about the laboratory.

"I'm beginning to think you're basically a voyeur." She put

her hand on Victoria's leg. "That's a different planet up there. Let's stop talking about it and turn on the boob."

Stop talking about it? They hadn't started. Janie pushed herself up and switched on a color television set almost as big as her little car. She left the sound low and didn't adjust the color. Everybody on the screen looked a little seasick. It seemed to be a comedy, involving some misadventure in the life of a pleasantly goofy middle-class American family.

Janie took the brandy glass out of Victoria's fingers and kissed her.

Victoria's thoughts were skittering. Should she or shouldn't she? But what choice did she have, if she wanted to get back into the project? And maybe she ought to find out what it was like, on a kind of laboratory level. There was no such thing as too much knowledge in this shadowy area.

"That's a nice dress," Janie observed. "Bonwit's?"

"Paraphernalia."

They helped each other off with their clothes while the television family, heterosexual of course, went on quarreling in soft voices across the room. The father of the family tumbled downstairs carrying a tray.

"Yours are so beautiful," Janie whispered. "I'm embarrassed about mine."

"You shouldn't be."

"It's so funny, that thing in the laboratory. Didn't it scare you at first? When I was a girl I used to have nightmares that this huge male organ was trying to poke its way into me. Then I walked into the laboratory, and there it was! I nearly went up the wall."

Victoria drew a deep breath.

"My friend's galloping around Asia for CARE," Janie continued, "and for me it's not such a bad solution. I stay away from the butch bars. I've got too good a thing going here. Of course," she added, "she *is* a bit freaky."

"It's a lovely apartment."

"Isn't it?"

Janie kissed and fondled her breasts. Victoria wasn't feeling a thing. She wished Janie hadn't mentioned the machine. Her memories of it didn't excite her, they made her sad.

"You're tired," Janie said.

"I'm exhausted."

"Well, listen. I mean, have you ever done the brain thing?"

Victoria didn't move or breathe; possibly her heart stopped beating. "I don't know what you mean."

"Measuring the electrical potential in your brain when you come, not that I really understand it. I'll do you," she offered excitedly, "and you just lie where you are. Don't move a muscle, not one single muscle!"

"Is that so special?"

"It's beyond belief! Then you can do me."

She started to go down, but Victoria squirmed away. "Wait a minute. You mean when you have an orgasm your brain gives off some kind of sparks?"

"I don't know about sparks," Janie said doubtfully. "And you can't see it with the naked eye, you use the encephalograph. Four electrodes. They explained it to me. The minute you start getting excited there's this low-voltage jiggle. And the waves get bigger and bigger, until when you bang off it looks as though your hair must be standing on end. Which isn't such a big deal in the world of science. Everybody's known about it for years. I don't mean you and me—people in the business. But in the textbooks the brain waves are all mixed up with these up-and-down marks, don't you know, from twitchings and spasms. Prescott's trying to get a few good tracings, just the waves themselves and nothing else. That's why you have to hold so still."

"But how can you?"

"Well, it ain't easy! I'm still not too perfect. But I get better every time, and they think after a couple more tries I'll be like frozen. What they don't seem to realize is that they've got something terrific here. These red and green and yellow wires running out of your skull. You're under orders to be selfish—don't do a thing. I like to speed up the action and have it get bigger, just the teeniest little bit. So Doc makes the adjustments for me. It's luxurious! You breathe very slow. You build up sort of a dam against it. But it sneaks up on you, all that power. And suddenly crash! The dam breaks. It's great, just great!"

Victoria shivered. She had known they were lying.

"What did you do last week when the rheostat was broken?"

"What rheostat? I had three appointments last week, three big O's. On and on and on."

"Congratulations," Victoria said softly.

She lay as still as if she had electrodes taped to her head. Her own dam had been breached. It wasn't just Martha, it was Prescott, DiVito, everybody. They had tricked her with the machine. They had fixed her so she would never be able to make it in any other way. She wished she was dead, really dead, just not alive anymore.

"What happens when you get the perfect tracing?"

Janie hugged her. "Then I go into the homo program! And is it overdue!"

"I didn't know they had one."

"They have to be sure you're reliable. Listen, why don't I arrange for you and me—" She pulled back. "Are you crying, by any chance?"

Victoria shook her head, but Janie's face was a dazzle of indistinct lines. Janie untangled herself.

"Out!" she said briefly. "And don't tell me what brought this on. I've got my own troubles."

Victoria began to grope among the clothes on the floor. After she was dressed she blew her nose hard and started for the door.

"No, you don't," Janie said grimly. "There's an elevator man and a doorman, and if they see you coming out like that— You're an old childhood chum from P.S. 232. I can get away with that if she finds I had a female guest, but not if you walk out bawling. I didn't think anybody I met at the laboratory—" She pointed. "Use the john."

Victoria locked the door behind her. When she saw her face in the mirror she almost broke apart. She looked like a mental case, and no fooling. All she could find in the medicine cabinet was Anacin, Bromo-Seltzer, a bottle of prescription tablets to be taken as directed for menstrual discomfort. She swallowed a couple of those and dumped all the other bottles in the big square bathtub. There was a pleasant sound of breaking glass.

Janie rattled the knob. "Tell me what's wrong. I want to help you. Don't break anything else."

Victoria dashed cold water on her face. After a bad time that may have lasted only a few minutes, she combed her hair and put on lipstick. She unlocked the door. Janie, in a half-slip and bra, was standing a step away, looking worried.

Victoria slapped her with her full strength. Janie went careening back against a table, and a potted plant went over. Victoria found her brandy and drank it in one long gulp.

"If you want to see some real EEG's, ask them to show you the file on Number 91."

She let herself out.

At home, she tumbled out of her clothes and fell asleep instantly. Something woke her at three, always her bad hour. Frightened, feeling sick, she got into bed with Anne.

The alarm went off at seven. Anne silenced the bell, then stiffened. After a moment she said, "You have to talk to somebody, Vicky. It might as well be me."

"There's nothing to talk about."

"Do you want to wait till they start giving you shots to keep you from screaming?"

Anne rolled over. Her hair was up in a plastic bag, and she looked so safe and familiar that Victoria had to grab her.

"Well, I love you," Anne said, kissing her forehead lightly. "Maybe you ought to see a doctor?"

"I've been seeing a doctor."

"I don't mean a sex doctor. If you won't tell me about it, tell a specialist."

"But would he believe me?"

Anne squeezed her. "Vicky, when you say a cute thing like that I think things can't be as bad as they seem. Come on, open up. It's good for the soul."

Victoria pressed her face against her friend's shoulder. "I don't know if I can trust you."

"On account of Woods? Don't worry—all I told him was that it seemed to do you good for a while, but lately you've been gobbling Seconals like salted peanuts."

"I had sex with a lesbian last night."

Anne groaned. "You idiot. What did you do that for?"

They held each other for a moment.

"I'm so conflicted about you," Anne said. "You need somebody to take care of you, Vicky. I want to tell you what Woods was saying. It's only a theory, remember, because what have we got to go on? Not a hell of a lot. I think you decided there was something wrong about what you were doing, and that's why you quit. Right?"

Right? She was so wrong it was funny.

"And then the guilt business started," Anne said. "Maybe you did something for them you never told me."

Victoria nodded. "I didn't see how I could refuse."

"That's what we figured. But it's definitely over?"

"I wouldn't go back there now for any amount of money."

Anne sat up. "That's the way I like to hear you talk! I've had a certain amount of experience with guilt-feelings, thanks to Mother. I've been an emotional cripple most of my life. Well, that's over, knock on wood."

Victoria swung her knees up and around. "I never thought masturbating was all that awful."

"Because you had a rational bringing-up! I never learned how to handle it. That night we talked started me in the right direction. It's not enough to just blame somebody, you've got to take steps! I never told you—I called Mother in Sarasota and gave her a piece of my mind. I don't suppose she's heard the word masturbation in years, and I said it a number of times. I told her she ought to do it herself because she's so obviously knotted-up on the subject. It was lovely! And I hung up on her and turned out the light and masturbated and enjoyed it!"

"Anne, you're a heroine!"

"I think so myself. Do you see what I'm getting at? You don't want to drag around in this self-destructive way. Pick out the guilty party and give it to him! Right in the kishke!"

"I don't see how you can compare—"

"I know it's not the same thing, dumbhead. But right now you're blaming yourself. You had intercourse with a machine in front of everybody, so you're going to punish yourself by getting stoned every night. Not that you aren't darling when you're tight. But you're taking it out on the wrong person! Who's the mastermind behind the machine? Prescott."

Victoria looked at her uneasily.

"In the kishke! Why not? I was cleaning out bureau drawers and I came across those photos I took at Fire Island last summer. Remember, Vicky, you were with that Princeton boy? With the shaggy hair, Mike something? You've changed so much. You've got new little lines at the corners of your mouth, you're so jittery—"

"Going up there was Woods's idea in the first place. You backed him up."

"Don't think I'm not sorry!" She took Victoria's shoulders firmly and looked into her eyes. "Why did you quit?"

"Maybe I'll tell you sometime, but not now. What does Woods want me to— No, don't tell me. I feel bad enough as it is. If I get them in trouble I'll feel a hundred times worse."

"How could you feel worse? Just keep quiet a minute and listen. If you got disgusted and quit, that's not too sensational, but if you were hurt in some way—"

"Hurt!"

"Now don't fly off the handle. This is still in the idea stage. But if something went wrong with the machine—"

Victoria stared at her. "What could go wrong? It's loaded with safety features."

"Vicky, use some imagination. No machine ever went out of control? What's wrong with stretching the truth a little? Dr. Prescott thinks he's entitled to do *anything*, anything at all, so long as he gets a few facts out of it. That's the scientific method. Well, two can play at that game."

Victoria shook her head. "I don't think you know me very well."

Anne patted her. "Well, I told Woods you wouldn't. In a minute I'm going to give you a hug and get up and make breakfast. Of course, if nobody does anything to stop Dr. Prescott he's going to be rich and famous. Out of your orgasms."

"I don't give a damn."

"What's really wrong, Vicky?"

It was so direct and personal that Victoria threw herself forward into the bigger girl's arms. She needed Anne badly. She had to think of something binding, or Anne would move out and get married, and then what would happen to Victoria?

She said in a whisper, "I can't come anymore."

"Because of the laboratory?"

"I don't know. Whenever I'm on the edge I keep thinking if only he was a little bigger, if only the bastard would move a little faster—"

"You mean *not at all?*"

"Most of the time I don't even get started."

"Why, that son of a bitch Prescott!" Anne said with feeling.

"Vicky, we're going to put our heads together over the weekend. We'll think of something."

"If you tell Woods I'll murder you."

"Of course I won't tell Woods. First a quick shower, then coffee, then we'll talk about it."

Feeling slightly more cheerful, Victoria began brushing her hair. Any help Anne could give her would be on the *Reader's Digest* level, but there was some truth in the old saws, after all. It had helped to share her troubles, even though she had stopped a long way short of the full truth.

The phone rang; apparently somebody still knew the number. It was a man's voice. Victoria might be hooked on a machine without vocal chords, but a male voice on the phone could still start the juices flowing.

"I don't suppose you remember me. Matt Hinkle?"

"I think that rings a bell," Victoria said doubtfully. "Tell me more."

"From Chicago. About a year ago now? A guy I knew in the service arranged it, Woody McChesney—"

Victoria felt an unaccountable reprieve. How could she have forgotten that night? She had come so close!

"But the way you stalked out of here—"

"I had second thoughts later. It wasn't your fault. Well, here I am in New York, and I thought I'd ring you up and find out what's been happening."

"Not a thing," Victoria said, lying in her teeth. "Still live in the same place. Same roommate. Still got the same job."

"I was wondering if you'd be free for dinner tonight."

"I don't know—I had tentative plans. How long will you be in town?"

"Just through tomorrow. I didn't think there was much of a chance—"

She made up her mind. Not dinner. There was too much conversation at dinner.

"Matt, where are you staying? I could meet you for a drink at four."

It was quickly arranged. As she hung up she remembered those scarred knees. Things might be taking a turn for the better.

Anne called her to breakfast. "Vicky, here's your solution!

Psychological anguish. It's not the kind of injury Woods was thinking of, but it's an injury."

Victoria brought her mind back. "Anne."

"I can see why you wouldn't want a lot of doctors arguing about tissue damage and internal bleeding and so forth," Anne ran on, "but you wouldn't be faking about this. You never had trouble having orgasms before, and we can prove that from Prescott's own records."

"You're insane!"

"You could even sue him," Anne said, more and more taken with her mad idea. "Would you turn down half a million bucks? They give that much for a leg."

"For heaven's sake—the jury can look at you and see you only have one leg."

"Now don't reject this out of hand. Think about it. They give awards for things they can't see. I'd be glad to stand up and testify how you've changed. Then they'd have to put Prescott on the stand and make him admit what he's been doing. You'd hurt him even if the jury only gave you forty-nine cents. It's the only way you'll ever get back to normal."

Well, it wouldn't happen, but it made a ridiculous daydream. With Matt in the offing, she was able to play around with it during breakfast almost as if there was nothing important at stake. She did the dishes while Anne went to the supermarket. She would have to hire a flashy lawyer, someone like F. Lee Bailey. Nobody would doze off while she was testifying, she could guarantee that. She would wear her dark wool with the high collar. "What made you join this experiment, Miss Orr?" Knees together, hands in lap. "I wanted to contribute to the enrichment of human sexual experience." "I know this will be painful to you, my dear, but will you describe to the jury in your own words the equipment they forced you to . . ."

No. This was black humor, neither funny nor soothing.

She poured herself a drink. Nine-thirty in the morning, another first. But somehow she had to get through to her date with Matt. When she heard Anne's key in the lock she looked for a place to hide her glass. But it was *her* life. If she wasn't a normal person, and apparently she wasn't, she didn't have to behave normally.

Anne's glance took in Victoria's highball, which was a nice, deep Scotch color, and went on with the joke that had been current an hour ago. "I got lobster tails. We're going to have a lavish lunch to celebrate that half-million-dollar settlement."

Victoria raised her glass and drank deliberately. "Don't push me, Anne," she said in a voice she hardly recognized.

"I'm trying to help."

Yes, by advising Victoria to get up in a public courtroom and testify under oath that she was a sexual clam! That had been half a joke but also half in earnest. What was she trying to do, drive Victoria around the bend? And all to ingratiate herself with that freak McChesney. If she wanted to get married that much, why didn't she pay ten dollars and sign up with the matrimonial computer? Anne started drinking in self-defense, and soon they were screaming at each other like any long-married couple. They both said things they didn't mean. Victoria felt herself beginning to panic. If she broke down completely and let Anne comfort her, she knew they would cross an invisible line, and she wasn't ready for *that* yet. She snatched up her bag and her cigarettes. Anne said her name in a small voice as she went out, but Victoria decided the hell with it. She was tired of having Anne run the errands and make the arrangements. Anne wanted the pleasures of a relationship with none of the headaches, and the next time they were in bed together Victoria was going to put an end to this shilly-shallying! It was too schoolgirlish for words.

And before the thought had had time to fade, she withdrew it in haste. Of course she wouldn't. She wasn't the type, and Anne wasn't either.

She was alarmed by the effect of the early drinks. She didn't want to be out of control when she met Matt. She wanted to dominate the meeting from the word "hello." She wouldn't insist on the full trip, just an indication that it wasn't totally hopeless.

The sunlight was as painful as the floodlights in the laboratory. She entered a cluttered drugstore to buy shades. Everything was marked down, the old prices and the new printed on tiny, flag-shaped signs. She wandered along the aisles. There were no clerks. Suddenly she stood still, surrounded by bargains. A terrible thought formed in her mind. When she entered the laboratory for the first time and saw the machine, so stripped and pure, it had seemed an expression of the clarity and relentlessness of science. Then she had come to think of it as a symbol of physical pleasure, again in a pure form. But it had fooled her. It was a symbol, all right, and she knew what it symbolized. *Everything!*

People were looking at her, not the way they did usually, but as though her name had been crossed off all the mailing lists it had ever been on. She left the store and turned into a side street.

A middle-aged woman came down some steps. Her face looked peaceful, and Victoria took out a handkerchief to cover her head and went in through the church door. Vigil lights winked at her with a certain complicity. She smelled the old smells of her girlhood, wax and incense. It came back with a rush. She longed desperately for the kind of contentment she had seen on the face of the woman coming out. Eyes were looking at her again, and she looked around. This time it was only a painted wooden figure hung from a nearby pillar. To Victoria's imagination the wounds seemed real.

The temperature inside the confessional had to be 103 at the least, and Father Dolan, approaching middle age but still, for his sins, a curate, could feel himself dissolving slowly into his separate components. He panted in the moist darkness. On a day like this the sheep and the goats, the shriven and unshriven, all sweated alike. Thirty minutes more, he thought hopelessly. He slammed one partition and opened the other. This had turned out to be the difficult side today. That was the way it went. Sometimes everything serious—blasphemy, lewdness, incest, disbelief—came in at one side of the confessional while the other produced nothing but envy and pride and an occasional simple fornication. He could smell perfume and whiskey. He sighed. Not that anything could surprise him, but it was the way they put things sometimes, the women especially, God love them.

A woman's voice: "Father, bless me. I've sinned terribly, against God, against nature—"

"In what way, my child?"

"I've committed the sin of impurity with an object."

Father Dolan rested his head in his hand. Priests had been

known to drop from the heat before the end of the two and a
half hours, and he prayed to God that it wouldn't happen to
him today.

"You've had unlawful connection with an object. How many
times?"

"Many times, Father. People stood around watching. They
made movies of it."

"That is a crime. You know the Church forbids it. How
long since you made your last confession?"

A hesitation. "I don't know, Father."

"When did you last attend Mass?"

Silence. A little sullenly: "Three years ago."

The priest sighed heavily into the sleeve of his cassock. Three
years since the last Mass. He was in for it now, the full cata-
logue.

"It is the law of the Church that you attend Mass on Sundays and holy days. You can subdue this evil with God's help,
but you must make use of the sacraments." He gathered himself and said more sharply: "You know that as well as I do!
Did they pay you to exhibit yourself?"

"Yes, Father. Fifteen dollars a time."

"That is a bad sin. You must stop it at once."

"I'll never do it again, you don't have to worry about that."

A queer thing to say, surely, and a queer voice to say it in.
Now Father Dolan began the hard task of finding what had
brought her to his confessional, a true desire for repentance, or
the whiskey she was breathing at him through the wicket. He
said abruptly, his tone hardening, "An object. What kind of
object?"

"It's shaped like a—like a penis. And it's so lifelike, Father!
Except longer. It runs on electricity—"

He was beginning to listen more attentively. Everything had
to be electrified these days. Anything like that would require
a bit of capital, and they'd have to operate on a sizable scale to
get their money out. He could see this ending as a police matter. And if Father Dolan had a share in driving a major source
of temptation out of the parish, the bishop, who was down on
him for some reason, would have to acknowledge his existence.

"Who supplied you with this thing?"

"A doctor. He has hundreds of people doing it for him, men

and women. He wants to know what happens inside." She was speaking more rapidly, running her words together. "I could turn dials and make it go faster and go in deeper and get bigger and bigger. There's a button you press to make it come—"

The priest relaxed. They could fool you sometimes, at least for a while.

"Is there anything else, my child?"

"Anything else?"

"Anything else to confess?"

"Well, I committed an act of impurity with a woman. And with men, many times. I did it in unlawful ways."

He waited patiently.

When she didn't go on: "You must pray. You should realize that you can use God's help. Stay away from erotic motion pictures. Think about your duty to the Church instead of fleshly things. If you are heartily sorry for your sins, for your penance say the rosary daily for one week and say ten 'Our Fathers' and ten 'Hail Marys' and pray for my intention. Make a good act of contrition—"

"Ten 'Our Fathers'!" she said incredulously.

"And ten 'Hail Marys' and the rosary."

"Is that all you're going to give me?"

Responding to the excitement in her voice, he put on his trouble-light. "You've sinned in thought—"

"I've sinned in more ways than thought! I've sinned in fact! Don't you believe me? They have a camera that's part of the machine, and it takes pictures away up inside. It's on West 158th Street, in the Research Building! They made tracings of my brain waves while I had intercourse with the machine."

They all thought no one had sinned before in the history of the world. In the Middle Ages, after fasting, unmarried female penitents would tell their confessors they had been entered by the Devil. It had been real enough, they had smelled him and felt him. Now Satan was a machine, with dials and buttons and a cord that could be plugged into the nearest outlet. Anti-Christ was a doctor in a white coat. The imagery was the only thing that had changed.

"You must rely on prayer. Pray to the Blessed Virgin for help in fighting these strange fancies."

"They aren't fancies! It happened!"

"No, my child," the priest said quite gently. "Nothing happened."

"It did! You don't know what's going on in the world, Father! You ought to read the medical journals."

He was losing her before he had given absolution. "Wait!" he said sharply.

She was gone.

Victoria stumbled into the sunlight. Kicked out of the laboratory, kicked out of the confessional. She only wished the priest was right, that all those multiple orgasms hadn't really taken place except in her mind. No such luck. ". . . through my fault, through my fault, through my most grievous fault. . . ."

The father had warned against erotic movies. One was playing at a nearby theater. Unlike the confessional, the theater was air-conditioned. She arrived in the middle of the big scene, which had earned the picture its condemned rating. The screen showed two apparently naked people. Coming in after the beginning, Victoria couldn't convince herself that she was witnessing an actual event. Probably this one lengthy embrace had taken as long as a week to film. She could imagine the small army of technicians clustered about the bed, photographing each change in position over and over until they were satisfied that an audience would believe it was real. In the laboratory, at least, sex came to a real climax, with the appropriate muscle groups in genuine spasm.

She had a headache when she left.

Now she had an hour and a half. She returned home and put together another drink without speaking to Anne, who was in the bathroom shaving her legs. By the time Victoria was dressed she looked okay externally, she was happy to see, in spite of the emotional turmoil of the afternoon. Just for luck, she slung a jeweled watch around her neck. Her mother had given it to her on some long-ago birthday. It no longer ran, but she had worn it to the laboratory the day of her first machine penetration, and on most of her lab dates afterward. She couldn't remember if she had taken her antiovulation pill, probably not, so she took another. Anne watched in silence as she put on the finishing touches and transferred her money and tools to a new bag. They still hadn't exchanged a word.

But at the top of the stairs Victoria suddenly whirled, fumbled the door open, and they ran into each other's arms.

"You aren't going to that woman, are you?" Anne said.

"No, it's a man this time. Back to normal, I hope. Keep your fingers crossed." She laughed uncertainly. "Maybe I won't have to sue."

"That would be wonderful, Vicky."

In the subway, she was getting the right kind of looks again. She had been told to stay out of erotic movies, but what about erotic subway trains? The car cards all promised certain orgasm, if she only wore the right brand of bra to her rendezvous and hadn't forgotten to spray herself with the latest sexy deodorant. A half-naked badman advertising a movie was pictured with a naked six-gun at his hip, cocked at an upward angle that was surely no accident.

Matt was waiting for her in the lobby of his motor inn. One thing she had forgotten was what awful clothes he wore. Who had given him his suit, Nikita Khrushchev?

"You look different," he said.

"I hope so. I'm a year older."

"Still kicking around?"

"Now what do you mean by that question?" she said with a smile.

"You haven't got married or anything?"

She took his arm. "Definitely not. All the interesting men I meet turn out to be queer. Or they seem to live in Chicago."

That pleased him. He suggested a drink in the creep bar off the lobby. They had three, one over the limit Victoria had set herself. She looked at her dead watch.

"This has been nice, but I've got to be going in a minute."

"Why not forget that date and have dinner with me?"

"I couldn't do that." She touched the tip of one of his fingers and looked suddenly into his eyes. "Well, I could be late."

He dropped a bill on the table and rose without answering. He held her arm all the way to the elevator, as though afraid she might change her mind and break for the street. And for a moment she considered it, because of his suit, because of his leaden conversation. None of her friends frequented this kind of place; nevertheless, she didn't dawdle. In the elevator he stood too close, exhibiting none of the cool charm of the men in the cigarette ads. He couldn't wait, but began kissing her in the hall. His hands started on her buttocks; they didn't stay there, but slipped down and around. Her mind leaped like a mountain goat from one erotic image to the next: the man with the naked gun, Dr. Prescott, the machine of course, the priest. What a scene, that confessional! Father had sounded quite young and innocent and had actually managed to get her a little excited at the end. She wondered about confessionals, if any randy penitent had ever . . .

Then they were in Matt's room, her back to the door with her skirt around her hips. She thought for a minute that he was going to come into her standing, skipping the early moves. Which might not be bad, for she was miles ahead of the point she had usually reached by now. She tore at the buttons of his shirt without breaking the kiss. A real fire was blazing this time. He did rough, exciting things. It was almost as though they had been deprived of all forms of sex during their year's separation. She gasped for breath and laughed.

"Jesus!" he said huskily.

Now the tempo changed abruptly. They took off their clothes slowly, facing each other. He had even more scars than she remembered. When they closed with each other, naked, she didn't stop to plot her place on the curve. They ran neck and neck. He was already excited and she made him more so. Talk about pistols! Lying back, she drew him inside her. He was under control. She didn't do it with dials but with her fingers on his back and with her body. Then was *that* the secret? It was going to happen today, for the first time outside the laboratory. She was all but over, and only the tiniest nudge . . .

Then there was a slippage of gears. It occurred to her that this was a man she was ashamed to be seen with in a motel lobby. Instantly, her mind was loose and away. It was an important milestone, her first nonmechanical orgasm, and shouldn't she keep it for someone who mattered?

She began to fight. He overcame her and made her join him. His moment was an instant ahead of hers. Entirely against her will, she felt an explosive release and then the throbbing started. She grabbed him with her whole body, including her teeth. In the next thirty seconds she fulfilled every textbook requirement, and it made her furious. Fury swept through her body with the receding blood. She made him withdraw at once. She felt for her clothes.

"God, I'm going to be late!"

"Sweetheart, don't go."

She had to get out before she screamed. Intelligence began to return to his eyes as he watched her. All her clothes were scattered and inside-out and took a fantastically long time to find and put on. She was dizzy, without coordination. One of her stockings had been kicked back beneath the bed. She went down on her knees to reach it. He rolled off the bed and caught her.

She kept her voice steady. "Darling, I really do have to go."

"Let's do it again."

She tried to shrug him off. An ex-ballplayer with scarred knees, he was strong enough to hold her with one arm. He thrust against her limply from behind until she felt his power beginning to return. He grunted that he wouldn't take long. She could have hurried it up if she had helped, but this one was going to be without her. His tongue, when he used it on her, was like a rasp. He hurt her continually, doing many of the same things she had liked before. There was no dial she could turn. When she resisted he hurt her more. He decided he was ready and ripped into her again, taking a secondary route. And then he began to labor. It took a long time. ". . . through my fault, through my most grievous fault . . ." It was like being worked on with a rattail file. She began to plead with him. He ignored her.

He was desperate at the end, and Victoria may have fainted.

As soon as she felt him relax she wrenched herself free and left him on the floor while she quietly finished dressing. He was breathing raggedly, really done.

"I'll be back next month. How about it?"

By the time she had her lipstick on, he had pulled himself around. He looked his age, a lean, middle-aged man thrown up on the beach after a losing struggle with a shark.

"Don't bother calling me," she said, dropping her lipstick in her bag.

"What?"

"You didn't think I enjoyed that, did you?"

His mouth was open. "You mean you don't like it that way?"

She kept her views to herself and opened the door. He called after her, and actually came into the hall, stark naked, and ordered her to come back. She didn't turn around.

Downstairs, she found the public phones. Sealing herself in, she dialed Woods McChesney's number and asked if he still wanted to have that talk.

chapter 20

The sex Jake Burgess was having with Betty Quinby was a little artificial at first, but it began to improve. She came to his apartment almost every day, theoretically for lunch. The meal consisted of martinis and sandwiches. Soon they began to omit the preliminary chatter over the martinis. Then they began omitting the sandwiches, and finally the martinis. She was working for Hubie Sachs, and Hubie had to speak to her more than once about getting back late from lunch.

Betty had a fondness for leisurely phone calls, which sometimes continued for hours. The play Jake was supposed to be working on was still stuck in his typewriter, but he refused to worry about it. Betty had introduced him to a producer named Gregory J. Granby, a rabbity man who was always accompanied by some tall, strikingly beautiful woman; it could happen in no other profession. He liked one of Jake's plays and more or less promised to do it. Money was tight at the moment, but as soon as it was easier—

Jake had been given a battered desk at 100 Center Street, in the bullpen outside Woods McChesney's office. The Democratic nominating convention was now only a few days away. Bobby Quinby had told Jake that McChesney was doing some hard conniving for a place on the ticket. He had clawed his way out of the swamp of assistant D.A.'s, and this had to be his year. As Bobby Quinby's vicar, the Bobby Quinby who had access to the top-circulation magazines, Jake was welcome, and McChesney had done everything for him except give him a set of skeleton keys to the Tombs.

But this seemed to be an off year for New York murders. The best they had been able to come up with was an acidhead who had dismembered a woman. Jake talked to him all one afternoon. Turned off, he was nobody. Jake was typing his notes—they were hardly worth typing—when the door of McChesney's office opened, and McChesney appeared with a young woman.

"Everything's going to work out, Vicky," McChesney said.
"For you," she answered.

She was extremely pretty, with well-marked breasts under a tight black jersey. But she radiated tension. Her face was drawn tight, as though being stretched from behind. McChesney touched her shoulder and she gave a slight jerk.

"I appreciate this," he said. "I'll send you something."

"Why bother?"

McChesney watched her cross the room to the outer door. There was a queer, taut look on his face. He felt Jake looking at him and raised his eyebrows, as though all he was doing was admiring the way a pretty girl looks from behind.

Jake had been told to meet Betty at a cocktail party, and he was already late. Nevertheless, after McChesney retreated into his office, Jake sat down in the creaky swivel chair and tried to remember where he had seen that girl before. She was somehow significant, as though she had planted herself in a part of his brain that was heavily trip-wired. She couldn't have anything to do with the Prescott project? Like a psychiatrist's office, the laboratory had a separate exit, so the departing subject and the arriving one wouldn't meet in the doorway. Then Jake made an involuntary movement, and the chair nearly threw him. Sunday morning, after the Hubie Sachs party in Central Park. He had been reading the Sunday paper on 158th Street, across from the Research Building, hoping to intercept Number 89. A girl had come out of the building. He had pursued and overtaken her. He couldn't remember her face, but like the girl who had just left McChesney's office she had been wearing a little watch on a chain around her neck.

And if so? If she was actually the same girl, if she was informing on Dr. Prescott—

Getting up, he tapped lightly on McChesney's door. McChesney asked him to come in. There was an air of cerebration here, too; the desk was bare.

"Oh, Jake. How was your afternoon?"

"Pretty lousy. Can I talk to you a minute?"

"Certainly."

McChesney was sucking a mint, to give himself the illusion that he was smoking a mentholated cigarette.

Jake said, "Bobby's in Spain and I haven't checked with him

about this, but I don't think he's going to be too crazy about the East Village murder. LSD is the big topic now, and there could be a magazine piece in it. But a book? By the time it could get researched and written and published, the public's going to be interested in something else. I've had another idea. Let's forget about homicide. What else is likely to be hot eighteen months from now? I don't know if you've heard about a sex-research laboratory that's—"

McChesney sat forward abruptly. Bull's-eye.

Jake continued, "I see it's not news. I've heard a dozen different versions, and it's obviously no great secret. For some reason, nobody's done anything with it. As I get the story, it's fantastic. Somebody told me it's been cleared with the D.A. and the Police Commissioner—"

"Not true."

They both waited. Jake spoke first.

"They're probably breaking the law. I don't say that critically—I know everything has to be buttoned up before you can move. My idea was to walk in and start asking questions, but if you have anything in the works I don't want to spoil it."

McChesney came out of his chair and crossed to the window, where he turned. "Where'd you say Quinby is, in Spain?"

"Yes, he's doing a piece about a director who's shooting a picture there." He paused briefly. "It's after five. I'm on my own time."

"Jake, will you wait outside a couple of minutes? I want to make a phone call."

Jake got out fast. He had no idea where this was going, but at least it was no longer standing still. He was on his second cigarette when McChesney called him in.

"I may have sounded abrupt," McChesney said. "I thought for a minute you'd bugged the office, because that's what I've been talking about all afternoon." He pushed a document across the desk. "Ever see one of these?"

Jake read it quickly. In one long paragraph, dense with legal quibbles, an unnamed person or persons covenanted and agreed that any material written in collaboration or by each severally, on the subject of the so-called Genital Physiology Research Project, conducted by Dr. Chalmers S. Prescott and Mrs. Martha Freeman, or their associated clinic, or any papers, articles, speeches, reports, minutes, or memoranda prepared by said Dr. Prescott and Mrs. Freeman, individually or as co-authors, could not be published in the form of a book or a magazine article or become the substance of a radio or television presentation or a newspaper interview, or communicated publicly in any way or form, without the written agreement of Woods McChesney, Assistant District Attorney of New York County.

"Bobby never signs this kind of release," Jake said.

"Then it's just as well he's in Spain."

Jake laughed and scratched his name at the bottom. "Now what?"

"This will take a little explaining," McChesney said, leaning back. "You don't have to be anywhere?"

"Not right away."

"To start with a generalization—most of the time this office doesn't get involved with anything until we get a complaint. Somebody comes in and tells us he's been swindled. In a murder case the victim's the complainant, if you get what I mean. This laboratory has been a touchy assignment. I can't just notify the precinct and have them arrested for staging lewd and indecent exhibitions. The fact that it's scientific gives them a certain immunity. You'd better read this."

He handed Jake a two-page deposition signed "Victoria Orr." McChesney himself had witnessed her signature. It described her adventures in the laboratory, beginning with observed masturbation, moving into machine coition, ending finally with a series of oral-genital contacts with another female as part of a brain-electricity program.

"Is she serious about this last part?" Jake said. "I thought it was straight man-woman stuff."

"So did I. But it's not something they'd want to have bruited around. You can see how they reason. They want to find out everything there is to know about orgasms, and when a scientist says everything he means *everything*. This is going to make a difference. I don't see the Civil Liberties Union coming in as a friend of the Court to defend his right to find out what happens when one fag rams another, or the subtle distinction between homo and hetero tongue-jobs. It's too marginal. Maybe someday we'll see it in the new Madison Square Garden, but right now I think the press is going to be on *our* side for a change. Looking ahead to the trial, he'll bring in a troop of experts to testify how much we need to know the truth about homosexuality, but I eat that kind of expert alive."

"So you've got your complainant. What's the problem?"

"The girl herself is the problem. If I bring her into court to repeat that in front of a jury, she says she'll deny the whole thing. Cute as she is, she's a little flakey, and I'd be a hell of a lawyer to put her on the stand and open her up to cross-examination. But I can get a search warrant on the strength of this deposition."

The phone rang.

"Yeah," he said into it. "He did? Did you try anybody in the Tenth? Try Piselli. I've got somebody with me now. I'll call you back."

He hung up and said "Shit!" under his breath. He returned to Jake.

"I don't have to tell you this is off the record—all the way off, Jake. The nominating convention opens Friday. My name's been mentioned for District Attorney."

"Congratulations."

"Congratulations at this point are premature. The D.A. isn't sure he's going for governor. If he does—*if* he does—and if my name's put in nomination I have a fifty-fifty chance."

He forced himself to unclench and sit back. "I'm thinking of the impact of this on the convention. Luck has a lot to do with it, but here's the way I work out the timing. Tonight I'm going to be busy. Tomorrow night, that's Wednesday, actually I think I'll wait till after midnight to cut down the chance of leaks, I'll get the warrant from Larry Hamp, who's the one judge in town I can trust not to phone the papers the minute I walk out the door. I'll use three detectives on the Squad. They won't know where they're going until it's time to leave. We'll hit the laboratory at five A.M., which will give us three or four hours to horse around. If the girl's story holds up, we'll find some lab notes and hopefully some movie film. Then we won't even have to bring her before the grand jury."

Jake was listening attentively. To take off some of the strain, he started another cigarette, and McChesney popped a fresh mint in his mouth.

"There's going to be no press coverage of the raid, because

if this thing leaks we're dead, dead, dead. It could blow back on us. On me, specifically. This is New York, New York. The egghead vote is only about four hundred thousand, but you have to have it to win. Unless I can identify some clear-cut homosexual material, I'll put everything back the way it was and walk out. But, assuming that the breaks go my way, I'll call in the press that afternoon, to make Friday's papers. The delegates are going to figure that this isn't a two-day story. It's going to be page one all summer, keeping my name in front of the voters. It should put me over."

"Five in the morning is pretty early for me to get up," Jake said, making it a question.

"You're not invited. We're talking in terms of a book, not a news bulletin. You'll get first crack at the records, first and only crack. You'll have access all the way through to material that won't be available to anybody else. If you could get a crash publication schedule so it's out before election, so much the better, but of course we have to stand for reelection every four years. Incidentally, it could make you some money."

The phone rang again. He looked at Jake.

"I guess that's it for now. Are we in business?"

"Damn right we're in business."

The party was thinning out by the time Jake arrived. The noise level remained high. Betty took these things seriously, and she didn't want the competition to think she couldn't come up with a suitable man when her husband was out of the country. Jake went over to kiss the air near her cheek and say he was glad he'd finally managed to make it. He had invented a very good excuse in the taxi, but she looked so mad he decided not to bother.

She didn't think they should take any chances merely because her husband was reputed to be across the Atlantic— Madrid was only a few hours away by jet. She had one of her best plans worked out for the evening—dinner with Hubie and a few friends, separate departures, all-night sex in a neutral apartment. So far they hadn't spent a night together, though they had been talking about it incessantly. The Quinby house was out of the question, and even with Bobby away she didn't want to run the risk of being seen leaving Jake's building in the morning. Now at last a friend of hers was going to Mexico for two weeks and had left her the key to an apartment in Lincoln Towers, which had the advantage of being a rabbit warren with numerous entrances and exits, an ideal spot for an assignation. Could Jake imagine how she had felt for the last two hours, with this piece of news bottled up inside her and no one to tell it to?

He drank from her glass. Having just arrived, he was on a different level of consciousness from everyone else. In theory, Betty was the cautious one, and yet here she was shouting about sleeping together, assuming that all the other guests except Jake had been deafened or somehow stunned. Jake didn't want to spend the night with Betty or anybody else; he needed time to think.

"Betty, as nice as it sounds—"

She caught the rest of the sentence before he spoke it. "You have an important business appointment. Someone to interview in connection with the book." She looked away. "I hope you're not going to turn out to be a typical bastard."

"I'm not sleeping with another girl, if that's what you mean."

"Am I being too much of an organizer, Jake?"

"Don't be silly. I want a drink."

"Don't disappear. Have some more of mine. I don't enjoy all this hugger-mugger any more than you do, darling. Wouldn't it be lovely to do something corny together for a change, like getting tickets to a terrible television show?"

"And then afterward," Jake said, watching her, "if we didn't feel like making love we could do something corny like going to sleep."

"You really are disaffected, aren't you?"

He decided he'd gone far enough. "No, it's just that when we make these elaborate arrangements, we both feel we have to come up to a certain standard or the effort will be wasted. Publish or perish, if you see what I mean."

"I see what you mean," she said, almost too quietly. "And I feel it, too, darling."

While they talked, Jake worked away at the snacks and watched the dying party. This was Betty's environment, and he was beginning to see how it worked. A California man, a middle-aged youth with a haircut like Julius Caesar's, had designed a revolutionary new line of men's sportswear. But he couldn't simply sell these clothes to stores for resale to the public. The public would be too frightened and ashamed to wear them. The party was to give the clothes some validity, to show that they were acceptable because so many people had been willing to come to a party in their honor. The *Times* was here. That couldn't have been easy.

To become part of this world, all Jake had to do was keep quiet about the raid and go along with McChesney's proposal. The Prescott story had to break sometime, and, if it broke in a way that would benefit Jake, why fight it? Bobby Quinby would howl if a book on the subject made money, but he didn't have much of a moral case, having hired Jake to hold a towel for him in his game of matrimonial chairs. Dr. Prescott would welcome the legal challenge. He would have a chance to bring in his own witnesses. The trial would make him famous, and if the jury found against him and sent him to jail, so much the better—all the great innovators have suffered for their beliefs.

Jake's argument with Betty—it was less shrill toward the end, but still an argument—ended in a compromise. They had a quick dinner by themselves and went to Jake's apartment. She left at eleven. Jake picked up his calculations where he had left off. Like it or not, he had contributed some fifteen orgasms to the Prescott-Freeman data. The cards McChesney's cops would finger through looking for titivating morsels would include his production-line sessions with Number 187, as well as the one superlative session with Number 89. He would have to warn them. But did this mean he couldn't ask for some information in return?

He knew he would have a better chance with Dr. Prescott than with Mrs. Freeman, who was already committed to a "no" answer. In the morning, after rehearsing his lines most of the night, he called the clinic. A girl's voice informed him that Dr. Prescott was out of town and offered to put him through to Mrs. Freeman, the doctor's associate.

"No, it's personal. Will he be in later?"

"I'm afraid not. He's been attending a conference in Seattle but what with the airline strike and all we don't know when to expect him."

He called Prescott's Leonia, New Jersey, number, and again he heard about the Seattle meeting and the airline strike.

"Who's calling, please?"

"Associated Press," Jake answered after an instant's pause.

"I see. Well, this is Mrs. Prescott. I'm afraid there's just no way you can reach him. He left Seattle yesterday morning, would you believe it? He's beating his way back across Canada in the most hit-or-miss fashion, on the dinkiest sort of airline. I'm sure I'll hear from him later this morning, if you'd care to call again."

Jake put in a good morning's work. Bobby had left him a list of people to talk to, but he decided to go on a one-man strike himself and see if he could finish a scene in his play. The new distractions seemed to be just what he needed; the dialogue came snapping onto the page as though real people were whispering it in his ear.

When he tried Mrs. Prescott again, he found that her husband had arrived in Toronto at noon and been promised a flight that would bring him in at the Newark Airport around four. No doubt he would come straight home instead of going into the city, because they were having guests for dinner.

"I don't suppose there's anything I could do in the meantime?" she said cheerfully.

Jake said he couldn't think of anything and promised to keep calling her. He went back to the typewriter, but the flow had stopped for the day. A faint note of vagueness in Mrs. Prescott's voice made him think that he'd better not trust her with a message. McChesney, unlike Prescott's airlines, was working on a firm deadline, and Jake decided he'd better be in Leonia himself when Prescott arrived. He called Betty and asked if he could borrow her Bugatti.

"Of course. You know where to find the keys. But don't scratch the fenders, love—you know how Bobby feels about that car. Jake?"

"Yeah."

"I can't talk now, but maybe we ought to review our situation. Will I see you tonight?"

"I'm not sure yet. I'll call you."

After picking up the Quinbys' car, Jake had the problem of finding Leonia, a commuting town somewhere on the western approaches to the George Washington Bridge. Coming off the bridge into a maze of concrete, he was given conflicting directions by policemen and gaspump jockeys and it was midafternoon by the time he found the house. He was surprised by a wrought-iron stork on the front lawn. True, Prescott had begun as a baby doctor, but the stork couldn't have been his idea unless laboratory work had changed him. A mysterious arrangement of aluminum in the rose garden reminded Jake of a similar piece in the project's waiting room. The turf was a beautiful deep green, like an advertisement for fertilizer.

The woman who answered the door was another surprise. She had lion-colored hair which seemed to have been blown into place on her head. She was wearing a tight pair of tapering slacks and she had the drawn look of the compulsive dieter.

"He's still not here," she said when Jake asked for her husband. "Are you the reporter who's been calling?"

"Yes. Have you had any news from him?"

"He's still in Toronto. It must be chaos up there. I'm expecting a call any minute, if you'd like to come in and wait?"

It was 3:45; the day was sliding rapidly past. This was a hell of a time for Prescott to be stuck in Toronto. If he wasn't back by five, Jake would have to take his chances with Mrs. Freeman.

A dog began barking angrily in a back room of the house as Jake entered the front hall.

"Ignore her," Mrs. Prescott said with a wave. "She overprotects me. This isn't New York, but we do have our burglaries."

The living room, with its thick pile carpet, its freshly cut flowers, its Paul McCobb furniture, again was not the kind of setting Jake associated with Dr. Prescott. The three most recent Book-of-the-Month Club selections were scattered around carelessly, still in their bright jackets.

"Forgive me if I'm slightly—" Mrs. Prescott said. "I'm always reduced to a state of absolute terror when my husband flies, and he flies all the time! He's been on unscheduled airplanes since yesterday morning. That word has such a treacherous sound, don't you think? Unscheduled—disorganized, haphazard, ramshackle. Did you see the motion picture *Those Magnificent Men in Their Flying Machines?* It frightened me half to death!"

She ran her hands through her hair. "I was about to pour myself a cup of coffee."

Jake had been hoping for a drink, but he told her coffee would be fine. She left the room, and he heard her rebuking the barking dog. He was looking at a photograph of a young man in army uniform when she returned with a tray.

"That's our son James. We're fearfully proud of him. Twelfth in his class at West Point." She added in a troubled voice, "How long will this terrible war— We'll have to put up with that barking, I'm afraid. The doctor's the only one who can quiet her. She knows I'm worrying—she can sense it through a closed door."

Jake accepted a coffee cup. "I don't suppose there's any way we could call him?"

"Quite impossible, I'm afraid. I imagine him camping out in one of those dreary airport lounges. But he's quite good about letting me know. He promised to call before four. This strike! I'm very much a prolabor person, but it does seem to me that anybody who flies airplanes has a public responsibility." Her spoon rattled and fell. "I know it's none of my business and I really know very little about the doctor's professional work, but could you give me some inkling as to why you want to talk to him?"

"I have a few questions about some of the things he's been doing."

"I certainly wouldn't be able to help you with anything technical." She put her cup down and said decisively, "I'm going to add a little cognac to this coffee. What about you?"

"I think that's a fine idea."

She went back to the kitchen, setting off another outburst from the dog. Jake shook his watch to be sure it was running. He was going to be as jumpy as Mrs. Prescott in another few minutes. She came back with a bottle and poured a strong slug of cognac in each cup.

"I feel so helpless! If there's some kind of crisis, I'd like to be doing something. I could be rounding up people."

"I'm sorry—I've been told not to say anything except to your husband himself."

"Couldn't you even indicate in a roundabout way— I suppose not. It doesn't come as a surprise! It's been hanging over us for years. Dr. Prescott is absolutely fearless—not so his wife, I'm afraid. Naturally, I don't have the faintest idea what sort of story you plan to write, but I do think you might find room for something— He's been working desperately hard. He comes home pale with exhaustion. There's never enough money or enough people or enough time. He used to help with the lawn and the flowers. When we first moved here—"

The phone rang, and she came up out of her chair like a rising pheasant. "That's the doctor."

She snatched up the phone. "Yes? Yes! Oh, finally. But what kind of plane is it? I know, yes, but are you sure you're not saying that because you know I'm worried? Of course you're in a hurry to get back, it's been a real ordeal, but I know how you are, sweetheart. No. No. I'm being sensible. At least size up the pilot, make sure he's a responsible person."

She covered the mouthpiece. "He'll be at Newark at four-fifty. Do you want me to ask him—"

"I'll meet him there," Jake said quickly.

To her husband: "Don't forget we're having the Petersons for dinner. Now Chuck, it's nothing to groan about. It's been scheduled for weeks. Be careful!"

She hung up. "I know it's some old-fashioned plane they've pressed into service because of the emergency." She gave Jake a searching look. "Will you tell me one thing at least? Should I phone our guests and tell them not to come to dinner?"

Jake hesitated. "I think so, Mrs. Prescott. He's going to have things to do."

"I knew it was serious." She filled her half-empty cup with cognac without adding more coffee. "One thing I'm thankful for, it didn't happen when James was at the Point. Donna's at Sarah Lawrence, but that's not so—"

Jake stood up. "I'd better be going."

"Please stay," she said sharply, looking up. "You zip straight down the Turnpike from here, and you'd just have to wait after you get there. Let me give you more cognac."

She poured it into his cup, and Jake had to sit down.

"Thank you," she said. "I won't worry so much when I know he's in the air. Getting up out of those crowded airports and then getting back down—that's when most of the accidents happen. I don't trust the people in the signal towers. They have other things on their minds. I forgot to offer you coffee."

"This is fine."

"I find it difficult to talk to my husband about his work. When he had an active practice he always used to be a part of the community. He used to take Jim to Yankee games. I hope you'll bear in mind when you write your story that you're dealing with a living person, not some horrible abstraction."

"I just phone it in, Mrs. Prescott. Somebody else writes it."

"I know I'm ignorant. Please don't tell the doctor I said anything to you. But I'm glad you could see his home." She waved at the ordered, careful room. "He isn't a cold-blooded— I can see you're not completely devoid of feeling, like those newspapermen on *Meet the Press*. Once a newspaper story gets rolling, I know there's not much one individual can do. But if there could be just one account written with sympathy—"

"I really have to be going, Mrs. Prescott."

"People will think he picked this field out of some unnatural compulsion, but that's just plain not true. He was one of the finest college basketball players in the Midwest. That man has sacrificed himself. Sometimes he's in the laboratory eighteen hours straight. He's had to cut himself off from ordinary life. When he comes home at night, what can we talk about? He used to like to play bridge, he was a crackerjack player. Now— somebody will tell some anecdote about what happened at work—"

Jake stirred.

"Are you married?" she asked.

"No. I don't want to be late. I'd better—"

"Did you notice the houses along this street? When you see a house like that in a movie, you know that somebody like Jack Lemmon lives inside, with a handsome wife and funny kids. The truth is that most of the women on this street are miserable! Don't tell him I said this, I beg you. Marriages are crumbling all over town—and for no reason. The boy next door killed himself at Yale. Just getting along pleasantly these days, two people, it's just about impossible. My father was a dairy farmer. He knew exactly what he was doing. Everybody we know works in New York in offices." She stared down into her cup. "Doing terrible things."

Jake stood up, but that didn't stop her.

"There are fewer divorces among doctors. Their wives

know there are certain things they can't demand. I've made
my peace with that. But because of the nature of his research,
there's a—lack of communication. I haven't wanted to meet
the people he works with. He's absorbed in his work; naturally, he can't stop thinking about it merely because his observations are over for the day. And those laboratory couples, I
must say this, I insist on saying it, how can he help com-
paring—"

That was enough for Jake. He broke in, "I'll do the best I
can, Mrs. Prescott."

"You're going? I suppose you must. If anything had happened while his plane was taking off, they would have called
me by now, don't you think?" She came to her feet, blinking
to keep her balance, and accompanied him to the door. "I've
been talking too much. I do that when I—"

He wanted to assure her that things might not be as bad as
they seemed, but by now he didn't believe it himself.

She gave him her hand. "You'll be in plenty of time. After
his plane gets in you'll have a few minutes, won't you, while
the luggage comes out? I'd appreciate it if you'd call me. Call
me collect."

Jake promised, and Mrs. Prescott told him to drive carefully. Sometimes she thought the highways were almost as
lethal as the airports.

"Damn," she said. "I shouldn't have given you that cognac.
It was criminal of me."

The dog was barking again. "Hush," she said uncertainly.
"There's nothing to worry about."

Prescott's plane was behind schedule, and Jake was beginning to share Mrs. Prescott's distrust of nonscheduled aircraft.
It dropped down finally through the smoke and steam, and
proved to be an ordinary jet-prop, with ordinary numbers on
its tail. He called Mrs. Prescott to tell her the plane was down
and the passengers were disembarking.

"I really knew it would be all right," she said with an embarrassed laugh. "It wasn't too bad this time—you ought to see me
when I really worry. You were sweet to hold my hand. I don't
know what I was babbling about— In a way, you know, it's a
relief to have this out in the open at last. I'm afraid I've become

something of an ingoing person. But what the devil do I care? We can always move. We're not sentenced to Leonia for life."

"There he is, Mrs. Prescott. I don't want to miss him."

Unlike most of his fellow travelers, Dr. Prescott had shaved recently, but they all looked equally beat. They collected at the luggage counter, looking as though they wouldn't be surprised to be told that their belongings had been thrown overboard to lighten the aircraft. Jake waited till Prescott's suitcase shot into view and met him in an eddy at the edge of the crowd. Prescott knew instantly that something was wrong. He was squinting with fatigue.

"I'm Jake Burgess. I've got some news about the project, and it's urgent."

"We can talk in my car. You were in the control program."

"That's right, 42-A. Fourteen hits and one miss."

They said nothing until Prescott unlocked his car and tossed his bag in the back seat. They got in.

"I've never been able to sleep on planes. All right, Jake."

"You're going to be raided at five tomorrow morning."

Prescott was too tired to react quickly. "Raided by whom?"

Jake told him about McChesney's plans and then said abruptly, "Did Mrs. Freeman tell you I've been trying to get the name of a girl I met in your laboratory?"

"No."

"She wouldn't give it to me because it might set a precedent. I want to be tough about this, but I don't know exactly how to do it. It's the first time I ever tried to blackmail anybody. McChesney has a statement from one of your volunteers. I think it would make a difference if you knew her name. I'll trade with you."

"I don't think that's possible."

"It might make a difference between a bad court case and no case at all. She had a couple of homosexual sessions, and I thought if you took her cards out of the files—"

After a moment Prescott said, "What would you do with the name if I gave it to you?"

"Go and see her. And if she doesn't want to talk to me I'll let her alone. We only had about forty-five minutes together, and I think I can keep it in proportion. I just want to find out if there's a chance of starting over. It was a pretty big forty-five minutes for her, too."

A clock on the dashboard gave the time. Prescott began setting his watch.

"I'm still on Seattle time. Very well, Jake. Do you have to have the name before you tell me the rest of it?"

"No, I think I'll trust you." He gave a sudden relieved laugh. "I didn't think you'd do it. Victoria Orr."

Prescott's fingers slipped on the winding knob. After a moment he corrected the setting and returned the watch to his wrist.

"Victoria Orr had no homosexual exposures in the laboratory. None whatever."

"She said she did. I only had time to skim through the statement, but it sounded authentic to me. Are you sure? She must have kept a calendar—most of it's dated. In one series with the machine she was trying to have orgasm without muscle tension. Does that sound right?"

"Yes, she worked on that."

"And then you talked her into having sex with a lesbian. She was new at it, and the idea was that you wanted to compare her with somebody who'd been a lesbian all her life."

"That's absolute nonsense."

"It's not too different from the program I was on. She says she did it three times. But she felt horrible afterward, she couldn't sleep. She's been seeing a psychiatrist. Finally, she confessed to a priest, and he told her to go to the police."

Prescott said dryly, "Yes, that could hurt us."

"I haven't heard about any homosexual stuff. I almost told McChesney she was lying."

"She was. Her only productive episodes were in machine coition. There was an emotional instability we didn't catch in the screening process, and we had to drop her. Apparently she interpreted that as a rejection and made this statement to punish us."

"But you do have a homosexual program?"

"Not as such. We record homosexual material as part of our generalized study of reaction patterns. Why not?"

"Why not?" Jake burst out. "Because enough is enough! You're supposed to be working on sexual incompatibility. Do we have to start worrying about incompatible queers? You're too far ahead of the rest of us already."

"Be logical, Jake," Prescott said wearily. "Why should

homosexual data carry this emotional charge? I'm having conversations with a publisher about issuing some of our findings in book form. He's made only one condition—that we exclude our homosexual observations. Oddly enough, the editor who'll be working with us on it is clearly a homosexual. Homosexuality is a pressing social concern. The law on the subject is medieval—based on guesswork and prejudice. How can we deal with the whole range of human sexuality and leave it out? But there's never been the slightest compulsion in any of our laboratory arrangements. All our homosexual material has come from individuals with a long history of homosexuality. If this statement gets out—"

He gathered himself with an effort. "Follow me in your car."

chapter 21

Called by electronic voices, Fletcher Williams stood up, relieved that the waiting was over. He and Hanna really didn't have much to say to each other anymore.

"I'll miss you," she said. "I asked about phone rates, and they're surprisingly cheap after nine at night. Call me, darling. Please."

She put up her mouth for a kiss. Fletcher found himself clutching her buttocks, pulling her in hard against him. If they had done this before leaving home, they might have smashed through to each other, but that sort of miracle doesn't happen at airports.

He was the first to pull back. "A real kiss for a change."

She set a precedent by saying nothing. Actually, if his plane fell into the Atlantic, she would probably miss him. He picked up his TWA bag and his music case. "This is a hell of a place to leave from. There's nothing definite about it."

"Make a date with me—the first weekend after you get back. Let's have two days somewhere by ourselves."

He kissed her forehead. "All right, dear. Take care of everybody on Riverside Drive."

He entered the corridor leading to his plane. At the gate he turned abruptly and hurried back.

Because of the mechanics' strike on the domestic airlines, there were vast crowds all over Kennedy and he had good cover. Hanna wouldn't hang around to watch his plane blow itself into the air. He had planned carefully and he didn't have to rush, so long as he kept moving. Leaving the building, he went into the nearest parking lot, where he had left the rented Chevy. If you wanted to convict your wife of having a secret affair, you arranged to leave for Germany, then canceled that reservation and made another on a later flight. You rented a car and parked it ahead of time at the airport. When your wife drove you out the next day in your own car, you were all set to follow her. Ridiculously simple.

The strange thing was that Fletched didn't really believe what he was doing. The old jealousy rationale, the clear title in paternity, had been destroyed by advances in contraceptive technique, and, in any case, Fletcher could hardly be afraid that his wife was being impregnated by Dr. Prescott's machine. He himself hadn't hesitated to get into Mary Jane Mosberg when he had the chance. He didn't believe there should be one law for the husband and another law for the wife, but, unluckily, what he believed had nothing to do with the way he felt. He felt murderous. He literally wanted to kill everyone who had anything to do with his wife's scientific orgasms.

The day he saw her going into Max Sultan's apartment building he went home and wrote his first new piece of music since the directorship had been dangled in front of his nose. He wrote in fury, but the fury didn't last, he had too many responsibilities. In the office, he stopped being the music-loving slob who considered administrative routine beneath the attention of a grown man. Without the administrators, the world would fall apart. He dropped a few caustic remarks where they would do the most good and fired an incompetent Negro secretary who had been kept on because of her place in the larger picture. The students were agitating for a voice in policy questions, but they quickly learned from Fletcher that they were at the bottom of the ladder, and ladders have to be climbed in the old-fashioned way, one rung at a time. He no longer wasted any time balancing pros and cons but decided things fast and got them out of his way.

He and Hanna resumed lovemaking, after a fashion. No one could take exception to his sexual behavior. Once, in an unguarded moment, he asked her which she preferred. She told him not to be an idiot, of course she preferred it with him. She offered again to abandon the laboratory if he insisted, but he couldn't let her trap him that way. It would give her a talking point for life. "The one time I really felt I was making a contribution—and I'll call your attention to the fact that I didn't hesitate to give it up to save our marriage."

The Darmstadt orchestra still wanted him, but, with the needle of his mind wobbling back and forth between sex and administration, he hadn't given them a definite yes or no. He had often wondered where they got a copy of his score. That mystery was solved by a casual reference in one of the German letters to the kind offices of **Dr. Max Sultan.** Very kind indeed; also an ingenious dodge to get his mistress' husband out of the country.

He ran into Max one evening, at the hour when cocktail parties begin breaking up. Max had been drinking, whereas Fletcher had been working on a preliminary building budget. Dragged into a nearby bar, Fletcher had to listen to still another harangue on the subject of Darmstadt. Max had read an article about the musicianship of the smaller German ensembles, their willingness to experiment. The Darmstadt concertmaster had refused offers from Berlin and Philadelphia. Max, needless to say, was well informed about Fletcher's activities. He knew the Conservatory was about to expand. They owned a once-elegant apartment house, at present occupied by welfare families, and Fletcher had ordered a feasibility study of the relative merits of conversion as opposed to destruction. Soon a building committee would be named, and then it would really be impossible to get away.

"I don't claim that a few bars of original music are more important than a rehearsal building," Max declared. "They're utterly different things. But nobody can write that music except you. Anybody can head up a building committee. There are sixteen million committees in New York, approximately two committees per capita." He peered at his friend. "I notice a slight thickening about the jowls. You may remember I predicted it."

"In that case," Fletcher said equably, "I suppose I'd better go to Darmstadt. Will that satisfy you?"

"I know you probably won't," Max said, bending down to his drink. "You may mean it now, because we all like flattery. But tomorrow you'll look at your 'in' basket. If you don't get to work on that paper right away, it'll overflow. I see a torrent of paper flowing out the door, down the corridor, down the front steps, along Broadway—"

Fletcher was still fond of his friend, who might even be half sincere about the dichotomy between creative music and creative musical administration; he had no personal stake in it himself. Fletcher, in his place, might have done the same, persuading himself that he was helping a friend as well as clearing up a problem of access to the friend's wife.

The next day he cabled an acceptance. Hanna said, "I think

it's the right thing, Fletcher—get clear away, with new people around you and a hard job of work."

Later, in bed, she made a strong try. He ran the usual patterns. It was all predictable and machinelike, which was what she liked, after all. He applied certain pressures, set in motion certain circulatory disturbances, established an appropriate level of neuromuscular tension. She came while trying to outwait him, and that set him off. They grasped each other convulsively, and the local sensations were as described in the literature, except that Fletcher was grinding his teeth. Had Dr. Prescott ever recorded that extragenital reaction?

He passed one car and left another between the rented Chevy he was driving and his own older Chevy driven by his wife.

Every living person, he knew, had the makings of a schizophrenic. He was following his wife along the Van Wyck Expressway—"tailing," was the way it would be described in detective fiction—in an attempt to trap her in an act of adultery. (Who even used the word anymore?) One of his troubles was that he knew her so damn well. When he imagined her in the laboratory, stroking herself or being stroked by the machine, it was all fantastically real. He knew the kind of noises she made. Sometimes, when she didn't want to call it a night and he was too tired to help, she continued alone, with Fletcher holding her breast. He had liked to follow the play of expression on her face while she booted herself home. He remembered being proud of her lack of inhibitions, grateful for being included in this private matter. But no longer! He should have put a stop to it long ago.

A horn blared behind him. He had drifted over the line.

The only person he truly loved at this moment was his daughter Jennie. The day before, during a tense, wordless breakfast, he had found himself examining her intently to see if her features resembled his. And they didn't, really, except in the same ways that he and Hanna resembled each other. He'd been shouting at her lately, which was new in that family. She didn't understand it. How could he explain to a four-year-old that the reason he was mad all the time was because her mummy was letting herself be entered by a machine, in the interests of science and her own pleasure? It wouldn't be fair to Jennie or to any of them to go on living together. But it had to be done in such a way that everyone would know who had broken up the marriage. Hanna was convinced that there was nothing wrong with her laboratory activities. But, if he could catch her in bed with a living man, even she would have to concede that she was a bitch and a cheat.

It wouldn't be pleasant. He would stand exposed as a social reactionary who believed a wife had obligations toward her family. Played in a certain way, it could be farce, with Fletcher in the role of buffoon.

Was it imagination, or was she driving more recklessly than usual? She passed a slower car, accelerating and braking like a hotrodder late for a date. Suddenly he wished he had a gun. Unfortunately, he had a horror of guns, the same horror he had of jealousy. But it would have lifted the scene out of comedy. It was too late to do anything about it now, but Hanna would have been impressed with a gun.

In Manhattan, caught by a red light, he almost lost her. By slipping in and out of lanes, he had her in view again by the time she signaled for the turn into the garage. Jennie was eating with a nursery-school classmate and didn't have to be picked up at any fixed time. What better way for Hanna to celebrate her husband's departure than by having Max visit her in her own bed for a change?

He found a parking space. Upstairs, after relocking the door, he went directly to the back bathroom, a tiny room with no tub. The toilet here had a tendency to keep running, and the room was rarely used. Fletcher shot the bolt and looked at himself in the mirror.

Unquestionably, he looked different.

He heard a door open and close, and after a moment the first bars of the overture to *Don Giovanni*. He loosened his tie; no air had seeped into this bathroom for years. *Don Giovanni* —probably Max, when he arrived, would interpret her choice of background music as a tribute to his sexual powers. The melodic line, usually so pure, seemed warped and fuzzy, as though some component in the hi-fi needed to be replaced. Was this what jealousy did to the ear?

His plans were flexible. He had twenty-four hours, and if the adultery didn't take place here—that word "adultery" again—it would take place at Max's. Fletcher would ring the bell, and when Max opened the door he would be so taken aback that Fletcher could walk right past him. After that they would see.

A clanking in the plumbing indicated that the other bath-room was being used. Time passed, and where was Max? To the accompaniment of the famous diminished seventh, Don Giovanni slew the Commendatore. Fletcher felt oddly resentful. The son of a bitch wasn't in much of a hurry.

When the doorbell sounded, Fletcher jumped off the closed john, his hands flying. An instant later, composing himself, he was listening intently at the door. Two rooms and a long hall separated him from the action. He had to hang onto himself now and imagine exactly how long they were spending on each preliminary. He would blow the whole thing by appearing too soon. They didn't actually have to be in sexual contact, but they had to be committed to it, with their clothes scattered. He had kept track of Hanna's comings and goings during the last few days, and he was almost positive that during that time she had had no extramarital sex. As for marital sex, he had deprived her of that himself. One of her main contentions had always been that she had needs, like a man. Probably she and Max wouldn't waste much time on idle conversation. Something like: "Got him off all right. Won't it be fabulous, making love without having to look at the clock?"

Damn that music! The soprano was denouncing libertines and libertinism, and in another moment Leporello and the great seducer himself, the prototype, would give the male view of the matter. Fletcher, from his place of concealment, was all but certain that the voices he could hear beneath the taped recitative had moved to the bedroom. Now there was silence. The initial kiss, surely. Now the clothes would start coming off. They were old hands; they wouldn't be coy. He tried to remember what Hanna had been wearing, but he couldn't visualize her at all, as though he had already shut her out of his life.

He waited till the end of the aria, unbolted the door quietly, and tiptoed into the extra bedroom, where he stopped and listened again. Nothing but Mozart. He was wishing for a weapon, to have something in his hands. Someone changed position on the bed, and Fletcher crossed the hall, stopping just short of the doorway.

"Who's that hanging around out there?" Hanna said lightly.

Don Giovanni continued to insist that his way of handling the sex problem could be used as a model for everybody. Fletcher entered the room. Hanna, in a slip, was sitting cross-legged on the bed, painting her toenails.

"Fletcher! What happened to your plane?"

"The flight was canceled," he said hoarsely. "Engine trouble."

She swung her legs off the bed. "You scared me! I thought you were out over the ocean—"

The excitement in her voice was meant to carry. She was a junior-eight Phi Beta Kappa, in the 99th percentile, and her presence of mind had always been remarkable. If she could tie Fletcher up for thirty seconds, if Max used his head and moved fast—

But Fletcher was in control of this situation. He smelled her usual smells.

"Fletcher, my God, my heart stopped beating there for a minute. Why on earth didn't you call me?"

She hugged him hard, and his hands went to the sweet curve at the base of her spine. Eleven years of conditioning told him to return her embrace and pretend he had imagined the door-bell and the voices. Hanna would know he had caught her but was too nice a guy to do anything about it. Her self-satisfied look, which kept her from looking really pretty, was gone, possibly for good.

Fletcher followed the "Madamina" aria with one part of his mind, and when he heard the squeak of the bathroom door he took her by the waist and moved her aside. The light was off, but there was movement at the far end of the hall.

"Don't rush off, Max," he said, quickening his step.

The figure came around. It wasn't Max. It was Joe Ben Fox, who had been coming to Fletcher for viola lessons for the last ten months. He was barefoot and carrying his shoes. He glowered at Fletcher, as though Fletcher was the one who didn't belong.

"Aren't you supposed to be in Germany or someplace?"

Hanna ran down the hall. "Fletcher, where did you get this taste for cheap melodrama?"

Melodrama at least was a higher form of art than farce. The tape, unwinding, reached the first-act finale, the waltz and the minuet combining with the two-four country dance—clever music but inappropriate to the situation.

Fletcher hit the boy with a small bust of Beethoven he didn't even know he was holding. The noise of the impact was disagreeable. A little bubble popped in his brain, and he hit the boy again with the full strength of his bow arm. Joe Ben wavered and fell.

Hanna was clinging to Fletcher from behind. He tried to thrust her away so he could smash the boy's head to powder. She fought him in silence. And then in an instant he pulled up and away and saw the scene from somewhere above the ceiling—the three ridiculous figures, the soprano, the bass, and the tenor. What were they fighting about? The strength went out of his fingers. The bust dropped to the floor.

"You lunatic! I just hope you didn't kill him."

He had to breathe deeply several times before he was able to say, "We don't agree about anything. I hope I did."

He pulled out of the situation and went into the bathroom to wash his hands. There was no blood on them, but he had a confused idea that it was necessary to start thinking about fingerprints. He felt dizzy and sick.

The boy gave a creepy moan, rising to A sharp on an indrawn breath. At least that meant he was still alive. Fletcher swept several towels off the rack. Joe Ben was rolling his head from side to side to some inner rhythm. Fletcher heard the clatter of a phone in the living room, and Hanna came out.

"Max is coming."

"Max!"

"Fletcher, you damn, damn fool." She came toward him. "It wasn't important."

He repeated that to see how it sounded. It sounded insane.

"Do you think you ought to touch him?"

Her pubic triangle, the source of all the trouble, showed clearly through the slip, on a level with his eyes. "You must realize that we're finished," he said.

He forced himself to look more closely at the bloody head.

Wiping gently, he located the two wounds. A flap of flesh had been torn loose, and through the opening he could see the whiteness of bone.

"Fletcher, don't. Max'll be here in a few minutes."

"Shut up, will you?"

He pressed the towel against the boy's head to stop the blood. It was flowing steadily, not in spurts, so at least he'd been lucky enough not to rupture an artery. But what a stupid thing to do. Joe Ben had been nothing but a piece of meat snapped up by a hungry dog.

"Fletcher," his ex-wife said quietly, "I haven't been going to the laboratory, not that it makes any difference. I tried to tell you."

"Will you please shut up?—What happened, did the machine wear out from all the friction?"

She made a broken gesture. "I have Jennie. Billions of people have babies. I'm a good cook. There are billions of good cooks. If you won't make love to me, don't I have a right to—"

"Absolutely, a perfect right. We're all entitled to a minimum of one orgasm a day. And that's only the minimum. If we're capable of excellence, we shouldn't settle for mediocrity."

The buzzer rasped. Fletcher opened the door to Max, smelling of whiskey.

"God almighty, Fletcher!"

He drove them back from the boy. Fletcher watched for only a moment, then went into the living room. Hanna came after him.

"I know you won't believe this—"

Fletcher shouted, "Then don't say it! I want you to keep absolutely quiet!"

"Fletcher, please listen to me."

"Why should I, when I know what you're going to say? You've only opened up for Joe Ben two or three times, and he's not as good as I am because he's so young and inexperienced. But everything's relative. I'm not in the same league as the machine, am I? I know when I'm outclassed. Now do you mind not talking about it?"

If he had been alone he would have spun the tape to the big scene where the statue took Don Giovanni by the hand

and they both went out yelling. But it would have been a frivolous gesture, after establishing his seriousness by trying to kill a man.

Max called him. "You're a tiger. I didn't think husbands tried to kill lovers anymore."

"Of course they do. Read the *News*."

"Nobody we know makes the *News*. We're taking him to St. Clare's. Help me with him, and for God's sake don't drop him. Hanna? Hanna!"

She appeared. She was finally crying.

"Get the elevator," Max snapped.

Like all hospitals, St. Clare's discouraged visitors, and Fletched was permitted into the X-ray section only because he was under the wing of a staff physician. He sat on a narrow radiator cover at the end of the hall. If one of those bone splinters had been driven into Joe Ben's brain, society would arrange for Fletched to have plenty of time to regret his stupidity. He felt a sharp, steady pain over one eye, as though a skewer of bone had been driven through his own eyebrow. Whatever happened, he knew he wasn't going back to the Conservatory. Somebody else would have to wield the ceremonial shovel at the cornerstone laying.

A door opened, and Max Sultan came toward him, feeling for cigarettes.

"Now you can tell me, Fletcher. What were you on?"

"I did it sober. How do the X-rays look?"

Max was in no hurry to tell him. He struck a match.

"I feel like hell, not that you care. I was just getting a buzz on when Hanna called. I had to let the intern sew him up."

"What about the bone splinters?"

"What bone splinters? Those were chips of plaster."

"Don't be a prick, Max! *How is he?*"

"He's conscious. He just doesn't know who he is."

"Well, that's contemporary."

Max looked at the end of his cigarette. "What odds is Las Vegas giving against a divorce?"

"They couldn't get any takers. Doesn't it annoy you that she phoned Joe Ben first?"

"A little. But I'm twenty pounds over my best weight and

everybody knows I'm no virtuoso in the sack." He looked directly at Fletcher. "Do you think we've been sleeping together?"

"Hell, I saw her going into your building. And that Darmstadt ploy—that was a little transparent."

"Yeah, that was my idea," Max agreed. "I've been trying to make it with Hanna since the first night I saw her. And the only time I came close was when she was so mad at you she didn't care what she did. And, to be honest, I didn't come very close even then."

"Don't give me that, Max. She'll screw anybody."

"Not just anybody." Max blew out smoke. "Outside of the laboratory, and I don't know too much about that, I can't think of more than, say—"

"*Who?*" Fletcher demanded sharply.

"I'm just making a point," Max said in disgust. "If you've given up on her you shouldn't care who or how many. You've been putting her over the jumps, boy. I don't like this Joe Ben thing any more than you do. I think she could have done better. But God damn it—"

"So the whole thing is my fault?"

"Haven't you figured that out yet?" Max said wearily. "Of course it's your fault. Hanna's a bright woman. She hasn't done much with her mind so far, but I don't think it's going to continue. She's not only bright, she's emotionally very responsive and trusting. You faked her into thinking you had some talent as a musician. Now it seems you're only a bureaucrat. Do you expect her to like it?"

"Everybody has to live in this world."

"What world? You wanted an excuse to buy Brooks Brothers suits and that stupid little hat. Why do you think she hauled you up to 158th Street?"

"Because she can have a very good orgasm at the count of three, and she knew I'd fizzle. That gave her the high ground. I've been taking a pounding ever since."

"That wasn't the way it was meant to work. It's funny, when you think about it. I'd fiddle things around and get an hour alone with her, and all we'd talk about was you. She wanted to shake you out of your coma. Your domestic sex was going downhill, you were turning into Heinrich Himmler

at the Conservatory. A bureaucrat in the office is a bureaucrat between the sheets."

The hell with this! Fletcher pushed off from the radiator.
Max stayed where he was, smoking. Halfway along the corridor Fletcher turned and came back.

"Max, she talks about sex ad infinitum. If she thought it
was going downhill, why didn't she say so?"

"How could she? Every time she tried, you went into a
sulk. She thought the laboratory might get you interested in
the subject again. And why did it make you so mad when
she wanted to go on alone? I'll tell you why. Because you
couldn't stand the idea that she could be better at anything
than you are."

Fletcher rubbed his face. "Maybe so, Max. It goes back
a hundred thousand years. Husbands are supposed to be bigger
and stronger than their wives. When a woman comes it's all
right to shake a little, but a man's supposed to explode! Leave
us something. We can't have babies."

"You know she hasn't been going lately?"

"So she tells me. Can we knock it off, Max? What about
the X-rays?"

"They're clean. But don't relax yet. I'm in a position to do
you some damage. Until I fill out the admissions sheet I've
got a handle. If his memory comes back nobody has to know
who hit him or with what. A bust of Beethoven, for God's
sake. I can say we picked him up in a doorway."

Fletcher looked at him suspiciously. "He won't go along
with that."

"He will unless you really scrambled his brains. Why should
he swear out a complaint against his Acting Director? But—
and it's a big but, Fletcher—you've got to go back and talk
to Hanna."

"Not talking was never our problem."

"I mean talk honestly. What do you want me to put on
the sheet?"

Fletcher hesitated. "That you found him in a doorway,
I suppose. I'm not looking for trouble. You're a romantic,
Max. What good is talking going to do us?"

"Try it and find out."

"Max, is it really true that you and Hanna didn't—haven't—"

"It's really true."

After a moment Fletcher shrugged, more in anger than in resignation. "I don't mind if she does things better than I do, so long as it doesn't include sex. And the next time she fucks anybody else there isn't going to be any of this crap about plaster busts. I'll use a gun. Bear that in mind."

"Yes, tiger. Are you taking her to Germany with you?"

"How can I? What about Jennie?"

"It's a jet, not a covered wagon. She's crazy to go."

Fletcher shook his fists in the air. "Why didn't she *say* something? Max, call her. Tell her I'm on my way."

They looked at each other, with no emotion showing. Were they still friends? Fletcher was damned if he knew.

All the cabs were snug in their garages for the night, and he had to walk most of the way. He called her name as he let himself in. There was no answer. He looked in every room, including the extra bathroom, but she was definitely gone.

Where he had made his mistake was telling Max to phone. If he could have got her into bed while she still thought he might have killed Joe Ben— He stood at the window, looking down at the moving necklace of lights along the highway. The door opened before he went out of his mind, and Hanna came in with Jennie.

"I hear we're going to Germany."

Disciplining himself—for if the woman is cool the man has to be cooler, which is something else that goes back 100,000 years—he went toward her without running.

chapter 22

The girl's name was Birgitta Engstrom.

After Dr. Prescott left him, Jake sat in the car for a moment, the slip of paper trembling in his fingers. He had made them take some responsibility for one of the things they had done, but nevertheless he nearly crumpled the paper and threw it away. He couldn't remember what she looked like. The one thing in his mind was a cryptic phrase from Mrs. Freeman's notes, " 'Seemed forever' (24 sec.)." Even on that Sunday there had been another thirty-six seconds in the minute, another twenty-three hours, fifty-nine minutes in the day. And it had been one day out of many.

He found a phone booth and started to dial Betty Quinby's number. The action of the dial was sluggish, as though an incoming call was trying to force its way through. He hung up and retrieved his dime. More phrases from Mrs. Freeman's notes came back to him: "Ideal . . . completeness . . . low emotional content with previous partners . . ." The worst that could happen, the very worst, would be to be told in her attractive accent to disappear and not come near her again. He could stand that, probably.

The address was in the East Fifties. He didn't stop to hunt for a legal parking space but left the Bugatti against a white-painted curb in front of a private hospital. She lived in a locked building. The bell card said simply: "Engstrom." He pressed buttons at random, but not hers, and when a voice answered he called, "United Parcel." A buzzer opened the door.

In the elevator he thought of other ways he might be doing this. It was too late now.

The silence that followed the ringing of her doorbell might have lasted only another twenty-four seconds, but again it seemed forever. There was a faint clink as the peephole opened. Jake stared straight at the deadly little circle, his face grim. Her reactions, if she was indeed reacting, were concealed by the door.

A bolt was thrown, then another bolt, the door swung open, and there she was.

She was wearing a wrapper and no makeup, the way he had seen her first. She gave him the grave look he remembered, and did the one thing he hadn't considered a possibility. Coming into his arms, she kissed him hard.

"Now we can finish this properly," she said.

He followed her in, feeling as clumsy as he had felt that first Sunday morning.

"First," she said, turning, "I have a husband now, and he'll be here in a moment. Second, I am to have a child, though it's too soon for you to notice. I was sure you could learn my name from the people at the Central Park party. It was so incredibly stupid, the way I took one look at you and ran away."

"Are you really pregnant?"

"Yes. And I have hoped for a child because of my husband —it is important to him. What did you think of me when I kept away from the laboratory?"

"I thought I'd disappointed you."

"I was afraid of that. No, it was something different. Wait a moment and I'll tell you. I must first put on my dress. My husband works for the diplomatic service, and I think for diplomatic reasons I should be dressed if he finds us together. He knows nothing of Dr. Prescott, by the way. Perhaps I will tell him sometime—perhaps! Come in the bedroom with me, and listen carefully for the sound of a key in the door."

In the bedroom, she took off her wrapper without any hesitation. She was wearing only a half-slip. Jake remembered the ways her body had moved in his hands.

He realized that he was in a large room with many mirrors. A closet door was folded open, as though someone had wanted to make sure he saw the black fur coat inside, in its transparent bag. The dress she meant to wear was laid out on an enormous double bed. She disappeared into it. There was a zipper, which she closed.

"I know he will be fifteen minutes yet, but all the same I will hurry."

Her self-possession was complete and invulnerable, and Jake despaired. She turned to her dressing table and began work on her eyes. That completed, she picked over the objects in a jewel box. Jake was watching her in the mirror and he saw that her left hand was tightly clenched. The fingernails must be digging into her palm.

She turned with a bracelet. "Fasten this for me," she said with no sign of agitation. "Then I will put in my earrings, and we can talk. But I should know your name. It would be a great error to introduce you to my husband as Number 137."

He put the bracelet around her waist. The stones were probably diamonds. It was an expensive apartment in an expensive neighborhood, and the coat in her closet probably cost as much as a new Cadillac. But, after making love to Number 137, he reminded himself, she had used the word ideal.

"Jake Burgess," he said.

"Now, Jake Burgess, do I look presentable? Would my husband look at me and think, here is a woman who will make love with any stranger?"

"How long have you been married to him?"

"Three months only."

There was a bar filled with bottles and glassware, with two large windows looking south. She poured him some excellent bourbon and stayed inside the bar with an expanse of stainless steel between them.

"I asked Martha to tell you why I didn't return," she said, "but they are so terribly discreet there. They expect us to lay our feelings aside when we pass through their door."

She stirred the ice in her drink. "The day we met, you and I, it was a Sunday, do you remember? That afternoon I went to a reception for a new ambassador from I think one of the African countries. And there I met Per. I broke my next appointment because it was a night when Per wished to see me. All of a sudden I was in love, and I couldn't go back. I thought of writing you a letter but Martha told me it was forbidden. And then I saw you dancing. I was married already. I was so happy that night, Jake, everything was the way I wished it, and when I saw you I was frightened. Not of you! But of that time in my life, the laboratory time. Because what would happen if Per should learn I had been going there for some months, doing thus and so?"

"Can we meet tomorrow?"

She looked at him incredulously. "No! You must understand. If we ever meet after tonight it will be by chance, and we must arrange matters now so there will be no surprise or excitement."

He touched her left hand. There were two rings on the proper finger.

"I suppose that means you're actually married. But I didn't get your name from Hubie Sachs. I tried that and ended up with a girl who works for NBC. I found out from Dr. Prescott."

Her eyes changed slightly. "I thought they—"

"I had some leverage and I used it. What I really mean is, I blackmailed him. It was probably a mean thing to do, but every time I asked nicely they just said no. Well, I didn't do it so you could give me a quick kiss and let me watch you get dressed to prove how trivial this all is. I can't say anything serious to you with a husband about to show up. Maybe he's already in the elevator."

"I don't want you to say anything serious! It's not a serious thing."

"Then why did you lie about when you got married? The name you gave Prescott was Engstrom. That's the name on the bell downstairs. You left your rings at home but you were married that day we made love."

She paused. "Yes, Jake. I thought it would be easier if you didn't know it."

"Don't worry about me."

"Yes, I think you are a little harder on the surface than when we met. All of us, Martha and Dr. Prescott and I, too, helped make it happen. As for the truth—I've been married two years. My husband was away when I went to the laboratory, in Washington only, but we had quarreled before he left. The way a diplomat quarrels, with silences."

Jake took her hand across the bar. She had lost some of her color.

"But I can't have sex with you again, Jake."

"I'll meet you tomorrow, and we'll go to a hotel."

She shook her head. "Please. I thought it would be a game to offer myself at the laboratory. I like making love, you realize that."

"Yes."

"There were men who wondered about me, because my husband was away. But with people, they think they can order me, the way you think now, Jake, because of our one time together. I must go to a hotel with you! What if I truly do not want it? It is embarrassing in hotels. I want my life to run easily. Before I was married to my husband I sold perfume in a store, Best's. No more. When my husband and I quarreled, I thought I'd better not make love to someone while he was gone, or the marriage would be over. And I must tell you, I was curious about the machine."

His eyes narrowed, and she said quickly, "And I liked it! Jake, you're hurting my hand. You know nothing about me! It came into me, and afterward it didn't make a great crusade out of finding me so it could come into me again. It has hundreds of women. There is no confusion. I think I love Per because he is like the machine in some ways. He is an expert at sex, but he is always in command of himself—"

Jake let go of her hand. "He sounds like a pain in the ass."

"No, he's quite nice as a matter of fact."

"Are you afraid of what'll happen if you make love to me again?"

"Afraid, no. But I am practical about it. There is no need for it now, you see. We make love often, my husband and I, it is safe and quite legal and very pleasant."

"We don't have to make love if you don't want to. But I'm too jumpy right now to say any of the things—"

"Jake, no, you are wrong about this. At the laboratory, remember, with the others there, you thought nothing would happen, but it did, and so perhaps you thought it was more historic than it really was. You would be surprised to find I am quite ordinary. You were sweet, I loved you very much. But the earth didn't stop for me. The sun didn't set in the east. There were times with the machine when such amazing things happened! Please don't be angry. What I remember about you was the way you were at first, the way you looked when it was over."

Her eyes were dark, clear blue, like good diving water.

"That's not what you told Mrs. Freeman afterward," he said.

A quick wind ruffled the surface. When Jake touched her shoulder she struck at his arm.

"Don't touch me!"

"All right!" he shouted. "I played dirty and took it out of their safe! We weren't introduced at a UN reception. There's nothing ordinary about this, but that doesn't mean it didn't happen! If you don't want to see me again I'll stay out of this part of town and sooner or later I'll stop thinking about you. But don't tell me it didn't mean anything to you because I know different. I can give it to you word for word. I know how long it lasted, how fast your heart was beating, what you said about it after it was over. The reason you didn't come back was because it scared you!"

"Yes."

He continued more gently, "Don't you see that I *had* to find you? It hit us both at the same time. Now we have to take a few chances. You don't want to go through life half-alive. I can see that he's rich. It's a wonderful apartment, but what does it really add up to? Three and a half rooms. That's probably a diamond bracelet you've got on. I'll buy you a bracelet, and you won't know whether it's real unless you have it appraised. Don't say no before you find out what I'm like. Have an affair with me. Married women have affairs all the time."

"No."

"Why not, damn it? Because you might like it even more than you did the first time?"

She came out from behind the bar. "Sit down, and don't shout at me anymore. Dear God, let Per be late this once." She showed him the chair he was to sit in and sat down facing him. "I was married another time. At home in Sweden there is sex younger than here, I think, and I married at the university. Such a gay, funny person I thought, always doing mad things. He taught me to jump in parachutes, and our marriage was like that, the feeling of absolute freedom before the parachute opens. And then there was a bad, depressed time, much drinking and ugliness. Then excitement again. It is a picture of illness, of course. He began taking drugs, he wanted me to join him there. Thank God we had no children, though we did nothing at first against it. There were two years in all, my eighteenth and nineteenth year. He started to choke me once. I don't know why, I don't know why he stopped. When I left him at last he jumped from an airplane and his parachute never opened."

"It wasn't your fault."

"Perhaps not. But it left me very cold and suspicious. I came to this country. I was never a success, making love to Americans. There were too many differences. I don't know how to say it. But the machine at the laboratory, I thought it so wonderful. It makes me shiver when I think of it. But soon it became like a perfume essence—is that the word?—the concentrated perfume, so strong it has no smell. So much was missing. So I agreed to meet a person some Sunday. There would be no questions, no emotion, and yet someone to hold, to kiss. And so you and I met. I quite agree I was frightened. Too frightened! I want no more of that wildness."

Jake went to her and touched her hair.

"You can't live this way."

"Yes. I'm jumping from no more planes. I will save my feeling for the baby."

He went down on his knees beside the chair. "We loved each other for forty-five minutes."

She was shaking her head when he kissed her. Then the next instant she fell against him. Her fingers trembled against his face. Jake hadn't intended anything like this, but there was no way to stop it. He could hear a phone ringing in the distance, summoning someone else. It rang again and again. The sound broke through to the girl finally, just as it stopped. She pulled away from Jake, looking into his eyes in horror. She put both hands flat on her stomach.

"I must be crazy, really crazy."

When the phone rang again she caught it on the second ring. She switched at once to Swedish after saying hello. After a moment she hung up and turned back to Jake.

"I am to meet him at the restaurant."

She reached under her arm, and Jake heard the snick of a zipper.

"And in celebration of our close escape, we are now going to make love. Quickly."

"Do you really want to?"

"I want to very, very much."

They watched each other in growing excitement. After a long kiss, she pulled him onto the white sofa. He lost himself in a whirl of movement, and for a long moment—forever?—he

knew possibilities he had never approached before. But somehow he missed by inches, and knew with certainty, for the first
time in his life, that he was mortal. He came back to a different
reality from the one he had left. The girl was part of his flesh;
everything else around him was hostile.

"You see," she said softly.

"I love you."

"But we are back in civilization now. What rating would
you give this for Martha Freeman?"

"The same as before. Ten."

"Liar. You could never forget I have a baby inside me, not a
baby of yours. Eight perhaps."

"That's still pretty high."

"I agree! Now I must dress again and start inventing a story
to tell my husband."

"Will we see each other tomorrow?"

"No. My husband is arranging his job so the baby can be
born in Sweden. And then his next post will be in another
country, not America. I'll remember you, believe me. I'll remember I was ready to smash up everything, to go on kissing
you."

"It means something."

She smiled and kissed him. "Yes. It means—be careful."

He made no objection when she began to separate herself
from him.

"There are so many things about you that are marvelous,"
she said. "The machine can never grow small and helpless. The
change is what I love. I want you to let me think about you
sometimes when I make love with my husband. Please. Will
you say yes?"

"Damn it—"

"Now one serious thing, my darling. I think we are almost
the same age. If I had met you at my university, or if you can
imagine me as an American girl—did you go to a university?
You see, I know so little about you! If we had started together
at the age of eighteen much would have been different. But
we met otherwise."

"You could see me again before you leave."

"No, our average would go down, down. Dr. Prescott would
be ashamed of us."

He pulled her to him. As they kissed he felt the tears on her cheek.

"I cry whenever I part from somebody," she said. "You must let me go now."

They dressed. Each piece of clothing widened the gap between them. They touched by accident as they went out the door, and she shied away. Downstairs, Jake found a parking ticket under his windshield wiper.

"Ah—you are being punished for coming to see me," she said.

He made the turn onto Third Avenue. "I don't know if my last name registered on you. It's Burgess. I'm not in the book, but you can get the number from information."

"Jake, if I feel my mind beginning to change I will run away again, much farther away this time. The restaurant is on East Fiftieth Street."

It was called Lutece. He reached over in front of her to unlatch the door, and she pulled his arm for an instant against her breast. Getting out, she crossed the sidewalk to the restaurant.

Jake felt an almost uncontrollable desire to see her husband. He had to start resisting his impulses, but nevertheless, after driving a dozen car-lengths, he decided to give in. Didn't this mark the end of a period in his life? He double-parked. Walking back to the restaurant, he peered inside.

Number 89 and her husband were greeting each other at the bar. Jake had expected someone tall, austere, with hair lightly touched with gray. The man whose cheek she was kissing was only a little older than his wife. He needed a haircut almost as badly as Jake did himself. He was plump and sunburned; his nose was peeling. Strangely, he looked happy.

Jake called his answering service. Betty Quinby had left her home number but no message. And Bobby Quinby had called. Instead of still being on location outside Madrid, he was back in town and at the Absinthe House, on West 48th Street, where he wanted Jake to meet him.

Jake found him at the bar. He had his usual salon going, three or four lesser members of the writing profession. He was discoursing in a low, confidential tone, making the others lean in toward him. He introduced Jake. They all pretended to be meeting for the first time. Bobby waved his way to a nearby table.

"We didn't expect you for another week," Jake said.

"Spain," Bobby said with disgust. "Franco can have it. How are you coming with the Mad Butcher of the East Village?"

"To tell you the truth, Bobby, he's a little dull."

"Well, let's look at your notes tomorrow and see if we want to go on with it. The reason I came back early—how shall I put it?"

Jake had a feeling that he knew what was coming. Betty could go on ducking and dodging indefinitely, but Bobby had recently turned forty and he didn't have unlimited time.

"In a nutshell, Jake, I've got another lady and I want a divorce. You can't have a rational discussion with Betty anymore. She's making good money with Hubie. She's marriageable. So why should I pay her alimony?"

He threw more whiskey on the fire. Jake realized for the first time that, in spite of the glibness, here was a desperate man.

"I keep off the hot subjects like sex and money," Bobby went on, "but there doesn't seem to be a damn thing I can say to her that she doesn't resent. You're sleeping with her, I hope."

"Hell, no. What gives you that idea?"

"Maybe it was a piece I wrote for the Sunday *Times* about the breakdown of old-fashioned morality. Plus the fact that Betty believes in regular sex and I know she isn't getting any at Hubie's. Well, I won't put you under sodium pentothal. What do you think about article-writing as a way of life?"

"It's interesting, Bobby, but it may not be for me."

"I agree with you. You've turned in some first-class research, but it's not shallow enough. With a magazine you've got to know where to stop. If there's room for quotes from five doctors, why talk to seven? Greg Granby tells me he's considering one of your scripts."

"Yeah. *The 8:40 Train Leaves at Midnight.*"

"We'll have to do something about that title. I've known Granby for years. I'm one of the few people in town who know how he broke into the business. He asked me what I think about giving you a production."

"I've got another copy of the script if you want to read it."

"I don't think that's necessary," Bobby said, not unkindly. "I'm advising him to do it, and I'm putting in fifteen G's. He'll open in New York with previews. That automatically makes you less of a nobody. I've got a press release in my pocket.

'Gregory Granby has acquired for October production—' Of course, there's a quid pro quo. There generally is."

"You want help with your alimony problem."

"I want you to set up an ambush for me," Bobby explained. "The best place would be Christopher Street, but the kid's got a very sensitive radar, and it may have to be somewhere else. We'll synchronize our watches. At zero-minus-ten you get her undressed and start to neck. I walk in with Judah Sutro, and nobody has to sue anybody. We can fix it in one of two ways. It can look like an accident, so she doesn't know you were in on it. Or if you've been getting restless—"

"Bobby, why don't you take your quid quo pro—your quid po cro—"

His stuttering over the cliché Latin stopped him in time. Like him or not, Bobby had the power to send Jake on to his next employer with a reference or a curse. But the thing that annoyed Jake was that Bobby had been so sure he'd jump at it.

"I don't know what makes you think I could get her in bed in ten minutes. She barely tolerates me."

"I don't have the time or the strength," Bobby said. "I just got off the plane and I'm disoriented, so don't expect any crap or compliments. My lady's holding a gun on me—do I mean what I say or don't I? Granby won't do the play without my fifteen."

"Then he'll be the twenty-sixth producer who's turned it down."

"I'm not asking you to knife the girl! The whole conception of alimony is out of the Middle Ages. How much has she contributed to the marriage? If you'll let me touch an intimate note, I can't write a line while she's menstruating. Does she deserve a fifteen percent lien on my lifetime earnings?"

"That's something you'll have to work out without me."

Bobby wagged his beard. "Jake, I didn't foresee this. I thought that kind of speech went out with World War II. You'd be embarrassed for about five minutes."

"It's your premise that's wrong, Bobby. I've got another girl, and she keeps me busy. I just left her this minute. I've been careful with Betty because, my God, I'm the rookie in this operation and I know it. Was that all? Because I've got to see some people."

Bobby nodded gloomily. Jake finished his drink, waved to the semientourage at the bar, and walked over to Broadway. It was a pleasant night, and Times Square was filled with tourists. He entered a drugstore and dialed Betty.

"I don't want to say anything bitchy," she said, "but where have you been?"

"Scrambling."

"You weren't near a phone at any time?"

"Probably, but too much has been going on. I may tell you about some of it—I've got to tell somebody. Do you want me to come down?"

"Yes," she said in a softer voice. "I want you to come down *intensely.*"

"Have you had dinner?"

"No, but I'm not hungry. Baby, a psychological test. What do you think about when the word marriage is mentioned?"

"It's a grand institution," Jake said. "Are you serious?"

"Dead serious. I've been able to put up with all this surreptitious business because of the pot of gold at the end of the rainbow, but I sense a slight cooling on your part. I ask myself —is alimony that important? It would only last as long as I stayed single."

"Betty, I love you, but am I grown up enough for marriage?"

She laughed softly, and for the first time in days he felt a tickle of desire for her.

"You're so cute," she said. "Even if you turn me down I've decided to let Bobby off the hook. Let's not go out. I have some frozen soup and caviar, and Hubie gave me a loaf of his home-baked bread. After we have a drink or two let's, you know, fuck."

Jake said he thought the program as outlined sounded fine. "At your house?"

"Why not, for a change?"

"Well—Bobby's back. We've just had a sincere talk about money. So let's adjourn to that Lincoln Towers apartment. Bring the bread and the caviar."

"Wait a minute, Jake. What did he offer?"

"A Greg Granby production, and he'll put in fifteen thousand of his own money. It seems his girl gave him an ultimatum."

"Then let's do it! Jake, we'd be mad not to."

"Don't be a nut," Jake said uneasily.

"Seriously! What's wrong with it? Bobby's a talker in some respects, but he can swing this. Time's passing, and you need a production. And it would do my self-esteem a world of good. At least we'd be taking him for something. That play's going to be a hit, Jake. We don't have to be naked, or anything, do we, so long as we're in bed? It'll all be over in five minutes. Jake?"

He didn't answer, and she said again, less hopefully, "Jake?"

He hung up slowly. There wasn't much elbowroom in the booth, and that also seemed to be the way his life was shaping up. He slammed his clenched fist against the pebbled wall.

Then he returned to the Absinthe House, where he found Bobby still at the bar.

"One thing we forgot to cover," Jake said. "I quit."

"What?"

The next moment Jake heard himself yelling. For spur-of-the-moment stuff, the dialogue wasn't bad. There was even a bit of shoving. The owner hurried over, and with the help of several of the minor writers got Jake outside. Bobby stayed where he was, shaking his beard in amazement.

chapter 23

The girl in the cigarette commercial pushed back her hair, and Harry Royce saw a familiar face. She had been one of the main events of the previous year. He had seen her last on the morning of the Foundation meeting at which they had voted the money to build Dr. Prescott his celebrated machine. In real life she was a furious smoker, scattering ashes and frequently talking without removing the cigarette from her mouth, but cigarettes are smoked more deliberately on television. After lighting up she gave the camera's eye a sleepy, passionate look that nearly sent Harry to the phone.

He bumped into her two nights later at a charity ball at the Americana. He was about to leave. It was after one, and he had a meeting with a union grievance committee the next morning. She threw her arms around him.

"Darling!" They kissed. "I think this is the first time I ever saw you in tails. Don't go yet. Talk to me."

He found an empty table, ordered champagne, and lighted her cigarette, which was not the same brand she'd been smoking on television. They picked up the conversation at almost exactly the point where they'd dropped it over a year before.

"Harry, I thought of calling you a million times. Were you bitter about that weekend? I really tossed around the insults there at the end, and I hope you don't believe I meant any of them."

"How did your audition go that day?"

"I didn't show up for it. They wanted a second lead for a pilot, and I was giving off so much static I knew nobody'd want me around for thirteen weeks. The state I was in! I knew it was serious when I walked into a room and a damn cat leaped up out of a sound sleep and stalked out. One session with Ramon changed all that."

"Who's Ramon?"

"A wonderful man, Harry. He's expensive, but after I started going to him my income went up about ten times. Do you notice the clearness of my eye?"

"I always thought your eye was pretty clear."

"There's no comparison at all. Cats come up and rub against my leg now. Darling—I haven't missed in months! I don't know if you're interested—"

Harry laughed. She was one of the most beautiful girls in New York, and of course he was interested. He said so.

"Well, I think you may have a certain remote academic interest," she said, "but you're a man. You don't have the problem. Harry, he sits on one side of the desk, and I sit on the other. He has a little silver pencil and I have one of those marble anxiety-eggs. He has wonderful piercing eyes. Sexy eyes. He moves the pencil back and forth and starts to count. I'm a good subject. I've never heard him get as high as seven. Pretty soon I feel myself beginning to get excited. He tells me what he wants me to do and what he wants me to feel."

She was moving slightly in her chair. She put her hand on his wrist. "Harry, what are your plans for the rest of the evening?"

"The evening's about over. I've got to get up in the morning. Why?"

"You know very well why, damn you!"

"Finish the story first. Then what happens?"

She jumped her hands apart. "I come! With a skirling of bagpipes. And before he wakes me up he tells me I'll feel the same way the next time I'm with a man. And you may be relieved to hear that I do!"

"Are you sure he stays on his side of the desk?"

"I can't be a hundred percent sure, can I? I don't have to see him regularly anymore. If I feel that old panic setting in, I call him up and he hypnotizes me on the phone. Really—it never fails, as long as I'm holding that marble egg. I know he's probably a bit of a charlatan, but if it works?" She darted her cigarette at him. "What's the state of *your* private life?"

"Let's see. Did you hear about Mollie Ridder?"

"I think so. Didn't she get married or something?"

"Last month. We had a proxy fight on our hands, and I couldn't give her my full attention. She likes the water. She married a man with a fifty-foot runabout."

"So you're not spoken for?" she said casually. "How nice.

Neither am I, at the moment. Harry, what's this sex thing you're mixed up in?"

"I'm not mixed up in any— You don't mean the Prescott laboratory?"

"I think that's his name. I've heard stories about it—friends of friends, kind of thing. I thought they were exaggerating but apparently not. My guy at dinner works for the publishing house that's bringing out the book."

"You mean Prescott's written a book?"

"I thought you'd know about it. Read the afternoon papers tomorrow—they're having a press conference after they sign the contracts. They expect a huge sale, and I think I see why. They're putting up a fifty-thousand-dollar advance."

"That's just lovely."

"But why should it affect you, Harry? Is there some legal catch about putting money into sex research?"

"No, but we're having some Internal Revenue trouble at the moment, and any bad publicity right now could make a difference. Did he say anything about a machine?"

"Oh, yes! He went into it at length, watching me closely all the time. With perhaps a fleck of saliva at the corners of his mouth."

"The Royce paid for that. It cost us forty thousand dollars. Well worth the money, everybody thinks. Is this publisher still around? Could you point him out to me?"

"I guess so. I hate to, but if money's involved—"

In the Prescott clinic Martha Freeman was still functioning with all her old efficiency. The recovery rate remained amazingly high. Unresponsive women would sometimes wage a real battle, but Martha and Dr. Prescott had the times on their side. They almost always won.

It was in the laboratory that Martha had begun to slow down. In the early days, working by trial and error, failing more often than they succeeded, she had never for a moment questioned the importance and the necessity of what they were doing. She had been as exhilarated at the end of a long, grueling night as at the beginning. Now she hated to work after midnight. Some night, when her supply of adrenalin was low, she knew she would speak the crucial sentence and close the laboratory door behind her forever. With her conscious mind she still believed in the value of this research. The rebellion was elsewhere, not really under her control.

They had weeded out the more colorful volunteers, and there was a blandness and predictability about those who were left. In the prostitute days, if an hour passed without a crisis, there had been reason for celebration. Now everything was routine, with few surprises. She never lost a sense that some fatal deadline was rapidly approaching. As the subjects became more adapted to the laboratory requirements, accustomed to the presence of silent witnesses, two sessions could sometimes be scheduled in one hour. On a typical Friday night, Martha might observe and record as many as twenty episodes, some involving multiple orgasms. Sometimes, over a cup of hot chocolate before falling into her own bed, she wondered if perhaps Gevorkian had been right; if they had seen only what they wanted to see, if what they had been watching since six o'clock the previous night was not actually human sex at all, but something they and their subjects had conjured up to satisfy the apparatus.

Prescott, of course, never gave any sign of early-morning doubts. His catchword remained: *confirm, confirm*. An observed phenomenon meant nothing unless it could be seen again and again, in different subjects under different circumstances, becoming at last a part of a pattern as regular as wallpaper. Martha had a feeling at times that all their major discoveries had been made, and from now on she had nothing to look forward to but confirmation, and after that more confirmation, and then finally the definitive confirmation that would make their data unassailable.

Occasionally, oppressed by the hothouse atmosphere of the laboratory, she made an effort and went out to dinner with one of the men who still called her from time to time. These people dated back to previous periods of her life, and sooner or later they got around to asking what she'd been doing lately. Apparently the man didn't live who could be told that a woman worked in an environment of observed sex, and then go on to some other subject. In her own opinion she was the same person she had always been, but they couldn't seem to believe it.

She had become a great reader of novels, limiting herself to those published before *The Interpretation of Dreams.* Her chief amusement, a private one, was composing sex histories of the principal characters, pretending they had been referred to an imaginary Prescott-Freeman Clinic for the Treatment of Sexual Disorders. She and Dr. Prescott subjected them to the usual searching interview, and Martha then wrote it up in the mixed jargon used by sexologists, part medicine and part sociology. More and more often these days she fell asleep with a book and a yellow pad in her lap, with the light still on.

When the phone rang that night, shocking her awake, she almost didn't answer. She had been getting obscene calls. The perversions the callers wanted her to share were the commonplaces of her working day, but they brought her back into the disturbed sexuality of the time, which she read nineteenth-century novels to forget. But, remembering that her last word from Prescott was that he was about to start across Canada on marginal airlines, she picked up the phone.

"Harry Royce," a voice said. "Are you the Martha Freeman who—"

"Yes."

"I probably woke you up. I'm sorry."

Martha collected herself, her heart still moving unpleasantly.

"It's all right. I went to sleep with the light on, which I don't like to do. It shows lack of character. But it's late, isn't it?"

"About two-thirty. I'm trying to locate Prescott."

"He left Seattle yesterday, but this airplane strike makes everything so—"

Harry interrupted. "No, he's back. I talked to his wife. He got in at Newark Airport around five. He called to say he had to go into the city, and she hasn't heard from him since. She's pretty upset. I thought he might have been in touch with you."

"I didn't get in till twelve. Have you tried the laboratory? He had some films with him, and conceivably—"

"I called but there's no answer."

She hitched up farther in bed. "Can I help you with anything?"

"I've just heard about the book. I'm told you're signing the contracts tomorrow morning."

"That's right. But how does it concern the Foundation?"

"It doesn't, directly. We have nothing to say about what you do with your material. But I hope I can persuade you to postpone it."

"Why?"

"It's a tax matter, Mrs. Freeman. Nobody likes to think about taxes at this time of night—"

"I'm awake now. Go ahead."

"Our tax-exempt status has been challenged. That may not sound too important, compared to starvation in Calcutta, but it's important to us, believe me."

"Well, the fifty-thousand-dollar advance from the publisher is important to us too, Mr. Royce. We're out of money as usual. You gave us thirty-five, and most of that went to pay bills. We've had no luck with the other foundations. If you're afraid the government will think we're making a profit I assure you—"

"No, it's not that. Did you see the *Time* cover story about the new American morality? It was pretty ridiculous, but it mentioned the Royce Foundation's Genital Physiology Project, in passing, and I didn't care for that apostrophe *s*. Guilt by association. I doubt if you read the financial pages, but we've just come out of a proxy fight, if you know what that is. To keep control we had to vote the Royce shares in the Foundation portfolio."

"What's wrong with that?"

"*I* don't think there's anything wrong with it, but the law governing family foundations is murky, to say the least. The Royce family and the Royce Foundation are supposed to stay at arm's length. And that's Treasury Department language. 'Arm's length'—what does it mean, exactly? I know this is pretty dull compared to your subject."

"I think I'm following you. You didn't stay at arm's length."

"And there've been a couple of other things. I bought some Royce common from the Foundation. There's nothing wrong with that either, in the opinion of a very high-priced law firm, but it shifts that much control of the business from Dad to me, via a charitable deduction, and sets up a new cost basis for the stock without paying inheritance tax or a capital gain."

"Well, that I *didn't* follow."

"Never mind. Well, let me explain it, though I feel pretty

silly giving a lecture on income tax over the phone. We think it's legal, but if the government says it isn't we won't argue. We'll just wash out the sale. There's an Exempt Organizations Council in Internal Revenue which has to decide whether Dad was thinking about cutting his taxes or of giving money to charity when he set up the Foundation—which is absurd! Of course he was thinking of cutting his taxes. There wouldn't be any foundations at all if it weren't for the charitable deduction. But if they decide against us they can pull our exemption and make us pay income tax on everything Dad put into the Foundation this year. And I don't even like to mention the possibility, but if they make it retroactive—"

"I still don't understand how it connects with us."

"It can go either way, you see, Mrs. Freeman. The law's equally good on both sides. Officially the Council makes the ruling, but actually there's one man, the examiner. They're all little people, I don't know why. By little I mean short. I've never met a tax examiner who was over five-feet-six. Well, while he's thinking about it—he's longing to sock us, but he's not sure he can get away with it—the papers suddenly get hold of a big new foundation scandal. Congressmen start getting up to denounce the un-American foundations for undermining the nation's moral fiber—"

"There hasn't been any publicity about us so far, and the book won't come out for six months."

"The publisher's calling a press conference tomorrow. He thinks he's going to get very good coverage."

"How long a postponement do you need?"

"We hope to get a ruling in about two weeks. Mrs. Prescott said an AP reporter met her husband at the airport. It may already be too late."

"That's probably about a paper he read in Seattle, on sex education in secondary schools. He thinks if the schools are going to teach sex, they ought to teach sex, not the reproductive cycle or family living."

"You don't mean with living models?"

"Not quite." She laughed. "But have you ever seen the film strips that are supposed to teach high school students about sexual physiology? What the poor student makes of them I can't imagine. They're either schematic and unrepresentational, a long way from real life, or else they're impossibly sentimentalized, the genitalia as seen through the eyes of Walt Disney. A few companies try to be more serious, using the Dickenson cross-section diagrams, do you know them? The male standing, the female lying down, and unless you're an expert you can't tell an anus from a cervix. How did we get off on this subject? About the press conference tomorrow. I may as well tell you—I'm opposed to the book idea. I don't want to postpone it for two weeks, I want to shelve it. I wish there were some other way of getting the money, but there doesn't seem to be."

"I didn't know you and Prescott ever disagreed about anything. From your point of view, what's wrong with a book?"

Martha closed *Jane Eyre*, keeping the place with her notes on Mr. Rochester's early sociosexual conditioning. "People who read medical journals have the same frame of reference we have—they use the same vocabulary and think in the same terms. We've taken a first step, a long one, but that's all it is, just a beginning, and I'm sure they realize that. We don't present our impressions as scientific facts, proved for all time. But the ordinary book-buyer will look at the photographs—and we have some sensational ones—then he'll read the section about the machine, and then he'll turn to the index to see what we say about female orgasm."

"Isn't that what Gevorkian was saying?"

"I'm afraid it is. I didn't think he was really arguing against what we're doing, so much as against what the public will make of it. He didn't like the idea that the typical laboratory orgasm is more intense and continues longer with the machine than it does with a human partner. I still can't see why he thinks it's so surprising. When a woman masturbates, she doesn't fantasize about other masturbations, but almost always about sex in a human context. We aren't *advising* people to give up human partners and start having sex with machines. The multiorgasm was his other bugbear. We've seen it, we've measured it, over and over and over. But all we've ever said on the subject is that there's no physiological reason why a normal woman can't have more than one orgasm, if the stimulus continues. We don't say it's necessary for her health and well-being. Certainly we don't think it confers any psychological status. I don't quite see how we can bring out a book for the mass market without seeming to say just that. But I don't have anything so grand as veto power."

"You aren't thinking of defecting, are you?"

"Certainly not!"

They both listened to the echoes of that, and she went on, "The argument is purely tactical—we still agree on the main points."

He waited a moment and said abruptly, "Are you one of those people who need eight hours sleep?"

"We've been known to work twenty-four hours straight. Why?"

"I'd like to go on with this but I don't want to tie up your line. I keep thinking Prescott is trying to call you."

"Would you like me to give you some scrambled eggs?"

"Yes."

"All right." Martha had hesitated for only an instant; it was a pleasure to talk to a man who had got over his first feeling of shock at her profession. "Do you know the Beresford on Central Park West?"

"Sure. I used to have a girl who lived there. I'll be up in five minutes."

chapter 24

Victoria was feeling a recurrence of her old trouble, a sort of mental flutter. Her conversation became more and more fragmentary, and she had more time to worry about it because she was no longer working. She had wanted to quit for ages; she had a feeling her machine was trying to get away from her. Her supervisor jumped on her one morning for a trivial error, and Victoria came out with a few of the things that had been simmering inside her. As she walked out, she was followed by respectful looks from the girls at the nearby machines.

She decided her hair was too long and rashly cut it herself, taking off too much on one side. By the time she had it even it was too short. Fortunately, with her unusually pretty features she was still sort of attractive, she thought. She was spending hours in the tub, which was bad for the skin. She kept searching her face for signs of tension. Finding them merely made her look more tense.

Anne, her roommate, was a great believer in the magic of psychiatry. Victoria finally allowed her to make an appointment with a bearded disciple of the Karen Horney school they had met at a party. That was a day or so after the Matt disaster, her first interpersonal orgasm. She was given comparatively little coherent advice but some new pills. They made her feel even worse. Anne came into her bed to comfort her. Anne at this point was really all she had. Victoria decided to do something that would rivet them together, at least until the crisis was over. Next morning they woke up with their friendship on a new basis.

Anne was probably a good influence because of the way she reduced everything to the simplest possible terms. She blamed the Prescott-Freeman project for Victoria's trouble and she was sure Victoria would snap out of it as soon as Prescott was shown up as a monster. Victoria only half-believed this herself—it was far too easy—but it gave her something to look forward to.

Still, when two days passed after her visit to Woods McChesney and nothing happened, she began to believe that Prescott had some sort of immunity. She dreamed about him as a surgeon. She had always been fearful about surgery. She was ninety-nine percent certain that she had cancer, but she hadn't done anything about verifying it because she was afraid of putting herself at the mercy of some crazy scientist with a knife. Now, in these Prescott nightmares, he was sometimes himself, sometimes the machine, but he was always out for blood.

Having given up guilt as a way of life, Anne became rather demanding. Victoria did her best to accommodate her. She enjoyed it while it was going on, but it had no effect on the way she felt the rest of the time. She was spending her days in bed, in the tub, in front of the television set. She had stopped hoping that things would ever be better. Every time she went to the bathroom she counted her pills. One of these days she would surprise a few people.

The phone rang. Anne held her tightly and told her in a whisper to pay no attention, it was probably a man from her old life. But Victoria had no intention of giving up men; that hadn't been part of the bargain. She twisted away and freed an arm.

"*Vicky*," Anne said. One of her faults was the petulant way she held her mouth when things didn't go exactly her way.

"Maybe it's Woods," Victoria said.

A man's voice asked if she was Victoria Orr, and then: "This is Dr. Prescott. I know it's late—"

"Dr. Prescott! You're kidding!"

Anne bounced out of bed and tried to get an ear close to the phone.

"I didn't mean to shriek like that," Victoria said, "but I never expected to hear from you."

"Could we meet somewhere? Something important has happened. I need your advice and help."

"Gosh—I always sort of assumed it was bad for the subjects and the research people—"

"Ordinarily, but this is urgent, Victoria, and we can't do it on the phone."

"I'm in bed," she said, slanting a glance at Anne. "Does it have to be tonight?"

"Yes."

"Well, I'm getting a cold, and I'd rather not— Could you come here?"

Prescott assented readily, and she hung up with a whoop.

"Now there was an unconvincing act if I ever heard one," Anne said. "I bet you never said gosh before in your life."

"He found out about the statement! What else could it be?"

"Lust," Anne said coldly.

"Not the man of iron! Do you think I have to get dressed? He's hardly ever seen me with clothes on."

"Don't start getting worked up. You're supposed to cut down on the peaks. We'd both better get dressed."

"He didn't say anything about wanting to see *you*." She pirouetted to the mirror. "My hair! Why didn't you hide the scissors, you beast? Remember the movie we saw when Rita Hayworth seduced the missionary?"

"If you start seducing anybody," Anne warned, "I'm going to be out there so fast—"

"Keep out of it, Anne," Victoria said, completely in earnest. "You open that door one quarter of an inch and we're through!"

"You've been feeling so much better—"

"I feel fine. I haven't felt as good as this in years and years. He thinks he's Jesus H. Christ. Well, we'll see."

She only had five minutes, not long enough for a real bath. She washed partially and applied perfume. What pills to take was a problem. She wanted to be really up, so she swallowed a jumper, twenty-five milligrams of Eskatrol. She also wanted Prescott to take something. He had to be completely relaxed. She would force-feed him if necessary. She went into her cache with some reluctance, took four of the pretty spansules to the kitchen, and ground up the pellets in a spoon with a little water.

Returning to the bedroom, she put on a blouse and skirt over bare flesh. Anne watched suspiciously. Her eyes had a way of getting very small and beady.

"If you're coming down with a cold, don't you think—"

"Now Anne."

Before putting on lipstick she came over to kiss her friend. Anne wanted to restake her claim. Pulling back, Victoria left her with her tongue showing.

"It's a wonder Mrs. Freeman let him out by himself. Anne, be a good thing. After he's gone we'll have a party. We'll do it any way you want—it's your turn." She gave Anne a quick caress; she didn't want her barging in at the wrong moment. "I seem to remember we were in the middle of something."

"That we were," Anne said, softening.

Victoria closed the bedroom door and hurried about the living room. Anne had a light touch with a vacuum cleaner but she didn't bother about ashtrays and magazines. The doorbell rang before Victoria had everything in the right piles. She pressed the buzzer and checked to make sure of what was showing—*Ramparts, The New Yorker, Avant Garde.*

She opened the door to Dr. Prescott, touching her badly cropped hair as though only this short notice had kept her from doing anything with it. This was the first time she had seen him out of uniform. He looked like everybody else—tired.

"Victoria, I really appreciate this."

"I'm afraid I didn't sound too nice on the— I have a roommate," she added, "but she's asleep."

Anne was wide awake and listening at the crack, as Victoria well knew. She offered her guest a drink. He said what he really wanted was coffee. She pretended to look and reported an empty can. She made a Scotch highball without ice and stirred in the mashed-up Nembutal. But it had a medicinal taste, and she decided she couldn't risk it as a first drink. She made another highball. For herself, she filled a liqueur glass with Dexedrine elixir, which looked and tasted like cherry brandy.

"I don't know what this will do to me," he said, taking the drink. "I've been flying and waiting, flying and waiting, for two long days."

Sitting down facing him, Victoria pulled her inadequate skirt in the direction of her knees. "In that case you probably don't feel like making lo—" She caught herself. "Freudian slip. You don't feel like making polite conversation. Is there some kind of crisis?"

He grimaced as he tasted his drink.

"Too strong?" she asked.

"No, it's all right. Victoria, did you give the District Attorney's office a deposition about the project?"

"Yes, I did. I'm not sure if it was the right thing—"

"But why?"

She held the elixir primly in both hands, knees together. "I guess I—" she paused—"just wanted to get even. He said they're taking statements from lots of people—"

"Yours is the only one, so far as I know."

"Oh, no! He told me— Well, anyway, he promised not to publish my name."

"He's using it to get a search warrant, Victoria. That makes it a matter of public record, and you can be examined on it."

Victoria heard a noise in the bedroom, where Anne, no doubt, was jumping up and down with joy. Things were rolling! A search warrant didn't sound too serious, but, to judge by the look on Prescott's face, evidently it was.

"Victoria, did your statement include a claim that you had relations with another woman in the laboratory, at our suggestion?"

She felt a twinge of embarrassment. But she hadn't done it to be mean. It had been the only way to blast the real truth into the open.

"I don't remember exactly what I did say. But you can't deny you use homosexuals, because I know better. And what possible scientific value—"

"Let's not talk about it tonight. The point is, and it's a very big point, we haven't taken homosexual material from anybody who wasn't entirely willing to give it. We've done nothing in the laboratory that wasn't already part of the individual's behavior pattern."

"How can you say that?" Victoria cried. "What about the machine? That's not part of anybody's—"

"Victoria, did anybody force you to use the machine?"

"God, no!" she exclaimed with a glint. "I couldn't wait to try it."

A muscle flicked in his tired face. "We can bring in a complete schedule of everything you did for us and prove you're lying. It won't be pleasant."

"Well, what's pleasant? Do you know I went to a psychiatrist? I hate the whole idea of people paddling around inside my mind. I wouldn't have done it if I hadn't thought I was pretty far gone. Maybe I wasn't deliriously happy before I heard about you, but I was getting along, I was relating to people. I think a judge might decide you had something to do— You never for one minute cared how I felt, so long as you could get a record of what I did. Besides, I only exaggerated that one thing."

"You didn't exaggerate it, Victoria. You lied about it."

"All right, I lied! And I hope you don't have one of those tape recorders in your shoe. But I'm not the only liar! Mrs. Freeman told me you didn't need any more EEG's, and if that wasn't a lie— She knew I was beginning to get wrong ideas about—well, people. But she didn't have the guts to come out and say so, she had to invent a cock-and-bull story about— I know you're sleeping with her."

"You're mistaken, Victoria."

"Don't tell me you can watch all that sex all day and half the night and not want to get in on it."

"We've had to develop a certain—indifference."

"You're a man! And a damn attractive one in my humble— Just putting on a white coat doesn't turn you into a pair of pliers. We all have to breathe."

"Yes," he said heavily. "We all have to breathe."

She looked at him for a moment. "I wish you'd decided to turn human earlier, that's all. If he's already got the search warrant—"

"No, he's saving that for the last minute. I know what judge he's going to, and, if we can get to him first and explain that part of your statement is untrue, I think the whole thing may collapse."

She tried to look undecided. "One of the things the psychiatrist drummed into me was to stop changing my mind all the time."

"Victoria, whichever way this turns out, it's sure to be ugly. I know you were in sympathy with us at the beginning. Why are you so bent on wrecking everything now?"

She said sulkily, "It's time people started telling the truth."

"Sex is a complex subject. How much truth can be told about

it at the criminal court level? Hang this one major lie around our neck, and no one will listen to anything else we have to say. You're charging us with compulsion, with an implied physical injury—"

She broke in, "I've had to get a little indifferent too, Dr. Prescott! My indifference isn't as thick as yours because it's newer. I've never been very public-spirited, but I really felt— I couldn't wait till the card came in the mail! And then to pull the rug out from under me that way— I had to quit my job before I broke anything. I'll get you another drink."

"A weak one."

For a noncompulsive drinker, he had downed that first Scotch very fast. In the kitchen, she added ice to the Nembutal highball she had already prepared. There were few worry-lines on his face, but she was going to give him something he could worry about the rest of his life. With his help, she had broken through into orgasm country, and everything there had been pretty much the same as in the world she had left. They had taken away her hope that things would change. The psychiatrist had given her an instant diagnosis, not that it was such an earthshaking insight; Victoria had always known, even without an advanced degree, that her big trouble was that she didn't care about anybody. Anne, for example—Victoria wouldn't really mind if she never saw her again. Prescott and his friends had made her care passionately about a machine and then they had grabbed it away. What it really came down to was that they had had a big effect on her life, and she had had no effect on their lives at all.

She handed him the loaded drink. He was looking her in the eyes, too tired to pretend. And suddenly it broke over her. She saw something deep in his eyes that he himself probably didn't know was there. He thought he'd come here tonight to argue, but that wasn't the reason. She had it all wrong! It hadn't been Freeman's idea to get rid of her but his! Apparently that look she gave him during her last laboratory orgasm had really penetrated. So she'd scared him, had she? Well, well.

He absorbed a good slug of the numbing drink and tried to gather himself. But she decided to pick up the tempo.

"It's different, getting a chance to talk to you without other people around. I'm all mixed up, as usual. I guess you know, don't you, that—"

She came down to him slowly. Her skirt rode up as she settled against him. He was motionless at first, as though already drugged. He put out one hand, perhaps meaning to hold her off, but the instant they touched he pulled her against him.

"Victoria—"

The drink had really hit him. She was going to be doing most of the work, which had also been the case with Rita Hayworth in *Rain*. She kissed him very lightly, to make him concentrate. She kissed his cheeks, his neck, and, after undoing his shirt, his chest. She managed to guide his hand, so he could see that he didn't have to do anything: she was ready. When wasn't she! It had been a sexy conversation, full of threats and tension.

All the time she was wondering. He was the world's leading expert. Wasn't it likely to be a little out of the ordinary? They twisted and changed position. He had come back a short way. His hands were very gentle. He was good, she decided, but he wasn't exactly blazing any new trails. His mind might be stocked with knowledge, but he was an exhausted, middle-aged man who would regret this bitterly in the morning.

But to regret it enough, he had to participate more. She roused him by degrees and at the same time began working herself up against him. If she couldn't love him, and that went without saying, they were so different, she had to try hating him. Both feelings were almost equally good. He was ready for connection now. That psychiatrist was nuts. The real thing that was heading Victoria for the precipice was this damned masculine organ, always making demands on her that she wasn't able to meet. It hurt coming in; it always had. She had no protection against him. She couldn't trust him any more than she had been able to trust him in her dream when he had worked on her with a knife.

Then the machinery took over. He filled her with fire. Middle-aged he might be, but he was lithe and strong. He had come alive. He kept telling himself—she could see the thoughts running through his head like the headlines around the Allied Chemical building—that he shouldn't be doing this, but he kept on doing it, with increasing passion. They lashed about like a broken wire in a rainstorm. She had an instant's happiness. If that instant could have been expanded to fill the day, she could have thrown away her pills and lived to a peaceful old age.

But it wasn't designed to last. Her body fulfilled itself. This was the second time in her life—leaving Anne and the machine out of it—and it was much, much better than the one with Matt.

He tore himself from her too soon, and she realized, looking at him, that that effort would be his last of the night. The Nembutal had reached him, not quite in time to stop his orgasm. Victoria, meanwhile, powered by a couple of hundred milligrams of amphetamines, was traveling in the opposite direction at the speed of sound. Her eyelids were lit up from within. He smiled like a baby. Far from regretting this, he would be able to rationalize it. She saw more trouble ahead. He would convince himself that he felt some kind of perverted tenderness for her, to prove to his own satisfaction that he wasn't the kind of creep who uses sex as a weapon, that he hadn't done it just to make her withdraw her deposition. She hadn't succeeded in hurting him yet, but there had to be ways.

She pulled off the sofa. He was pitiful! The machine, by contrast, always looked just as *machismic* afterward, if never exactly pretty. Arrows of light stabbed her eyelids, and the floor tilted, as though somebody was trying to tip the island and spill the buildings and people into the bay. Was there any hope of getting through to him permanently? He was one of those people who make a habit of winning. He would survive the grand jury investigation and the trial and the publicity and be as important as ever. She had rocked him for a moment, but unless she did something else he would forget her in a month, the white mouse, who had snarled at him briefly, under the impression that she was a predator.

Opening the medicine cabinet, she checked her pharmacy. She still had more than enough, and wouldn't this be a perfect time? Let Prescott, that pillar of the Sexual Establishment, struggle up out of a barbed stupor and find her stretched on the floor beside the sofa, too far gone to be brought back. That would force him to realize— She wasn't too sure exactly what, but at least he would be a little less self-righteous from that point on. If everybody she had ever had sex with came to her funeral she could fill quite a few pews. Nick DiVito could help carry the coffin.

But how about Anne? She had become so enveloping lately, she would be sure to do something crude, like calling an ambulance.

Closing the medicine cabinet brought the mirror back into view. Victoria was surprised at how she looked. With her odd haircut, and ignoring some of the tension marks, she looked like a top model. She was certainly up tight. She was giving off so many vibrations it was a marvel they didn't shatter the glass. If she could only hold onto a thought for longer than a split second, she was convinced she could think of a way to hurt him. She wouldn't have a chance like this again. What did he care about, outside the laboratory?

And then she and her image exchanged a smile. There was always a random bombardment of ideas going on, and if she stayed in one place long enough something was sure to hit her. If she could convince him that the reason she had feigned a sexual interest was to get his keys— Absolutely, she told herself. She would be striking a blow on behalf of all laboratory animals.

He looked surprisingly helpless. She reminded herself again that he symbolized everything she distrusted most—sanity, logic, authority. Her father had slept like that, in that oddly collapsed way, with his mouth open. She had a sudden shaky feeling and wished her grasshopper of a mind had jumped in some other direction. Incest was one of the few variations she hadn't tried, fantasy-wise, and this was a hell of a time to introduce anything new. Except for their age, Prescott and her father had nothing in common.

She carried her clothes into the bedroom. Anne was awake, of course.

"So you did it," Anne commented bitterly. "You have the morals of an alley-cat. What are you trying to accomplish?"

"I've never been able to stand jealous people, Anne, so my advice to you—"

"What are you getting dressed for?" Anne demanded. "Are you going with him?"

"No, let him sleep. He couldn't relax, so I gave him a couple of pills and it was like hitting him with a hammer. Darling, turn out the light and go to sleep. I'm all dexed up, and if I don't walk it off I'll just lie there all night and sizzle."

"Vicky, you know this isn't the most law-abiding neighborhood in the world. I can see you don't want my company, but I'd better come with you anyway, in the interest of not getting raped. We can walk over to Stewarts' and have some cheesecake."

This was one of the maddest suggestions anybody had ever made in Victoria's hearing, and she went on dressing in silence. She dropped her makeup equipment into her bag. She had never gone to the laboratory without looking her best. Anne watched every move like a hungry eagle. Victoria unstoppered her best perfume, which she used for important dates.

"You must really want to be raped," Anne observed.

"Nobody's raped me lately but you. Anne honey, don't listen to me—I'm as high as a balloon."

"Vicky, who am I, somebody you just met this minute at a party? Aren't you going to tell me what he wanted? Was it about the statement?"

She was between Victoria and the door, wearing only pajama bottoms, and suddenly Victoria had a moment of real terror. Anne looked so scary, standing that way, as though about to grab Victoria and drag her off to Bellevue for observation. Victoria screamed, "Be careful, fats! Unless you want to go back to playing with yourself! I'm not your slave!"

"Vicky," Anne said in distress, "when you get that gleam—"

Victoria started forward. She had to break into the open or go jangling off in ten hundred different directions.

"You're the one who needs a psychiatrist, not me. All I'm trying to do is get out of a rut—"

"Sweetheart," Anne said, the expression on her face a caricature of mother love, and reached out to take her in her arms.

Victoria raked her fingernails across Anne's breast. When Anne continued to try to clutch her, Victoria seized one of her breasts and twisted.

"You overweight slob! I don't want you to go with me because people might get the idea I'm as kinky as you are. I only let you do it to me because I felt sorry for you. Woods is the only kind of man—"

Anne just stood there letting Victoria hurt her, the cretin. Victoria wanted to move along to even worse things. Anne was another one of the vultures who were picking her bones. If she hadn't kept lying there talking about orgasms constantly—

Then she went through another dizzying shift of direction.

"I didn't want to do that! I don't know why you're so nice to me."

She kissed her friend's breasts, licking the blood from the scratches. Anne shivered and touched the back of Victoria's head.

"I'm only going out for a minute," Victoria murmured. "You know how it is, honey—sometimes I've got to be by myself."

"I know."

"He says they want me to come back to the laboratory. They want me to be sort of an assistant."

"Don't do it, Vicky. It had such an awful effect on you."

"Well, I probably won't. But I have to decide by myself. I'll keep your arguments in mind, don't worry." She gave each nipple a final kiss. "Don't stay awake for me. I'll crawl in with you when I come home."

"Keep on the avenues."

Victoria went out, closing the bedroom door. Then she went through Prescott's pockets and found his keys. Feeling more friendly toward him, she arranged his clothing and slid a cushion beneath his head.

She hoped she looked all right, not too wacky or anything. Reaching Sheridan Square safely, she lingered on the curb hoping a taxi would materialize in front of her, its off-duty light unlit, heading uptown. But extrasensory perception, which Victoria partly believed in, didn't work with taxis, and she plunged into the subway.

This was a bad time of night in the IRT. All the faces had that special subway color. Loose pages of the *Daily News* blew through the car. The big double line on page one reported the suicide of a well-known actress, a charged-up girl Victoria had always identified with, so ESP wasn't something to laugh off, by any means.

There were two men across from her. One was a truck driver or a longshoreman. His pants were too tight in the crotch, and if Victoria had had a tape measure she could have whipped it out and taken his measurements for the Prescott files. The other man wore an expensive suit and concealed his genitals beneath a cowhide dispatch case. Both men watched Victoria rearrange her legs. Her mind went fluttering off after a new bug. Why shouldn't she introduce herself, making clear that she might be a little smashed but she wasn't usually a hustler, and ask them to ride on up to 158th Street and let her show them something really amazing? The three of them would have the run of the place, with no observers setting the limits. The truck driver had the muscles, the pinstripe the finesse. Queerer things happened every day.

One of the feats Victoria had been invited to perform in the laboratory was to try to reach orgasm by thought processes alone. She had never brought it off, but now, assisted of course by the motion of the train, she managed a pretty good imitation between 42nd Street and Columbus Circle. And ESP was working. Both men knew something was happening. There was a real flow of communication.

Victoria placed a hunch bet. If either man spoke to her, she would put off the laboratory to another night. She began sending them invitations, first focusing on one, then on the other. But they both decided to stay in their own rut. The truck driver got off at 72nd Street. The other, who looked less cute standing up, left at 96th. So much for longshots.

When she walked into the Research Building, she caught the lobby cop in the middle of a yawn. She had seen him before; she had had some of her highest-scoring sessions at this time of night.

"You're up after your bedtime," she said.

"God, am I! I haven't seen you around lately."

"No, I come in at funny hours."

Alone in the elevator, she permitted herself a smile. She never had trouble with men in uniform.

The lights over the door flashed explosively. As the elevator rose, Victoria rose even faster, and stopped more abruptly. She shook out Prescott's keys as she went down the corridor. None of them fitted at first because she was in too much of a hurry. She tried again and soon had the door open.

First she went through all the rooms turning on lights. There was one thing that had always unsettled her a little. She opened a metal cupboard containing various erotic visual aids. So this was science, was it? There were photographs of every conceivable sexual combination—and many inconceivable ones. If people knew the sort of things that went on up here! She picked out a dozen or so of the worst, found some thumbtacks in Freeman's desk, and tacked the pictures along the corridor, so when the cops arrived they would have a trail to follow. The elevator was still on her floor, and she wedged her last picture into the frame of the control panel. Somebody was going to be surprised.

Back in the consulting room, she unlocked the big safe, exposing the banks of drawers. She found her project number and pulled out her file. She wanted to destroy every scrap of evidence that anyone answering the description of Victoria Orr had ever had anything to do with this place. That would jar Prescott if anything could. She filled a wastebasket with paper and set it on fire. She watched for a moment, bemused. Thirty-eight contractions in one blow! Now nobody could prove it had actually happened.

While she was locating her own records she had emptied a number of other files, and somehow they caught fire too. Terrified, she raced into the darkroom for the portable fire extinguisher, came back, and squirted it on the flames. She emptied the extinguisher. After the fire was out she directed a stream at Prescott's diplomas. She left a puddle on Mrs. Freeman's desk.

She scattered more and more files. They had accumulated an ocean of paper! In a moment she was ankle-deep in other people's sex cycles. She didn't want to risk another fire, so she kicked the papers about the room, mixing everything up. She emptied ink and floorwax over the mess. She broke a window overlooking Fort Washington Avenue, and hurled double-handfuls of the sticky stuff into the night.

Now for the film. There was less of it here than she had hoped. She found a pair of shears and had just enough patience to slice up half a can of film as it came off the reel. She emptied the snippets out the window and strewed the rest of the film around like crepe-paper streamers, which gave the austere rooms a dissolute look.

Now at last she gave her attention to the apparatus. Here were her real enemies! The stylus jiggled violently as she smashed the EEG with a chair, recording a giantess' orgasm, one for the books. When she finished with the Arries, neither camera would ever again take a picture of anybody's masturbation. She smashed the electrocardiogram and the myogram. Finally, almost through, she approached the machine.

She felt ashamed of the way she looked. She was filthy. Her clothes were soaked with chemical foam. She would have been ruled out of a hippie parade. The machine, in contrast, stood untouched amid the wreckage, gleaming with pride and power, magnificent in repose. The connections inside her head were fraying rapidly. The machine seemed to grow larger, turning its single deadly eye toward her. She sucked in her breath and struck with the chair.

The stainless-steel armature buckled, and the chair dropped from Victoria's hand. Something had fused inside the machine. Slowly, it began to move. Her head whirled and a terrible noise roared in her ears. She reached out blindly and her fingers closed on a dial. It was the rheostat that controlled the size. The armature began to expand, the plastic peeled back. She screamed. It was so maimed, so damaged.

She wanted to take it against her. She knew the danger. Sparks flickered across the broken connections. Victoria had always feared pain. Yet she somehow understood that this was the only way her life could be made to mean anything and she reached out gladly. The object moved forward against her hand, sparking. She screamed again, terribly, as electricity poured across the break and entered her body.

chapter 25

With much difficulty, over a period of time, Martha Freeman
had put on a protective glaze, like porcelain over cast iron.
She didn't want to take on any new problems until she decided
what to do about her old ones.

But, when she finally forced herself out of bed after Harry
Royce's call, she dressed quickly. To prove to herself that this
was primarily business, she put on the works, from a girdle on
up. She was ready by the time the buzzer sounded.

He was in tails. They exchanged a look, and she knew she
had wasted her time; it would all be coming off again presently.

"This is a marvelous building," he said, coming in. "Prescott
hasn't called?"

"No."

"I talked to his wife again. She'll call us here if she hears
from him. One funny thing. The AP reporter who was phon-
ing him on and off all day told her his name was Burgess.
I have a friend who works for the AP and I woke him up.
They don't have any reporter by that name. He couldn't remember seeing anything on tonight's file about Prescott or the
laboratory. That means a small story if they used anything at
all. So why would they send a reporter to Newark to meet
his plane?"

"Was the name Jake Burgess?"

"She couldn't remember anything but Burgess. She kept
jumping around from one thing to another."

"We used a boy named Burgess on the project, but I don't
see— Come in the kitchen with me while I make coffee. I have
some whiskey, I think, if you'd rather have that."

"No, coffee."

It had been a long time since Martha had cooked for a man.
Would it be silly to put on an apron? She decided against it.
He sat on a tall stool while she began her preparations.

"I hate to pass up this opportunity," he said. "You're the only sexologist I've ever met. What does it do to you? I mean to you personally?"

"It's such an old, old story. How many times do you think I've been asked that question?"

"Hundreds?"

"Thousands. And always with a leer. It's what I do for a living." She began breaking eggs into a bowl. "I have to admit that the first few episodes were pretty searing. I knew I had to behave as though what was happening was the most ordinary thing in the world. It became ordinary later, but it wasn't then. My first nonprostitute couple! They were thirty-fivish, indoor people. Scientifically, it was wonderful. A huge success. Esthetically, I'd say it fell a little short."

"I guess you can adapt to anything."

She turned on him. "That's what I mean. You said that with a leer."

He laughed. "You're too sensitive. That's my regular face. I used to think working in a slaughterhouse would turn anybody into a vegetarian. I suppose they eat steak like the rest of us."

He gave her another man-woman look, of a kind she hadn't been getting lately. It was interrupted by the ringing of the phone.

"Prescott?" he said.

"Maybe, but I've been getting middle-of-the-night calls from people who don't know I'm a hard person to shock."

She picked up the phone and said hello. She thought at first it must be the man she knew as the Breather, a lonely soul who called her up to gratify himself by breathing in her ear.

"Martha?" Prescott's voice said faintly.

"Where are you?"

"My keys are gone. The lab keys. You have to—"

He stopped. She could hear him panting.

"Harry Royce is here," she said. "What do you want us to do?"

"Victoria . . . drugged me. She told the police we forced her into homosexual— A raid at five."

She heard another voice, and Prescott said more distinctly, "Benzedrine? Yes! Yes, let me have it."

A moment later: "Martha! Now listen carefully. They want

the homosexual files. She must be there now, to make sure they find everything. But there may be time. Hurry. We may be able to—"

He broke the connection. Martha hung up slowly.

"The police are going to raid the laboratory at five. One of our ex-subjects drugged him and stole his keys so he couldn't get there first to—" She threw up her hands at Harry's expression. "I know! But that's what he said!"

"Not one of your busy nights," the policeman in the lobby said as Martha Freeman signed in.

"No."

The name on the line above hers was an illegible scribble. Whoever had put it there half an hour before hadn't signed out. A car door slammed, and Prescott hurried in from the street. He nodded curtly to Harry. Martha was surprised to find him looking more or less as usual, except without a tie. It was only in the elevator that she began to feel his tension.

"They're due at five. Did I say that? It's four now. I want to try talking to her first. But we've got to get her away. The film—the film's the important thing, the twelve hundred feet that just came back from the lab. Try to find it while I deal with Victoria."

"What the hell is this?" Harry said.

He pulled a glossy photograph from the button panel. It showed a nude woman being lapped by a dog. Martha knew at once that it had come from their laboratory. They had used it in an early series of tests measuring the effect of purely psychological stimuli on vaginal lubrication. It was a legitimate subject for investigation, but in Harry's hands it hit her with terrific force.

Prescott swayed as the car stopped. They followed a trail of lewd photographs down the corridor. Martha unlocked the door. Inside, she was brought up short by the chaos in the consulting room. All their records, accumulated at such cost in human dignity, over long, painful months, lay strewn about in wild disorder. As Prescott ran into the laboratory, he set up little swirls of charred paper. Martha followed more slowly. How Victoria must have hated them!

In the laboratory, the battered machine was thrusting

clumsily forward and back. Martha's stomach clenched. Prescott, on his hands and knees beside Victoria's body, was trying to blow life into her lungs.

She felt Harry's arm around her shoulder. She pressed against him gratefully.

"Dear Jesus!" Harry said softly, seeing the crippled machine and the figures on the floor. After a moment he released her and pulled the plug out of the wall. The misshapen penis wrenched forward once more and then stopped for good.

Harry said quietly, "Is that the girl who made the deposition?"

Martha nodded, her hand to her mouth.

"Can you prove she was lying?"

She forced herself to look away from Victoria's body. "Probably not now. It depends on how much has been burned."

"What did she really do for you?"

"We used her in machine programs entirely."

"All right," he said after a moment. "A disgruntled ex-employee. That's the kind of simple explanation the cops like. Where do you keep the tools?"

"What did you say?"

"I need some socket wrenches or a hacksaw. Come on, Martha." He snapped his fingers. "We don't have that much time. Move!"

She took him to the maintenance closet, and he dragged out a toolbox. She didn't understand what he wanted it for until he started dismantling the machine.

He handed her a chisel. "Put some gouges in the doorframe so they'll think she broke in."

By the time she returned he had freed three of the bolts holding the stainless-steel arm and was working on the fourth. Prescott sat back on his heels. He lifted Victoria's burned hand and after a moment laid it gently on her still body. He looked across at Martha.

"We killed her."

A nut clattered to the floor, and his eyes jumped to Harry. "What are you doing?" he said sharply. "Leave it alone!"

"You don't want to get caught with this thing still intact."

His face darkening, Prescott came to his feet. "She killed herself with it."

"There's no point in letting the public know that," Harry said through set teeth.

"Everything has to be the way she left it! I can't permit you to interfere. Don't you understand? She hated the machine for what it did to her. Perhaps she was right to hate it."

"It did what you designed it to do. That's the most you can ask of a machine."

"Martha, we have to stop him!" He put out his hand. "Royce, I have to ask you to give me that wrench."

"They can check the book downstairs and see when we signed in, so we'll have to call the police in a minute. What makes you so sure it was suicide? She wasn't depressed, she was high. While she was smashing the machines she happened to touch a hot wire."

"No!" Prescott said. "We're going to tell the truth about this, however inconvenient it may be for your stores."

Martha watched Prescott pick up a hammer. A vein was beating in his forehead.

"Get away from that table!" Prescott snapped.

"I'm almost finished."

The hammer came up. Harry's hand shot forward and caught Prescott's wrist. Prescott's face was unrecognizable. Martha had been holding back, in the observer's role she had filled so long, but now she seized the hammer with both hands and twisted it away.

"I'm not afraid of the truth," Prescott said.

"You should be," Harry said. "Look at your wonderful machine. Do you want to see a picture of that on the front page of the News? 'Sex Machine Runs Wild, Girl Dies.' How does it sound?"

Prescott managed to free one hand and tried to hit him. Harry closed with him again.

"You know him better than I do," Harry said. "What are we going to do with him?"

Martha pulled Prescott around and made him look at her. "You're not responsible! Whatever was wrong with her started long before she came here."

The awkward struggle continued for a moment more, then ceased abruptly. Prescott's face took on its familiar look of disciplined intensity. Harry could feel the change, and let him go.

"But we helped," Prescott said. "We certainly helped! She went to a lot of trouble to get my keys, so she could kill herself in a way that would have some point."

"She made the point," Martha said. "She smashed the machine. Now where do we go from here?"

He stared at her for a moment. "I thought I knew you, Martha."

"Apparently not."

He started to say something more but Harry interrupted. "We have to get rid of that film. Prescott, you'd better be the one to call the police. Take down the pictures in the corridor. Then get working on the files. If you see anything you don't want the D.A. to have, burn it. We only have about ten minutes."

Prescott looked around as though seeing his laboratory for the first time, hesitated, and went out to phone.

Two plainclothes detectives from the local precinct appeared at 4:20. The consulting room was still a shambles, but the laboratory itself was no different from the others in the building except for the broken glass and the absence of cages. Harry had taken the machine apart. Before throwing the main component into the garbage can, he hammered it flat, destroying the last traces of its original design. The loose film had been rewound. Martha hadn't been able to find the homosexual footage. When she was clearing up afterward she came across a few scraps; apparently Victoria had cut it up and thrown it out the window, and the pieces had been blown onto the West Side Highway or into the river.

She found the homosexual file virtually intact. She didn't hesitate, but dumped it into the same wastebasket Victoria had used, and set it on fire, adding the pornographic photographs before it had burned all the way down. The fire was still smoldering when the detectives arrived.

Prescott had withdrawn to his office, and Harry did the explaining. What had happened was clear. Obviously, Victoria had touched one of the broken connections on the EEG machine. Her feet were wet. She took the full 220 volts and died instantly.

She had been employed here, on a part-time basis, but she had been discharged for refusing to follow orders. She was under a psychiatrist's care. Possibly she had been taking drugs; that could be checked. Within a very short time, Victoria Orr lost her final claim to individuality and became a statistic. There was a routine for dealing with this kind of death, and the detectives had made the preliminary moves by the time Woods McChesney walked in at the head of his little raiding party, on the dot of five. There was a smell of anticlimax in the air, along with the smell of burned paper.

"What the hell's going on?" he demanded.

One of the precinct men explained: an ex-employee with a grievance, a splintered personality, a splintered doorframe, fire and destruction, an accidental death by electrocution.

McChesney stooped over the body and twitched back the sheet. He made an extraordinary sound.

"*Victoria!*"

His entire body clenched over the girl. After a long moment he looked up, and Martha saw the face of a small, frightened boy. Gradually that face faded and his other one returned. He stood up.

"I hope you bastards don't think you'll get away with this!"

"Let's talk about it in the other room," Harry said.

McChesney had taken two papers out of his inside pocket. As soon as the consulting room door closed behind them, Harry picked the papers out of his hand.

"A warrant for the arrest of Dr. Prescott and Mrs. Martha Freeman. You don't want to be a damn fool, McChesney. And a subpoena—complete files on all sexual experiments involving the presence of three or more people at one time. Look around you. Are you sure you want to get involved with this can of worms? How do you think the D.A. will like it if you bring in a truckload of raw files in this condition? If Mrs. Freeman asks my legal advice, I'm going to counsel her to ignore this subpoena until we can satisfy ourselves that you have evidence that a crime has been committed."

McChesney popped a mint in his mouth and began to chew.

"I hope you're not relying on a deposition from the dead girl," Harry went on, "because we'll have to challenge her competence on obvious medical grounds. Cigarette?"

McChesney checked himself as he reached for the pack.

Then he swore softly and took one. Harry waited till he filled his lungs and breathed the smoke out slowly.

"That was a very personal sound you made when you looked at the girl," Harry said. "You planted her here, didn't you? I think we might be able to claim entrapment. That's the legal angle. The human angle, the public-relations angle, is that you took an unstable girl, put her in a difficult situation as an undercover agent, and got her killed."

"That's enough," McChesney said shortly. "Mrs. Freeman, did Victoria have anything to do with lesbians here?"

"Definitely not!"

He smoked for a moment in silence. "I was so crazy about that girl. I thought if we worked together on this she might—" He ripped the warrant in two and threw it down. "The hell with the whole God damn thing."

"That's the last of them," Harry said as the two precinct detectives departed. He touched her shoulder. "Martha, you're astonishing. Will I see you tonight?"

She looked at him gravely. "I hope so. I'll call you before noon."

After he left she sat quietly for some minutes, surrounded by the wreckage of two years of her life. Finally, she tapped on Prescott's door and went in. He was at his desk, adding a column of figures. He looked up and said quickly, "Martha. Can we talk about something else for a moment?"

She sat down. "All right."

"I spent an incredible four days in Seattle. They showed us every human-reproduction film and film strip in the catalogues, all of them atrocious. The pulling of punches, Martha, the physiological howlers. You know how unsatisfactory—how repellent—most diagrams are, and there's nothing else on the market. The action starts with the sperm arriving in the uterus. No mention of how it got there, or that there's anything at all pleasurable about the process. It was grimmer than calculus."

He looked down at the figures he had written on a yellow pad. His fingers were trembling.

"I've worked out a tentative budget. We have nearly a million feet of film in the vaults. Our only expense would be for editing and sound. We could make a beautiful series of films, scientifically exact, without any romantic distortions or evasions, a true celebration of the human body."

It was a logical extension of their clinical practice, but for the first time Martha was chilled by Prescott's logic instead of being warmed by it. Noticing the edginess of her silence, he said sharply, "You don't agree?"

"But how many schools would be willing to—"

"Not many at first, but educational innovations spread with amazing speed. In a few years' time every high school in the country is going to be offering a course in sex education. It's an exciting thought. Imagine a generation which comes to maturity with no hidden fears or guilts, which finds nothing obscure or dirty about sex—"

His voice had steadied as he escaped farther and farther into the future. A few hours before, he had been threatening Harry Royce with a hammer, but he had come a long way. All the doors in his life had been blown open, and he was slamming them shut again, one by one.

"I think we finally know what an orgasm is," he said. "What do we do next? Do we want to go on piling up data confirming things we already know? Isn't it time for us to finish with the animal aspects of sex? I think that was what Victoria—"

He was digging his pencil into the pad. The point snapped.

"Her orgasmic proficiency didn't help her much, did it? I reread her history, and you were right about her, it's full of signals."

"I didn't believe much of that," Martha said dryly.

"Last night—" He thought for a moment, his eyes unfocused. "I can't explain what happened. I knew she must have hated us, to sign that statement. I could hear a sort of—dissonance in everything she was saying."

"I don't want to hear about it," Martha said flatly.

Surprised, he looked up from his hands. "But I have to tell you. We made love. She did it to get my keys, but what about me? Did I go there because I hoped it might happen?"

Martha couldn't let him entangle her in the problem. Victoria hadn't been that much different from the other naked girls Prescott had observed in the act of sex. It was the streak of wildness, the abandon, the cunning, that had appealed to something inside him. The same thing had happened to

McChesney, another zipped-up professional. All it meant was that there was more to sex than could be observed in the laboratory. Martha had known that all along, though she had lost sight of it from time to time.

"It's late," she said abruptly, to ward off further disclosures, and stood up.

Prescott swung forward against her, in an awkward movement without any of his usual sureness, and caught her around the waist.

"Martha, God, I'm in—such turmoil. Stay with me. I have to talk to you."

She twisted and tried to break free. "I have to go."

After a moment he released her. He looked up at her, his glasses askew.

"You know I'm in love with you," he said quietly.

She turned away from him. "There's no place for love in your kind of laboratory."

"Martha, dear, I had to—"

She broke in. "Don't explain! I know, I know. We couldn't run the risk of thinking about each other. We might see something in other people's sex that wasn't really there. We'd set up the wrong kind of vibrations. Divorce? I've always known it wasn't a possibility. The two children and the home in the suburbs were part of your credentials. Now all that has changed. It might be easier to sell sex-instruction films as a husband and wife team."

"That's wrong and unfair!"

"Perhaps it's unfair, but it's realistic, and realism is the only thing that counts around here. Damn you, what made you think I wanted to be told about your sex with Victoria? What an idiotic thing to do! Couldn't you tell she was—"

"Martha, you know why you and I never made love."

"Yes, there were always excellent reasons. And there were excellent reasons why you should have stayed away from that girl! You should have cleaned the homosexual records out of the files, and that would have been that. We could have had sex if you'd wanted to. If you'd really wanted to. Nothing so awful would have happened."

She realized she was shaking.

"Martha, we'll talk about it after we've had some sleep."

"No. We won't talk about it and we won't do it. Because I don't believe in the same things you do anymore! I don't want to make sex films for adolescents! You'll turn those poor children into—"

She took the top of her head in both hands, trying to stem the rush of images. "An erect penis is a frightening thing! I don't think a girl should see one until she's in love."

"Martha, for God's sake!"

"I mean it. Ignorance isn't entirely bad! The best thing about sex is its mystery. And I don't care what our films show—it's mysterious as hell. I've wanted to have sex with you. I still do, but it won't happen! We disagree about too much. I don't think you ought to publish that book. I want people to learn about sex from each other, not from a textbook or a movie. Maybe there ought to be something dirty about sex at the start."

"You don't mean that."

"I do!" She pushed back her hair. "All I'm trying to do is find arguments for not going on with you. Because I'm not. I'll help you straighten out this mess, but one week from today I start looking for another job."

He had forced himself back into his mold while she was shouting at him. "One week from today," he said coldly, apparently with perfect confidence, "you'll be sleeping with me."

"Will I?" she said wearily. "I have to go now."

chapter 26

Some months later, Dennis Cullihan, in an airy office looking out into the fog concealing the Golden Gate Bridge, placed a personal call to his friend Peter Hixon at the Royce Foundation in New York.

"Why!" Hixon exclaimed. "If we had that television attachment they keep talking about, you'd see me batting my eyes in wonder. Our calls usually go the other way."

"Just wanted to ask what's up," Dennis said, "and to let you know we've finally filled that Policy Studies situation. I tried to wangle another postponement, but Wickham's really gone into galloping senility, and it isn't funny anymore. We had to bolster him up with pillows for our television show. Did you happen to catch it?"

"Was that *Great Ideas of the Free World?*"

"That wasn't quite the title, was it? I believe it was something more portentous. I see from *Publishers' Weekly* that Dr. Prescott's book is finally coming out in the spring. It took long enough."

"Oh, that was always a hundred-to-one shot," Hixon said easily. "I'm learning to lose gracefully. I think in a way I misgauged the situation. Probably there won't be any public fuss about it at all. He must have a good fairy looking over his shoulder—speaking metaphorically, of course."

"Of course."

"They had an accident in their laboratory. A girl was killed. Electrocuted, actually. I thought that would surely blow everything open, but not at all. The story didn't even run through all editions. It's a crazy world."

"Crazy is right," Dennis agreed. "The papers can't touch it, television can't touch it, and now I hear a *play* on the subject is going into rehearsal, starring the great machine, the most indefatigable lover of modern times. How in God's name are they going to get away with *that?*"

"The leading man never actually appears," Hixon explained.

"All the interesting action takes place on the other side of a closed door. I'm told the playwright was one of Prescott's early volunteers, which adds to the piquancy of the thing, doesn't it? A Maine boy, handsome as sin. He's in the columns all the time, with this girl and that, unfortunately. Now let's put the subject of the Prescott laboratory aside for a moment. Is there any truth to the rumor— But I'd better not ask."

"What rumor, love? That I've been canned? It's only too true. And you know I blame you, in a way?"

"Now, Dennis. Fair's fair."

In distant California, Dennis giggled faintly. "Which version did you hear?"

"That everybody's mad at you for leaking the CIA story about channeling funds through foundations. I didn't believe it for a minute. I know you too well. But now if you want to tell me you're the one who leaked the story about leaking the CIA story about channeling funds through foundations—"

Dennis was giggling uncontrollably. Hixon had to move the phone away from his ear.

"Forgive me," Dennis said when he was able to get the spasm under control. "I'm drinking Cointreau to celebrate my imminent departure, and I'm sticky and half-crocked. The sheer physical relief! Everybody's so damn hearty in this shop. If I tell you what really happened, will you take a solemn oath on *Who's Who,* so help you God, that you'll keep it strictly between you and me and any buggers who may happen to be on the line at the moment, excuse the expression?"

"Absolutely."

"Do you remember those Prescott films you loaned me? I didn't tell you at the time, but I had a print made."

"You bastard," Hixon said fondly. "I hope it didn't get you in trouble?"

"Wait. I was giving a small sherry party, and the subject of our mutual sex laboratory happened to come up. My charming friends, the skunks, demanded an immediate screening. We adjourned to the projection room. Saturday night, eleven o'clock, who else would be using it? Well! Talk about aphrodisiacs. Things were rolling nicely when who should walk in but a party consisting of the Director, the publisher of the *Chronicle,* a local lady of great wealth, three members of the

Board of Regents—but why go on? There was a nice wild fracas for a minute. And now," he concluded soberly, "let's talk about you."

"Nothing much to report. The Hixons are about to move to Greenwich, Connecticut, after a long domestic debate. Ellen took her braces off and stopped seeing the shrink. Of course you know I'm leaving the Royce. Some low-down conniver, and I'm not thinking of you, Den, because I know how loyal you are to your friends, told them I was the one who made that match between Prescott and the publisher. They thought I was trying to call attention to myself, isn't that silly? So we had it out with rapiers, and I'm the one who got stabbed, which is the way things generally go."

"I did hear something about it. What are your plans?"

"I'm setting up as a consultant. I'll advise people who need money about what foundation to go to and how to phrase their requests. I already have a verbal commitment from the University of Pennsylvania, which should start me off with a bang, if not with a whimper."

"But great! What do you call yourself?"

"Peter Hixon Associates. Offices at 417 Madison. Drop in and we'll have lunch."

"Who's the associate, do I know him?"

"I'm quite sure you don't," Hixon said sharply.

Dennis laughed. "Lunch isn't a bad idea, baby, and I'll expect you to pick up the check. I'm one of those foundation contacts you want to impress. Have they told you who your successor's going to be?"

"No, but I've heard the drums beating in the jungle. You, Den?"

"Precisely."

"I would have said it was a slight comedown for you."

"Before you leave, ask them what they've budgeted for the new executive director's salary and expenses. You have to go high for a really good man."

"I know. Don't think I feel any resentment, because my tax man has opened my eyes to what you can do with your own business. I hope we'll be working hand-in-glove. What kinds of programs will you be looking for?"

"I haven't given it much thought. I just had the confirming

call before I called you. What about this film scheme of Prescott's? Sex education in the primary grades? I don't want to get off to a bad start by recommending something they won't go for."

"Dennis, I don't know what to advise you. Still, I don't see how you could go very far wrong."

"Oh?"

"One thing you may not have heard. Harry Royce is being seen, shall we say, with Martha Freeman, who used to work for the good doctor. Remember when it was Prescott and Freeman? And this is not one of Harry Royce's usual things. The word is that it's not exclusively physical. They're white, Anglo-Saxon, Protestant—and normal! It's a God damn idyll. So you can be fairly sure Harry will be receptive to the idea, and don't forget that he's the man you really have to sell."